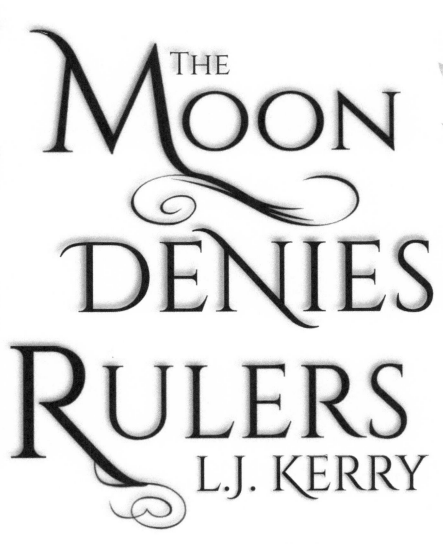

THE MOON DENIES RULERS

L.J. KERRY

THE FALLASINGHA CHRONICLES
BOOK 2

THE MOON DENIES RULERS

L.J. KERRY

The Moon Denies Rulers © 2023 L.J. Kerry

Editor: Dianne M Jones

Cover Design: Lucy Cooper

Under Dust Jacket Illustration (Dragon Eyes): MadSchofield

Map Illustrator: Z.K. Dorward

This book has been professionally typeset on AtticusText © 2023 L.J. Kerry

To all the people
who turn away from the dark

-

In memory of Dianne M Jones

WHAT HAPPENED IN...

THE
STARS
PLOT
REVENGE

L.J. KERRY

THE FALLASINGHA CHRONICLES
BOOK 1

RECAP

A month after Orison is kidnapped from the mortal realm, and imprisoned in Alsaphus Castle after being turned Fae against her will. She is forced to attend King Sila's birthday celebration. Unable to dance, King Sila humiliates her in front of his entire court, and then forcibly sends her back to her chambers. Inside her chambers, Orison receives the first of many mysterious letters. With roaring in her head, she ventures to the stables where she meets a Nyxite; a type of dragon with black fur and stars in his purple eyes.

In the days that follow, Orison endures Sila's wrath while learning more about her own powers and building a secret friendship with the mysterious Nyxite. Then one night she discovers that Sila's brother, Prince Xabian, has been missing since the night of her imprisonment and everybody is forbidden from looking for him.

Despite the risk of death, Orison is determined to find the missing prince in the hopes to overthrow the king. Orison and her friends work together to try and find clues in the castle library via diaries, and confides in a guard that has been sent to serve her. During one particular day of Sila's rage, Orison discovers a powerful protection spell has been placed on her and uncovers one of many secrets the new guard is hiding. Like the fact, the new guard is the Nyxite she met all that time ago—finding he is under a powerful curse that turns him into a dragon at night fall.

After Sila pushes Orison off the castle balcony, she is saved by the protection spell and once out of the confinement of the castle, Orison searches across the country to find the prince. Finding only riddles and warnings to stop her quest but she couldn't give up. Eventually Sila catches up to her antics and she is thrust back into the castle, where she discovers more secrets the new guard is hiding.

After Sila locks Orison in her bedroom, she calls upon her friends to enact a series of revenge tactics to make his life miserable and administer small amounts of poison into the kings food. However, a failed assassination attempt— with a more lethal dose of poison— foils her plan and Orison is forced to rethink. Then she is called to watch a public execution. Before the execution, she discovers the entire truth of what the new guard is hiding and reveals his true identity. Enraged by the discovery, she casts him out of the castle, feigning to deal with her situation herself. Until night falls and King Idralis of Akornsonia offers Orison refuge in his land—an offer she cannot refue.

Within the safety of Akornsonia, Orison is happy until Sila wages a ferocious battle to get Orison back from the elf kingdoms grasp. As the battle rages on, Orison researches the Nyxite curse and when she uncovers Sila's lethal secret, she rides into battle without a second thought; determined to take down the king. After a fierce stand off, King Sila summons an enchantress and in his rage exiles Orison to the mortal realm.

OTHEREAL

LHANDAHIR

GHARTAH

KARSHAKROH

KARSHAK CASTLE

HARANSHAL

TSUNAMAL

ENTAN

N
W E
S

NOTE TO READER

Despite working hard, through multiple rounds of edits, to give you the best product possible some grammar and spelling issues may have slipped through the cracks. Please direct any concerns to: ljkerrybooks@outlook.com

Chapters 28, 29, and 30 are intentionally shorter than normal. Nothing is missing from the book.

Content Warning

ONE

The devil appeared in the form of a flaming pitchfork, with an audience of demons.

A mob surrounded the clearing where Orison cowered, using her body as a shield to protect Xabian who lay unconscious in her lap. The heat of the flames brushed against her skin like a soft caress to somebody's doom; a sharp scent permeated the air. Her sobs echoed around the clearing, enhanced by the trees around them. Her palpable fear possessed her like a ghost.

Surrounding her were the people Orison had grown up with; who had shared her milestones, and smiled and laughed with her. Yet they acted like she was a complete stranger. Spittle flew from their mouths as they roared abuse. Some of them thrust their pitchforks towards her as they looked down at her with scorn.

"We don't accept Fae in our village!" one man shouted.

"Your kind took our villagers!" another bellowed.

Orison flinched as they threw rotten tomatoes at the filthy Akornsonian soldier's uniform she had stolen. Tightening her grip on Xabian's shoulder, Orison inspected him as he slept. She willed him to wake up with a gentle shake, but it didn't help. His head lolled to the side.

Hands grabbed Orison from behind. She let out an earth-shattering scream as they ripped her away from Xabian. She kicked and struggled against their hold, trying to summon her power, but nothing came. Out of the corner of her eye, a lanky figure presented itself in the flames. The dark silhouette chuckled as they dragged her closer to the gloomy expanse of the Nalan Forest. Another stocky figure tried to grab her legs, Orison groaned, kicking with all her might and smashing her boot into his jaw. His head snapped back and he fell into unconsciousness.

"Please spare me," she begged. Her voice was hoarse from all the screaming. Tears spilled down her cheeks. "I'm not here to cause harm. I need a doctor."

Her assailant threw her down at the edge of the forest. She cried out as he landed a kick into her ribs; Orison coughed and held her side. Tears stung her eyes as she glanced at Xabian. The mob jeered at his unconscious form, jamming sticks in fruitless attempts to rouse him.

"Don't harm him, please," Orison croaked and extended her hand.

Another kick to her ribs caused Orison to collapse onto her back, she coughed and wheezed from the impact. Her world spun as she tried to gain composure; the stars above swirled with the trees like a procession of dancers in the night sky. Orison turned her head to peer at Xabian. She was bewildered that night was upon them, but he was no longer in his Nyxite form; his black hair indicated the curse was still present.

"Burn them at the stake!" a heavy-set man with black hair ordered. She knew him as Darius; the bartender who had served Orison her first drink at her eighteenth birthday. His face was shrouded in shadow.

Orison lifted her head. "No!" she gasped.

A group of the rioters surrounded Orison; tears blurred her world as she continued to beg for mercy. The sharp scent of fire stung her nose. Warped figures jeered obscenities while they aggressively waved their arms around.

Nobody had taught her how to Glamour; the Luxarts had decided to leave it until she had mastered the basics. She wished they would have told her regardless, then she wouldn't be in this mess. Orison tensed when a terror-filled scream filled the clearing—a scream she recognised.

"Stop!" a male howled.

A feminine voice cried, "That's my baby!"

Orison shifted to get a better view, wincing at the pain in her ribs. "Mother?" she exclaimed. "Father?"

The mortals who had advanced on her paused, each lowered their pitchforks as they turned to face the intruders. Peering through the darkness, Orison saw two familiar silhouettes, one diverted towards Xabian and the other ran towards her. The stocky man with wavy brown hair—Orison immediately knew as her father—crouched beside Xabian. A thin woman, who was the spitting image of Orison, raced towards her and embraced Orison in a vice-like grip. Orison breathed in the fresh smell of chopped wood—the smell of home.

A shadow engulfed them and when Orison looked up, her father fell to his knees with a heavy thud. Marus brushed Orison's blonde hair away from her pointed ears and gasped at what had become of her. He covered his mouth to hide his horror, his eyes widened when he took in the blood-soaked armour. It was the first time he had seen his daughter after King Sila took her and turned her into a Fae. The faintest smile spread across his face as his shoulders relaxed, but it didn't meet his eyes.

"What have they done to her?" Darius spat; his face was aghast. He threw his pitchfork to the ground. It landed with a dull thud; the metal hummed from the vibrations. "What the fuck have they done to you, Orison?"

A tense silence settled over the clearing as two mortals dragged Xabian next to Orison. She panted heavily as she took in each of their faces, not daring to look away. "King Sila turned me into Fae for power, then exiled me here with Xabian."

Murmurs filled the crowd. Nobody paid any attention to Georgea as she crawled to Xabian and moved him onto her lap. She checked him for injuries, ignoring the blood on her hands from holding Orison. Georgea appeared calm as she pressed two fingers to his neck, taking in his pointed ears and pale face as she counted the pulse. The mob continued to discuss Orison like she wasn't around.

"We need a doctor," Georgea concluded.

Darius stepped forward. "Who can work on a Fae?"

The murmurs ceased and they glanced around for a doctor, but nobody volunteered their services. They were all too scared of the power that thrummed through the Fae's fingers.

"Find somebody," Georgea seethed. "I need men to help transport Xabian to my home. We must assist him."

The crowd split up into small groups, each discussing whose job it was to carry Xabian. At last, the mob diverted their attention to another task and their anger was like a distant memory; no longer concerned about spewing hatred to the Fae.

Marcus took Orison's hand, helping her stand on shaking legs. He caught her when she fell into him; her ribs sent jolts of pain through her side. She held her father's hand in a white-knuckled grip as she waited for the pain to subside. Marcus rubbed her shoulder and guided her towards their home.

Taviar woke with a gasp, clutching a hand to his chest as pain seared through his heart; he grimaced while waiting for it to subside. Beside him, Riddle reached over the twins—asleep between them—and touched his arm. Taviar looked at his husband as he massaged his chest.

"Are you okay?" Riddle whispered; his voice groggy from sleep.

Riddle's eyes were wide; concern written all over his face. He rested on his elbow and glanced briefly at Zade as he stirred. With a wince, Taviar nodded and looked down at his chest. He knew what this meant and didn't expect it to be as painful as this.

"The king is dead," Taviar announced as he ran his hand over the gold velvet duvet.

Riddle sucked in a breath, waking their children even more. "How do you know?" He looked down when Zade gripped his shirt.

"Our bond has just been severed." Taviar winced as he lay back down, the pain still persistent. "The bond we made when they appointed me as an emissary."

Unable to get back to sleep, Taviar stared at the window at the foot of the grand wooden bed. Moonlight trickled through a gap in the red velvet drapes, casting a distorted white line down their bed. He tried to calm down and forget about the pain; this was a good thing.

Akornsonia had succeeded in taking down Sila. Fallasingha would have a new king or queen soon.

Butterflies filled his stomach and a sense of foreboding settled on his shoulders. Something wasn't right. When Taviar should feel elated, he only felt empty. Upon Sila's death, Taviar was free; until he was bound to either Xabian or Orison when they took the throne. He would no longer have to endure being patronised every day, nor sent on impossible death-defying missions that made him tremble with fear.

"That means we need to prepare for a coronation," Riddle concluded, gently lifting Zade onto his chest. He kissed the top of his son's head as he held him. Yil rubbed his eye and sprawled out on Taviar.

Taviar held Yil close and stared at the oil paintings on the ceiling, which depicted cherubs flying through the clouds. "I have a bad feeling though."

Riddle looked across at him. "So do I." The room fell quiet as Taviar continued to stare into space and draw circles on Yil's shoulder. "Talk to me," Riddle coaxed.

Taviar faced his husband with a deep exhale of breath. "What if the bad feeling is that something happened to either Orison or Xabian?"

"Kins found out that the only way to break the curse was for Xabian to kill King Sila." Riddle held Taviar's hand and ran his thumb over his knuckles. "If he succeeded, I doubt anything bad has happened to them."

Taviar tensed and sat up. "So, it's Orison?" Yil groaned and rubbed his eyes. Taviar set his son back on the bed, tucking the covers around him. "Hush, go back to sleep."

Through the darkness, Taviar looked at Riddle and waited for his response. He was as silent as the room they were in. For the first time in years, his children were safe and Saskia would have a chance to reclaim her rightful position in the castle. It would make all the wrongs right; the opportunities were endless. Yet it all felt wrong.

Shuffling sounds filled the room. Taviar whirled around to discover a letter addressed to him sitting on the bedside table. With a wave of his hand, the bedside lamp flickered on, casting the light wooden walls into a soft yellow hue. He turned the brightness down, resulting in the shadows stretching ominous shapes up the wall. The bed creaked as the twins turned away from the light. Riddle hushed them back to sleep and held them close.

Another wave of his hand sent the letter towards Taviar. He didn't recognise the scrawled handwriting which depicted his name. When he turned the envelope over, he noticed the Fallasingha crest embossed onto the wax seal. Taviar eased himself into a sitting position to rest against the headboard as he stared down at the letter. The bad feeling worsened when he went to open the letter, but froze.

Mustering up all his courage, Taviar popped the wax seal and took the parchment out of the envelope. He didn't want to prolong fate and deny the inevitable. As his gaze scanned the contents of the letter, his stomach dropped to the depths of hell and his heart pounded painfully against his ribs. While he continued reading, the bizarre sense of foreboding made perfect terrifying sense.

"What does it say?" Riddle asked.

Taviar blinked back tears and exhaled a breath. "The king is indeed dead," he confirmed. He pushed back tears. "But... I'm now Regent of the Fallasingha Empire."

The twins stirred as Riddle sat up quickly and took the letter from his hand. "Regent?"

"King Sila exiled Princess Orison and Prince Xabian to the mortal lands."

A leech trapped between a set of tweezers squirmed, making a wet, slippery sound. Its black surface glistened in the candlelight. The doctor lowered it down onto Xabian's back; alongside several other plump creatures. He regarded the Fae Prince lying on the dining table. Xabian hadn't stirred once since arriving in the mortal lands.

Orison watched the doctor's performance from a stool beside the fireplace; her mother gently brushed her hair after a bath. She was thankful that her ribs no longer hurt, and that she didn't feel so disgusting after a change of clothes. Tearing her gaze away from the doctor, the giant with brown hair sticking up in all directions, and paid attention to her family dog—Morty—instead. The dog was fast asleep in front of the fire, looking more like a golden fur rug than a living being.

For the first time in a long while, Orison observed her childhood home, realising how much it resembled Saskia's cottage in Cardenk. There was the open-plan kitchen and living area. To the left of the stairs was a spare bedroom with white plaster walls. The only difference was that another spare bedroom was by the front door for her father's woodworking and mother's textile work.

"Will he be well?" Orison asked as she returned to the doctor.

The doctor turned and the goggles he wore showed reflections of the fire. "I'm quite sure he will be well; leeches always work." He returned to Xabian. "On second thoughts, we may need to heat some urine and get him to inhale it."

Orison pressed a hand to her belly, which churned like a storm at sea. After months in the Othereal, the barbaric ways they healed ailments in the mortal realm were foreign to her. The Healengales's magic she'd grown accustomed to was less invasive.

The doctor pulled off the plump leeches with a pop. Blood pooled along Xabian's spine where they had feasted on him. Orison watched as the doctor placed the leeches in a jar; remnants of Xabian's blood smeared along the sides as they writhed around. He shoved the jar in his bag and returned to the prince with another jar which was filled with an off-white substance. The label read *snail extract*.

After soaking a cotton ball in the extract, the doctor wrapped the slimy ball around his tweezers. He proceeded to rub the concoction onto Xabian's bleeding lesions. The doctor secured the cap back on and shoved the jar inside his bag.

"I will be back with a jar of urine from my clinic," the doctor announced.

Marcus held the door open for the doctor and bowed before his giant gait disappeared into the night. From her stool, Orison watched her father close the door and approach Xabian. He looked down at the prince with his hands on his hips.

"Georgie, we may need to see a witch doctor," Marcus announced.

Orison stiffened at the sound of a witch doctor. She didn't know if such a thing could work in the mortal realm or if such a doctor was even legitimate. There was a risk they could do more harm than good, if they were successful in channelling the spirit realm to fix Xabian. She had her doubts that the spirit world would help a Fae.

She glanced over her shoulder when her mother stopped brushing her hair. Georgea had her hands in her lap, her spine was ram-rod straight as she gazed upon Xabian with a look of longing. She sighed and approached the dining table. Morty woke up and followed her; she absentmindedly ran her hand through the dog's golden fur before inspecting Xabian.

"He looks so different from when he tried to prevent our baby from being taken," Georgea stated as she looked at Marcus. "We can't let him waste away."

"I'll send word for a witch doctor," Marcus announced as he approached the front door. He plucked the brown cloak from a hook on the wall and secured it around his stocky frame.

Orison thought back to Xabian's tellages in Alsaphus Castle before the Nighthex had prevented any more entries. Most of them were about watching her grow up. When Xabian wasn't doing that, he was arguing with Sila to call off the bargain her parents made in desperation. If her parents hadn't made that bargain, Orison would still be mortal and living in this very cottage.

The frigid night air cut into the warmth of her home, pulling her out of her spiralling thoughts. Orison sat upright as the cold seeped through her nightgown, making her shiver and tug her beige cardigan around her body.

"Be careful, Honey," her mother warned Orison's father. "Take Morty with you."

Morty approached with a wag of his tail. Marcus patted his thighs. "Come on, boy."

As the door shut behind them, Orison caught a glimpse of her father's cloak as he disappeared into the night with Morty in tow. Her attention fixated on Xabian and the thoughts of a witch doctor's legitimacy returned with a vengeance.

Her thoughts changed to the memories of their ordeal in the clearing; how she tried to use her magic for protection, but nothing happened. Orison was unsure if magic worked in the mortal realm, but hoped it did. She sucked in a shuddering breath as she remembered the last time she almost succumbed to magic starvation. It felt like her veins were burning and she struggled for every single breath; it wasn't something she wanted to relive.

Orison pushed herself off the stool and stood beside her mother. She lowered herself down to kneel beside Xabian. Taking his hand, she conveyed her Mindelate abilities towards him to coax him to wake up.

It was the first time that her magic didn't feel like her own. Her heart raced at the heaviness of pushing her magic towards Xabian. No matter how much she tried, it wouldn't budge; but worst of all, it *hurt*. Orison cried out and collapsed onto the floor. She panted from the exertion and her head pounded.

Misting the elves to Navawich to escape Sila's clutches was the only other time her magic had been painful. She used her entire reserve of power in her desperate need to save her rescuers. Khardell still died despite her best efforts.

"Ori, are you okay?" her mother exclaimed. She crouched beside her daughter and rubbed her back.

"There's something wrong with my magic," Orison panted.

"What do you mean?"

Orison shook her head as she tried to hold back the tears. "It hurts."

Georgea frowned. "Hurts in what way?"

"Like I've tried to lift one of Father's big crates of wood." Orison looked at Xabian. "I've never had trouble before. I don't understand."

Her mother pulled her close, breaking the dam inside her. Orison wept for everything she had endured—the tellage pages in the war camp, riding into the Battle of Torwarin full of rage and her exile to her home world.

After discovering her magic was snuffed out like a flame, Orison's body felt hot and she found it difficult to breathe. Whether she had truly lost her power or it lay dormant, she needed to learn fast to escape the undeniable. She refused to die in this realm.

TWO

A heavy cloud hung over Torwarin after the battle had ceased two days prior. The village was unscathed from the battle, except for the charred remains from when King Sila set fire to the wooden structures. Fog spilled through the narrow streets, casting the summer morning into a false dreary winter.

The sound of horses' hooves crunching on the gravel broke the silence of the village. A caravan of wagons entered the village; the women and children had returned. Those who were rebuilding Torwarin paused their daily tasks and gathered on the side of the road, ready to reunite with their families.

Taviar pushed the black curtains of his carriage to the side and watched all of the elves with beaming smiles on their faces as they waved to their fellow people. His stomach gurgled from forgoing breakfast; his nerves were too immense for him to eat. Orison was in the mortal realm—untrained. He turned away from the smiling faces, wringing his hands as he tried to force down malicious thoughts of the endless ways Orison could die. No matter how many times he told himself Xabian was with her, it never abated his concern.

He exhaled a heavy breath and glanced at Saskia. The clicking sound of her knitting needles filled the silence of the carriage like a metronome. Taviar wished he could be like Saskia, oblivious to the world as she knitted—lost in the mantra. His attention diverted to Riddle, who held Yil close and kissed the top of his head; then he glanced at Zade, who lay asleep beside him. All the adults in the wagon knew they would have to face the consequences of the battle; like ruling a country when only days before, they were mere staff at the castle.

The wagon rolled to a stop. Taviar looked out of the window when the sound of squealing tore through the tranquil silence. Children were the first to be let out of the wagons, free to run into the arms of their fathers or brothers who were left behind to fight. It was a joyous sight, filling Taviar with warmth, a slight smile appearing on his face. He watched husbands give their wives long awaited kisses to welcome them home.

Riddle opened the carriage door. "I'll take the boys while you speak to King Idralis."

Taviar gently pushed Zade on his shoulder. "Zade, wake up, we're here." His son stirred and his green eyes fluttered open, groaning as he rubbed his eye. "I know. Come on, we need to go."

The carriage rocked as Saskia stood up. Riddle held her hand and assisted her down the steps to the gravel below. She brushed dust off her mint green and black dress. Turning to Yil, Saskia groaned when he jumped into her arms; she set him down on the gravel and ruffled his black hair. Yil scowled as he fixed his hair, sticking his tongue out; Saskia's warm laughter filtered into the carriage.

Riddle scooped up Zade. "Come on, sleepy head." With a protective hand on his son's head, he climbed out of the carriage. He turned to Taviar. "Honey, are you coming?"

With a nod, Taviar climbed out of the carriage and adjusted his black lapel. He adjusted Riddle's golden waistcoat—which complimented his dark complexion—and gave him a kiss.

"I love you," Riddle said with a smile.

Taviar returned the smile. "I love you too."

Taviar remained by the carriage as Riddle walked off with their sons. He stayed until his family disappeared down a side street. A gentle touch on his arm diverted his attention; Saskia gestured at something behind a group of children playing. That's when he noticed Idralis approaching. He stopped briefly to check on his people, but his attention was on the new rulers of Fallasingha. When he was close enough, Idralis shoved his hands into his pockets.

"We have much to discuss," Idralis said solemnly. "Let's go to my cabin."

A wave of his hand and they were on the move. Taviar followed Idralis into Torwarin, leaving behind the cheery environment. Gravel crunched underfoot the deeper they ventured into the village—then he stepped into hell. Injured soldiers groaned as they lay on benches in the street, being tended to by nurses; others lay on tables taken from homes. Blood painted the street. Some men held their intestines in their hands. Others were clearly dead, with blue mottled skin. Taviar felt sick to his stomach as he witnessed some nurses amputating a soldier's arm in the middle of a bakery. A gag in a soldier's mouth muffled his screams. He glanced over his shoulder and prayed to Fallagh that his sons would never witness such atrocities.

Bypassing the grotesque site, which confirmed why Taviar hated war, he breathed a sigh of relief when Idralis's cabin finally came into view. The king moved briskly towards the front door. The stairs creaked as they ascended each step and the door opened on a phantom wind. Taviar followed the king into the cabin, which resembled more of a peasant's home than something made for royalty.

All the walls were wooden. Three doors on his left led to various rooms, with one directly in front of him. Nazareth sat in her wheelchair in front of the roaring fire; above the mantle was a painting of Idralis. She turned herself around and approached everybody.

"How was the trip?" she asked.

Taviar nodded. "It was pleasant, I'm not used to going through elf portals, though."

"I'm tired, but it was splendid," Saskia replied.

Idralis opened the door and waved everybody inside. He gestured for Nazareth to go first. She manoeuvred herself through the door and Taviar followed behind. The room was a small office with a wall of bookcases full of leather-bound books. Idralis sat in his red leather chair that creaked as he settled into it. He adjusted his paperwork on his desk and gestured for Saskia and Taviar to take a seat. Taviar settled into the seat opposite Idralis and glanced at Saskia when she settled down.

"How did the exile happen?" Taviar enquired. "I thought Orison wasn't fighting."

Idralis groaned and buried his head in his hands. "She rode into battle, despite many protests from your daughter and her boyfriend. She fought valiantly, but Sila opened a portal and threw her in. Xabian jumped in after her."

Murmurs filled the room; Saskia squeezed her eyes shut. "We will figure out how to get them back to the Othereal," she declared. "Xabian is with her; he can teach her how to use her powers there so she can survive."

"That's the only good thing about this situation," Taviar said, looking at his hands.

Idralis shuffled some paperwork around. "Xabian appointed both of you to uphold royal duties. I took it upon myself to appoint you—Taviar—as Regent, with you—Saskia—as an advisor."

Taviar tensed and cast his attention to Saskia, who pushed her shoulders back and nodded—she accepted her duty. They had a monumental task to complete; taking over Fallasingha in the wake of the exiled royals, whilst trying to secure their return. He looked down when Saskia held his hand. They both knew that one wrong move would bring Fallasingha to its knees.

Despite the sweltering summer heat outside, everything felt like an eternal winter to Orison. It had been two days without using magic. Orison couldn't get warm, to the point that her teeth chattered painfully. She hadn't felt this bad since she first became Fae, when she didn't know how to wield her powers and Sila had refused to teach her. Orison was different now; *this* experience was different.

Orison threw herself out of bed, groaning as she flopped onto the wood flooring; too weak to stand. Her body trembled as she dragged herself out of the downstairs bedroom that she occupied. Each breath came out in a rasping wheeze; her veins sent burning waves of pain throughout her body. Orison was thankful that her parents listened when she insisted that they go to work; they couldn't see how much she was struggling or the pain she was in.

Every effort to use her magic was fruitless; either nothing happened or it gave her pain. Xabian was still unconscious in Orison's childhood bedroom; she couldn't wake him or ask for help. She knew she had a day left to live at best.

In the living room was a chest of blankets behind the sofa. Orison winced as she dragged herself over. Tears streamed down her cheeks; each breath was like she was in a marathon. Her hands wrapped around the lid of the chest. She grimaced as she tried to push it open, only to cry out when collapsing against its wooden surface. It was too heavy to move. All she wanted was another blanket; it would be selfish to burn precious firewood.

Giving up on the chest, Orison rolled onto her back and focused on her laboured breathing as she stared at the wooden beams on the ceiling. It felt like a thousand sacks of flour had been placed on her chest; all she wanted to do was throw them off and take her first deep breath—she couldn't. Tiredness weighed her down; she felt safe enough to close her eyes for a little while.

A loud wheeze filled the living room in the cottage as Orison woke up. Hacking coughs overwhelmed her; she curled up as she waited for them to subside. She was too delirious to realise how long she had been asleep. Her heart pounded painfully, working overtime to keep her alive, as she lifted her head and dragged herself towards the sofa. Orison heaved out several more coughs along the way.

Grabbing the edge of the sofa, she slumped against the plush surface. Laying down was fatal, but she was so tired. She stared at her hand and willed some magic to present itself. Her theory was that she'd feel better if she had even an ounce of power; she could only wish that was true.

"Please, please let this work," she rasped.

It took all of her energy to click her fingers—nothing. Tears blurred her vision as she tried over and over, becoming more frustrated when each effort resulted in nothing. On the tenth try, Orison gasped loudly when a red apple appeared in her hand. The sickly feeling partially ebbed away, as did the weight on her chest.

"Thank you," she breathed out a sigh of relief.

Clicking her fingers again, she tried to conjure up anything. Once more, nothing happened. A loud sob tore out of Orison as she placed her forehead against the sofa, punching the sofa as she pleaded for it to work a second time. With a heavy wheeze, she clicked her fingers more furiously in quick succession, until another apple appeared. A small amount of strength returned. Her legs and feet no longer felt like spiders were crawling underneath her skin.

It was like a breath of fresh air to regain small fragments of her power. The thought that it could run out filled her with terror. Orison didn't want to conserve the power she had regained, but the risk that it could run out was too great. It would be the only way to survive.

THREE

Deep in the belly of the Temple of Lioress lay the deity's tomb. With the assistance of the Othereal lights in their sconces, shadows danced around the golden walls. In the burial chamber were copious amounts of treasures spanning over millennia—offerings for luck and prosperity in battle or life.

A hand lay flat against the golden sarcophagus of Lioress. The air was thick with a prayer in the Elven language. Nazareth knelt at the foot of the deity, with her head bowed and eyes closed—a single tear rolled down her cheek. It was a prayer begging for forgiveness, for the lives she had taken in battle and the families she had destroyed.

This was a pilgrimage that Nazareth made after every battle. Things happened so quickly after the Battle of Torwarin that it took a week for her to pay a visit. There was only one time she hadn't been able to complete the ritual; when King Sila had poisoned her with Necro's Kiss.

She took her hand off the sarcophagus and knelt before Lioress; her blood-shot eyes were fixated on the final resting place of her maker. Battles weighed heavily on Nazareth; each one chipped away a bit of her soul. Regardless, she would fight for Akornsonia. It was her home and she would risk her life to defend it.

Nazareth kissed the ground at Lioress's feet and bowed her head. Using the sarcophagus for support, Nazareth eased herself to her feet and bowed once more to say goodbye. She started to leave, but paused when a scraping sound filled the chamber.

In case she had overstayed her welcome, Nazareth inspected her surroundings. She half expected the monks to come out of the shadows to escort her off the premises. When she turned around, she staggered back with a gasp. Lioress's sarcophagus was open; in its centre was a beautiful woman who sat up. She had brown curly hair and luscious red lips; the white tunic intensified her make-up. The woman stretched like she had awoken from a nap. She turned to Nazareth with a peaceful smile. Nazareth couldn't deny that she faced Lioress.

"Hello, Emissary Nazareth," Lioress said.

Nazareth straightened up, then bowed. "Hello, Your Highness."

"I'm going to ensure Princess Orison remains safe in the mortal realm." Speechless, Nazareth rubbed her eyes in case this exchange was a dream. "You aren't dreaming, Emissary."

"Princess Orison is untrained. It's been a week; she could already be dead."

Lioress shifted in the sarcophagus. "I can assure you she is still alive. I will give her some allies for training. She will be fine."

"And Xabian?"

"The curse holds him in sleep." Nazareth closed her eyes; she was afraid that would be the case. "He sealed his fate when he went into the mortal realm during recovery. Prince Xabian will never return to the man he once was."

Nazareth looked around the temple. "How do they stop him from dying in the mortal realm?"

"They have to wake him up until the curse reclaims him."

"How?"

Lioress yawned. "I do not have that answer, but they will figure it out."

"Thank you, Your Highness. I shall relay this to King Idralis."

She bowed once more when Lioress laid back down. The stone lid of her sarcophagus moved to seal her back into eternal sleep. Nazareth turned to the stairs and began the long walk to the surface of Irodore. She held the cold railing for support as she thought about the message. At the top of the stairs, a monk stepped out of the shadows with her weapons and her extendable walking stick.

Nazareth thanked the monk as she retrieved them, unfolding her walking stick and swiftly exiting the temple.

The sun blinded her when she stepped outside. Shielding her eyes from the glare, Nazareth squinted. Her eyes adjusted and she entered the bustling bridge that was crammed with tourists. They pushed against each other until they noticed Nazareth's presence; only then did they give her a clear path into Irodore's centre.

On the other side of the bridge, Nazareth navigated her way through Irodore's many platforms. She found her favourite café, which was carved into a tree, ironically named *Tree House.* The bell rang as she pushed the door open. Inside were tree stumps for tables, littering a large area with wrought-iron chairs. Nazareth approached the wooden counter where a barrel of steaming hot coffee bubbled on the back shelf, flanked by shelving units that displayed tea and syrups. She placed a bag of coins on the counter in front of a blue-skinned pixie with purple hair.

"The usual, please," she requested.

The pixie pushed the bag of coins back to Nazareth. "Royal staff don't need to pay."

"Idralis always pays; let me do so, as well."

With a sigh, the pixie took the bag and placed it in a drawer. She dived into the kitchen to prepare the chicken and jalapeno bagel that Nazareth always ordered with a coffee. Nazareth walked away from the counter. Patrons gawped at her as she passed them and settled in a secluded area away from them all. With a click of her fingers, a leaf appeared with a stylus. While she scribbled a message to Idralis, her food was served. She relayed the information Lioress told her and sent it off into the oblivion. Only Lioress knew Orison's fate from here.

Everything overwhelmed Orison as she stumbled through Nalan Forest. The sun blinded her and the world spun. Each step felt like the earth beneath her feet was a sponge. Sweat clung to her skin as she struggled through each breath, bracing herself against trees when she tripped over tree roots. Morty was none the wiser as he trotted beside Orison; his tongue lolled out the corner of his mouth as he ventured through the forest.

It had been a week and Orison had managed to regain only a miniscule amount of power. Though it made her feel slightly stronger, it wasn't enough for what her body required.

Morty pulled on his leash to chase a bird; Orison didn't have the strength to stand her ground. The strength of the dog dominated her and she fell face-first into the soft soil. The ground appeared to have encapsulated her; every attempt to get up was useless. She let out a weak groan. Through half-closed eyes, she watched two versions of Morty disappear into the dark forest. Her teeth chattered and her body shivered as a wave of coldness washed over her.

"Come back," she tried to shout. All that came out was a feeble whisper.

The two dogs returned to Orison, their tails wagging; but when the dog touched her face, there was only one cold, wet nose. She sneezed and the two dogs retreated. Orison grimaced as they barked; the sound was raucous. Her arm felt too heavy to move, even though she tried with all her might to pet one of the dogs. Rasping wheezes escaped Orison's chest and her veins burned; her body shuddered as she wept.

"Get help," she whispered as the world went dark.

For the first time since her exile, Orison no longer felt weak as she awoke on the forest floor. She felt as strong as when she was in the Othereal. Sitting up, she took in the surrounding forest and realised she hadn't woken up in Nalan Forest.

Unicorns galloped through the canopy of trees. A roar diverted her attention to the sky, where dragons flew overhead. She felt a heaviness settle on her shoulders; causing her to look at her arms, where a cloak of flowers settled around her. A group of pixies fluttered near her face and ogled her in awe. Laughter bubbled out of Orison as she tightened the ensemble around herself. A line of trolls—small things which looked like freshly picked potatoes—waved Orison along a cobblestone path. She pushed herself to her feet and followed them, accepting the bouquet of flowers they gave her.

The path led to a blinding white light which cut across the forest; she staggered back and shielded her eyes. As her eyes adjusted, she felt compelled to reach out to the light. It crawled up her arm in a warm embrace, offering peace and tranquillity. Through the haze, she saw a street like Parndore and childish giggles filled the air.

Orison looked behind her shoulder when she heard a dog barking. There were no dogs around the forest; only the unicorns, trolls and pixies were present in the darkness.

"It's not your time. Follow my voice," a rich voice sang to her. "Follow my voice."

Ignoring the comfort of the light, she was like a moth to a flame. She followed the voice, which was exotic, with a thick accent. She'd never heard such a beautiful song before.

As she stepped through the forest, the cloak of flowers fell from her shoulders. The darkness consumed her; even the beautiful creatures of the Othereal disappeared. Orison screamed when she fell into a hole and tumbled into a dark abyss.

Orison's eyes flew open. She gasped loudly and tried to take a deep breath. Her teeth chattered violently while observing her surroundings. She was in an unfamiliar bed with a thick patchwork blanket on top of her. Something heavy prevented her from moving her feet. Groaning, she propped herself onto her elbows to inspect the obstruction and saw Morty asleep on her legs.

The room was unfamiliar too. Shadows on the cream-plastered walls flickered from the candles in the chandelier. A half-vaulted ceiling sloped down to where the bed was sitting. The fireplace in the centre of the cramped room sat in darkness; to its left was a dining table and a door where the handle rattled.

Orison tensed and tried to click her fingers to obtain one of the fire pokers from the fireplace; alas nothing happened. Cringing, Orison eased her feet out from under Morty and rolled out of bed. Pain shot through her ribs when she crashed to the floor. She army crawled over to the fireplace, grabbed the fire poker and whirled around.

Two broad chested people walked into the room; their glowing eyes indicated they were Fae. One had yellow eyes, the other had green eyes. Both had dark brown hair to their waist and light brown skin. They spoke amongst themselves in a foreign language and shared laughter. Green eyes had a tray in his large hands. A strange pulling sensation filled Orison's chest, but she refused to disarm her weapon.

"Stop, don't come any closer," Orison squeaked as she aimed the pointed end of the fire poker at them. She was trying to sound fierce, but her lack of power took her voice as well.

The pair stopped and looked at one another; their laughter bellowed out of them. Green eyes leaned into his companion and spoke in that language again. Yellow eyes shrugged and crossed the room towards her; the pulling sensation in her chest intensified in his proximity. His round face was mesmerising up close and dare she say—he was handsome. She baulked when he wrestled the fire poker from her grip; she was too weak to fight him. He threw it across the room with a metallic clatter.

"I will scream," Orison threatened.

Green eyes leaned on the chair. "And who will side with you? Two Fae Glamoured to look like mortals; or you, who does not have her Glamour on?" His voice was so deep it vibrated the walls; his accent was thick and sounded familiar. Her eyes widened when she realised it was the one from the magic forest. The pair conversed in that foreign language again.

"What language is that?" Orison demanded.

Green eyes turned to her. "Karshakir." He drummed his thumbs on the chair. "My name is Erol and my companion is Ashim."

"Karshakir," she muttered. "Karshakroh?"

"*Halek*," Ashim, replied.

Orison gasped loudly and scrambled away from them, her back smacked into the wall. Xabian had told her Karshakians were untrustworthy; that they could break people in the most gruesome way possible and torture them for fun. She panted and brought her knees to her chest as she tried to calm down. The enemy had captured her.

"We buy food," Ashim said. His accent was so thick it was difficult to understand him and his voice was as deep as Erol's.

Her attention diverted to the tray on the dining table. The smell of beef stew awakened her hunger. Orison's mouth salivated at the promise of food, but she wouldn't accept any from Karshakians—they could have poisoned it.

A cry of pain escaped Orison as her veins burned. She collapsed to the floor and squeezed her eyes shut as she waited for it to pass. It was a pain like no other and one she'd been experiencing for days—she wanted it to stop. If these men were from Karshakroh, she didn't know which realm she had woken up in.

The feeling of a hand on her forehead made Orison quickly sit up; she hit her head on the corner of the mantelpiece and yelped. Ashim winced apologetically and crouched beside her. He looked over his shoulder at Erol as she inched away.

"If it wasn't for the dog, you'd be dead," Erol grumbled. "Princess Orison, why aren't you using your powers?"

She breathed heavily and gawped like a fish, taken aback by his friendly disposition. "My powers are gone," Orison admitted. "Every day I keep trying to get it back, but I can only manage a spark. Are we in Karshakroh? Othereal?"

"Mortal realm," Ashim clarified.

The pair resumed talking in Karshakir. She frowned. If they were trying to stop her from dying, then they must have other motives. Orison gazed longingly at the bowl of stew Erol had kept out of reach from her. Her mouth salivated for the food underneath the metal cover and her stomach let out animalistic noises.

Erol glanced at her. "You aren't eating or leaving until you use your power."

"So, you are planning to hold me captive," Orison grumbled. "I told you, my power is gone. It vanished when I was exiled."

Erol rolled his eyes with a shake of his head. Ashim held his hand up, but she pushed it away. He held it up again and despite her struggle, he made Orison hold her hand up. She shifted further back as Ashim waved his fingers in a circular motion. Her eyes widened when an apple appeared out of thin air. Ashim gestured for her to do the same. Orison sighed and copied the circular motion; an apple appeared in her hand, causing her to gasp.

"Magic work not same," Ashim said. He spoke slowly, as though he had difficulty with talking in the common tongue. Orison's hunger betrayed her judgement and she tried to take a bite of the apple. It disappeared with a click of Ashim's fingers, then reappeared in his hand. She glared at him. "Get it back."

The apple returned when she clicked her fingers. She attempted to take another bite, but Ashim snatched it back again with his magic. Glowering at Ashim, she gave into his game, finding the more they continued, the better she felt. Her body had the first semblance of energy in days. Setting her sights on the other target, she clicked her fingers and the tray of food appeared in her lap.

Orison tore into the bread roll like she hadn't seen food before and shoved a large piece into her mouth. She was too hungry to care if they had poisoned it.

"You'll get stomach ache if you eat fast," Erol warned.

She drank the water with her mouth full of bread, then tried to slow herself down. Once again, Erol and Ashim talked amongst themselves. Orison glanced at Morty, realising he had woken up and was watching the interactions. Doubt settled in that these men would hurt her. They had helped her regain her power and fed her after all; neither had made crude advances.

"If I'm in the mortal realm, where am I?" Orison asked, realising she didn't have a clue.

"Roseview," Erol stated. "In The Goblin Tavern."

Orison relaxed to know she was still in her home town; she knew her way home from there. She finished her food quickly and drank more water. The men continued to converse amongst themselves as she staggered onto her feet, her legs trembling. It was the first time in a week that she hadn't felt dizzy.

"I should get home; my parents will be worried." She grabbed Morty's leash. "Thank you for the food and for saving me."

"We walk home," Ashim said as he opened the door.

Orison baulked and looked at Erol. He let out an exasperated sigh, "Please trust us, he just wants to walk you home so that you're safe."

Orison nodded as Morty pulled her out of the room. She turned around to ensure Ashim followed and watched him close the door behind them. He gestured for her to continue walking and they both made their way back into civilisation.

The moon illuminated the path to her parents' home. Orison's rejuvenated energy had her wanting to run home or jump into the nearest river for a swim.

All thanks to the man who walked silently beside her; and his companion in the tavern. Something told her Xabian lied about them being untrustworthy.

Morty tugged on his leash as they walked; he sniffed at a tree and then moved on. Though Orison would have preferred to walk home alone, she was comforted that Ashim walked beside her. With the night dragging on, the forest adorned an ominous mask and she felt safer with him by her side.

"Sorry for thinking you were going to hurt me." Orison looked at her feet in shame. "A friend told me all Karshakians torture people for fun."

"We aren't like that," Ashim replied. "And it's okay, most Fallasingha people think so."

"You shouldn't be used to it." Orison folded her arms across her chest. "Which part of Karshakroh are you from?"

"Haranshal." His accent was thick and strong.

"Haranshal," she repeated, poorly imitating his voice. She stopped when Morty found a mushroom to sniff.

Ashim tilted his head. "Please don't repeat my accent. It'll sound better in yours."

"Sorry. Haranshal sounds beautiful the way you pronounce it."

Morty sneezed on a mushroom and bolted. Orison nearly tripped over her feet, but Ashim caught her. The dog yelped when his leash went taut and forced him to retreat. She shook her head with a groan as she continued walking. Morty had always been skittish. There were countless times a bird scared him and he bolted.

As they cleared the tree line, the thatched roof cottage came into full view with candles in the windows to guide somebody home. Orison came to a stop, allowing Morty to sniff around her feet. She petted him while wondering if Ashim would take her to the front door. Her father would ask way too many embarrassing questions if so.

"Your royal carriage awaits," he said, gesturing to the cottage. Orison looked at the cottage and let out a laugh. Ashim frowned. "What?"

"That's not a carriage."

He muttered to himself in Karshakir. Ashim tapped his chin. "What is a carriage?"

"A carriage is something pulled by a horse and helps you travel across the land," Orison explained.

"Oh! A diacerre." Ashim said, scratching the back of his neck. "Sorry."

Orison noticed his cheeks turning red. "You're doing okay." She pointed to her parents' home. "That is a cottage."

"Thank you."

"Good night," she said with a smile.

Morty gave up waiting and snorted like a pig as he pulled against his leash, attempting to drag Orison towards their home; his tail wagged furiously. She rolled her eyes as she nearly tripped from the strength of the dog. Orison wanted to stay with Ashim. The odd pulling sensation in his presence was a persistent entity that she couldn't put a finger on, making her wonder if he felt it as well.

"Little Queen," Ashim called. The nickname made her pause and turn around. Morty growled and barked at the interruption. "Have a safe journey to sleep!"

She let out another laugh and shook her head. "Good night!"

Ashim's mistakes in the common tongue were only funny to Orison because she understood everything he was saying. If Orison ever saw Ashim again, she vowed to teach him how to sound more natural in this environment. The common tongue was difficult, yet he wasn't incompetent at holding a conversation.

With a final glance at the Karshakian man, Orison gave in to Morty's demands to get home. The strange pulling in her chest dulled to nothing, the further that Orison strayed from Ashim's side. She cast a glance over her shoulder with her hand on her chest. Through the darkness, she could make out Ashim's silhouette as he watched her from the shadows; ensuring she got home safely. Shaking off the sensation, Orison's attention turned to her parents' front door. At the sound of a creak, her mother hurried to her and pulled her into a hug.

"Where have you been?" she asked in a shrill voice.

"I fell asleep in the forest, then got dinner in town," Orison lied. She let go of Morty's leash and let him disappear into the house. In her mother's current state, Orison didn't want to tell her about the near-death experience. "See, I'm fine."

Georgea pulled away, checking Orison's face. Her thumb ran over Orison's cheek and her hair. "You don't look as ill, baby." She ushered Orison inside with a hand on her back. "Are you feeling better?"

"Much better. I learned how to use some of my magic while outside."

"That's good."

The dull thud of a hammer emanated out of the spare bedroom; indicating that her father was hard at work. Orison glanced at her bedroom door, wanting to curl up and fall asleep after her ordeal in the forest—but needed to convince her mother she was fine. Georgea hurried to the kitchen and grabbed the kettle. She placed it on the stove, humming as she grabbed tea leaves from a cupboard.

Orison settled on the sofa. She looked at her hands, then at the stairs as her thoughts drifted to Xabian. With the return of her power, she could figure out a way to wake him up.

FOUR

Crockery clinked against each other as Orison carried a tray through the darkened upstairs corridor. She hummed as she walked, keeping her attention on the door at the end, which was ajar. Orison pushed it open with her hip and stumbled when Morty shoved her to the side as he ran into the room. She swore under her breath as orange juice splattered across the tray.

"Morty!" she reprimanded.

Orison rolled her eyes as she stepped into the room; Morty leapt onto the bed and curled up at Xabian's feet. The room had two windows that sandwiched the bed in the centre and a third window to the right of the room with a chest of drawers underneath. The left wall had a bookcase carved into it, which was filled with books from Orison's childhood; most had seen better days. Beside the bookcase was a small fireplace, where the mantel displayed some carved wooden figurines. The white plastered walls with vaulted ceilings gave it an illusion of being bigger than it was.

She made her way over to Xabian and sat on the edge of the bed. Her gaze roamed over his unconscious figure. To her surprise, his skin didn't take on a sickly green hue, as a result of not using his powers for over a week. He appeared as though it was last night he went to sleep and had yet to wake up.

She placed the tray of chicken broth on the bedside table. She frowned when she waved her hand to conjure wind to clean the spilled orange juice—nothing happened. With a huff of breath, she returned her attention to Xabian.

The bed creaked when Orison stood up. She placed her hands underneath Xabian's armpits and propped him into a sitting position, with a heave. She breathed heavily and collapsed onto him from the exertion, still weak from not using her power. When she pushed away from Xabian, his head lolled to the side. This was supposed to be her mother's job, but her mother had to run off to a client's house for a dress fitting.

Orison sat on the bed and dipped the spoon into the broth, blowing on it until it was lukewarm. She spoon fed Xabian, moving his head back until she saw his throat bob to indicate it went down.

"Can you hear me?" Orison inquired.

With bated breath, she waited for him to stir; like her magic—nothing happened. Only the rise and fall of his chest showed he was alive. It was ridiculous to think he could wake up. Shaking her head, she continued to feed him. The spoon clattered in the bowl as she set it down, replacing it with the cup of orange juice and helping him drink.

Orison tensed when the door opened. Morty lifted his head to inspect their intruder. Looking over her shoulder, she relaxed when her father strolled in; his brown hair was swept to one side. The sleeves of his white shirt stretched over his muscular frame and rolled up to the elbows as he crossed the threshold of her room. Marcus extended a white pouch to Orison with a smile. She took the pouch and tugged on the pull string to open it up; inside were three vials of white powder.

"The apothecary said smelling salts might work," Marcus suggested. He settled into the rocking chair in front of the bookshelf. "We could give it a go."

"But the urine didn't work," Orison pointed out.

"This might be different. It won't hurt to try," Marcus urged.

Orison toyed with the vials in her hand. Taking one vial out, she slipped the bag into the drawer of her bedside table. Time was running out for Xabian. She couldn't let her parents see him waste away in the bed any longer. Morty nudged at the vial in her hand with his nose. She petted his soft fur with a kiss as she prepared to open the concoction.

She popped the cork and retched; the pungent scent of body odour attacked her senses. Orison made quick work of waving it under Xabian's nose before snapping the cork back into place with a cringe. Placing the vial in the drawer, she vowed to be prepared next time.

While waiting, she tapped her foot anxiously. She observed her father when he picked up the wooden figurines on her mantel—a king and queen with their princess. Although the faded paint had chips, they were the toys from her childhood and she refused to part with them.

"Do you remember when I carved these?" he asked.

She nodded with a smile. "They're still beautiful."

A gasp dragged her attention away from her father. Xabian's purple eyes flared as they flew open; he clutched the duvet closer around him. Orison covered her mouth to see that they had succeeded, despite the foul smell.

"Xabian?" Orison asked. She inched closer to him.

He slowly looked at her. "How long has it been?"

"A week," Orison explained.

"How are you alive right now?" Xabian asked, his eyes widened in surprise. "You... you should be dead at this point. You don't know how to use your powers in the mortal realm."

Orison gawped and looked at her father. She pushed her hair behind her ear, then turned to Xabian, "That's your first thought?"

"Sorry, just surprised," Xabian admitted as he shrank into bed.

"I've been teaching myself," she lied. With her father in the room, she didn't want to mention the men from Karshakroh who saved her. Xabian made to speak, but she changed the subject by reaching for the broth. "Look, we made you food."

Xabian grabbed the bowl and guzzled the broth down, forgoing using a spoon. When the broth dribbled down his chin, Orison itched to clean it from his face and flexed her hands to stop herself. The bowl skittered on the tray when it was down to the dregs. Xabian used his powers to make bread appear and wiped the bowl clean. Watching him devour the food like an animal made

Orison's jaw fall open. He grabbed the orange juice and glugged it down in one go, dribbling on the white shirt her father had given him.

Xabian patted his belly and belched. "Sorry."

"We can get you more, if you wish," Marcus offered. "Though we've been feeding you broth, you must be starving."

He covered his mouth when he burped again. "I'm fine for now, thank you."

Unable to control herself, Orison grabbed a handkerchief from the bedside drawer. She wiped the broth and orange juice off him. "Did you have to eat like an animal?"

Xabian ignored her question. Instead, he Misted away with a flurry of purple smoke. She straightened up and bit her lip as she tried to figure out where he'd gone. Marcus was aghast at Xabian's power; evidently new to Fae power.

Orison jumped when Xabian reappeared a few moments later. He staggered towards the bed, then froze. His eyes widened and his face blanched, like he had witnessed something horrific. As though sensing the horrors that Xabian witnessed, Morty barked and stood on the bed with his hackles up. Orison tried to calm Morty down by petting his fur, but he continued to bark.

A scream tore out of her when Xabian fell to the floor. His muscles convulsed and he twitched violently on the floor.

"Xabian!" she screamed.

"Get him onto his side," her father instructed.

She crouched beside Xabian and pushed him onto his side with a grimace. Orison's heart raced as her hand wrapped around Xabian's clenched fist. His eyes rolled to the back of his head and pain-filled groans passed his lips. Her father appeared next to her, placing a pillow underneath Xabian's head. Orison inched back; tears burned her eyes, which she blinked away quickly.

"Father, what's happening?" Orison asked.

Xabian's purple eyes flared as his muscles seized once more; he let out a pained cry. For the second time since arriving in the mortal realm, Orison felt powerless. Her father rubbed Xabian's arm, offering hushed words of comfort as the convulsions subsided, continuing long after the prince returned to his unconscious state.

Saskia pressed herself against the wall as two Akornsonian guards vacated King Sila's former bed chambers—a golden chest of drawers between them. She watched as they disappeared down the servants' staircase. Confident that the coast was clear, she moved into the vacant room, which was void of furniture.

A metallic clink, from hammers on chisels, filled the space where elves worked to seal the reflection pools. Other elves mulled about to remove furniture from the bedroom. They had volunteered to aid in removing Sila's belongings throughout the castle, alongside Fallasingha guards. They both worked in perfect harmony.

Saskia's high heels clicked as she entered King Sila's bedroom. The white walls with gold embellishments appeared lighter without his presence. Minimal furniture remained inside; the bed was the first to go. She frowned at the bookcase which spanned the entire length of the room. All the books were bound in black with no exterior text to show their titles. She had never noticed it before. Every time she came in here, that wall was like the others—except for the bay window.

Taviar, Riddle and Kinsley inspected the bookcase. Sitting backwards on a chair, Nazareth frowned at the discovery as she drummed her fingers on the wood. They all appeared puzzled, like the bookcase wasn't supposed to be there.

"Did you install a bookcase in my absence?" Saskia asked as she neared.

Everybody turned their attention to Saskia. Nazareth straightened up on the chair. "Kinsley noticed a groove in the wall while cleaning. When she pressed on it, this appeared." She gestured to the bookcase.

"I didn't know he had a secret bookcase behind the wall," Saskia admitted.

"Me neither," Taviar cut in.

Riddle approached the books, tapping his chin. "They are all enchanted," he pointed out absentmindedly.

"Have you opened any of them?" Saskia enquired.

Taviar directed his attention back to the bookcase. "Not yet. Who volunteers?"

"As royal advisor, I feel I should go first," Saskia said. Though her racing heart deceived her confidence. "But Kinsley is the one who found the bookcase."

Kinsley gestured to it. "You open a book, Sas. I'm too scared."

She smoothed out her buttercup yellow dress and cleared her throat. With her shoulders pushed back and chin set high, she approached the bookcase and scanned the shelves for the best book to choose. Saskia pulled one from the shelf; it hummed in her hand from the magic it possessed. Though her stomach twisted with nerves, Saskia resolved her fear and opened the book.

To her surprise, a blank page stared back at her. She made to address the group, however, before she could get any words out, she was thrown backwards by a blinding white light. Saskia cried out as she crashed to the floor. Riddle was at her side in an instant and helped her sit up. He checked her for any injuries, eyes wide with horror.

"Othereal above!" Kinsley exclaimed.

Saskia and Riddle turned towards Kinsley. In unison, they gasped when their eyes fell upon somebody who had appeared in the centre of the room; seated on the book. The person had wet tendrils of hair; their bones protruded out of the dirt-riddled rags they wore. They shivered violently and loud sobs filled the room.

"I can't perform any more spells, My King," a timid lilting voice rasped. "I'm so tired."

Taviar approached the stranger slowly and crouched in front of them. "King Sila has passed away," he announced. "May I get your name?"

"Enchantress Emphina," she recalled. "Please don't make me perform spells."

"No, we're here to help. Are you the only one here?"

Saskia followed Emphina's trembling hand as she raised it to point at the textless books. A horror-filled gasp escaped Saskia as she covered her mouth at what this meant. The entire wall was filled with imprisoned enchantresses.

Nazareth pressed a hand to her stomach. "I think I'm going to throw up."

Without further ado, Saskia staggered to her feet and approached the bookcase, taking down each book—one by one—with careful precision. Riddle came to her aid soon after.

"Get Eloise and take the books to the infirmary," Saskia instructed quickly. "When you free them, they will need food and water."

As a team, they handed each book to Kinsley or Nazareth to place in a pile by the door. Taviar relayed orders to the guards. Hurried footsteps sounded outside of the room, making Saskia glance over her shoulder to witness guards getting to work.

Emphina looked at Saskia with a bewildered look. "You're freeing us?"

"Of course, we're freeing you," Saskia explained between passes of books.

Though they needed an enchantress to get Orison and Xabian out of the mortal realm, they couldn't do so with enchantresses so weak from neglect.

The Roseview Market, a maze of wooden stalls with colourful canopies, had a bustling aura. Over the sound of patrons chattering, vendors hollered about their sales and the latest goods from lands far away. Giggling children ran through the labyrinth, bypassing the crowd of people looking at the latest wares.

Amongst them, Orison strayed from her father's booth and walked through the cramped environment. She wore a red cloak over her head to conceal her purple eyes and pointed ears; the bag of coin on her hip jingled with each step. She was grateful nobody batted an eyelash at her, not wanting a repeat of the night of her arrival.

Leaving the confines of the market, Orison stumbled upon the Goblin Tavern again. She was so lost in her head she didn't know why she had ended up here. The timber-framed structure eclipsed the sun, towering over her. Pot-bellied men—roaring with laughter—filled the tavern's veranda as they sat around wooden tables. Orison cringed, knowing that their beer was warm—judging by the lack of condensation on their glasses.

With a hand pressed to her stomach that growled loudly, she made her way towards the tavern's open door. Once inside, Orison remembered how packed this place always was; tables were crammed together, with too many people around them for their intended purpose. Servers struggled to navigate their way around to fill orders—they all looked exhausted. Various decorations adorned the dark wooden walls. The smell of alcohol and food, along with sweat, lingered in the air.

Orison leaned against the bar. "Hi Darius, a beer and a steak pie, please."

The man behind the bar cast a scrutinising glance at her. "We don't serve the Fae."

Her heart skipped a beat when the tavern fell silent—aside from the creaking chairs—as the people of Roseview turned to stare. Orison audibly gulped and tapped her thumb on the wooden edge of the bar. They knew her parents weren't there to protect her this time.

"It's me—Orison. You saw me in the clearing and assisted my parents," she explained.

Darius spat into the cup and waved it in the air. "Go on."

Orison baulked and glanced around when three men surrounded her. A yelp filled the silenced space as the men wrestled the cloak off her, exposing her Fae-like features. Her heart pounded painfully against her ribs when their laughter skittered around her. She screamed for help as they grabbed her from behind. Thrashing in their grasp, she tried to kick them until they lifted her in the air and carried her towards the entrance.

"Please!" she cried.

At the doorway, the men threw her to the ground like she was a piece of rubbish. Orison landed hard on the cobblestone path. It sent pain through her hip as she skidded to a halt; the scraped skin on her hand burned. She flinched when the men snorted and took it in turns to spit on her; causing her to retch as she curled up on the ground, refusing to cry.

She struggled against a hand on her back until she felt the strange pull in her chest. "Shush." Orison ceased her fight and whirled around. Ashim stood over her. "Can you walk?"

With a nod, Orison allowed Ashim to help her. His dark brown hair brushed against her skin, where it fell over his shoulder. His gentle hands aided Orison to her feet. She fell into his chest, her breath taken away. Ashim stepped back to brush down her green peasant dress, ridding it of the dirt that had accumulated from the assault. He took a handkerchief out of his pocket and handed it to Orison. She thanked him as she wiped the spit from her face and folded it over to dab away at the other spots.

"I should have known," Orison grumbled, allowing Ashim to take her hand. He inspected it before he blew on the cuts that marred her skin. She cried out and held her hand to her chest. "Fuck, that hurts!"

"Sorry," Ashim said quickly. She hissed as she inspected her hand. "You cannot Glamour?"

"What gave that away?" she snapped, harsher than she intended to. Orison noticed her hand wasn't healing immediately, like injuries usually did. "Do injuries heal slower here?"

Ashim nodded. "*Halek*."

With a groan, Orison looked at the sky, exasperated at this turn of events. The pull in her chest disappeared. She turned her attention to Ashim, realising he was nowhere to be seen. Orison swallowed the lump in her throat, turning her

back on the tavern in defeat. Her belly still growled and one of the only other
Fae had abandoned her.

She re-entered the labyrinth of stalls, too numb to react to the people who
pushed into her at all angles. It was the first time she felt like a foreigner in
her own home. Everybody regarded her as a stranger since her return. Orison
Durham, the naïve mortal who these people grew up with, died when King
Sila kidnapped her. That's the only story these people would believe.

The strange pulling in her chest returned. "Excuse me, ma'am," Ashim
exclaimed. Orison gradually came to a halt. She turned around in surprise that
he had come back. In his hand was a wicker basket. "Can I eat you out?"

Orison guffawed and let out a laugh. "Do you ask that of all women you've
just met?"

"What?" He frowned and muttered to himself in Karshakir, turning his back
on her. Ashim whirled back around with wide eyes. "No!" he exclaimed. "No,
no, no! Lunch. Do you want lunch with me?"

Orison's body shifted as a laugh bubbled out of her. "Othereal above." She
ran a hand down her face. "Yes, I will eat lunch with you."

A laugh escaped him and he cringed as he scratched the back of his neck.
Orison was relieved he didn't leave her like she thought he had; the gesture
made her feel warm inside. Ashim puffed out his chest and extended his elbow
to her. Orison looped her arm through his and they set out on a quest for a
picnic spot.

"Where are we going?" Ashim asked.

Orison laughed again. "Aren't you supposed to be the one taking me to
lunch?" She grinned. Ashim shrugged. "Come on, I know a place."

Orison's cheeks hurt as they began their quest. She hadn't laughed so much
in a long while. They walked side by side out of the market. At the Goblin
Tavern she veered Ashim to the right, leading him to a park he might like. It
would be much better than a stuffy tavern full of men drooling over their pints
and fighting. Having Ashim in town made Orison not feel so alone.

FIVE

At the top of a hill in a secluded park, Roseview was put on a pedestal. The Nalan Forest encompassed the town and stretched like a veil out to the horizon. Roseview Market's colourful canopy displayed like a patchwork quilt over a section of the town.

Ashim had never been to this part of Roseview, despite it being his tenth visit. It was a peaceful place, full of birdsong and a scarcity of mortals. The mortals mulled around at the bottom of the hill, basking in the summer heat. Being this far away from civilisation was liberating. He could drop his Glamour under the cover of trees and breathe a sigh of relief. Ashim let the bottle of beer hang between his fingers as he looked across the distant horizon.

"Tell me, what is a guard doing in the mortal realm?" Orison spoke with her mouth full, muffling her question. It pulled Ashim out of his thoughts; his gaze fell to where she licked pieces of pie from her fork. "Did King Raj exile you out of anger too?"

Nobody assumed he was a guard before; the mere thought made him laugh. Shaking his head, Ashim held his leg to his chest. "Anesh," he managed. "I'm King Raj's Runner."

She raised an eyebrow. "Runner?"

"My ohrahnarsh sell... sold." Ashim shook his head. "Sell me to King Raj." He cringed.

"Sold," Orison corrected. "What's an ohrahnarsh?"

Ashim frowned. "When you have no parents; it is a home."

"Oh! Orphanage," Orison said.

"*Halek*. My orphanage sold me to King Raj at ten years old; now I work for him," Ashim explained. He pulled down the collar of his shirt, revealing the brand of a lion over his heart; the lion had a *K* for a third eye. It signified his loyalty to Karshakroh. "*Lohar.*"

Orison gawped at the brand, astonished at its very presence. She reached out to touch it, but Ashim adjusted his shirt and kept the brand out of her reach. He didn't know her well enough for her to touch his brand. Ashim returned to his beer and took a long drink as Orison cleared her throat.

"How old are you now?"

Ashim frowned and counted on his fingers. It had been too long since they had assigned him a job in the mortal realm, so long that he didn't remember the numbers. "Two, one. Twenty-one. I'm twenty-one," he stammered. His cheeks heated and he shied away. "Sorry."

Orison shook her head. "Don't apologise. Do orphanages always sell their children to the king?"

"Karshakroh is poor," Ashim stated. "My orphanage had to sell me to pay a tithe."

"But you were ten, bound to a king for work. Doesn't that make you a slave?" Orison accused.

"No!" Ashim snapped, harsher than he intended. "Ten is normal for work, I chose this. King Raj treats me with respect, I get freedom and he lets me look after my baby."

To most people, ten years of age was too young to work; Karshakroh was very different. Raj had raised Ashim, teaching him everything he knew, Ashim had chosen to be a Runner and the king paid handsomely with each assignment completed. By the age of fifteen, he could own his own apartment in the capital city of Haranshal. Few people in Karshakroh got that luxury, even as adults. The one bonus the home had was that his cat, Mahavu, had a roof over her head.

"You have a baby?" Orison widened her eyes. "You're a father?"

Ashim cringed and rubbed his neck. "Cat father." His cheeks heated; many called him silly for considering Mahavu as his daughter. "I know she's just a cat, but I raise her."

"Of course, she's your baby, regardless of species," Orison assured.

Ashim huffed out a breath as he placed the bottle of beer in the basket and stood up. He tightened his ponytail, then extended his hand out to her. "Nobody is around, let's play Faerie tag."

Orison threw her head back and laughed. "What?"

"You Mist how you do at home. So..." He tapped her arm. "Tag, you're it."

Ashim Misted away from her in a flurry of beige smoke and sand. He landed nearby behind a tree, not straying too far away from the picnic area. He observed Orison as she tried to Mist. A flurry of purple smoke enveloped her and she disappeared from where she sat. His heart skipped a beat, hoping she would land safely. When Orison materialised, she crashed face-first into the grass with a squeal.

"Orison!" Ashim ran to her aid, crouching beside her and rolling Orison onto her back. "Alright?"

To his surprise, Orison held her stomach in a fit of laughter. "Yeah, I'm fine. I lost balance because it feels heavier." Ashim lowered his head in relief. He tensed when she tapped his arm. "Tag, you're it!"

Ashim gasped when he realised that she had tricked him. Shaking his head with a smile, she Misted away before he could react. He loved a challenge and he would win this game. Anticipating Orison's direction, he Misted towards it. His judgement proved correct, as she materialised in front of him, making her skid to a stop. She almost fell, but Ashim caught her. He tapped her arm and with a flurry of beige smoke and sand, he Misted to a different tree.

Ashim landed three trees away from where Orison materialised. She smirked as she stalked towards him, but he Misted to the other side of their picnic area, hoping to evade her before she made her move. Feeling a small tap on his arm, he turned around and swore when Orison stood before him.

He was pleased that Orison quickly got the hang of it. Each time they Misted, she got a fraction quicker; to the point that avoiding her keen eye was nearly impossible. To get away, Ashim Misted onto a tree branch and watched Orison look around for him with her hands on her hips.

"Okay, come out. That's not fair," Orison called out.

Jumping from the tree, he stirred up only a handful of dirt as he landed with grace. "Boo."

Orison jumped with a hand over her heart. "Othereal above." He chuckled; ready to go again until she shook her head. "We should stop before the mortals see and get their pitchforks out."

Though deflated from having his fun stopped, Ashim agreed it was better to be safe than sorry. He pointed to their picnic location and walked her back to their basket.

Their little private picnic area was where Ashim talked to Orison well into the afternoon; until Erol found Ashim to begin their next assignment for King Raj.

A light shower of rain fell onto the cobblestone street of Merchant's Row. Despite the depletion of staff, it was still full of families and soldiers going about their daily business. Some crossed from one timber-framed shop to the next. Neighbours helped bring children home. Off-duty guards crowded outside the local tavern, regardless of the rain; their laughter roared through the street, along with their hands slamming on tables.

One of them placed their fingers in their mouth and whistled to Saskia as she walked past them. "Hello, pretty lady; want to join us for a round of drinks and a party after?"

Saskia turned; heat rose to her cheeks at the exchange. "Maybe another time, Harold."

Harold blanched at the realisation of who he catcalled. "Apologies, Advisor."

"I'm sure after this meeting I shall join you for drinks," she promised with a grin.

She continued to walk with a smile spread across her face. It wasn't every day she got catcalled; it was affirmation she was doing something right. Saskia lifted her chin and approached the illuminated façade of Riddle Me This Antiquities.

It was a mystery why Taviar had summoned her to the shop and not one of the many meeting rooms within the castle. Her heart raced at the thought that something happened to the children. Saskia quickly shook that thought away.

The bell rang as she pushed the door open and stepped inside. She was thankful for the delicious warmth that seeped into her wet clothing. She used her magic to dry her emerald green dress and blonde wig; another click of her fingers put her make-up right. Zade and Yil were behind the counter, grinning from ear to ear.

"Grandma Saskia!" Yil shouted as he ran up to her. She staggered back with a laugh when he hugged her waist. "Hello!"

She ruffled his hair. "Hello, where's your father?"

"He's upstairs with Papa," Zade said from the counter. "He has some friends around."

That made her pause. Yil stepped away from her and she made her way to the stairs that led to the apartment where the Luxarts lived. They had rooms in the castle to reside in, but Riddle and Taviar couldn't bear sleeping there while remnants of Sila remained inside.

"Look after the shop while the adults talk, okay?"

Zade nodded as his brother joined him; he was scribbling something on a sheet of parchment. Confident that the twins wouldn't tear up the place, Saskia picked up her skirts and ascended the stairs. The further she went, the more she could hear the crescendo of voices—making her tense.

Through the baluster, she could see that Nazareth sat on the green armchair, nursing a glass of amber liquid. Kinsley, Aeson and Eloise were sitting on the sofa—laughing amongst themselves. Her attention snagged onto Emphina. She looked healthier than the last time they met—her flowing dark-brown hair fell to her elbows, though her bones continued to protrude through her white dress.

They had removed 284 books from Sila's bedchamber. At first, it did not convince the enchantresses that they were free; until Saskia aided Taviar in burning all the books and allowing the enchantresses to join in.

The floorboards creaked when Saskia got to the top of the stairs; the room fell silent as everyone looked in her direction. "Hello," she greeted with a curtsy.

"Hello, Sas." Riddle exclaimed from a nearby corridor. "How are you?"

Saskia fidgeted with the bodice of her dress. "I'm fine, thank you. Is Taviar here? I received his correspondence."

"I'm here." His voice filtered from his bedroom.

The stairs creaked as Taviar jogged down the stairs and pulled her into a one-armed hug. Saskia inched towards the sofa, thanking Kinsley when she moved to sit on Aeson's lap to accommodate her. She sat down and waited, hearing commotion from the kitchen behind her. Wood scraped on wood as Taviar dragged a chair from the nearby dining table to sit on for this meeting.

"I thought the twins got hurt," Saskia admitted with a laugh.

Kinsley scoffed. "For once, they're behaving," she joked. Taviar shot her a stern look, she swiftly averted her gaze to the floor. "Sorry."

"We should get this meeting started," Taviar announced and gestured to Emphina, who looked up with wide eyes. "Emphina, you suggested it, so you should go first."

She cleared her throat and fidgeted in her seat. "I am forever in your debt for allowing me to escape, along with my sisters. To thank you, I will perform a spell for you when I have regained strength in my powers."

Saskia tensed. This had to be a blessing from the gods. "Oh, you don't have to."

"I insist," she said sternly.

Taviar tapped his nose. "Actually, we need your services. Queen Orison and Prince Xabian are in the mortal realm. We need a portal to bring them home."

"That would require several sisters to bring them home," Emphina pointed out. Saskia looked down at her hands in remorse; she knew this task was difficult. "However, I think we can come to an agreement. My sisters and I need a territory, so if you can give us that, then our debts are settled."

Taviar was silent for a long moment, his brow furrowed in deep thought. "I think your clan can do great things within Cleravoralis. We can send an escort there to ensure you're settled," he declared. Saskia straightened up and looked at him. There wasn't any point in asking for her opinion; it was the only solution they had. "When can you expect the portal to be completed?"

"I can't make promises, but at the latest—a month."

Saskia closed her eyes; it was the worst-case scenario. When her eyes fluttered open, Taviar and Emphina shook hands in agreement, then they turned to her. Saskia hesitated, but thought better of it; she extended her hand and sealed Fallasingha's fate.

SIX

A ball of dough thudded against the countertop. Flour rained down like snow and a rolling pin flattened out the dough. Orison huffed out a breath to rid a stray hair from her face. When that didn't work, she pushed it back with her hand, smearing flour across her cheek. A small bark made her look down at Morty, who licked his lips as he watched; his large brown eyes pleaded for a bite.

"This is raw bread dough, you silly dog," she groaned. "You can eat some after it's cooked."

He whined as he laid on the floor, giving her puppy-dog eyes. Orison shook her head and pulled off pieces of dough to create little balls. She placed them on the greased baking tray, casting a glance at Xabian sitting at the dining table.

Xabian glanced at Morty. "Is he always like that?"

"Yes, he will eat anything," Orison grumbled.

Orison stepped over Morty to get to the oven, finding it difficult to move around the kitchen with him in the way. She placed the bread in the oven and fed more logs into the compartment.

The chair creaked as Xabian shifted. "What's the worst thing he's eaten?"

"The sofa." Orison laughed at the memory of the stuffing that was strewn around the floor. She laughed even more at Xabian's perplexed expression. She crouched to Morty's level. "You're so silly," she said to Morty in a high-pitched voice reserved for babies.

A knock at the door drew her attention away from the dog. Orison stood up and winced at the fact that dough and flour caked her hands. She hurried over to the door and did her best to open it with her power. She gasped to see her visitors were none other than Erol and Ashim.

"Hello!" Orison exclaimed.

"Ahnes," Erol replied. "May we come in?"

"Yes, of course." Orison stepped out of the way for them, hiding her dirty hands behind her back. "Erol, Ashim, this is Prince Xabian; I'm sure you've heard about him."

Orison clicked her fingers to clean her hands and the mess she made from baking—glad that Ashim and Erol had taught her. They communicated amongst themselves in Karshakir; laughing amongst themselves.

The room fell silent when Xabian smacked his hand on the table. "Orison," he said sternly, his purple eyes flared. "Why are there Karshakians in your home and how do they know your name?"

Her mouth fell open. She looked at her saviours; clearing her throat, Orison gestured to them. "I lied. I didn't teach myself how to use my powers here; Erol and Ashim have been teaching me."

Xabian stood up slowly; she took a step back with an audible gulp. "Are they selling you?" he snapped.

"What?" Orison scoffed and regarded them. "No, they've never touched me!"

"*Why* are you being a reckless bitch?" Xabian seethed. His tone made Morty bark in Orison's defence.

Erol stepped forward, fury written along his scowl. He spoke sternly in Karshakir to Xabian, Orison could feel the vibration of his voice in the floorboards. She found comfort when Ashim came closer to her. Leaning against the chair, Xabian snarled at them both for coming to Orison's defence.

When Xabian froze, Orison stepped forward to catch him—judging by the seizure he had the last time he was awake. He crumpled to his knees, taking Orison down with him. She cried out as she crashed to the floor; narrowly missing her head on the dining table. Xabian's muscles tensed as he convulsed on the floor. With all her strength, Orison wrestled her way out from under Xabian and shoved him onto his side.

Erol crouched beside Xabian, shouting instructions at Ashim in Karshakir. It happened in a blur of movements; Orison couldn't focus as groans escaped Xabian. She covered her mouth upon witnessing the convulsions a second time.

"Is this normal?" Ashim asked.

Orison slumped against Xabian with heavy breaths as the seizure subsided. "No, this is new." She moved her hair from her face and noted Erol's bewilderment.

She went to explain, but Erol cut her off. Ashim grabbed Xabian by the foot and dragged him across the floor. Witnessing Orison's horror at how they were handling the prince, Erol muttered under his breath before he lifted Xabian's torso. Together they carried Xabian into the bedroom to the left of the stairs Orison had been occupying.

Xabian had changed. Since the moment he woke up, he was colder and more callous with his words, unlike the man she met in Alsaphus Castle. Part of Orison wanted to keep her distance from Xabian, but a foolish part of her wanted to remain friends.

The library welcomed Ashim and Orison, like it did with all its visitors.

Roseview Town Library was small with two levels. Wooden columns held the second floor up and the ground level had little alcoves for seating areas. People sat at desks, reading or writing under candlelight. Other than the scratching of styluses on parchment, everything was silent.

The smell of old books drifted through the air, along with the smell of leather. Within the maze of bookcases, adventures awaited. This was a sanctuary for dreamers; as any library should be.

Ashim hadn't stepped into a mortal library before. Usually on missions for King Raj, he had been too busy to explore Roseview. However, on this mission, Ashim had a year to find a new mortal servant for his king. Between searches, he had time to relax and explore the village to his heart's content. Roseview Town Library gave him the opportunity to learn the common tongue and to be good at it.

"They say that this library is the oldest in Roseview," Orison whispered as they dived into the maze of bookcases. Ashim raised an eyebrow and made a noise. "It used to be the mayor's house before he moved to an estate on the outskirts."

Ashim glanced at the titles which glistened to him in the candlelight; he had difficulty understanding half of the words. He hated his inability to be as fluent as Erol in the common tongue. His listening skills were better than his reading or speaking skills. In this library, he could improve his language proficiency in all areas.

"I want to use books to improve my speaking," Ashim admitted.

She nodded. "I'll help you."

He followed Orison as she navigated her way around the shelves. Ashim lowered his head and shied away with embarrassment when they entered the children's section. Orison tapped her finger along the books as they made their way down the aisle. A loud gasp had Ashim's heart racing and he hurried to check if she was okay—only to relax as she pulled a book out of the shelves.

"I love this one," Orison whispered. The spine creaked as she opened it and traced her finger along the oil paintings inside. "Cinderella."

"Cinderella," he repeated slowly.

She sauntered over to an empty table and sat down in a darkened section of the library, hiding from the librarian's view. Ashim knew she still couldn't

Glamour yet—he'd teach her in time—but at this moment he was more focused on seeing the library.

Ashim settled beside her; he took the book and looked at the writing. His voice was shaky as he read to her quietly; nervous in case Orison judged him for his mistakes. Instead, she jumped in with any words he didn't know and corrected his pronunciation when he went wrong. His confidence with reading aloud soon grew.

A loud hum tore him away from the book. Following the direction of the sound, Ashim's eyes widened to witness the librarian leaning on their table. The formidable woman looked skeletal with the shadows from candlelight. Her black hair was bound in a bun, with glasses on the tip of her hooked nose.

She glared at Ashim and Orison. "We don't allow the Fae in our library. You must leave."

With an exasperated sigh, Orison slammed the book shut and stood up. "Libraries should be a place where people can be themselves." She rolled her eyes. "Guess not. Come on, Ash."

The librarian gawped at Orison's defiance. While the librarian was distracted, Ashim swiped the book and tucked it into the inside pocket of his jacket. With the woman being a bitch, she deserved to have her books stolen. He hurried after Orison when she stormed out.

Ashim had never encountered such discrimination from the mortals; his Glamour was a perfect mask in the mortal realm. He ran after Orison when she turned towards the Goblin Tavern. He grabbed her hand and led her back towards her home.

It didn't take long for them to return to the cottage, where anger still simmered through Orison's veins at being kicked out of another establishment. She sat on the edge of the armchair, tapping her feet in quick succession as her father and Ashim spoke in hushed whispers. Orison gnawed on the side of her nail and tried to focus.

Her gaze followed the two men as they sat on the sofa. She noticed her father fidgeted and squirmed in his seat. Orison frowned; things rarely affected her father. She raised an eyebrow at Ashim, who had a smug smile on his face. Her curiosity grew as Marcus cast glances between the two Fae and exhaled a breath.

"If you hurt my baby girl while doing this, I will throw an axe at your head," her father threatened.

"What?" Orison and Ashim cried in unison.

"I never intend to hurt Orison," Ashim defended.

Her father let out an exasperated sigh. Marcus shifted in his seat and cleared his throat, rubbing the stubble on his chin. Orison didn't know what made her father threaten Ashim, nor why Ashim made her return home.

"What am I needed for then?" Marcus asked.

"I'm going to teach Orison how to Glamour and I need your eyes," Ashim replied.

Orison gripped the arms of the sofa until her knuckles were white. "You are?" She gulped audibly.

Ashim ignored her fear. "It is like Misting. You tell yourself what mortals see." He sat back. "You can't appear as a bug, though; it's too small."

The room fell silent as Orison concentrated. She closed her eyes as she tried to think of what she looked like as a mortal. Something stirred within her, like a swirling sensation in the pit of her stomach. Orison opened one eye, then the other as she looked between them.

"Did it work?" she asked.

Orison looked at her father. The only downside to Glamour was the fact other Fae couldn't see if it worked. Her ability to Glamour successfully was solely on Marcus's shoulders. His mouth pulled into a straight line and he shook his head.

"No, it didn't work."

"Try again," Ashim instructed. "Tell Marcus what you want him to see."

Orison sat back on the armchair; the only sound in the room was that of her foot tapping on the wooden floor. She closed her eyes once more and tried to conjure up all the power she could to Glamour. A headache developed at the top of her head.

"What do I look like?" She opened her eyes to look at her father.

Marcus sat forward. "No, you still look Fae."

With a loud groan, she glared at Ashim as he scoffed. She could see he was trying not to laugh and wanted to smack the smirk from his face. Orison had tried to Glamour in the Othereal, but it was clear why that didn't work. It probably never worked if it took this much concentration.

Orison buried her head in her hands, humming loudly as she tried to concentrate on Glamouring. She attempted to adapt to what Ashim had told her. She repeated a mantra in her head until she convinced herself it worked.

"How about now?" Instead of answering, Marcus looked at Ashim. "Don't look at Ashim; I need to learn."

"If you can't do it, I can wipe the mortal brains," Ashim admitted. The comment earned him a look from both Orison and Marcus. "What? I'm a Mindelate."

"Mindelates can do that?" Orison asked. Ashim nodded. "Teach me that."

"Glamour first. Think of somebody you're close to."

Orison threw her head back against the armchair when Ashim adorned another smug grin. This time, she didn't bother to close her eyes and concentrate. She'd given up. Her mind wandered to the fact that Ashim could wipe minds. She didn't know Mindelates could do that; if she mastered the skill, she'd be a formidable weapon. Ashim was teaching her more in only a few days than she was ever taught in the Othereal. It was revolutionary.

She jumped when something smacked her head. Orison frowned and looked around, finding a sponge at the side of the sofa. Orison glared at Ashim, then back at the sponge. Using her magic to pick it up, she threw it back at Ashim. He flinched when it smacked him in the face.

"Careful, Little Queen," Ashim retorted with a chuckle.

"Don't throw sponges at me then," Orison snapped.

Hearing a snort, Orison looked at Marcus who appeared amused at the interaction. She glared at him. Ashim shook his head and chuckled, then focused on Orison. She rubbed her forehead profusely when the headache became like a pounding drum. Orison leaned back on the armchair and let out a huff of breath. She placed her hands over her face and screamed.

"You know, this isn't working," she grumbled at Ashim. Marcus gasped, making them stare at him. Something mesmerised him as he gestured to Orison. "What, father?"

"You look like your mother," he said.

Orison's head lolled to the side as she glanced at him. "I've always looked like my mother."

"No, I meant you don't look Fae."

As if it was fate, Georgea returned home from work. "Good afternoon!" she sang out. When she turned around, she yelped and fell against the wall. "Orison?"

"Yes, mother?"

Georgea glanced at everybody. "You look... mortal."

Realising that her Glamour worked made Orison's eyes widen. She was unsure of how she achieved it. She'd been telling herself it wouldn't work, but it did. Ashim had a proud grin when she looked at him.

"You did it!" he exclaimed.

Orison pushed herself off the sofa and threw her arms around him. "Thank you, thank you, thank you!" Ashim was tense under her embrace.

Marcus looked at him. "Thank you for helping Orison."

"Helping with what?" Georgea asked.

Orison released Ashim and beamed. "Ashim taught me to Glamour!" She looked down at herself, realising she didn't know how to change back. "How do I change back?"

"Do the opposite of what got you like that," Ashim replied.

It took only a few moments of doing the opposite, her parents were deflated. Georgea's smile vanished, along with Marcus's.

Orison felt giddy with excitement. She couldn't wait to run into town and explore everything without being turfed out. Ashim had saved her life and now he had given her freedom.

SEVEN

Through an open window, Ashim observed a woman curled up on a brown armchair reading a book; allowing the sound of rain to enter her space and provide a tranquil environment. Her dark hair fell to her waist, half tied up, allowing the rest to spill like ink over her shoulders.

Ashim lowered his telescope and glanced at Erol crouched behind an adjacent tree. His companion unrolled a piece of parchment to read over his observations. The surrounding shield kept them and the parchment dry. It didn't prevent the cold from seeping into Ashim's clothes from the wind and rain; his Fire Singer abilities battled to keep him warm.

"She works as a baker in town; that skill would come in handy in Karshakroh," Erol explained in Karshakir. "We need to do further investigations on what she's like at cleaning. That's another desirable skill."

Ashim peered back through the window. "Do you know her name?"

"What's the point when she might not accept the role?" Erol explained as he rolled up the parchment. "This is our strongest contender."

Ashim shifted. "Family?"

"You need to stop being compassionate," Erol reprimanded. He glared at his companion. "This is why the king rarely assigns you to the mortal realm."

Ashim rolled his eyes; he didn't need the reminder.

The king assigned the mission to Ashim and Erol after a horse trampled one of his mortal servants. He was relieved when King Raj bestowed this task upon him because no other Runner could fulfil the position. Retrieving diamonds, artefacts and gold from undesirable places had grown boring.

The last time he was tasked to retrieve a mortal, Ashim returned home crying because he couldn't bring himself to wipe the mortal's mind after transportation. Erol had forced Ashim's hand with his Protelsha abilities. Protelshas were dangerous business, they could bend anybody to their will with an improvised song. His powers were the only reason why Orison lived.

With a huff of breath, Ashim returned to his telescope to inspect the potential servant. His attention snagged onto the crib beside the woman. Inside the crib was a plump, pink baby that wriggled around. This wasn't moral, the baby needed its mother. Erol was right, Ashim was too compassionate for such a task.

Through the telescope, Ashim scanned the woman again—from her dark-brown hair, to her dark peasant dress and to the gold wedding band on her finger. He scanned down to her feet and around her ankles were bands of black beads—Normahlef Berries. The only thing that could nullify Fae powers. She wasn't the one. Ashim froze and lowered the telescope in horror.

"She's not the one, we need to find somebody else." Ashim slipped the telescope into his bag and turned away from the thatched roof cottage.

"What are you on about? This is the best we got," Erol hissed. "We need to interview her."

Ashim pointed to the house. "She's wearing double Normahlef Berries. No matter what we do, she won't accept and our magic won't work on her."

His companion frowned and looked through his telescope. "Fuck."

Ashim trudged through the woods, glancing over his shoulder when the leaves behind him rustled; Erol ran up to him, holding the strap of his satchel. He continued swearing as they ventured back to town.

"I really thought we had one then," Erol grumbled. "That is all Orison's fault. If only she knew how to Glamour before coming here, people wouldn't make our job more difficult!"

Ashim whirled around and slammed Erol into the nearest tree. "None of that is Orison's fault. You know the shit she's been through," he seethed.

Erol's green eyes flared as he struggled against the arm that pinned him against the tree. He panted from the anger simmering beneath the surface. Ashim stared him down, awaiting his answer, but his companion remained silent. Pushing away from Erol, Ashim continued on a brisk walk through the forest.

Ashim's hand dived into a pocket sewn into the seams of his black tunic. He tugged out a piece of parchment, unfolding it to reveal a drawing of a cat—Mahavu. Though it was nothing more than a pencil sketch, Ashim could see Mahavu's sand coloured fur with black stripes on her front legs and tail.

"Since you found that fleabag, you carry that photo everywhere," Erol snapped.

"Mahavu is not a fleabag; she's my baby," Ashim retorted.

Erol rolled his eyes. "It's a cat, Ashim."

"Mahavu might be *just a cat* to you, but to me, she is my family." Ashim folded up the parchment and placed it back into his pocket. His companion was silent. "She was like me when I rescued her, no family and needing a companion."

"You're right. Sorry, just frustrated," Erol grumbled. "Let's go back to town."

The wheels of Nazareth's wheelchair bumped along the gravel path as she headed to the lakefront. She pushed on the push rims while steering herself onto the dock; her eyes fixated on the soldiers training on the water. At the water's edge, she applied the brakes.

Nazareth remembered the days when she could be up there, training on the logs and feeling that rush when she got slammed into the lake. Training like that was too dangerous after losing her leg, but it was a happy memory she held close to her heart.

She was grateful she could still train like any other soldier. They all saw her as a worthy opponent; even when she used her chair on the training field. Sometimes the soldiers deliberately pushed her harder to test her full strength.

The men on the logs clashed swords against each other, moving swiftly when a sword came towards them. She clapped when the one to her right fell in the water with a tremendous splash. Nazareth gasped loudly, then laughed when he dragged the other one down with him.

"I warn you. The prince won't be the same when he returns," a voice next to her claimed.

Nazareth jumped and turned. An old crone, hunched over her walking stick, was looking out over Torwarin's lake; the sun glistening in her white eyes. She was a seer. Unlocking the brakes of the wheelchair, Nazareth turned to face her.

"What do you mean?" Nazareth asked with a tilt of her head.

The crone's wispy white hair flew about in the breeze. "You can't save him." Nazareth frowned and pushed her blonde hair out of her face as the wind stirred. "Nobody can."

"I don't understand."

"You can trust the Karshak men, they're good men," the crone continued.

Nazareth looked around. "What Karshak men?"

"Trust them!" the crone screeched, making Nazareth jump. "Don't trust the prince."

The crone turned and walked away, Nazareth's curiosity peaked and she followed in her wheelchair. She grimaced as the wind picked up, leaves battered Nazareth's face, causing her to shield her eyes. When the wind dissipated, the crone was gone.

Nazareth spent the next few moments searching for the crone—alas, she was nowhere to be found. Where the crone came from was another mystery. *Don't trust the prince.* As far as Nazareth was concerned, Xabian was a friendly face—unlike his brother. The thought something detrimental occurred in the mortal realm made her shudder.

The encounter left her perplexed and shaken. Many powerful forces were giving her strange messages, but all were indecipherable.

Everything Lioress and the crone had told her contradicted one another; Nazareth couldn't find the truth. If they couldn't trust Xabian, how could Orison be safe in the mortal realm? The big mystery was the men from Karshakroh.

The tavern greeted Nazareth like a friend as she pushed herself up the ramp to go inside. Patrons moved seats for her so she could sit at one of the lower tables. She thanked them and conjured up a stylus and parchment. She needed to write everything down and present it to Idralis when she figured it all out; *if* she ever did.

Extending her arms out, Orison balanced along a log in the forest. She teetered off balance before righting herself. She averted her gaze to Morty, who splashed in the water below and tried to bite at it, then shook the water off. Her attention soon fell on Xabian. He sat on the riverbank staring into space, completely silent—the way he had been since she woke him up and took him outside.

"What if I have a seizure? How will you get me back?" Xabian finally asked.

Orison crouched on the log. "My parents' house is only up the hill; I could drag you."

"I'd get injured." Xabian folded his arms over his chest.

"You're Fae, you can heal." Orison sat on the log and swung her legs.

She hadn't thought that far ahead when bringing him out here. Orison couldn't admit to Xabian she could call upon Ashim and Erol for help if the situation became dire; Xabian would only get angry again.

A loud splash made her pay attention to Morty. He belly-flopped into the water; his tongue lolled out of his mouth with each pant. Orison rolled her eyes, knowing he would get extremely muddy on the walk home. It would be her task to clean him off—another reason being Fae was an advantage; she could clean Morty with the click of her finger.

"Why aren't you changing into a dragon anymore?" Orison asked.

Xabian stared at the water. "The curse ended." Orison's eyes widened. "But I don't understand why my appearance hasn't returned to normal yet."

"Ashim told me magic works differently here." Orison tensed when she realised what she said and covered her mouth.

The man before her couldn't know she was still talking to her saviours from Karshakroh. He couldn't know she trusted them profusely; though she was still figuring Erol out.

Xabian's attention snapped to where she sat on the log. His purple glowing eyes flared with anger at her mistake. Orison lowered her head in remorse, remembering how he called her a reckless bitch for trusting them.

"You need to forget the men from Karshakroh, Ori," Xabian said with lethal calmness, showing his anger.

"They're helping me train," she announced. "Well, Ashim is helping me train."

"Ask me!" Xabian spat. Orison scoffed as she jumped off the log and welcomed the cool water as she approached him. "What's that scoff mean?"

"I have to live in the mortal realm while you can barely stay conscious for longer than an hour!" Her shout echoed around the trees. "I need help around the clock, not just ten minutes."

Xabian stood up so fast Orison staggered back. He grabbed both of her arms. "Your alliance lies with Fallasingha and Fallagh people do not ally with Karshakroh!" he seethed. Morty barked in warning and growled.

Orison winced in pain and struggled in his grip. "You're hurting me, let me go!"

"Not until you swear your alliance to Fallasingha," Xabian simmered.

She balled her hands into fists. "I said, let me go." Pulling her fist back, Orison slammed it into Xabian's face.

He cried out as his hold on Orison released. She staggered back and watched Xabian drop to the ground. Orison cried out as pain made her hand go numb. It was rare that she punched somebody.

A dull thud drew her attention to Xabian. She gasped when she realised Xabian had fallen onto a rock and the river ran red underneath where he landed.

EIGHT

Water sloshed around Orison's feet as she ran through the shallow river with Erol close behind. He was the only one she found quickly to help. The sound of Morty's bark guided her back to Xabian. Although she had told herself to Mist to Xabian, it brought her further downstream than she intended. Ducking under low-hanging branches, she stumbled upon the correct spot. Morty stopped his incessant barking as soon as he sensed her return.

"I'm here, baby," Orison crooned as she crouched beside Morty, petting his damp fur. She smiled as he licked her hand. "Good boy."

Orison turned her attention to Erol when he crouched beside Xabian. Her hand still hurt from punching him and he had a bruise on his cheek to show for it. Erol pressed two fingers to Xabian's neck and waited. He glanced at Orison when he noticed the prince's swollen cheek; then he saw the bruises on Orison's arms.

"Did he touch you?" Erol enquired. "What happened?"

Orison looked between Xabian and Erol. "He accused me of being a traitor of Fallasingha for trusting you and Ashim." She shuddered as she cast her sights on the water. "And then he grabbed me. He wouldn't let go."

"He deserved the punch." Erol shifted and checked Xabian's other injuries.

Her heart wanted to give Xabian the benefit of the doubt, but her mind screamed at her to run. Orison needed to bring Xabian home whether she trusted him or not. She couldn't leave him to rot in the mortal realm.

Standing up, Orison secured the leash onto Morty. "We need to get him back to my parents' house."

Erol looked down at Xabian. "I'll Mist there with him and meet you in town. Does that sound good?"

"Why meet in town?"

"Have you had lunch?" Erol asked. Orison shook her head. "I'll treat you to lunch."

Orison tightened the grip on the leash when Erol disappeared in a flurry of red smoke, leaving nothing but the bloody rock behind. Guilt tore at her conscience.

With a click of her tongue, she pulled Morty out of the water. She clicked her fingers to avoid the inevitable shaking of water from his fur. He looked squeaky clean, like he had taken a bath. Morty shook his body anyway, resulting in a smile from Orison.

As they traversed through the woods towards town, Orison dared a glance at her hand. She swore under her breath as she inspected her bruised knuckles. Orison was unsure of what the mortal realm did to Fae's healing, but it was agonisingly slow. However, she didn't regret punching Xabian. It was better that he was unconscious by her punch than by another seizure; even if her hand pulsated with pain from it.

She Glamoured at the edge of town and walked into the throng of people. Morty sniffed his way around the cobblestone streets. Orison let him continue with his adventure to sniff every single surface as she looked for Erol. He emerged from a nearby alley, adjusting his green tunic.

"Let's get some lunch," Erol offered.

Orison smiled and tugged Morty until she pried him from an interesting piece of stone. He sneezed and tried to bolt, yelping when the leash went taut. She shook her head and reprimanded the animal as she walked alongside Erol.

"I'm sorry that Xabian doesn't think that we can trust you," Orison divulged. She pulled on Morty's leash as he tried smelling somebody.

"Years of being told a lie makes it difficult to believe the truth," Erol responded. "I'm glad you're not so easily swayed."

Orison tugged Morty's leash again. "Maybe when I take the crown, I could form an alliance with Karshakroh and make people realise the truth."

"You can try, Princess. I'm sure both Fallagh and Karshak people will like you." A group of people made the pair separate; after they had passed, Erol returned to Orison's side.

"I heard Sila started a war in Karshakroh over bread. Did he really start a war over something so small?" Orison pressed a hand to her stomach as it growled. "They have ingredients to make bread in Fallasingha."

He burst out laughing. "Of course he did. The people of Karshakroh live in fear of another war."

Orison's heart was heavy. The people of Karshakroh didn't deserve war if they were like Ashim or Erol. They shouldn't have to sell children to pay for tithes. Her blood boiled. The wars sounded petty and childish that only left damage in its wake—summing up Sila perfectly.

"Are you well?" Erol asked.

"I'm fine," Orison replied.

Erol raised an eyebrow. "You were pretty deep in thought."

He led Orison to a nearby sandwich shop. The smell of freshly baked bread hung heavily in the air. Orison's mind reeling with information.

"Order for me," Orison said, petting Morty's head.

She watched Erol order while she stayed near the door. Erol and Ashim were good men, Orison knew that much was true. The actions of a few people from their country didn't mean everybody was like that—she had come to realise. The Karshak men she had met were kind and were keeping her alive.

"Let's find somewhere to eat these," Erol said with a smile.

Orison followed him outside and stepped back into the bustling town of Roseview.

Lightning cracked around the throne room as the portal cleaved the air in two, spinning in a purple vortex. Taviar stood behind Saskia in front of the portal, his shoulders pushed back as he steeled his nerves for this meeting. Guards flanked the pair. Edmund, now guard captain, stood to attention with his hand on the pommel of his sword.

At first nothing happened, only the swirling vortex presented itself. Then somebody with light-brown skin and dark-brown hair tied in a ponytail, stepped out of the portal—King Raj. His angular face was moulded into a look of indifference. He seemed bored by the mere fact he was in Alsaphus Castle. His brown eyes glowed as he took in the throne room—until they settled on Taviar and Saskia.

It was Taviar's first time meeting with King Raj as Regent of Fallasingha. Every other time he had been a mere emissary. The Karshak King wore a long black tunic which fell to his knees. It was embroidered with gold, matching the jewellery on his neck and wrist—Karshak mourning attire. Taviar held back his laugh at the irony of wearing such a garment for a king he despised. Behind King Raj, a man with short hair stepped out, wearing similar attire. He wasn't like most Karshak men who kept their hair long.

"What kind of tea do you like, Your Majesty?" Saskia asked with a curtsy.

King Raj clicked his fingers, each one weighed down in a multitude of gold rings. A servant appeared at his side. "Get me green apple tea, make it hot. Two sugars," he said in pure Karshakir. The servant looked at him blankly.

"Green apple tea, two sugars. Extra hot, please," Taviar translated.

King Raj looked at the servant. "I don't pour my own tea, it would be much obliged to do it for me," he announced in the common tongue.

It was a sign that this was going to be a long meeting. Taviar knew this was one of King Raj's many masks, his true demeanour was shrouded in mystery to Fallagh citizens.

The servant curtsied and hurried off. King Raj gestured to the nearby table and chairs that the servants had set up for this meeting—like he owned Alsaphus Castle. They walked across the throne room and settled into their seating arrangements; Taviar against a king who'd rather be doing something else. His gaze snagged on the stranger.

"May I ask your name, Sir?" Taviar asked.

The male looked up; his brown eyes glistened. "Hello, Regent. I'm Bahlir."

"Why did you call me?" King Raj interrupted.

Taviar held his tongue at the interruption. "Princess Orison is the next heir to the throne. However, the late King Sila has exiled her to the mortal realm."

He chortled and smiled at the servant when she returned with his tea. "Really?" King Raj watched the tea making process closely. "I bet she wasn't exiled and instead fled to a far-off land. Considering what Sila did to her."

"No, he exiled her. King Idralis confirmed it; he watched," Saskia announced.

King Raj sipped his tea and laughed. "A shame, really."

"A seer recently contacted Emissary Nazareth of Akornsonia and told her we can trust some of your citizens with Orison," Taviar said.

The announcement made King Raj pause in the middle of a sip; Bahlir tensed. Raj set his teacup on its saucer with a clink; he sat back on the seat with a raised eyebrow, shaking his head. Clearing his throat, Taviar sat forward, thanking the servants for giving him some tea.

"There are thirty-four million people in my country, Regent Luxart. They wouldn't be seen dead with a Fallagh citizen," Raj intoned.

Saskia shifted in her seat. "With all due respect, Your Majesty, a seer's prophecy is almost always correct."

Raj sighed heavily, rubbing the stubble on his chin. If by some miracle, Orison had befriended some Karshak men, the king had to answer for it.

Swearing under his breath in Karshakir, the king shifted in his seat, shaking his head. Raj drummed his fingers on the table and cast his attention to the window. The change of demeanour caused Taviar to frown; so far, Raj had acted like this meeting was beneath him.

"Is it Mahrishan and Beshankar?" Bahlir whispered to Raj.

Taviar raised an eyebrow as the king turned to look at his companion. He noted Raj cast a glance to Taviar before he spoke to Bahlir in hushed whispers.

"It'll be Mahrishan," Raj uttered. With an exasperated sigh, he shook his head and tapped his foot on the stone floor. "He's always been too compassionate."

When Raj manifested a pipe out of thin air, Taviar made to protest when he lit the herbs inside, but thought better of it. Instead, he watched Raj puff on the pipe and sit back, staring off into the distance with a stern facial expression.

"Do you think Mahrishan will have befriended Orison?" Saskia asked.

Raj's brown eyes bore into her. "His name is Ashim Mahrishan. He befriends everybody, despite trying to toughen his skin."

It took everything for Taviar not to react to the claim. "Is he in the mortal realm?"

"Yes, looking for a mortal servant to replace one slain by a horse." Raj took a puff of his pipe. "I will have to talk to Beshankar too."

Saskia sat on the edge of her seat. "If Mr Mahrishan or Mr Beshankar return with Orison, please inform us. We'll pay for her lodgings and create a portal to Karshakroh, so she leaves as soon as possible."

"I'll see what I can do," Raj stated nonchalantly, staring at his nails. "I have to attend to my duties. We shall see each other again, Regent and Advisor."

As Raj and Bahlir stood up, Taviar baulked, wanting to get more answers. By the calm and collected way Raj was behaving, it was like he expected this meeting and knew something nobody else did. It left Taviar perplexed, wondering what the Karshak King was hiding underneath his calm and collected mask.

NINE

Orison knocked on Ashim's door in the Goblin Tavern. She chewed on the side of her nail, wondering how his journey went. Orison knew he was inside by the pull in her chest; it only happened around him. It had been three days since she last saw him.

Two days had passed since she punched Xabian. Since then, his anger had been unfathomable each time that she woke him up. It made her reluctant to offer him further help; he was acting too much like Sila for her liking. Also, he said the two words she hated more than anything—"*You're weak.*"

"Come in," Ashim's voice filtered through the door.

The sound of his voice eased the roaring in her head as she turned the doorknob and stepped into the room. Orison didn't know why Ashim could calm the storm in her head or why he created the pull in her chest, but he did and she craved his comfort. She paused in the doorway; the last time she had been in this room it was neat and tidy. Since then, Ashim had acquired two stacks of books which were piled against the foot of the bed. Ashim lay on his stomach with an open book in front of him while he ate apple pieces.

Clearing her throat, Orison eased the door shut. "Did you borrow these from the library?"

"No, I buy them while on journey," Ashim announced. "I want to sound like Erol when speaking in common tongue."

She approached the bed and held her brown skirts up as she knelt on the floor to inspect the books. Orison saw a couple she'd read as a child, others she hadn't seen before. It made her admire Ashim's efforts all the more. Within the stack was the unmistakable golden lettering of *Cinderella*. She realised he had bought his own copy; instead of blue binding like the library had, this one was red.

"Your mind is heavy, Little Queen, want to talk about it?" Ashim asked. He bit into a slice of apple with a crunch.

Her eyes slowly rose to his, tearing her hand away quickly from his books, when she realised that he was looking at her. "Sorry, I should have asked," Orison said.

"I don't care."

At first, Orison hesitated; then her words spilled out easily. "I'm worried about Xabian. He has never lashed out at me, and now... and now, he's acting like Sila." With a huff of breath, Orison looked down at the wooden floor. Ashim remained silent as she explained. "Now he's calling me weak and a reckless bitch. In the Othereal, Xabian was the sweetest man, he saved a child when Sila burned down Torwarin. "

"Did King Sila teach you how to use your powers?" Ashim asked.

Orison shook her head. "My Fae fathers—Taviar and Riddle—taught me and I taught myself when I had the chance."

"Then you aren't weak." Ashim's book rustled as he turned a page. "You almost died here, but you fought to survive. That's not weak."

With a huff of breath, Orison fixated on Ashim when he muttered in Karshakir. Sometimes she heard Xabian's name and could only assume he was insulting him. It made her stifle a laugh as she watched him pretend to read. Inching closer to him, she wondered what book he was so engrossed in.

"Where's Erol today?" Orison asked. "You haven't been working together recently."

Ashim placed a bookmark in his book. "A brothel."

It took everything for Orison not to cringe; she didn't need to know *that* information. Plucking up the courage, she dared to ask. "Why didn't you go with him?" She looked at her hands. "When I was sleeping with a guard while imprisoned in Alsaphus Castle, he used to go with a group of his friends to a brothel and I heard they shared the women."

"That's disgusting," Ashim mumbled. She felt her cheeks heat from sharing that detail about Edmund. The room fell silent until Ashim continued with—"Sex with a stranger..." Ashim looked at the ceiling as he tried to find the words. "I don't find attraction."

"Oh." She tapped her chin. "So, all strangers?" Ashim nodded.

"The healers called it dohrashmah." Orison squinted. "Unless I have a bond with somebody, no attraction for sex."

Orison's eyes widened in realisation. "In my language, we call it demisexual." She tilted her head, leaning closer. "Why did you go to a healer?"

"Demisexual..." He repeated the word a couple times, testing it on his tongue. "This is embarrassment. I thought something wrong." Ashim grimaced and fiddled with the end of his braid that sat over his shoulder. He clicked his fingers, trying to think of the words. "But the... the healers told me nothing wrong. So, I accept it."

"That's like me, in a way. I don't have romantic feelings for anybody without a bond first," Orison explained as she played with her hair.

Ashim smiled. "It's like we're equal."

When the word *equal* passed his lips, something snapped in Orison's chest. To her surprise, the snap wasn't painful; it was like a jigsaw puzzle finding a missing piece. She placed a hand over her heart, realising Ashim had the same reaction with a frown. Although no windows were open, wind stirred in the room. The wind flapped the pages of the book on Ashim's bed and played with Orison's hair. The strange pull towards Ashim had increased tenfold and she wondered what it meant.

"What was that?" Orison asked under her breath.

Ashim cleared his throat and looked at Orison warily as he massaged his chest. "I don't know." He shifted uncomfortably, avoiding eye contact. "Erm. That was unusual."

"Do you need me to teach you any words?" Orison asked quickly, trying to take her mind off the weird experience.

He scooped up the book from his bed, opened it and took out the crumpled piece of parchment he used as a bookmark. He laid it out flat. "I write a list."

Orison took it and taught him how to pronounce each word until it sounded natural. He listened intently. She picked out *Cinderella* again and told him to read it aloud to her. As Ashim told the story, his voice made one of her favourite childhood stories sound different. Each word was captivating and transported her into the story; to the point she didn't need the oil paintings to guide her way. His pronunciation improved the longer she taught him. Orison couldn't help but smile at his progress; proud she could help him achieve his goals.

Night had fallen over a sleepy town of Lowehum. At this time of night, only a handful of people walked around the town's main square. They were mostly drunks coming out of taverns or prostitutes standing on street corners looking for work.

Ashim and Erol stepped out of the shadows of an alleyway which was filled with closed shops after a day's work. They kept their heads down, shying away from the glow of candles in the tavern's bay windows; or from the occasional shops which remained open well into the night. It was another opportunity to scope out a potential servant for King Raj. They had to find a way into their residence to secure the mortal for transportation.

They hurried stealthily through the streets and Ashim pressed himself against a wall, ensuring it was the right place. The dark, decrepit building confirmed it. Vines crawled up the exterior, knocking on windows when the wind blew strong; demanding to be let in. Some windows were smashed and the bricks were black, like someone had painted them with oil or soot from the chimneys. On one side of the building, the roof had caved in. If this was their chosen servant, Karshak Castle would be luxurious—compared to this work-house—even if they lived in the castle's servant quarters and slept in a hammock suspended from the ceiling.

"Is this where the mortal lives?" Erol asked in Karshakir.

"Yes," Ashim said. "His name is Harry."

A loud groan made Ashim turn his head. Erol rubbed the bridge of his nose. "I told you not to get their names until we've vetted them."

Ignoring his companion, Ashim looked at the house. "He's an orphan, he might accept the job. Harry works at the local blacksmiths as an apprentice. The servant that the horse trampled was a blacksmith and Raj needs a replacement."

"Age?"

"Fourteen."

Ashim jolted when Erol smacked him over the head. "Dufflepud," Erol argued. "King Raj does not like mortals that young. I keep telling you, eighteen or over."

"He's good, Erol," Ashim said quickly. "Despite his age, engaged couples ask for him personally to make their wedding rings. Men who need horseshoes want him as well."

Thrusting his finger into Ashim's face, he leaned back. "You're going to be in so much shit, Mahrishan. I won't take the fall for you," Erol spat.

With a sigh, he watched Erol dart out of the shadows and towards the work-house gates. Ashim hated being considered as less important than the other Runners because of his compassion and his tendency to bend the rules. Eventually catching up to Erol, Ashim couldn't see anything inside the workhouse, apart from a silhouette in the window, which was illuminated by candlelight. Other than that, the place was deserted.

The men had no intentions of proposing the job to Harry tonight without seeing his work first. Ashim only needed to observe where he lived and check if he had high security. Judging by the lack of guards stationed in the security outposts, it would make their job even easier. They could slip in and out in minutes.

Taking Erol by the hand, Ashim Misted them to Harry's bedroom. It was even more cramped than the one in Roseview Tavern. Ashim pointed to a thin boy with curly blonde hair. Harry slept soundly under the window, with nothing more than a thin scrap of material to cover him. In Karshakroh, with Raj providing him with a blanket, it would be another luxury.

"Your ridiculous risk had better be a good one. We need examples of his work. If it's up to par with what King Raj likes, we'll give him the proposition." Erol scowled, Misting away in a flurry of red smoke.

Ashim remained standing at the foot of Harry's bed, staring at the small boy. His work had better be good enough. He knew from first-hand experience that this was no way to live.

The brisk air outside and the rain beating down on the cobblestones, was like a bucket of ice being thrown over Orison; especially after the warmth of the library. She itched to go back inside, curl up by the fire and read. Instead, she tugged her cloak tighter around her as rain drummed on her head.

Orison shivered violently as she walked; jumping over puddles to avoid drenching her shoes. A sudden heavy weight on her shoulders made her slow down; it was the undeniable feeling of being watched. Orison looked over her shoulder, but nobody presented themselves. She shook the thought away, picking up the pace of her walking. As she passed an alleyway, her assailant struck, grabbing her from behind. Orison screamed as she was dragged into the darkness.

She blindly kicked and punched, connecting with her assailant a couple of times. They dragged her further into the alley until a hard fist smashed into the side of her head. She screamed for help until her voice cracked, earning another punch and being thrown to the floor in a puddle of God knows what. A whimper escaped her lips, the cold seeped through her dress. Her head and hands pounded with pain.

The assailants were two mortals; one with blonde hair and the other light-brown. Both sneered at Orison as they advanced on her, ignoring the rain that beat down. Orison's eyes burned with tears as she crawled backwards to try to escape, but the blonde one grabbed her bag. Clutching the bag tight to keep it in her possession, Orison gasped when the glint of a knife presented itself and he cut it from her shoulders. He chuckled as he rifled through her bag; both laughed as they pulled out the book she'd borrowed. Orison's heart sank when they tore the book in two; pages flew around her and some landed in a puddle. She stared at it with sorrow.

"No!" Orison pleaded, then cried out as the brown-haired one gripped her hair.

She groaned and grabbed his wrist as more pain laced its way around her head. A scream tore through her when he kicked her in the stomach. The blonde one pinned her legs down to stop her from kicking him as she tried to get away with all her might.

"A little birdy told me you're a Fae. Let's see it then; show us your true self," the brown-haired one mocked.

Orison struggled against him, panting. "I don't know what you're on about."

A groan filled the alleyway as he punched her in the mouth. "Change!" Orison tasted the blood which filled her mouth from their assault. She spat it out on the floor. "I want to see the actual monster that you are."

"No!" Orison whimpered. She screamed when he punched her again, feeling the warmth of her blood as it ran down her face. "Stop."

"Change!" The man was shaking with rage. "I need to make a bargain."

Orison cowered before him. "I don't know how; please let me go."

The blonde-haired one pulled his arm back, ready to join his companion in using her as a punching bag. Orison squeezed her eyes shut, bracing for them to do their worst. Xabian was right, she really was weak.

Yet the punch never came. The grip on her hair disappeared, resulting in her crumpling onto the ground. The feel of rain no longer pounded against her skin. Orison opened her eyes slowly and immediately recognised Ashim's bedroom in the Goblin Tavern. She lay on the floor like a drowned rat—bloody and bruised. She saw the familiar bed underneath the sloping roof and the dining table near the door. Ashim was nowhere to be seen.

Pain sliced through Orison's body while she dragged herself across the floor, sobbing with each breath that came out as a wheeze. She gripped the bed with a violently shaking hand as she tried to get to her feet. Her legs gave out on her and she crashed to the floor with a yelp. Orison was freezing and this time it wasn't from her powers. Water dripped from her hair and sopping wet dress. Orison jumped and struggled against the hands which settled on her shoulder. She screamed to alert somebody that she was in trouble—the mortals had followed her.

"Shush," Ashim said repeatedly as he pulled her into his embrace. "It's only me. Calm down." He turned her around, eyes widening when he took in the bloody state of Orison's face. There was a large cut on her cheek, nose and lip which poured blood. She had gashes on her hands from how much she had fought. His yellow eyes flared with anger. "Who did this to you?"

"Two mortals," Orison managed to divulge. "Help me." She wanted to say more, but the world started spinning. Ashim's face doubled before returning to its natural state; then her entire world went dark.

TEN

In a flurry of beige smoke, Ashim Misted into his room at the Goblin Tavern. His attention immediately fixated on Orison; she was curled up asleep in his bed where he left her, cuddling his pillow for comfort. Orison's hair fell like a golden waterfall over her shoulder. With quiet steps, he eased the wardrobe open and pulled out a red tartan blanket, which he placed around Orison to give her added warmth.

Orison stirred with a groan; she pulled the blanket tighter around her. His gaze lingered on her split lip and nose, noticing a black eye forming, plus the bump on her forehead. *Bastards.* Though it would be gone by morning, she didn't deserve this. He froze when he noticed her eyes had opened and she was watching him.

"Did you kill them?" Orison asked.

"Anesh." Ashim sat carefully on the end of the bed, to avoid sitting on her feet. "I wiped their brains." He glanced at her when she gasped. "They can only remember their names."

Orison shifted. "Thank you." She looked down in shame. "I would have protected myself, but I don't know how to shield."

"We'll learn that soon." Ashim rubbed her shoulder. "You're safe now."

She rolled onto her back and covered her face. "Fuck. I don't want to go home; my father will kill them. But I need to for Xabian."

"Anesh. You aren't going home tonight," Ashim said quicker than he anticipated. She lifted her hands to look at him. "I want you safe."

"But…" Orison looked around. "There's only one bed."

Moving to the floor, Ashim created a tiny unicorn made of fire with his Fire Singer abilities. "I don't mind taking the floor."

The unicorn's appearance was like a moth to a flame. Orison sat up with her mouth ajar; then she chuckled. Ashim couldn't help but notice her wince with pain.

"You're a Fire Singer," Orison pointed out with a mesmerised smile.

He made an identical unicorn and allowed them to dance around on his palm. Ashim had Orison's full attention; her purple eyes glistened. With a wave of his hand, the scene changed to a night sky made of flames. Her jaw fell open.

"In the Othereal, I've always loved watching Fire Singers," she said. She observed the night sky that changed to a flock of birds fluttering in his hand. "They're beautiful."

"Thank you." Ashim extinguished the flames. "I don't like using it." She raised an eyebrow. "I'm scared of hurting people."

Orison settled back on the bed, observing Ashim as he waved his hand; a book bound in leather appeared in his hand. It was the book he found in the alleyway, where the mortal men were growling like dogs when searching for Orison; it was how he found them so easily. Someone had ripped the pages out and strewn them about in the rain. With the use of his magic, Ashim painstakingly made the book appear brand new. He flicked through the pages before running a finger over the title embossed in the spine—*The Castle of…*—he had difficulty making out the last word.

"Do you know about this book?" Ashim asked.

Orison sat up again and gasped when she saw the book in his hand. "That's the book I loaned from the library… How? The muggers destroyed it." Ashim returned to his seat at the edge of the bed; settling beside Orison. "You fixed it."

"Can I try to read it to you?"

She smiled. "Can I cuddle up to you while you do?" Ashim raised an eyebrow. He looked down and noticed her cheeks turning pink. "Sorry, that was weird."

"*Oneshir*. As long as you help with the title," Ashim said.

"*The Castle of Otranto*," Orison said slowly.

Ashim repeated her pronunciation; they worked together to strengthen it and make it sound natural. Eventually, Ashim liked the way *Otranto* rolled off his tongue. Orison shifted into a sitting position, allowing Ashim to settle against the headboard. She settled in beside him, until her head rested on his chest. The surreal pulling in his chest grew exponentially; it was something that he'd grown accustomed to since meeting Orison. It was his one constant sign to know where to find her.

While adjusting the blanket to fit around them both, Ashim sent a message to Erol's mind to retrieve clothes for Orison and check on Xabian. Getting comfier, Ashim opened the book; the bindings creaked as it opened. There were no remnants of water damage or torn pages from when Orison was attacked; it was pristine, as it should be.

This story was much more advanced than Ashim expected. He stumbled over his words and felt his heart race from fear of judgement. Orison took it in her stride, only correcting him when absolutely necessary, until he found his footing. Once Ashim eased into the story, he was on a roll. Both got lost in the words and forgot the ordeal with the mortals who attacked Orison in the darkness. They read well into the night and eventually fell asleep in each other's arms.

When Orison woke up in Ashim's arms, she was fully healed—to her delight. Orison wouldn't be questioned by Xabian or her father. During their walk to her home, Ashim found it the perfect opportunity to teach Orison how to wipe somebody's mind, in the form of a game. It went on for quite some time and each time she wasn't successful.

"I once shoplifted fabric from my mum's shop," Orison announced as she walked beside Ashim through the Nalan Forest.

Ashim tensed and looked at her. "Did you now?"

She smiled and took his hand, diving into his mind. Through her mind's eye, she could see what appeared to be cavernous alcoves built into desert rocks; each one holding a memory etched into the floor. In this place, she didn't have a body and flew around like the pixies she saw in Lake Braloak. After scoping out memory after memory, she found the one which spoke of her admission and tried to scrub it away from its alcove—as Ashim had taught her to do countless times since this game started. Triple checking that the sandy floor of the cavern was clear of the memory, she retreated.

"What do you remember?" Orison asked.

"You did something to your mum's shop," he replied.

Orison swore under her breath. It hadn't worked again, after the fifth attempt of trying to learn this new trick. While navigating the winding labyrinth of trees, Orison thought of more things to say to Ashim, more secrets. He still remembered her darkest secret after her first failed attempt. She should have started with something mild, then later with something more extreme—but no, she had told him she poisoned King Sila months before her exile.

Holding her hands in front of her, she blurted out, "I think you're really handsome."

Startled by her confession, Ashim tripped over a root and steadied himself on a tree. It wasn't a lie. From the day Orison met Ashim, she had found him handsome. Swiftly taking his hand, Orison jumped into his mind and removed the memory like she was picking a book from a shelf.

She had a theory that adapting the way she used her power would help her to be successful, in the same way as how she altered her Glamour. Orison had realised that learning something new about her power was a game of trial and error.

When she let go of his hand, Orison watched Ashim's face go blank. He frowned and continued walking like nothing happened. Her heart raced in case he could remember her admission, but reminded herself she had nothing to fear around Ashim.

"Did you say something?" he asked. Orison shook her head with a pleased smile, it was proof her plan had worked. "Well done."

"I've never known Mindelates to do this. Is it common knowledge?" Orison questioned. She held her hands behind her back while awaiting his answer.

Ashim picked up a stick. "In Fallasingha, it's illegal because it can kill. Over there, the knowledge has been lost." Her eyes widened. "The first time I tried doing it, I made a mortal turn to mush." He jammed the stick into the forest's soft soil.

"You turned a mortal to mush?" Orison asked.

"It was my first mission. I got scared and erased all of the mortal's memories; he was like a new-born," Ashim explained. It made Orison wince. "If I didn't stop, he would have died."

"I don't understand." Orison turned. "You're scared to use your Fire Singer abilities for nearly killing somebody. Why aren't you scared to use your Mindelate powers?"

He scoffed and looked down. "With this, you can re-learn all the things you erase. But, like I say, fire is different. You can learn from your mistakes, but there will always be scars."

She couldn't argue with that concept. When her childhood home came into view, Orison picked up the pace; Ashim comfortably kept in sync with her stride. Part of her wanted to run and burst the door open, pet Morty and check on Xabian—but she was reluctant to face the Fallasingha Prince.

"Why did you Mist into my room last night?" Ashim asked.

Orison frowned. "I didn't Mist. I closed my eyes and when I opened them again, I was in there." She looked at Ashim when he fell silent; he walked beside her, rubbing his chest. "What's wrong?"

"Nothing," Ashim said as they reached the front door. "Let's go inside."

Orison opened the door and stepped inside, with Ashim close behind. She breathed in the familiar scent of home—freshly carved wood, along with baked bread. She could hear the familiar sound of her father working on his sculptures.

She leaned into the room on her left, where there was a mishmash of various hobbies. In the centre was her mother's pedestal for dressmaking, along with her supplies. Sculptures were scattered around the floor, accompanied by Markus's woodworking table where he worked diligently. There was also a small bed squashed into the corner. Her father's hammering stopped and he looked up from his woodworking table, staring at her with goggles, which magnified his eyes.

"Father, I'm home!" Orison exclaimed.

"How are you, Ori?" he asked. "I heard you got rained out and stayed in the tavern. Your friend came over."

Orison nodded. "My shoes got stuck in the mud. It was safer to stay there."

Her father returned to chiselling away at the wooden sculpture that he was making. Morty sneezed as he entered the room, panting as he rubbed against Orison's leg. He laid down on her feet; the weight made her wince.

Orison laughed and pried her feet out from under the dog. She tapped her thighs to get him to follow, which he more than obliged—with a big wag of his tail. Orison closed the door behind her and Morty ran across the home to Xabian's room. She shook her head at the dog's silliness as Erol had a play-fight with him.

"I guess it's time to wake Xabian up," Orison said with a sigh, reluctant to see what mood he was in.

"I'll be here," Ashim said, settling onto the sofa.

Orison smiled as she crossed the threshold towards Xabian's room, where he lay resting since the last time she had woken him. The empty bowl of his breakfast sat on the side table with an empty glass. Erol had composed himself enough to stand beside him with a vial of smelling salts.

"I was just about to wake him," Erol said with a smile.

He leaned down to the prince, popped the cork and waved it under his nose. Erol replaced the cork with a cringe at the smell, placing the vial back in the drawer. Orison stood in the doorway, waiting for it to work. She glanced out of the room when Morty darted past her.

Xabian woke up with a gasp; the grip on his blanket tightened as he looked around. "I think something is wrong," he mumbled, turning to look at Erol.

Curious, Orison stepped forward. "What do you mean?"

He didn't look at her, he only continued to watch Erol standing nearby. "My head hurts all the time when I'm awake. Then I get overwhelmed with a rage I can't explain. Just know I'm not mad at you." Xabian finally looked at Orison, his eyes glazed over with tears. "What is wrong with me?"

Orison swallowed the lump in her throat as she looked at him. "I wish I had an answer."

He sat up, his black hair hung limp over his shoulders. Orison had only seen him look this defeated once before, when admitting he wasn't Kiltar. With a wave of his hand, the window opened and closed; it was the same routine they had created for the past week to ensure he used his power. Xabian looked over Orison's shoulder when Morty barked.

"Why are they here?" Xabian asked.

Orison rolled her eyes. "Last night, mortals attacked me; Ashim and Erol rescued me—again!" she explained. "They brought me home safely."

She expected his rage to surface. Instead, Xabian merely climbed out of bed and walked out of the room to disappear upstairs. Orison watched the stairway, speechless and confused about what had occurred.

A thud drew her attention to the sofa. Ashim and Erol had taken it upon themselves to play with Morty, who snorted and wagged his tail while lying on the floor. Her heart ached, knowing she had to leave her dog behind again so soon.

Xabian finally returned. He used his magic to move objects and conjured up a ball of lightning—anything to give himself a sustainable life. Orison came out of his bedroom when he opened the front door and stepped outside. She didn't like him straying too far from the house in case he had another seizure.

Xabian cried out for Ashim, who stopped playing with Morty and glanced at the door as another cry from the prince filled the house. Erol kept Morty occupied as Ashim got to his feet and hurried outside. Orison followed close behind.

"Orison and I need to go home," Xabian announced. "I think that's why I don't feel well and why I keep going into unconsciousness."

Ashim glanced over his shoulder at Orison, then back to the prince. "My mission isn't complete yet."

"It needs to be sooner rather than later," Xabian pleaded.

Orison could see the fear on Xabian's face. She knew that wide-eyed look, the look when somebody knew their time was close. She had seen it multiple times on the battlefield in Torwarin. There was something that made Xabian scared and desperate to get back to the Othereal.

Ashim nodded. "I'll do what I can."

"Thank you," Xabian said, closing his eyes and basking in the sun. "I might heal if I'm home."

Orison glanced at Ashim; his nod made her pause. It told her he intended to do as the prince requested. They were going back to the Othereal, leaving her parents and Morty behind again. She would have to face whatever lay back in Fallasingha. Orison hadn't heard what had happened to Sila, but in her home town, she was free and she didn't want to be made a prisoner again.

ELEVEN

The mouth of an alleyway opened up to a large square that was surrounded by timber-framed structures with thatched roofs. Children played near a fountain, where their giggles bounced around the alley's walls. Some men and women walked together peacefully with their arms interlocked. In the town of Lowehum there was no market with rainbow canopies.

Ashim took Orison's arm and looped it through his; he was thankful she didn't protest. It was like she already knew they had to blend in and play a role. Erol led the way out of the dark confines of the alleyway. The sudden change in light made Ashim squint and blink a few times until his eyes adjusted. He checked on Orison as she rubbed her eyes and took in the surrounding sights.

"Are there many women who go on these missions?" she asked.

Following Erol down the street, Ashim nodded. "*Halek.*"

"There's many genders in the Runner team," Erol explained over his shoulder.

"King Raj allows that?" Orison asked.

Erol stopped abruptly and turned around. "Is that a problem for you Fallasingha folk?"

"Not at all," Orison said defensively.

"Good." Erol resumed walking. "King Raj treats us well. He doesn't care what we identify as. All he cares about is us doing our jobs."

The duo continued to follow Erol. Ashim kept checking on Orison to ensure she was okay. With the speed that Erol was walking, Ashim could tell he was eager to see Harry's skills. He hoped he had chosen the next servant wisely in their haste. With Xabian slowly deteriorating, they needed to finish this job quickly.

From the brief glances around him, most mortals in this town just mulled about; some looked through shop windows and a few mothers ran after their toddlers.

"If he is right for us, are we going home?" Ashim asked in Karshakir.

Erol pointed to an isolated hut at the edge of town. "Yes. Xabian's health is of great importance. There's no help for him in this realm."

As the trio approached the hut, the smell of smoke and heated metal hung heavily in the air. It told Ashim it was the blacksmith they were looking for, especially with the black smoke escaping from one of its many chimneys. When Orison's grip tightened, he patted her hand. It would be okay, only a routine check of a potential servant—a mortal servant, no doubt.

Orphans were even better than the people with families. The workhouses never reported the orphans missing; to them, they were just another pay check from the government. It would delight King Raj that he had a replacement blacksmith and he would pay handsomely as well.

The clink of hammers on metal bounced off the surrounding trees, growing louder with each step they took. Ashim could see sparks of molten steel flying out of the open windows before dying on the dirt outside. The men inside were silent, working hard on what Ashim observed as chains and swords. It was perfect.

An older man with silver hands stepped out of a side door. "May I help you three?" A white beard adorned his chin and silver embedded into his wrinkles. His brown eyes fixated on Orison. "This is no place for a lady."

Ashim turned to the silver man. "We have come from distant shores to obtain a wedding ring for my fiancée." He nudged Orison, a silent gesture to be quiet. "My partner here told me you make the best in the land."

The silver man gestured to the hut, "My apprentice, Harry, can sort you out for two silvers."

"We can pay," Erol said. "How much for some swords thrown in? For a wedding present."

The silver man replied. "One gold."

Erol nodded. "We have a deal."

The silver man walked off to speak to Harry. Ashim allowed Orison to step closer to look into the blacksmith's domain. Ashim recognised Harry immediately; he looked different in his waking hours, compared to when he was asleep. It amazed Ashim how tall he was.

"It's scorching hot in there," Orison said as she returned to Ashim's side, watching the men work from a distance. "Working there must be tough."

Ashim chuckled. "*Halek*."

Both watched as Erol kicked at a stone. "I hope we can go home when everything has settled," he grumbled in Karshakir.

"What's he saying?" Orison asked.

"He's grumpy," Ashim replied.

Ashim watched through the window as the silver man talked to Harry. He nodded and approached the window, where he peered at all three of them. Though his hair was blonde at the roots, soot had accumulated on the ends—along with pieces of metal. His hands shined with silver.

Harry reached up to a shelf and produced some string. "Let's measure your finger for the ring, ma'am."

Orison held out her left hand and Harry meticulously wrapped the string around her ring finger. He cut off the string and set it to one side. Harry ushered for Ashim's hand, who extended it and allowed his finger to be measured. A pang of guilt slammed Ashim in the gut. This was a teenager—and they were testing him for a job he might not even accept.

He tugged some parchment from a drawer. "May I get a name?"

"Mahrishan," Ashim said. Harry scowled at the parchment. "M-A-H-R-I-S-H-A-N. Ashim Mahrishan."

"And what kind of swords would you like, Mr?"

"Beshankar," Erol said, spelling it out for him. He pulled out a knife from his waistband. "Something like this, but with inscriptions for a happy marriage."

Harry noted it down. "The rings should be ready by sunset. The knives about a week. Are you okay with that?"

"That will be ample time to show the future Mrs Mahrishan the beauty of this land," Erol boasted as he slid the coin to Harry. "We will be back."

Ashim noted the way Orison's cheeks had turned a deep shade of pink. Was she blushing?

He guided her away from the blacksmith and they walked back to the town. Erol had a beaming smile on his face as he skipped ahead. Ashim knew that smile from their many missions together.

"Is that our servant?" Ashim asked in Karshakir.

Erol pouted. "I have a good feeling about him," he replied in the same language. "Harry has nice people skills. For now, good job, Mahrishan."

"We go home in a week," Ashim said to Orison. She looked up at him. "If his work is good and he accepts the position."

Orison's eyes widened. "Then we can get Xabian some Healengales."

"*Halek*," Erol replied.

Ashim pulled the piece of parchment from his inside pocket and looked at the picture of Mahavu. He rubbed his thumb over the cat's small face. On these types of excursions, he liked looking at her picture. It reminded him of why he did these missions—to make money and give his cat a good life. His heart ached, hoping his baby would remember him when he returned. Of course, she would.

"Is that your baby?" Orison asked. He nodded.

"This is Bastard," he said with a chuckle.

Ashim flinched when Orison smacked his arm. "Bastard is not a name for a cat; why be so cruel like that?"

"She always bites me." Mahavu had stopped biting him when she realised that she had a forever home, but it was fun to see Orison's reaction to her nickname.

Orison glared. "No wonder she always bites with a name like Bastard."

"He's messing around, the cat's name is Mahavu. It means sand in Karshakir," Erol interjected, spoiling the joke. Ashim shot him a glare.

"That's a much better name than Bastard." Orison clicked her tongue.

Her reaction made him chuckle. They navigated the town of Lowehum to find something to do until they collected the rings from Harry. It meant that Ashim was closer to going home—to being in his own bed and eating Karshak food. His mouth watered at the thought of eating pohamak; a potato pancake with chicken inside.

Ashim yearned to be home.

Taviar's foot tapped on the floor as he looked at the map of the Othereal. His gaze darted between Alsaphus Castle and Karshak Castle. It was a long way to travel; five days on a boat across the Falshak Sea, to be exact. When Orison and Xabian returned to the Othereal, they would have to make that voyage.

A toy horse landed on the map, breaking Taviar's concentration. Zade scooped it up and made it gallop across Fallasingha. Taviar wrapped his hand around his son's wrist and moved it away from the map as he tried to focus. He sighed and ran a hand down his face in frustration when Yil placed another toy horse on the map. The chair creaked as he sat back and regarded his sons, while they giggled in unison.

"Boys, I'm trying to concentrate."

Zade picked up the horse and smashed it against his brother's. A growl from Yil had him jumping off the desk and running; only for Yil to zap him with magic. Anger simmered beneath the surface, Taviar needed to work—not deal with his children trying to kill each other. Zade twitched around on the floor and when he recovered, he put Yil into a headlock.

The boys jumped and parted ways when Taviar slammed his hands on the desk as he rose from his seat. "I'll get Papa to take you both home if you carry on and you'll both be grounded!" Taviar reprimanded. "Yil, apologise to your brother immediately."

"Sorry," Yil said to his brother. He picked up his horse and toyed with it in his hand.

"Sorry, Father," the twins said in unison.

It had been a week since the meeting with King Raj and Taviar hadn't heard anything. Also, there was no word from Nazareth who was using a discovaker almost daily to locate Orison and Xabian. Butterflies waged war in Taviar's belly from the unknown, as his mind wandered to Xabian's well-being. Taviar asked himself if they were running out of time so often that it became a mantra.

He settled back into the chair and glanced at his sons as an awkward silence settled in the room. They were playing with their horses silently—unlike the destructive way beforehand. He shook his head as he grabbed the correspondence letters. The leather chair creaked as he leaned back and placed his feet on the desk to read them.

The letters were the usual stuff he had grown accustomed to, including dates of when supplies would come in from Karshakroh, Marona and Akornsonia. With the change of season, higher tithes would be charged when sending supplies to other nations. There was some advertisement about new produce, as crops flourished in the harvest season. He could probably indulge in such luxuries, but he had bigger things to think about.

Using his magic, Taviar opened a drawer to retrieve a stylus and some parchment. He needed to draft another letter to request some undersea fruits from Marona. He looked up when the office door opened. Saskia's emerald dress swished along the floor as she approached the desk. The Luxart twins gawped at her and she gave them a little wave with a smile. Her cheerful demeanour told Taviar she had news.

"Do you have news?" Taviar asked, as he impatiently tapped the stylus on the desk.

Saskia leaned against the desk, inspecting the map. "The enchantresses have regained some of their powers."

He stood up so fast that the chair toppled over. Taviar covered his mouth and tried his hardest to remain composed. They had found a way to the mortal realm, to get Orison and Xabian back far sooner than Ashim Mahrishan ever could. They could prevent both of them from falling into King Raj's hands.

"Can we go tonight?" Taviar asked quickly.

Saskia folded her arms, looked down and shook her head. "It's not enough time."

"When?"

She shrugged. "Maybe another week."

Taviar's hands trembled against the map. He had one week to make plans with Emphina and find a way to get the portal secured. He needed to ensure Orison and Xabian were retrieved from the mortal lands. With King Raj's behaviour, Taviar didn't want to witness what he had up his sleeve for the two Fallasingha royals.

He pushed himself off the desk and approached his sons. "Come on boys, the adults have to talk," Taviar said, guiding his sons towards the entrance of the office. He turned to face Saskia. "What if we're too late?"

"Don't think such negative things, we'll be fine," Saskia assured.

Ever since Taviar had met Saskia, she had always known the right things to say when he was in a time of need. It was probably why she was such a great guard captain before her banishment from the castle.

The knowledge that Taviar was responsible for his children's safe future made him more determined to ensure that he did this right. With Orison in power, she could guarantee they were cared for, with unlimited choices in their future careers. Kinsley could get a job without limitations. Everybody would be better off.

He could do that for his children. He could go into the mortal realm and bring back their future with this hope for better days. Now he had to reach out and grab it.

TWELVE

The necklace dangled over the map of the Othereal and the ruby pendant swayed from side to side, like a pendulum. Nazareth's eyes narrowed as she watched it. After a few moments, it flew out of her hand and landed on the neighbouring map of the mortal realm. She ran a hand down her face and surveyed the location—Roseview.

It confirmed Orison was alive and still trapped in the mortal realm. Nazareth picked the necklace up and toyed with it around her fingers. It was a necklace from Orison's former cabin in Torwarin and Nazareth used it almost daily to check her location. Her amber eyes watched the necklace sway once again. It flew out of her hand and onto the map of the mortal realm. Further confirmation she was alive.

"How is it going?" Idralis asked.

Nazareth jumped at his sudden appearance and looked up at him. The Elven King approached the picnic table. He drummed his fingers on the wood as he regarded the map, then the pendant. Scooping up the pendant, Nazareth wrapped the chain around her hand.

"Well, she's still alive, if that's what you're asking," Nazareth grumbled. "Despite having something of Xabian's, the discovaker doesn't work on him."

"How odd," Idralis said as he settled beside Nazareth.

Nazareth looked at the map. "I wonder why. The curse ended, didn't it?"

The king was silent for a few moments, then nodded. Nazareth made to hold the necklace over the map again, but Idralis' hand wrapped around her wrist and lowered it to the table—enough. He was saying it was enough, that she should stop hoping the necklace would land anywhere but on the mortal realm. But she couldn't give up on Orison and Xabian, not yet. They were her allies.

With an exasperated sigh, Idralis looked at the map. "We should stop."

"I can't. They need our help," Nazareth responded.

Her hopes diminished when Idralis made the maps disappear with a click of his fingers. She would continue tomorrow, if they managed to get back to the Othereal in that time. Idralis stood up and brushed off his black trousers.

"Take a walk with me," Idralis requested.

Nazareth nodded slowly and eased herself onto her feet. She brushed tree sap from her brown trousers and approached her king. Idralis moved towards the town, opening a tin of glazed fruit and eating an orange. He offered some to Nazareth who shook her head. Casting her gaze to the lake, the afternoon sun shimmered on the calm water. Part of her wished to be that calm. Maybe it would happen after they solved this situation.

"Naz?"

"I'm fine, just worried," she insisted.

"How long have you worked as my emissary?" She didn't answer the question. After fifty years of being in his service, Idralis knew her like the back of his hand. "If the discovaker says they're alive, Lioress is doing her job well."

She kicked up some gravel like a defiant child. Idralis ate another orange and looked off into the distance, deep in thought as he chewed. He looked down at the tin of sweets in his hand and pulled his mouth into a tight line. There was no denying Idralis shared the same worries as Nazareth.

Footsteps made her look over her shoulder. "Excuse me, King Idralis!" Bara called from behind them, wringing his hands together. "If you would be so kind, when you know the date of Taviar going to the mortal realm, may I go home?"

Idralis smiled. "Of course, we can arrange that, Sir. I'll send the Regent a message and we'll get the plans in place."

Nazareth noticed the way Bara's shoulders slumped. He was homesick, craving his mortal life. Though they had been keeping Bara safe in Torwarin since the battle, they both knew this wasn't where he belonged. They didn't need a mortal in Akornsonia.

They ushered Bara to join them on their walk. He took the piece of orange Idralis offered him and they discussed his life back home. It allowed Nazareth the chance to mull over the information she had from the discovaker. They needed a seer and more answers from Taviar.

Five days had passed since retrieving the rings from the blacksmiths. Orison's ring dangled in front of her as she lay in her bed, held in mid-air by her magic. She inspected how different Karshakir looked in writing compared to Fallagh. Jagged brush strokes with harsh lines were used in Fallagh writing, whereas Karshakir had smooth brush strokes with perfectly curved lines.

The writing glistened when the sun hit it at just the right angle. Ashim had translated what it said—*My Equal until the sands take us.* It proved how isolated she had been when under King Sila's imprisonment. When she took possession of the ring, Erol explained the Fae had soulmates, or what they called Equals—*Tahanbashri* in Karshakir.

He informed her that the Equal bond between two Fae could enhance each other's power when in proximity to one another. Neither Ashim nor Erol knew anything beyond that. Yet the idea was beautiful. Part of her wanted to find her own Equal and strengthen her powers with somebody who matched her perfectly.

A knock at her bedroom door made her lower the ring into her hand. She didn't know why she felt inclined to keep it; the ring was merely a pawn to gage Harry's worth for servitude. Orison sat up and threaded the ring through a gold necklace chain to secure it around her neck. The bedroom door creaked open and her mother walked in, in her hand she held an embroidery hoop which she absentmindedly worked on as she settled on the bed.

"I heard you're leaving soon, going back to that place," Georgea said. Her face was crestfallen as she returned to working on her embroidery.

Orison knew they needed this talk. "Yeah. In two days, if the swords are satisfactory."

"I'm proud of you, Ori. Even though I don't want you to go, you don't belong here," her mother admitted with a heavy sigh. "You've got a crown to steal."

Orison scoffed; a smile spread across her face. She couldn't admit she feared facing Sila and the possibility of being caged in Alsaphus Castle again. If that was the case, Orison would happily hide in Karshakroh to avoid her captor's wrath—until Xabian crossed her mind. She needed to face Sila to get Xabian the help he needed. Her mother was right, the mortal realm was no place for a Fae.

"You've made some good friends with Ashim and Erol," her mother said as she looked up from her work with a tired smile. "How about we go to the circus? There's one coming into town tomorrow and we can go to the arcade games. We could celebrate your birthday before you return to the magic world."

The circus always came into town on the first day of autumn. The temperature outside had already started to decrease and the leaves dropped in hues of red and orange. Orison nodded profusely, wanting a taste of normality.

"I'd love that," Orison beamed.

"I'll tell your father to get tickets," Georgea said with a smile. "We should invite those nice boys from Karshakroh to join."

Orison sighed with a smile. "Mother, they'll be busy getting ready for the journey back. Let it be just us three, like old times; as a final goodbye and celebrate my birthday."

Her mother nodded as she continued her stitching, tapping her feet on the wooden floor. Orison pushed her mother's blonde hair away from her eyes as she worked. She inched closer as she watched her mother.

"What's your favourite place in the magic world?" Georgea asked.

"Probably Parndore."

Georgea frowned. "What's that?"

Orison explained everything Parndore offered; including the Fire Singers at night with their performances, the valley with compact houses and the castle on the hill. Orison didn't end there; she told her mother about Tsunamal and how she saw a dolphin in Lake Braloak. She had longed to talk about this with her parents, so they knew there was much more than the mortal realm out there.

The next day a thunderous roar engulfed the large tent, drowning out the symphony of trumpets that announced the next act. Orison clapped her hands and inched closer to the edge of her seat so she could see the jugglers as they took centre stage. The audience gawped at the jugglers as they set their pins on fire and juggled to the beat of a bass drum—ramping up how dangerous this act was.

As Orison watched them, it reminded her of Parndore, where she watched the Fire Singers. She had danced the night away with fire running between her feet; where alcohol was passed around generously, and she was free for one night. Her heart ached. Orison wanted to be back there and see their performance with Kinsley and her friends.

"Ori, are you okay?" her father asked.

"Yeah, why?"

Her mother leaned forward. "You're crying, baby."

Orison pulled a handkerchief from her pocket and dabbed at her eyes. She hadn't realised until her parents pointed it out. A shaky breath escaped her as she returned to the jugglers who reminded her so much of Parndore. They were encouraging the crowd to add to the bass of the drum with their feet. She stamped her feet on the ground and clapped her hands in tune with everybody else.

The jugglers bowed to the audience and their fires were extinguished, plunging the tent into darkness. Markus pulled Orison into him as the crowd gasped. She looked around, only seeing the slit in the tent at the bottom which allowed in some daylight. Candles against the support beams lit up the tent and in the centre two people held a sign: *Thank you for watching*—signalling the end.

Everybody stood up, providing the circus with a standing ovation; some of the audience whistled before applauding. As the crowd vacated, their chatter about the performance bounced from person to person. Orison squinted from the sun as they entered the warm air outside. When her eyes adjusted, she gasped at the performers who stood around showcasing other tricks; some were on stilts and juggled, with smiles on their faces.

She shuddered as she watched a clown playing peekaboo with a child in between some crates. Orison had always hated clowns, especially this one. The way the mischievous smile was painted on their face made her skin crawl, especially when its actual smile revealed yellow rotten teeth. She was thankful her father steered her in the opposite direction, where fewer patrons were. She heard the familiar ringing of bells and the calls of vendors—the games area.

"Father, you know they rig these games; don't pressure yourself to win something," Orison stated as she glanced over her shoulder.

"As a goodbye present, I want to win you something," Markus declared. "Remember when I won you that fish when you were a child?"

Reluctantly, she nodded. Orison faintly remembered—it was at a duck pond game when the travelling fair came to town and she was five.

Orison followed her father towards the ring toss game and looked around. Vendors bellowed to step up to their games and spend money. It was encouragement to waste money on something they knew people couldn't win.

"Let him do this, Ori. We don't know when we'll see you again," Georgea announced.

The declaration hit her like a punch in the gut. Her mother was right, she didn't know when she'd see her parents after she left. Orison had to allow her father to do this, like old times. If it came down to it, she would make him win. In her heart, she knew her father would give everything to win her something for one final joyous memory.

There was a plethora of prizes to be won. Most were fish swimming around in glass jars that were far too small for a substantial home. Other prizes were small wooden figurines and marionettes.

"A bucket please, good sir," her father said with confidence.

"If you fill the board, you can pick any marionette in my collection," the man beamed.

Markus picked up the wooden rings. "I will."

A wave of nausea passed over Orison as her nerves kicked into high gear. She noticed he was staring at a princess which looked like her, with a blue dress on. It would be easy to manipulate the game. A plan formulated in her mind; she would allow her father a couple of misses before discreetly using her magic to change the trajectory.

Markus got into a power stance and flung the ring from his hand. It was a perfect hit, but the second one missed. When the next one went flying, she faked a yawn and with a wave of her hand, the ring went directly on the pins. Her father didn't seem to notice anything. Another ring flew from his hand and as Orison wiped her hand along the wrinkles in her green dress, it landed home.

Orison knew it was wrong to cheat, but for her father's happiness, she would do it. If he went home empty-handed, he would be distraught. Her attention snagged onto her mother's piercing blue gaze; it was as though she had caught on to Orison's trickery. Georgea shook her head and scratched her nose before clearing her throat. Another two rings and they had won. Beginner's luck, the vendor might say; little did he know it was all Fae magic. He clapped when Markus had emptied the bucket of rings.

"Well done, that was impressive," the vendor said. "Which marionette would you like?"

Her father pointed to the princess. "That one, please."

The man used a hook to pick it from the shelf and handed the doll to Markus. Orison watched her father cradle it in his arm, careful not to tangle the strings; he smiled at her proudly. She was happy about her father winning, even if it was fabricated.

Georgea looped her arm around Orison's and steered her away from her father. "You should have invited the nice boys to come with us, they would've loved it."

"Mother," Orison groaned, leaning into her.

"What?" Georgea baulked. "I don't know if they have this stuff in the magic place."

Orison rolled her eyes. "I'm sure they do. And I'm sure Ashim and Erol have been to a circus. I told you they're preparing to travel back."

Her mother's grip tightened. "You're always happier around Ashim. He would have loved the circus."

"Mother, stop," Orison hissed. Her cheeks heated and she pressed a hand to them. "Ashim and Erol are friends."

Though her mother fell silent, Orison still noticed the smirk she gave to her father. Orison nudged her mother and shot her a look that told her to stop meddling. Her mother was a matchmaker when she got going.

"Do you want to go on the roundabout, baby?" Markus called.

Orison looked around the fair, finding the wooden sign that said *Mr Unif Roundabout* and a smaller sign stating three bronze coins. Horses were tethered to a rotating wooden contraption, which was being led in circles by children. Markus looped his arm around Orison's and guided her towards it.

"Let's all go on together," her mother proposed.

Her parents walked her over to the roundabout. After paying, they strolled around the area until they found some horses close together. Even though Orison had ridden enough horses in the Othereal and could perfectly mount one by herself, she still allowed her father to help her up. She knew he would feel better in doing so. When they were settled, they waited for the ride to start.

Orison looked across at her father when he put the marionette in his lap. "The knight in shining armour has rescued the princess. On guard!"

Her grip on the reigns tightened. Her father's words resonated within her about her escape from Alsaphus Castle. Orison's heart thundered in her chest and she found it difficult to breathe. The circus was reminding her too much of the Othereal.

The horse beneath her shifted as the ride started. Orison shook away the intrusive thoughts and forced a smile, trying to enjoy what little time she had left with her family. The ride began slowly, until eventually, the horses galloped around the circle; their hooves thundered on the compact dirt underneath their feet. It took Orison's breath away.

The ride came to a gentle stop. Orison dismounted from the horse and staggered to a nearby fence. She took a moment to catch her breath as she stood hunched over with her hands on her hips.

"What's wrong, baby?" Markus asked. "Did you enjoy yourself?"

Orison nodded. "The horses went a little too fast; I'm just winded, that's all." She winced as she straightened up. "Should we walk around and get some more rides in?"

Despite the concerned looks from both her parents, they both guided her away from the roundabout and towards the other rides. At least they could talk and catch up while at the fair, before she would have to leave them again.

THIRTEEN

On the pedestal, Orison looked at herself in the mirror. She looked like a Fae queen with her back straight, shoulders pushed back and hair tied into a bun. Her clothes ruined the entire look. A moss-green skirt with floral embellishments hung from her waist; pins stuck out haphazardly as they held it all together and poked her with every movement. The only thing covering her chest was her crème-coloured stay. Georgea held up a matching green top and presented it to Orison.

"Hold that for me," Georgea instructed.

Orison held it to her chest as her mother pinned the fabric around her. She watched her mother work from the mirror, feeling the bodice conform to her figure.

"It looks beautiful," Orison said.

"It does." Her mother held her as she inspected her art in the mirror. The dress clashed with her mother's brown ensemble. "I look like I'm in rags."

"No, you don't." Orison gasped. She tried to move, but the pins stabbed at her skin, making her flinch. "You look lovely."

Her mother pointed a finger at her. "Stop telling porkies," she said with a smile. Orison giggled, looking down at the dress. "I need to lift the dress off you." Not wanting to be stabbed by any more pins, Orison Misted to the bed behind the pedestal. "Or do that."

With a click of her fingers, a white dress draped over Orison with her other hand poised to hold up the dress for her mother to sew. She was glad she could assist her mother; the dress couldn't get ruined that way. Orison gasped and nearly dropped her hold on the dress as Xabian stepped into the room. He looked paler than normal, but he was awake; she could only assume her father had woken him.

"Morning, Sweetheart," Georgea said.

Xabian smiled at her. "Morning." He looked at Orison. "Hi."

"Hi. How are you feeling?"

He shrugged. "Just a little weak."

"We're going back to the Othereal tonight, we'll get you a healer."

Xabian tensed as he looked between Georgea and Orison. He navigated his way around the cramped spare bedroom, which was filled with boxes of fabrics and her father's tools. He crouched in front of Orison.

He took her hands. "I hope going back to the Othereal is going to fix this."

"Me too," Orison declared.

"We're going to land in Karshakroh, aren't we?" Orison nodded. "I don't know how we'll get home from there."

Orison ran her thumbs over Xabian's hands. "We'll find a way."

She noticed her mother watching the interaction over Xabian's shoulder. Orison was relieved that Xabian acted like his old self, but she could see the monster simmering behind his tired eyes, trying to claw its way out. The mortal realm had made him weak.

"I'm nervous, but it'll help us." Xabian looked at the dress. "That's beautiful."

"Thank you," Georgea replied.

Her mother had always been the best seamstress in Roseville, where people flocked to get her dresses. Georgea's dresses weren't as extravagant as the ones Orison wore in Alsaphus Castle, but Georgea made them with love; they would always be Orison's favourite.

Xabian pulled away from Orison and his jaw tensed as he looked at the window. It was like he was having a fight with himself, trying to tame the beast inside his head. He tapped his foot on the floor, biting his lip as he looked

down. Orison didn't know what he was thinking, but she could tell something
was bothering him. When Georgea huffed out a breath, Orison approached
her mother to help with the dress.

A loud thud made Orison jump and her mother rushed to Xabian's side as
he convulsed on the floor. His eyes rolled to the back of his head as his muscles
tensed. A pained groan escaped his lips and his purple eyes flared. Georgea
rolled him onto his side and watched until he passed out.

A full moon illuminated the forest clearing in a pale light. It was a fitting place
to open a portal and step into another world. Ashim stood close by, observing
Erol as he lit torches where the portal would be.

He then focused on Harry, who was sitting on the forest floor. Harry pawed
at the air like there were butterflies fluttering around him. That was the worst
part of transporting mortals. Then there was Xabian, passed out in a stolen
wheelbarrow. It would be funny if the situation wasn't dire. Under normal
circumstances, they would deem it embarrassing for a prince to be in such a
state.

Loud sobs made Ashim turn towards Orison, who sat on a nearby log
and was inconsolable. She cuddled the princess marionette and wept into its
blonde hair; her shoulders shook with each sob. Ashim made his way over and
crouched before her. He itched to place a hand on her but thought better of
it. On her lap, along with the marionette, was her bag for travelling.

"May I comfort you?" Ashim asked as he sat beside her.

Orison said nothing, only rested her head on his shoulder. He rubbed her
back to soothe her; the scent of mint clung to her hair and her red tunic was
soft to touch. Ashim cast his attention to Erol as he chanted the spell to open

the portal. The spell was the strongest on a full moon. Ashim looked down when he felt his shirt dampening from Orison's tears.

"My shirt is raining cats and dogs," Ashim muttered.

Her body stopped shuddering as she slowly pulled away to look at his face. "What did you say?" It was her first smile since they left the cottage. "Your shirt is raining cats and dogs?"

"Is that wrong?"

Orison nodded, wiping tears away with a chuckle. She glanced over his shoulder as Erol's voice boomed with power around the trees. Ashim helped Orison to her feet as the wind stirred; dirt on the forest floor swirled and leaves rustled around the clearing. He shielded his eyes as a blinding white light erupted around them. Ashim gritted his teeth as he staggered back by the force of the wind. Orison nearly fell, but he swiftly caught her.

When the light and wind dissipated, a shiny silver portal had appeared in the centre of the clearing. Lightning crackled between the trees from its power. It was done—this was their ticket home! Orison looked at the portal with her mouth agape and wiped the remaining tears from her eyes. Ashim let go of her as he approached Xabian; he pushed the wheelbarrow and stepped towards the portal.

"Come on, it'll close soon," Ashim instructed.

She picked up her skirts, bag and doll; then moved closer to Ashim. Erol stepped through the portal first, with Harry on his arm. Ashim allowed Orison one last look at the mortal realm before the silver portal engulfed them; transporting them back to Karshakroh.

The portal opened up to a mountainous cavern. It was cool inside the stone walls—a stark contrast to the stifling humid air of Karshakroh. Ashim set

Xabian down, then caught Orison as she stumbled out of the portal. He looked at Erol who guided Harry to sit on a rock. It was a successful return home, landing right where they needed to.

"Let's drop our belongings off at my home and afterwards, present Harry to King Raj," Ashim instructed in Karshakir.

His attention veered towards Orison, who yelped when someone yanked her from his embrace. Ashim flinched when the cold press of a gun pushed against his head, his heart pounded against his ribs. Orison held her hands up; her eyes glazed over with tears as King Raj's guards pressed a gun to her head. Her lips trembled as she held back more tears. Ashim's mouth went dry; confused about what was happening—this wasn't normal.

"You are not going anywhere," the guard spat.

Ashim raised his hands, his eyes shifted between Erol and Orison. "What's going on?" he demanded in Karshakir.

Some guards yanked the blankets from Xabian. The cavern quickly filled with more guards, all with varying degrees of weaponry. Ashim tried to keep his cool while they discussed their instructions from the king. When they talked about all the things they wanted to do to Orison while sneering at her, Ashim's blood boiled. He would cut off their hands before they went near her.

A guard patted him down and did the same to Erol and Orison. He wanted to protest, but the gun to his head told him to hold his tongue. If he had a bullet in his skull, he wouldn't be able to protect Orison.

Don't say anything, Ashim said to Orison's mind.

I won't.

"Stop talking!" a guard shouted. Ashim winced when the pressure of the gun increased.

He forgot some of the guards were Mindelates, like him and Orison. Two other guards flanked him, forcing his hands behind his back. The chilled feeling of manacles pressed into his wrists as they forced them on.

"Sir Mahrishan, you are under arrest for treason." The guards kicked him behind the legs, his knees crashed to the ground with an excruciating bite of pain. Ashim didn't understand what treason he had committed.

"Orison of Fallasingha, you are under arrest for trespassing." Orison winced when they slapped manacles around her wrists and forced her onto her knees; her head lowered as she accepted fate.

"Sir Beshankar, you are under arrest for treason."

"We've completed our assignment; there is no treason!" Erol screamed.

He grunted when a guard smashed the butt of a gun into the side of his head. He crumpled to the ground—unconscious. The guards talked amongst themselves while they snapped manacles around Xabian's wrists. A guard opened the prince's eyes and checked his pulse. Ashim briefly heard them mention Xabian's disappearance. His hopes of showing Orison everything that Karshakroh had to offer were ruined.

Ashim watched in horror as three guards picked Orison up; her face sculpted into forlorn horror. She struggled and thrashed against them, letting out a terrified scream as they dragged her into the shadows of the cave. Using all his strength, Ashim briefly pushed himself off the ground.

"Get off her!" he screamed, as he was forced back onto his knees. "Orison!"

Ashim struggled against the manacles that held his hands together. The guards forced his head to the floor and pinned him down with a heavy knee on his back. He could do nothing except watch the guards take Orison into the darkness. When agonised cries from where they had taken her filled the cavern, Ashim struggled with all his might to get to her.

"Orison!" Ashim screamed.

Something heavy slammed into the side of his head. He cringed from the force as the world spun. Orison's cries turned into loud sobs, with male laughter at her misery. Ashim let out a pain-filled groan as a guard slammed the butt of their gun into his head once more, casting him in darkness.

FOURTEEN

Rain sliced through the sky like a thousand tiny knives, each seemed to find their way into the slits in the dungeon walls, which substituted for windows. It turned the dirt floor into an ankle-deep pool.

Orison groaned as her eyes fluttered open. She winced from a burning pain that pierced her side. Shivers from the cold were not helping the wound to heal; the pain intensified as she propped herself up onto her elbows. Her hands shook violently when she touched the large red stain on her left side, which gradually grew with each intense shiver. Orison bit her lip as she pressed the heel of her hand on the injury to stop the bleeding; she cried out and wept from the pain which turned her numb.

The torches on the wall behind the bars were the only thing that illuminated the cell. Orison watched the flame turn the water to an orange colour. Two adjacent walls had holes in them; allowing her to peek into the neighbouring cells, but the shadows gave only a little away. Her bucket to relieve herself bobbed in the water, banging against the bars like it wanted to escape. Orison's only luxury was the suspended bed, which kept her out of the water and a burlap sack to use as a blanket.

A tap on the shoulder made Orison jump. She stifled her yelp as her side burned from the sudden shock. Orison peered through a hole in the grey stone wall, feeling relieved to see Ashim. Orison knew he was in a nearby cell, because of the tugging in her chest, which added to her misery. He fed his hand through the hole and Orison clutched it like her life depended on it.

"What did the guards do to you?" Ashim asked.

"They carved something into my side," she explained.

He looked through another hole in the wall. "Anything else?" Orison shook her head. She was being honest and was relieved nothing else happened. Ashim pressed his head to the wall and closed his eyes. "I'm sorry. I should have protected you."

Orison had never seen him look so defeated. His brown hair hung limp around his face; he tapped his head against the wall while muttering under his breath in Karshakir. She ran her thumb over his knuckles to comfort him.

"Don't blame yourself for this. You couldn't have known." Ashim looked at her. "I'm not mad at you."

A loud, exasperated cry filled the dungeon. Orison eased herself onto her back and turned her head. Erol's face peered through a hole in the adjacent wall. He was yelling something in Karshakir. The sound of him smacking the wall echoed around the dungeon. He yelled even louder, earning a retort from a guard; Orison could only guess it meant *shut up*.

Orison yelped when a heavy weight settled on her side. She looked down and grimaced as Ashim inspected the wound. She didn't understand why it wasn't healing. The guards hadn't given her any dressings for it; she was sure an infection would spread soon.

"Sorry," Ashim said, moving his hands. "King Raj hasn't treated us like this before."

"Where is Xabian?" Orison asked. Aside from Erol's rant, the dungeon was silent. She turned to Ashim, who was slumped against the wall with his eyes closed. She reached in and pushed on his shoulder. "Ash."

"Yeah?" he grumbled sleepily, keeping his eyes closed.

"Thought you'd fallen asleep."

"Nearly." He reached his hand through to her cell as she settled down and held his hand. "Try to get some sleep."

Upon closer inspection of his hand, Orison noticed it was full of scars. She looked at him. "You can call me Ori if you want to."

"Ori's a cute nickname," he mumbled.

Orison pressed her cheek into his hand when she realised that she couldn't stop him from falling asleep. It comforted her that Ashim was in the same situation. She wouldn't feel alone while trapped in a castle once again. She knew nothing would change in the Othereal.

With the drumming of the rain outside and the icy breeze blowing in, exhaustion caught up with Orison. Her teeth chattered together from the cold as she pulled the burlap blanket around her frozen body. The heat from Ashim's hand was a small bit of warmth.

As she drifted off to sleep, she thought of everything that Haranshal might have been. Orison could have bought a boat ticket and ran up to the entrance of Alsaphus Castle to claim her throne and overthrow King Sila. She would have held her family close, informing them she was safe and they may have rejoiced in her safe return. But nothing ever went according to plan. She went to sleep with these thoughts, hoping some day she might escape this new prison.

Reflections from the sun painted water ripples across the ceiling of the dungeon. They wavered as a warm breeze pushed its way into the dungeon and played with the knee-deep water. Ashim was thankful the rain had subsided for now. The sloshing of water echoed through the dungeon as guards waded through it. They used sticks to unblock the drains, which allowed the water to flow out. They completely ignored Ashim, Erol and Orison as they passed.

Ashim pressed his back to the wall, waiting for whatever was coming to them. Out of boredom, he watched the water trickle out of his boot from when he had to relieve himself. His wet trousers had scraped the skin on his knees raw.

Despite being in King Raj's service for almost his entire adult life, he'd never been in the dungeon before. It was abysmal and he never wanted to see the inside of it again. The guards were grumbling amongst themselves about unblocking the drains.

"When we get out of here, we can try Ferkowl," Ashim said to Orison when he noticed she had been silent all morning. "It's a bowl we have for breakfast. It has eggs, sausages and bacon in there. You'd love it."

He peered through the hole in the wall when she didn't reply. Orison seemed to be asleep, her breakfast was still on the shelf in the wall. Ashim frowned and knelt down to look at her; she was pale with dark circles under her eyes.

"Orison?" He reached through the hole and pushed her shoulder—she didn't stir. "Ori?"

"Ash," Erol drawled. He looked up at his companion. "I think something is wrong."

His gaze travelled to the wound she received last night. The blood stain on her side had worsened since the last time he inspected it; the stain showed a green circle in the centre. Ashim gasped and staggered backwards. His feet sloshed in the water as he waded to the bars of the cell. The guards had their backs to him.

"I need a healer!" he shouted in Karshakir. Ashim banged on the metal bars. "Hey! We need a healer over here!"

A guard approached him with a snarl. "Don't try to use that as an escape tactic."

"Orison isn't waking up. She's gravely sick. Please!"

The guard smirked at him as he unclipped his keys, which jingled together as he moved to Orison's cell. Ashim pressed his forehead to the bars, knowing the guards didn't believe him. When the lock of her cell clicked, Ashim waded back to the hole and peered inside Orison's cell to check on her. The guard approached, placing two fingers on her neck.

"Shit." The guard waded through the water. "We need a healer over here, now!"

As soon as the guard gave the instruction, the entire dungeon erupted in chaos, with the sound of whooshing water echoing around the cells. Ashim reached into her cell and held her hand; it was cold to the touch. Pressing his forehead to the wall, he closed his eyes, wishing he was in that cell with her.

A guard hurried to Orison's cell. "King Raj has ordered for Orison to be brought to the infirmary immediately."

More guards filtered into her cell, this time with a stretcher. Ashim blinked back the sting of tears, the world around him was blurred and distorted. He quickly pushed the tears away with an exhale of breath. His stomach dropped when the guards pried his hand from Orison's. He cried out in protest, but the guards ignored his pleas as they scooped her up.

Pushing off from his bed, Ashim waded through the water to the bars. His knuckles were white as he watched the guards carry Orison away. He pressed his face to the bars to try and get close to her. Regardless of the water level, he fell to his knees out of despair. Ashim screamed loudly and succumbed to the emotions of the past twenty-four hours.

FIFTEEN

Ashim had counted three days since Orison took ill and she still hadn't returned. They had moved Erol into her cell. Every time Ashim asked for an update on her wellbeing or why he was being kept there, guards took pleasure in ignoring him. He flexed his fists, furious and confused as to why King Raj acted so differently—after three months in the mortal realm. It wasn't his usual welcome home.

"You're like a lovesick puppy," Erol said in Karshakir.

"Fuck off." Ashim snapped, as his nails dug into his palms.

Erol's chuckle was his only response. Ashim felt protective of Orison. He didn't know why, but he couldn't stay away and there was the pull which he felt in her presence. Ashim cared for Orison deeply. Her smile lit up the room for him and made his hard days better.

"She'll be okay; don't torture yourself," Erol said. Ashim shook off Erol's hand when he tapped his shoulder through the hole in the wall. "Come on."

"I'd prefer to suffer if it means getting answers," Ashim muttered.

Ashim wanted to suffer, especially if King Raj had decided to turn his back on him completely and signed him up for an execution. However, executions were only for extreme crimes, none of which Ashim had committed.

Heavy footsteps came closer to his cell. Ashim looked through his hair at the guard, keys clinked together as he unlocked Ashim's cell. The door swung open with a squeal and the guard walked into the cell with manacles.

"Has my time finally come?" Ashim asked.

The guard snorted. "No. King Raj has need of you."

It made him wonder what he was in for. As the guard opened the cell, he gestured to go outside—there were no manacles slapped around Ashim's wrist—the guard simply ushered him to stand. Doing as he was told, Ashim eyed the guards with suspicion, not knowing their intentions.

"What is my mission?"

The guard gestured to the open door, pointing him towards the exit. Ashim regarded the guard for a moment, convinced this was a trap. Hearing keys jingling, he turned his head, eyes widening when he realised the guards also released Erol from this pit of despair. It made little sense after what King Raj had done.

"What are you doing?" the guard snapped. He grabbed Ashim and shoved him out of the cell. "Get to work; you're being released."

"Move!" another guard ordered.

Ashim staggered into a nearby wall, glancing at Erol. It was the first time in days he had seen the outside of his cell. Shaking off the peculiar encounter, he used the wall to navigate his way out of the dungeon. Ashim's heart raced because of the unknown and what King Raj might have up his sleeve.

Guards flanked Orison as they guided her to King Raj's throne room. They walked her through corridors which were the colour of sand. Arched glassless windows overlooked a bustling city, full of mismatching architecture; timber-framed structures mingled with clay structures that spread close to the ocean. A push on Orison's back made her return her gaze to the corridor before her.

The arched throne room doors opened on a phantom wind and the barren walls of the corridor turned to gold. Sheer red curtains billowed through the windows, allowing a cool breeze to spread across the space. It was a welcome reprieve from the heat, which Orison wasn't accustomed to. Golden tables piled with fruit made Orison salivate from hunger; they had denied her any food since leaving the infirmary. Her thoughts of eating were diminished when she saw who sat in the centre of the space. King Raj lounged on a plethora of pillows with his dark-brown hair tied into a bun. His all-white ensemble was pristine and a female wearing next to nothing fed him strawberries.

An unusual tugging sensation from Orison's wound lowered her to her knees until she knelt before the Karshak King. The wound sent a jab of pain through her side; Orison winced and placed a hand to it. When she looked through her hair, the man smiled.

"Welcome, Orison," King Raj said. His brown eyes glistened with adoration as he leaned forward. "I'm King Raj."

She remained silent, glaring at him as she gripped her thin white dress, feeling the wound's dressings that lay underneath. This man had nearly killed her with whatever his cronies had cut into her side. She hadn't inspected it yet. Orison detested how happy King Raj appeared.

The king shifted on his pillows. Orison cringed at hearing him moan with pleasure at the strawberry being fed to him. Her stomach growled loudly and she pressed a hand on it. King Raj couldn't know she was ravenous. Even while trapped in Fallasingha Castle, she had never felt hunger like this. The clicking of King Raj's fingers made her wince, reminding her of Sila.

Raj shouted something in Karshakir. Orison listened to the sound of retreating footsteps as he slurped on something she refused to look at. "Did King Sila take your voice when he exiled you?"

They had met briefly when she was trapped in Alsaphus Castle, on one of her first days with King Sila. As expected, the meeting went horribly wrong, with King Raj and King Sila arguing until Raj left in a fit of anger. He appeared nice back then.

"No," she growled.

"Ah, she speaks!" King Raj clapped his bejewelled hands together with a grin. "Welcome to Karshakroh, Orison."

Orison raised her head ever so slightly. "You haven't provided a very warm welcome."

With a pout, Raj nodded. "I can only apologise. I wasn't aware Ashim had given you knowledge of my true nature." Orison glared. "King Sila is dead, Orison. You were destined to be queen."

Orison frowned. "Were?"

"It has come to my attention that you are in danger, so I made some arrangements," Raj explained as he leaned forward.

Orison sucked in a breath at the king's explanation. If she was truly in danger, she refused to believe King Sila was dead. Xabian would have boasted about it otherwise, regardless of his illness. Orison had convinced herself that she was never destined to be queen; she was a false princess to fill Sila's ego. She tightened the grip on her dress from the rage clouding her judgement; she was seconds away from punching King Raj.

A servant set a plate loaded with food in front of Orison—brown meat, rice and slices of mango. Orison salivated from the sight of it all; she wanted to dive into the delectable meal, but the risk of poisoning was too great. It took all her might to ignore the plate and stare at the king.

"It's not poisoned. My tasters have checked. You look like you're about to collapse," King Raj commented, leaning back. "In my country, it's rude to refuse food from an ally."

Reluctantly, she picked up the spoon and gave in to her desire. When the spices danced along her tongue, her hunger grew exponentially. She devoured each morsel until the plate was clean, even licking the fork and knife to get every last bit; not knowing when her next meal was coming. Her hands wrapped around the goblet and guzzled down the crisp water, letting it dribble down her chin. Orison sank back on her heels, with a comfortable fullness in her belly. She regarded King Raj's words about arrangements.

Her attention snapped to him. "What do you mean by arrangements?" A pair of beige trousers and a white tunic replaced the empty plate. Her eyes widened.

King Raj smirked. "You're now one of my Runners, Orison Durham." Her heart raced as she stared at the clothes before her. "Don't worry, you are going to be accompanied by Mahrishan and Beshankar."

"I am nobody's slave," Orison spat.

King Raj gawped. "Runners are not slaves, Orison. You'll do well to remember that." It took everything for Orison to hold back a retort. "The brand in your side merely ensures you do your duties. These clothes are your uniform. While you're not on errands, you must wear it to clean the castle."

"No, I refuse." King Raj grimaced and buried his head in his hands with a groan. Her heart pounded against her chest. "I don't have a home here," Orison whimpered. Her breath came out in heavy pants as panic set in, tears stinging her eyes. "I have nothing here."

"Please trust me!" Raj pleaded. "Your life is on the line if I don't do this. Speak with another Runner for a place to sleep. I can't offer you a room because you are not a guest, but an employee; it's inappropriate."

Her body shook violently as she hugged her arms. Ashim was in the dungeon and so was Erol. Orison didn't know either of their addresses; she knew nothing about Haranshal. Daring to look at King Raj, he appeared remorseful; like he hated seeing her misery.

"Show her the way out," King Raj reluctantly ordered the guards. She tried to protest, not knowing where she was going. "See you tomorrow, Orison."

"Please," she begged as they led her away, placing the clothes into her arms.

The guards didn't listen. They continued to lead her from the golden throne room and into the castle. She never got to ask about Xabian, Erol or Ashim. Eventually, Orison gave up the fight, just as she did in Alsaphus Castle.

Ashim chuckled with Erol as they crossed the drawbridge which led from Karshak Castle into Haranshal. It was like old times in the castle, despite everything that had changed. He had spent the day cleaning the rooms, ensuring King Raj was comfy; at mid-afternoon, he and Erol were dismissed. Only when Ashim crossed the last archway out of the castle did he pause; he had been so busy he hadn't thought of Orison.

"I'll see you tomorrow. I have to check on Orison," Ashim announced as he turned around to return to the castle.

"Okay," Erol called. Ashim whirled back around, he jumped when a hand clamped around his shoulder, jostling him into a guard outpost. Ashim came face to face with Erol, "Something's wrong, there's an unfamiliar sound coming from the castle walls."

Frowning, Ashim walked with Erol back through the archway. Ashim made to take a step further, but Erol held him back and signalled for him to listen. The sound of loud cries made him tense, then he felt the inevitable pull in his chest.

"Orison," Ashim breathed.

Erol cast him a bewildered look. "What?"

Pushing his friend's arm away, Ashim rushed towards the cries. He leaned against the outer wall to balance himself against a tumble down a steep hill, following the pull in his chest to guide him to Orison. He found her curled up figure; her shoulders shifted with each sob. Her blonde hair cascaded down her back and she cuddled the bag she had brought back to the Othereal.

"Orison, I'm here," Ashim said and crouched beside her.

Her head shot up at the sound of his voice. She grabbed both his hands and spoke so quickly he had difficulty understanding her—despite his understanding of the common tongue being far superior to everything else. With a shuddering intake of breath, she broke down again.

"King... Raj...." She swallowed audibly. "Job."

"King Raj gave you a job?" Ashim asked.

Orison nodded quickly as she tried to catch her breath. She spoke in that hurried way again and the conversation was lost on him; but he listened, regardless. "I'm so confused, Ashim. I don't know what to do," she cried.

He tensed when she held him close. His attention was on Erol as he approached. After a few moments, Ashim ran his hand through Orison's hair and pressed his forehead to her shoulder. He was glad he found her when he did. Raj's change of demeanour lately had confused him; the king never treated anybody this poorly. Rubbing her back, Ashim tried to soothe Orison, but she kept crying.

"It's okay, you're going to be okay," Ashim soothed. She gripped his shirt harder and her body shook as she wept. "What kind of job?"

"Runner, he made me a Runner," Orison gasped.

"Okay, that's not bad; you're going to be fine." Ashim glanced over her shoulder. "I think I'll meet you tomorrow, Erol. I need to take Orison home; the king has made her a Runner," he said in Karshakir.

"She's joined us?" Erol gasped, eyes wide in shock. "Othereal above. Take her to your place, make sure she's comfortable."

Ashim nodded, securing her bag over his shoulder. With a dip of his chin as a goodbye to Erol, he Misted in a flurry of beige smoke and sand towards his apartment. They landed in his living room; the large space was simple, with a small beige sofa facing an unused fireplace. The green walls were bare, aside from shelves with a couple of books on them; now he could fill them with his common tongue books.

Orison lifted her head and looked around. "Where am I?"

"My house." A quiet meow came from his bedroom and Mahavu stepped out. With determination, the small desert cat with sandy fur and black stripes on her forelegs ran up to Ashim. He picked up Mahavu with a smile. "Meet Orison, give her comfort," Ashim instructed in Karshakir.

He placed Mahavu in Orison's lap. Reluctantly, she sat on the floor and cradled the small feline. She petted her soft fur, smiling at the loud purring; she held Mahavu to eye level. Ashim could already tell they were going to be friends.

"Ahnes," Orison said to Mahavu. It surprised Ashim to hear her say *hello* in Karshakir. When Mahavu meowed, it sounded like she was growling. Orison jumped and held her to her chest. "Oh, did I hurt her?" Orison looked down and petted Mahavu's head.

He shook his head. "Her voice is a little different."

Leaving Orison to play with Mahavu, he stood up and approached the kitchen. Ashim put the kettle under the tap to fill it with water. He placed tea leaves inside and began making tea to calm Orison's nerves.

"Ash?" Orison called from the living room. He watched as she kissed Mahavu's head. "Can... can I stay here?"

"*Halek*," Ashim said as he placed the kettle on the stove. "You have nowhere else to go."

Orison stood up. "I can sleep on the sofa."

"Second bedroom." He pointed to the spare room next to the front door.

She placed Mahavu on the floor as she looked around the apartment, opening doors to familiarise herself with the rooms. Ashim closed the lid on the teapot, feeling the familiar weight and the jabs of claws as Mahavu jumped onto his shoulder. He petted her head and earned loud purrs as he watched Orison disappear into the spare bedroom. At least with Orison staying there, she was safe and not outside in an unfamiliar country.

Giving Mahavu a kiss, Ashim smiled. "Do you like Orison?" he asked in Karshakir.

The cat meowed in response; he winced when her claws pierced through his white tunic. Mahavu was like a parrot—she always insisted sitting on Ashim's shoulder—but the claws always came out when he moved, to maintain balance.

Orison re-emerged from the spare bedroom. "Thank you."

"Have you found the bathroom?" he asked. Orison nodded. "Get cleaned up. Then you can relax until tomorrow."

She nodded and hurried into the bathroom. Ashim needed to tell her the conditions of being King Raj's Runner, but that could wait. This latest development had caused Orison to be shaken up enough. As the kettle squealed, Ashim returned to the stove and got to work, making her a refreshing fruit tea.

SIXTEEN

Deep in the belly of a cavern outside of Cleravoralis, enchantresses—naked as the day they were born—swayed around in a rock pool while chanting. Taviar followed Emphina down the carved stairs and walked to the edge of the pool. His hand clutched the piece of fabric which held his robe together and kept his modesty. It had been three weeks and the enchantresses had regained their power enough to allow passage into the mortal realm.

Emphina stripped off her robe and stepped into the water to join her sisters. "Join us, Sir Luxart, for luck and prosperity in the mortal realm."

Reluctantly, Taviar let go of his robe and shrugged it off. It fell to the cavern floor, exposing his skin to the enchantresses; he covered his crotch with his hand and waited. Emphina held his other hand and guided him into the warm water.

An enchantress approached him and smeared blue powder on Taviar's forehead as she chanted in a foreign language. The other enchantresses smeared the blue paint on his limbs before turning him around to the entrance. He gasped at how overwhelming and invasive this was.

"Take a deep breath," Emphina instructed.

After doing so, the enchantress pushed on his chest and dragged him under the water. Hands held him down for what felt like an eternity. Taviar's lungs burned and his eyes felt like they would bulge out of their sockets. When he came to the surface, he gasped loudly as he gulped in some oxygen. He took another deep inhale before they dragged him back under the water. It seemed a never-ending journey of being pushed beneath the surface with only limited reprieve.

Once the pool cleansing was over, they dressed Taviar in an all-white outfit, then laid him down on a rock. The enchantresses surrounded him and threw coloured powder all over his body. They chanted and hollered at the top of their lungs; their magic filled the cavern in pinks, blues, purples and reds. Drums were added to the mix, along with tambourines. Some enchantresses burned herbs as they worked through the cleansing. In the past, Taviar had never done this when he went to the mortal realm; Sila didn't believe in it.

As per Emphina's wishes, Taviar had spent the morning undertaking various other cleansing rituals. It was like a weight was lifted off his shoulders and he felt free. During his two nights in Cleravoralis, Idralis—along with Bara—had joined them. It was Taviar's job to bring Bara home in exchange for Orison.

Once the cleansings were complete, the enchantresses led Taviar into the forest, where they walked along a path to a clearing filled with people. Some banged on drums and others danced with tambourines as they hollered to the sky. It made Taviar delirious as they led him into the centre; where Bara waited patiently, looking around at each of them. Some had blue or black face paint on, smearing it into their white dresses.

The cries of the enchantresses turned into a crescendo; it took everything for Taviar not to cover his ears. When they all slammed down their staffs, the ground shook and he could feel the magic radiating through the clearing.

Emphina stepped up to Taviar with a book in her hand. She recited a spell from the book in a foreign language and the surrounding air churned up into a whirlwind. Taviar's hair whipped around his face as he looked around and saw the other enchantresses chanting together with Emphina. With a crack of lightning, the portal opened up; it resembled liquid metal that swirled in mid-air.

Taviar's heart was racing as he prepared for what this entailed for Orison's return. He nodded at Bara and waited for Emphina to finish her spell before he moved towards the portal. With a final chant, she closed the book and placed it behind her back.

"Wait!" somebody cried. The three of them whirled around. An enchantress with wispy white hair hurried through the crowd; her all-white eyes indicated that she was blind. "The princess has returned to the Othereal!"

Taviar tensed; his face blanched in horror at her words. He stepped away from the portal and towards the seer. Leaves rustled behind him as Emphina stepped closer.

"You can stay in the Othereal while I return Bara," Emphina offered.

"Please do. I have a duty to uphold," Taviar gasped.

Turning to the other enchantresses, Emphina smiled. "See you soon."

Emphina guided Bara to the portal's entrance. He took one last look at the forest surrounding them before they disappeared into the abyss. Wind whirled around the clearing as the portal sealed shut behind them, leaving Taviar planted on Othereal soil without a plan to get Orison home.

Water splashed onto the stone floor of King Raj's throne room. Orison grabbed the brush and scrubbed out sand that had accumulated in the crevices. Her arms burned from exhaustion and her hands were wrinkled from the water, but she kept her head down and continued. It had been two weeks in King Raj's service and this day was her birthday, but she hadn't told anybody; she had forgotten until she saw a calendar in the castle kitchen.

The sweltering heat in Karshakroh made Orison's clothes damp from sweat; a thin beige scarf kept her hair up and out of the way. Over the past two weeks, the suffocating heat made her feel like she was wading through warm syrup. With a grimace, Orison scrubbed the floor faster with the sound of approaching footsteps.

"Lovely to see you, Orison," King Raj drawled. She braced herself, waiting for him to walk through the section she had cleaned. Instead, he diverted his trajectory to a dirty section she hadn't cleaned yet. He skipped over the parts she'd cleaned and settled on his chaise. "How are you?"

"Hot," she grumbled.

Orison sat back and wiped away the sweat on her forehead with her tunic. The heat made her pant as she tried to keep cool, but to no avail. Every day was torture in Karshakroh.

Worried he would reprimand her for taking a break, she dipped the brush into a bucket and returned to cleaning the sand from the crevices in the floor. Her attention briefly settled on Raj when he clicked his fingers. A servant appeared with a glass of ice water which Orison would have died for. Raj extended the glass out to Orison. Tentatively, she took it and gulped it down greedily.

"Take a break and speak with me," King Raj instructed. Orison held the glass to her chest, scooping out an ice cube and rubbing it against her forehead. "Do you know why Xabian fails to awaken?"

Orison turned to King Raj. "No. He's been like that since our exile to the mortal realm. Before then, Xabian has been cursed with the Nighthex."

He pouted, muttering something in Karshakir under his breath. He beckoned for Orison to come forward and she staggered to her feet. The wet patches on her coarse trousers made her knees itch with each step. She curtsied to him before she returned to running ice cubes along her hot skin.

"Did King Sila curse him?" Raj asked. Orison nodded. "Thank you for the information. Please return to work."

King Raj pulled out a pipe and used his magic to light the herbs inside. She curtsied once more, placed the glass on his side table and rushed back to her bucket of water. Dipping the sponge into the bucket, she continued to scrub the floor. The ice only gave her a slight reprieve from the heat; she wasn't desperate enough to pour the glass of ice over her head to chill her to the bone.

She paused scrubbing when a servant placed another glass of ice water beside her.

Keeping her mind from how hot she was, Orison thought about how far she had fallen. Ashim explained this was a job and she would get paid for missions and manual labour around the castle. She didn't mind either of those things; the fact was that she had to do this to remain safe from a threat. Orison should have been on a ship to Fallasingha at this point, reclaiming her throne, not scrubbing floors.

She tried to eavesdrop on King Raj talking to a servant in Karshakir. She wondered who had set her up to this. King Sila came to mind—to teach her a lesson—but Orison had to remind herself they were sworn enemies. If Raj was telling the truth about his death, then somebody from Fallasingha had to know she was there.

Orison yearned to explore Haranshal after Raj dismissed her, but she didn't know if they would allow it. She was unsure if they had confined her to Ashim's home and Karshak Castle. It would be fitting if so, because all kings wanted to lock her up. Orison had to hold on to the hope she could escape one day.

Taviar settled down at the dining table, staring down at the map before him. He had to figure out where Orison was in the Othereal and why she could not come home. Riddle settled down beside him with a bottle of amber coloured alcohol and two glasses. His husband popped the cork and poured equal amounts into the glasses.

He knocked back his alcohol and cringed when it burned on the way down. Taviar watched Riddle conjure up a hair clip—which Orison often wore from her former chambers—and recited the incantation of the discovaker. The hair clip twitched in Riddle's palm as they waited for it to work. It flew out of Riddle's hand and onto the map where Haranshal, Karshakroh was located.

"Am I reading that right?" Taviar baulked and inched closer to the map. "She's in Karshakroh?"

Riddle's hand trembled as he knocked back his alcohol. "Othereal above."

"King Raj said he'd contact me if she returned. He lied!" Taviar gasped, his attention fixated on Karshak Castle where the hair clip sat. "He had no intention of contacting me when she returned, did he?"

The chair creaked as Riddle sat forward and ran his hand over his head. Taviar drummed his fingers on the table. He had to consult Saskia and tell her about this latest development. He vowed he would when he picked up the twins from her care; he had to form a plan to get Orison out.

"I'm unsure of his intentions," Riddle stated as he inspected the map. "It's how long she's been in the Othereal—that's the issue."

"I failed her," Taviar gasped.

Riddle took Taviar's hand as he bowed his head in shame. He regretted not having soldiers constantly checking her location, to ensure Raj followed through with his plan. If he had found out sooner, he might have saved Orison from whatever horrors she faced. Taviar could only imagine how scared she was over there. The hair clip only reassured him she was still alive and that she would fight her way out.

"You haven't failed her, she's a fighter," Riddle reassured.

Taviar poured himself another glass of alcohol and knocked it back in one gulp, savouring the burn in his throat. He knew he hadn't failed Orison, yet he still felt guilty. Taviar still held hope that he would see Orison healthy. He wished for her to become her true self and to flourish—free from Sila's tyrannical grasp. She was a queen without a crown, trapped in a far-off land away from the comforts she knew.

His eyes widened in awe when the hair clip moved around the map. It left the confines of Karshak castle and appeared in the heart of Haranshal. Taviar's curiosity peaked and he leaned into the map to inspect it further.

He prayed they had released her from the dungeons and she could now board a ship towards Fallasingha to reunite with everybody. Yet the longer he stared at the map, the more he realised it wasn't the case.

"Do you think the king has another dungeon in the heart of Haranshal?" Taviar asked as he viewed the clip. "If he let her escape, surely she would run to the docks to catch the first ship home."

"Why would the king have a dungeon in the heart of the capital?" Riddle enquired. Taviar gave him a look. "Even if it was to keep the citizens in line, I don't think he'd parade around somebody from an enemy nation."

"Sorry," Taviar sighed, running a hand down his face. "I know little about Haranshal, we rarely visited."

Riddle tapped Taviar's hand. "I'm sure she'll be in contact when she's allowed."

Taviar looked at his husband's brown eyes, which gave him so much comfort. He knew Riddle was correct; he was his voice of reason. Though he'd only travelled to Karshakroh a few times, it was King Raj in particular who really stuck out as peculiar. None of the citizens appeared to be in ill health or living in fear like Fallasingha. A strange thought crossed his mind—that Orison willingly stayed in Haranshal to avoid Fallasingha. He knew she didn't know Sila was dead so he wouldn't put it past her.

"Maybe Orison ran away," Taviar suggested as he inspected the map. "King Idralis told us it was before King Sila's passing, so maybe she's avoiding Fallasingha."

Riddle's jaw tightened as he regarded the notion. "That is a very strong possibility, but we know she was in the castle."

"Maybe she befriended King Raj; she's good at making friends," Taviar suggested.

Taviar knew the idea was absurd, but it helped quell his fear for Orison's safety. Dark memories of his time on the battlefield between Karshakroh and Fallasingha came to the forefront of his mind. His heart quickened in pace as he recalled the screams of his fellow men. He shook his head quickly; it was normal in war and they weren't at war now.

"We still need to get her home to take the crown," Riddle reminded him.

"And there's the crown," Taviar repeated with a murmur.

Whatever kept Orison tied to Haranshal, he hoped it was good and not something sinister. Taviar knew he couldn't be Regent forever. Though he was a good leader and could keep Fallasingha safe from any threats, he was ultimately a leader with no power. He was merely the babysitter of a country until Orison claimed her throne.

SEVENTEEN

Orison faked taking a nap after King Raj dismissed her. Her birthday had fizzled down to her being curled up in bed, where she cried over every event that had occurred since returning to the Othereal. To muffle the sound of her sobs, she shoved the corner of the blanket into her mouth as she succumbed to her emotions.

She cried until she choked on tears and her head pounded. Orison jumped when something soft brushed against her face. She slowly opened her eyes to the dark-green room, blurred from her tears as she went to inspect what touched her. She felt it again, followed by something being shoved under her chin; she found Mahavu trying to snuggle into her. The cat purred as Orison gently placed a hand on her back and looked at the door, which was firmly closed. Orison wiped her tears.

"How did you get in?" Orison asked, inspecting the feline. "Animals can't Mist."

Orison sat up, curious about Mahavu's point of entry. Cats couldn't open and close doors, as far as she knew. The bed creaked as she leaned over to check underneath, wondering if she had been hiding under there the entire time. Her eyes widened to uncover a small brown door, large enough for a cat, carved into the skirting board. It was the only way she could have gotten in. She returned to the bed, where Mahavu lay on her side and blinked slowly at Orison, with loud purrs.

She couldn't help but smile as she reached out and scratched under Mahavu's chin. The cat grabbed her finger and gently chomped on it, making Orison jump. The animal's scratchy tongue scraped across Orison's skin. She wasn't used to having cats around, but she enjoyed the company.

Scooping up Mahavu, Orison crossed the room and sat on the window ledge. In the bustling street below, chariots pulled men along, their hair flowed behind them; women sold kebabs, fruit juice and coffee on the side of the street. Orison itched to experience it all and indulge in this rich, vibrant culture outside her window.

"Today's my birthday," she told Mahavu, while petting her. "I can't celebrate because I'm trapped here." The cat wriggled and looked up at Orison with large yellow eyes. "You can't understand me either, huh?"

She didn't care. Mahavu was a cat—they would lie there and listen, regardless of the language barrier. Mahavu purred loudly as Orison petted her head and looked outside. Orison sighed, wondering what the coffee or juice tasted like; or the kebabs that the meat vendor was selling. She jumped when the door opened.

"Why didn't you tell me it's your birthday?" Ashim asked.

"You were eavesdropping?" Orison baulked when Ashim nodded. "I forgot what day it was until I saw a calendar."

"Come on, let's celebrate instead of being in here." Ashim waved her along. Orison went to stand, but settled back on the seat and returned to gazing outside. "You aren't trapped in my house, you know."

Orison blinked a few times, then turned to Ashim. "I can leave? Like leave the country?"

"You can travel the entirety of Karshakroh; but you can't leave the country without telling King Raj," Ashim explained.

"What happens if you leave the country without permission?" Orison petted Mahavu, who was asleep.

"The brand turns black and if you try to return, you're put in the dungeons." His explanation made Orison gasp and cover her mouth.

She touched her hip where the brand was. "Why is my brand on my hip?"

Ashim frowned and looked at her hip. "That's odd, it's usually over your heart," he scratched his head while muttering something in Karshakir.

"We'll go celebrate when Mahavu wakes up," Orison stated as she stroked Mahavu's head.

He sat beside her on the window ledge, leaning his head on the window. It gave Orison some comfort to know she could come and go as she pleased; but she was unsure how she felt about never leaving the country without permission.

"What are you thinking about?" Ashim asked.

Orison rubbed her thumb over Mahavu's paw. "King Raj never explained why he made me a Runner. He only said it was to keep me safe." She frowned as she looked at the street. "I don't understand."

"The King never acts this way," Ashim admitted. "It's odd."

She shrugged, looking at Mahavu, hoping she would wake up. Then Orison could see what Haranshal had to offer and celebrate her birthday with some freedom. She thought about riding on the chariots or trying some street food. If she was supposed to be confined to this country, Orison had to get used to it—whether or not she wanted to.

The bazaar heaved with people, packed shoulder to shoulder. A domed ceiling shielded them from the elements; it was adorned with mosaic tiles in the shapes of stars and musical instruments. Fabrics of all colours hung above stalls; flags flapped across the entire market. The smells of rich spices, including tea and cinnamon hung heavy in the air. They had propped bags of them outside various vendors. Men shouted in Karshakir, bartering for the best prices.

In one of the stalls, Ashim leaned against a support beam as he listened to a handful of giggling women who surrounded Orison. They lined her eyes with kohl, placed lipstick on her lips and adorned her hair with curls and gold. They talked amongst themselves in Karshakir. Orison's purple gaze kept shifting to Ashim, who was smiling. The women had made her look like a goddess. Ashim eyed her purple and gold dress, which hugged her curves in all the right places. He shifted and cleared his throat.

"Ashim!" He looked around when his name was called. Another Runner—Bahlir, hurried over to him, with a crate of beer under his arm and a basket in his hand. He smiled at Ashim as he approached and it didn't falter as he looked at Orison. "Welcome home, is this Orison?"

"Yes, I thought I said to meet you at my house," Ashim reminded him.

"I had to pick up some of my elixir, so thought I'd get snacks for the party," Bahlir explained, allowing Ashim to take the crate of beer.

Most Runners knew Bahlir was transitioning. He took a weekly elixir to help him achieve a deeper voice among other things. Since he announced it five years ago, King Raj had supported Bahlir every step of the way. Unlike most men in Karshakroh, Bahlir kept his hair short, with a long fringe across his left eye.

"Have you told the others?" Ashim asked.

Bahlir nodded. With the Runners always on various assignments, it was difficult to set up a last-minute birthday party. However, the ones who could make it were better than none. He turned to check on Orison; the women were now placing golden sandals on her feet. They showed her various pieces of clothing and jewels. When they first arrived, they noted her distinct Fallasingha dress and vowed to change it.

"Why has King Raj decided to recruit a Fallagh?" Bahlir asked. "Has he not told Regent Luxart? He promised he would."

"We're wondering the same thing," Ashim mumbled. "The king is not acting himself."

"Your lady friend is ready for her birthday!" a woman announced, who was wearing a sunshine-yellow gown.

Ashim gasped and nearly staggered into a nearby stall, as the women parted ways to reveal Orison. She stepped forward with a blissful smile as she regarded Ashim and twirled to show off the ensemble. He extended his hand out to Orison. She slid her hand into his and Ashim pressed a gentle kiss onto the back of it. The women behind her giggled like schoolchildren, hiding behind fans that they were holding, as they watched the interaction.

"You look beautiful," Ashim commented, noticing the gold in her hair. "The women did a really good job at everything."

"Hello, I'm Bahlir," he interrupted in the common tongue. Bahlir stepped forward, extending a hand. "I'm one of the Runners and I'm helping celebrate your birthday."

Orison beamed as she shook his hand. "Nice to meet you, Bahlir."

When Ashim tried to pay for Orison's makeover, the women at the stall shooed him away. They had shoved a plethora of bags into his hands; insisting Orison's transformation was on the house. He staggered away from the stall with a *thank you* and joined Orison and Bahlir; ushering them out of the bazaar.

Orison looked over her shoulder. "They gave me clothes to be cooler in the heat. It should help to not feel dizzy all the time."

Bahlir swiped an apple and flicked a coin into the jug. "Are you drinking enough water while on the job?"

"I... I wasn't sure if I was allowed to," Orison admitted.

Ashim and Bahlir baulked at her as they pushed through the crowd. Bahlir shook his head, furious. "Of course, you're allowed. The drink stations around the castle are for everybody, so we don't collapse."

"Sorry, I'm used to King Sila." Orison looked down, her cheeks turning a rosy shade of pink. "I'll drink more water; I didn't know King Raj was different."

"As long as we've finished the job by the end of the day, the king doesn't care how many rests you need to take between tasks," Bahlir explained. "We live in the desert, for fuck's sake."

Ashim nodded in agreement. All the Runners looked out for each other and ensured they were okay. Though the job was gruelling, it was the found family that came with the job, which made it all rewarding.

Orison's birthday party would be good for her to be introduced to the other Runners and get to know them. Ashim knew they would protect her. They would welcome and guide her while she was on this new journey.

Ashim approached a flower vendor. Even though he knew Mahavu would eat the flowers, he still picked out a bouquet full of pink flowers in the shapes of stars and roses. He paid for the bouquet and handed them to Orison; her eyes lit up as she looked at each flower. Ashim smiled at her happiness. Having her enjoy his country was something that filled him with bliss. It showed her that Karshakroh wasn't a desolate wasteland like the rumours around Fallasingha suggested.

"Is my husband allowed to the party?" Bahlir asked.

"Of course," Ashim replied.

Orison looked between them. "Runners are allowed to get married?" Ashim and Bahlir nodded in unison. "That's awesome."

They wound their way through Haranshal and back to Ashim's apartment to get the party started. Orison pointed out some ancient architectural designs, which even Ashim hadn't seen, despite living in Haranshal his entire life. It made him appreciate his home city more.

Ashim's living space had come alive. People created music with drums and guitars by the fireplace. Others stood around with cups as they conversed in Karshakir and some danced in circles, wherever there was free space. The minority shouted loudly after drinking too much faerie wine.

Orison pushed through the crowd, as she sipped on her alcohol. The Runners seemed nice. She watched Bahlir play with his husband's hair as they talked on the sofa. His husband, Kharhem, seemed friendly and tried to make Orison feel included. She retreated to an isolated spot by the kitchen to speak to the other women. One woman had light-tanned skin and red-wine hair—named Ahkeeva. The other woman had dark skin with black hair. Though both could speak the common tongue, they kept slipping into Karshakir, which made Orison feel awkward after a while. Despite the language barrier, she was enjoying herself.

Her gaze fell on Erol as he stood on a chair. He held something in his hands as he searched the crowd. When he made eye contact with Orison, he got down and approached her quickly. Some Runners moved out the way to accommodate him. Erol stopped when he reached Orison; in his hand was a box with an envelope.

"Is this my first assignment from Raj?" Orison said with a laugh. "Happy birthday to me."

"No, I found it on a table. It's addressed to you."

Orison frowned as she put her mug on the window ledge and took the box and parchment from Erol's hands. She smiled when she recognised Kinsley's handwriting. The box popped open and Orison gasped at the golden chain with a rose pendant. Placing the lid back on the box, Orison opened the envelope; '*I didn't know if you'd get this, but happy birthday! –K.*'

"Does anybody have a Teltroma?" Orison asked. "Or parchment?"

Nobody understood her request until Erol translated. She didn't mind if she had to settle for parchment, as long as she told her friend she had received the gift. Kharhem shifted on the sofa, then fished out the golden disk of a Teltroma, extending it out to Orison. She crossed the space and thanked him multiple times. Seating herself on the floor behind the sofa, Orison dialled for Kinsley. The golden disk pulsated with varying colours until Kinsley materialised; Orison watched as her eyes widened.

"You're *not* in a dungeon!" Kinsley exclaimed upon greeting.

Orison scoffed. "I haven't been in a dungeon for two weeks."

"Father said you're in Karshakroh." Kinsley shifted as she got comfier. "We'll come and get you."

"I'm in Karshakroh," Orison confirmed. "But I'm bound to King Raj and expected to help with assignments. I can't leave the country without the risk of death—the king says I'm in danger. I'm safe, aside from that and I have friends here."

Aeson appeared beside Kinsley; he smiled at Orison and waved. She waved back with a grin and glanced to her side when Ashim sat next to her on the floor—nursing his alcohol.

"Happy birthday!" Aeson exclaimed.

Kinsley cleared her throat. "As long as you're safe. Are you having a good birthday? It sounds like a party over there."

"Thank you, we are having a party," Orison grinned. She moved the Teltroma around to showcase the party. The device panned around until it settled on Ashim; Orison tapped his arm. "This is Ashim, he's helping me while I'm in Karshakroh. He threw me the party. He helped me in the mortal realm, too."

"We'll get you out, Orison," Kinsley promised. "Buy your own Teltroma so we can talk often to update us on your safety."

She knew everybody in Fallasingha would fight to bring her home, regardless of how long it took. Though Orison was used to the notion that she was safe, she was ready to return to Fallasingha and to everybody she knew. Orison was ready for true freedom.

EIGHTEEN

Nazareth pushed her wheelchair at the highest speed she could manage. Each time somebody got in her path, she shouted at them to move—on emissary orders. People dodged Nazareth with surprised gasps.

She coasted through the streets with great pushes on the push rims—when she lost momentum—as she hurried to get to King Idralis. They had built her prosthetic leg for running; but she didn't have time to put it on when she received the call for an emergency meeting with Idralis in his office.

Using a wall to zip around a corner, she was relieved when Idralis's cottage came into view. Another large push on her push rim and she quickly approached the wooden cottage. Nazareth groaned as she glided up the ramp and onto his porch; it weakened her strength and made her desperation grow. Moving her chair through the entryway, she rolled all the way into Idralis's office; kicking the door open and making her way inside.

"What's the emergency?" Nazareth gasped, approaching the desk and putting the brakes on her wheelchair.

Idralis's chair creaked as he sat forward. "Orison and Xabian are back in the Othereal."

Nazareth breathed a sigh of relief. "Thank Othereal, when's the coronation?"

"The coronation isn't happening any time soon. King Raj has decided to employ them in Karshakroh," Idralis announced. "That's the emergency."

"They're working for King Raj?" Nazareth covered her mouth in abject horror.

"Apparently they've been there three weeks," Idralis stated.

Nazareth lowered her hands and huffed out a breath. She placed a hand over her racing heart and scanned the room. "The king has to have an ulterior motive."

Releasing the brakes from her chair, Nazareth brought herself closer to the desk and leaned her elbows on it. Idralis drummed a stylus on the desk and glanced at her with his forest-green eyes. She couldn't comprehend why King Raj would do something so reckless—it could start a war. Many possibilities ran through her head as to why he made the decision, but none of them seemed accurate.

"How did you receive the information?" Nazareth enquired. "I thought Taviar went into the mortal realm to retrieve them."

"A seer prevented Taviar from going," Idralis assured.

When Idralis returned from Cleravoralis, he had informed her it was a successful handover—Bara had gone back to the mortal realm with Taviar and Emphina—only for Nazareth to discover in this meeting that it wasn't the entire truth. She thought about the men who the seer had mentioned to her.

She shifted in her chair. "A seer approached me a few weeks ago, saying there were some men from Karshakroh who are trustworthy. It's got to stem from them."

Idralis sat forward and looked slowly at Nazareth, with a raised eyebrow. "You've been having visits from a seer, saying men from Karshakroh are their allies?"

She felt her cheeks burning. "I didn't know how to approach you with the subject."

The Elf King took out a stack of parchment and a stylus. "Tell me everything."

With a sigh, Nazareth told Idralis everything the seer had to say—about the men from Karshakroh and her encounter with Lioress in the temple—it all tied to the men there.

She hadn't checked the discovaker since Idralis told her to stop; because of his command, the two heirs to the Fallasingha throne were taken. With Taviar still ruling as Regent, Fallasingha continued to hang in the balance and its future was unstable.

Idralis drafted a letter to both Raj and Taviar regarding this discovery. His face was stern as he signed them off. The letters disappeared to their respective recipients, then there was a third one.

"I've sent a letter to our export captain," Idralis muttered. "I hope Vex can get Orison and Xabian on the next run from Karshakroh soon. It'll help get some stability in Fallasingha."

Nazareth looked at her hands. "Yes, that way they'll have a safe passage home."

"I've requested for Vex to give them passage to Fallasingha for free and to be put into a stateroom," Idralis said as he looked at the map. "This whole thing has gone to shit."

"I warned you this would happen."

Idralis sighed and closed his eyes, indicating he admitted his mistakes. They sat in silence for a few moments. Nazareth had to trust a seer's judgement on how safe Orison and Xabian were in Karshakroh.

"All we can do is wait to see what Raj or Taviar have to say, then we try to contact Orison to let her know we're looking out for her," Idralis stated.

"We can only hope they make it back safely," Nazareth mumbled.

Nazareth's chair creaked as she sat back. If it was Xabian helping Orison navigate her way around Karshakroh, she'd be safe. Or the men who the seer prophesised about were more than likely helping hands. However, if Orison was navigating Haranshal alone, Nazareth didn't want to think of what could go wrong.

The door creaked as Orison stepped into the training area outside of Karshak Castle. It took her a moment to realise it was situated on a cliff edge, with no railing to prevent guards from falling to their death. Sand coated the entire floor and her feet sank as she ventured deeper into the space. Swords sang as guards unsheathed them and arrows flew into targets with dull thuds. Men bellowed orders that echoed around the landscape. Orison fiddled with the note in her pocket and unfurled it. This was her first assignment with King Raj and he had placed her here—of all places. A yelp tore out of Orison when a dagger flew towards her; she narrowly dodged it and it jammed into the door behind her with a hum.

She audibly gulped when a guard approached and towered over her, blocking out the sun with his gargantuan size. He wore gold-plated armour that glistened in the sun. Orison trembled in his presence; especially when he shouted at her in Karshakir and she couldn't understand a thing he said. When Orison extended the note out to him, he snatched it up and read it. Everything screamed at her to run and never look back. The door behind her opened, making Orison tense. A tanned female Runner with red-wine hair appeared—Ahkeeva. She wore a black tank top and bandages adorned her arms; she had brown trousers with boots. The guard shouted at Ahkeeva, causing her to shout back.

"Why am I here?" Orison squeaked.

"The king wants you to learn how to shield," Ahkeeva stated. Her accent was thick, like the other Karshakians. "And I'm to assist."

"Oh."

Ahkeeva grabbed Orison's note and guided her to an isolated spot away from the other guards. Orison held her arms as Ahkeeva muttered under her breath in Karshakir while tying the laces of her boots. If Orison thought learning magic in Fallasingha was difficult, learning it in a country where she barely spoke the language was nearly insurmountable.

"Do you know how to Glamour?" Ahkeeva asked. Orison nodded. "This is like that, but you think of what you want the shield to do."

She had figured out how to Glamour in the mortal realm. If a shield worked in the same way, it would be easy. Orison thought of a protection shield surrounding her; she could feel her magic tugging from her centre and settling around her. When Ahkeeva's fist swung at her, Orison yelped and dodged out the way; the shield hadn't worked.

"What'd you do that for?" Orison exclaimed.

"How else am I supposed to see if it worked?" Ahkeeva rolled her shoulders and cracked her fingers, making Orison grimace. "I won't actually hit you. Try again."

Orison glared at Ahkeeva as she focused again. She could feel her magic pulling a shield around her—it had to work if she could feel it. While Orison figured it out, Ahkeeva watched the guards training. She exhaled a breath when the pull from her magic reserve stopped. Once again, Ahkeeva swung her fist towards her. Orison flinched and when she realised the shield hadn't worked again, she ducked with only inches to spare. Her breathing became heavy.

"What country are you from?" Orison asked, noting the differences in Ahkeeva compared to other Karshakians.

Ahkeeva's blue eyes flared. "Karshakroh, my parents were Fallagh." She gestured to Orison. "Continue."

Orison tried again. She bounced on the spot, honing in on the magic that tugged at her as she tried to reinforce the shield. Ahkeeva held her fists up, ready to strike. As something whizzed past her, Orison held her arm up and a jolt of electricity shot through her arm. Her eyes widened when an arrow landed in the dirt nearby.

"Did I shield?" Orison asked. She spun around when Ahkeeva shouted something to the guards—she understood the Karshak word for *sorry*.

The Runner tapped her chin with a frown. "Maybe we can start with small shields like the one you created, then work our way up."

Orison nodded. "I think that's a good plan. But I don't know how I did that."

She chuckled as she stepped closer. "Maybe I need to fire arrows at you."

"Don't you dare."

Ahkeeva tightened her ponytail and flexed her hands. She ushered for Orison to continue creating shields, while she got into a fighting stance. Orison was fixated on Ahkeeva; she tried to recreate the shield she had made when an arrow was fired at her. As Ahkeeva flicked shards of ice at her, it bounced off a small shield in her hand.

"Nice," Ahkeeva complimented and watched the ice melt. "Maybe think of an umbrella shield."

Orison looked up at the sky. "What type of Fae are you?" she asked, as she thought of an umbrella over her head.

"Ice Singer. I can control ice and snow," she replied, throwing a snowball at Orison's head. It didn't hit a shield. Instead, Orison gasped from the sudden cold as it slammed into her. "Sorry."

"Again," she insisted, now shivering.

Ahkeeva smirked at the challenge. Together they spent the entire day practising, until Orison achieved a full body shield and could stand independently against a threat. When King Raj dismissed her for the day, she felt renewed.

Palm trees rustled in the park as Orison sat cross-legged on a bench at sunset and listened to the waves crash onto the shore. She drank from a coconut that she bought from a street vendor and smiled. She glanced at her first payment from King Raj—five hundred bronze coins and fifty gold coins glistened in the sun—a small fortune for a commoner.

Tearing her attention away from the coins, a warm wind played with her hair. Across the ocean, autumn was in full effect, with trees of all different colours. Orison wondered if it would be more spectacular than it was in the mortal realm. She suspected it would be—everything in the Othereal was more sensational.

The sound of footsteps made her whirl around and the familiar pull in her chest told her it was Ashim. She wondered how he found her, but didn't mind his company. He settled on the bench next to her with a sigh and watched the ocean with her.

"How did you know I was here?" Orison asked.

"Just had a feeling," Ashim admitted. He noticed the coins in her hand. "Put your coin away, somebody might steal it."

Orison placed the coins back in the leather pouch Raj had given her. "Sorry, it's the first money I've earned on my own in the Othereal." She watched the waves crash to the shore. "I got my first assignment today."

He tensed. "What?" Ashim turned. "You should have told me, where is he placing you?"

"Don't worry, it was in the castle. I had to learn how to shield with Ahkeeva," Orison explained.

Upon hearing that, Ashim relaxed and continued to observe the ocean. It brought a smile to Orison's face, knowing he cared about her wellbeing while they committed her as a Runner. Ashim made the whole ordeal tolerable and ensured she was safe in Karshakroh.

"You learned how to shield?" Ashim said. His eyes lit up when he looked at her. Orison nodded. "I'm really proud of you."

"I still need to continue training, obviously." She tensed when Ashim brought out a pocketknife and took the coconut from her hand. "What are you doing?"

He cut into the coconut and scooped out the flesh, handing it to Orison with a gesture to eat it. She was surprised at the refreshing sweet taste. Ashim ate some too, as he continued to cut into the coconut.

"King Raj usually doesn't assign a Runner to do that on their first run," Ashim muttered, with his mouth full. "This whole thing is confusing."

"It is, but I'm enjoying it," Orison admitted as she accepted another piece of coconut. "Mostly because of how much I'm learning."

Ashim smiled, his eyes glistened when they caught the sun. "I'm glad."

She had learned more about powers while in Haranshal than she had in the entire time she was in Fallasingha. Every assumption made about Karshakroh was false. The people were welcoming and kind; and a rich culture lay across the ocean. As much as she wanted to believe the lies, Orison couldn't ignore how comfortable she had become in this country. For the first time, she felt powerful.

Nineteen

Ashim stirred clothes in a large water basin—like mixing batter when baking. His arms burned as he churned the white fabric through warm soapy water, sweat beaded on his brow from the exertion. Orison hung the wet sheets and clothing on ropes suspended from the ceiling. Her skin glowed with a fresh tan since being in Karshakroh for a month; a red scarf around her hair to keep it out of her face amplified the tan.

The room was silent aside from the sloshing of water. Ashim set the paddle down, stretching his arms which had grown tired. He leaned against the basin and looked down at the submerged fabrics, drumming his thumbs on the side of the basin.

"Do you want to switch jobs?" Orison offered.

Ashim's gaze swept over her. "You can try it. Your arms will get tired."

"So... no?"

He straightened up. "I didn't say that." Ashim gestured to the paddle. "Try."

With a smirk, Orison stood next to him. He saw the challenging look in her purple gaze. Taking the paddle, Orison sloshed the water around. He knew it was the wrong way to do things and they would get reprimanded by Captain Haranah if caught.

"Like this?" she asked.

Ashim shook his head. "It's like baking."

The moment he said baking, a new side of Orison presented itself. She mixed the washing with vigour he hadn't seen before. He knew she'd been a baker's apprentice before the Othereal, but Ashim didn't expect the gentle person before him to mix the laundry so well.

With a nod of approval, Ashim took over her job of taking the soaking-wet laundry and hanging it on the line. He watched the water drop into the drains below his feet. The washroom wasn't anything special. The mud walls cooled down the blistering heat to a moderate temperature and hay covered the red tiles under his feet. It was a place where King Raj wouldn't bother entering.

He kept his head down when a guard came into the room with a scroll. Ashim knew what those scrolls entailed—a job. He didn't know what King Raj had in store for him this time. Like a child, Ashim hid in the sheets to stop the guard from seeing him. Though it was his duty to go on missions, he didn't want to leave Orison alone in Haranshal. To Ashim's surprise, the guard wasn't here for him, but for Orison.

"Your second assignment," the guard instructed.

Ashim staggered out from the hung washing. "Wait!" The guard whirled around. "Whatever the assignment, I'm going with Orison. She still doesn't know what our job entails."

"You don't have an assignment; therefore, she goes alone," the guard reprimanded. "You know the rules, Mahrishan."

Ashim tried to come up with a retort, to beg the guard for a resolution. He turned to Orison in the hopes of her telling the guard he needed to assist. The thought of her next assignment being out of the castle terrified him because she would be in danger. Orison unravelled the scroll and read its contents. Her calm demeanour unnerved Ashim.

"It's okay, it's in the castle again," Orison announced.

Relief flooded through his veins and he sank against the wall. He knew how brutal some assignments could be; she got off easy again. For his first assignment, Ashim had to collect a rare ruby from a manor, sleeping in a sewer for three days while scoping out how to collect it. He had to steal a relic from a crypt for his second assignment and got impaled with a poisoned arrow while doing so, almost dying in the process.

"What is it?" Ashim asked. When he looked over his shoulder, the guard was gone. "Is there something he wants stealing?"

Orison shook her head. "The king wants dinner with me."

"Dinner?" He frowned. "What?"

Orison shrugged and placed the scroll on the window ledge; she returned to work like nothing happened. Ashim guffawed at the king's odd behaviour—it resulted in a raised eyebrow and she slowed her mixing. He paced in a circle with his hands on his hips, looking down at his feet. The king rarely gave Runners such menial assignments. If he was acting normally, she'd be on the first horse out of Haranshal and off into the desert to retrieve something.

"I guess that would be nice," Orison stated with a shrug. "I don't have to cook."

"Something's wrong with the king, he doesn't act like this," Ashim reminded her as he returned to his job. "Somebody died on their first assignment and you get shield work—now dinner."

Orison's eyes widened and her jaw fell open. "I guess the way he is treating me is a little odd. I see Runners coming and going all the time, but I've not left Haranshal yet."

With a tight-lipped smile, Ashim nodded. He had to question the king about why he was treating Orison differently; getting the answers that he sought was another story with King Raj's busy schedule. The other Runners would catch on and get jealous; he didn't want them to hate her. Giving Orison one last look, he returned to work.

Guards flanked Orison as they led her towards a small dining table in the centre of a balcony, which was covered by a wrought iron veranda. King Raj sat at the head of the table, observing the servants who laid out plates and filled glasses with alcohol. His attention landed on Orison as she approached. Beyond the balcony, Haranshal twinkled like the stars at dusk.

Orison had been so enthralled with Haranshal, she didn't realise the guards had come to a stop and walked into the back of one. They stood before the table, which was surrounded by leather high-back chairs like the king's chair. She made to sit at the foot of the table—how Sila had demanded when she was his captor.

"Sit beside me please, Orison," Raj said softly, tapping the seat the guards had assigned.

The guards bowed, then parted like doors to stand at their stations. Orison curtsied with a wobble; no longer used to the heaviness of royal garments like the red and gold dress Raj had picked out for her. Orison straightened up and reluctantly sat down.

She stared him down, still unsure if she could trust him. The king ladled something—resembling orange soup with large chunks in it—into a bowl, along with a large serving of rice. He set it down in front of her with some flat bread. Orison inspected it; the smell was decadent in spices. She watched as he poured her a sparkling white wine into a glass.

"Is the dish poisoned?" Orison asked with a wince.

Raj chuckled. "My tasters are alive and well." He handed her a spoon. "I want to share some of Karshakroh with you."

Her hand trembled as she took the spoon. Orison stared down at the steaming bowl. Steeling her nerves, she dipped the spoon into the orange sauce and took a sip. Fire fizzled along her tongue; she coughed a few times and grabbed the nearest goblet of water, guzzling it down. Raj chuckled as he ate and he dipped some flat bread into the mixture.

"In Karshakroh, we call this dish Cuhlar," Raj explained calmly. "Bread and rice help the kick."

"Cuhlar." The spices still stung her tongue as she lowered the goblet. She had to ask the vital question, "What is the danger I'm in?"

Raj dipped his hands into a bowl of water in the centre of the table. "Knives in your back can be twisted like curses."

Orison frowned as she continued to eat the Cuhlar, despite the burn. She found the large chunks were pieces of chicken and vegetables; the rice did help take the edge off the spice. The chair creaked as Raj sat back, wiping his mouth with a napkin.

"Stop with the riddles and just tell me so I can prepare. I'm tired."

King Raj was silent as he drummed his fingers on the table. "I think you already know the answer, Orison."

Orison paused with the spoon halfway to her mouth; she thought of everything that had transpired since her exile to the mortal lands and the one person who had changed the most. She ate her spoonful quickly while contemplating his words, seeing them in a new light rather than just simple riddles.

"If you can be trusted, you would tell me where Xabian is."

"Xabian's whereabouts isn't a secret, he's in the infirmary," Raj explained, looking out over Haranshal as he ate. "We've just created the medication to help him wake up."

The spoon fell out of her hand and clattered into the bowl; she swore when Cuhlar splattered across the table. Orison grabbed a napkin to clean up, petrified of being reprimanded and having bands of fire wrapped around her wrists. Instead, King Raj clicked his fingers and the mess disappeared with Orison's napkin hovering. She looked at him and he shrugged. Orison slowly seated herself down.

"What will happen once he's awake?"

King Raj swirled the contents of his wine glass. "He will become a servant. Not a Runner, I need to keep a closer eye on him." Orison gave him a pointed look. "Now for your third assignment."

A scroll appeared in King Raj's hand and he handed it to Orison. She eyed the king as she took the scroll from his hand and popped the wax seal to read the contents. Her eyes widened with each line she read; dread roared in her heated ears and it felt like the veranda had sucked all the air from the balcony. Orison looked at the king.

"I refuse to sleep beside you!" she shouted, slamming the scroll down on the table.

"For your peace of mind, I deem a sexual relationship with any of my Runners highly inappropriate. I hold you to the same standards. I will erect a shield down the centre of the bed so we don't come into contact," Raj explained.

Orison wiped her mouth and pushed herself away from the table. She made it two steps to the door before the pressure on her brand made her pause. It wasn't painful, just extremely uncomfortable. Holding her hip where it sat, the pressure intensified until she returned to the table where it eased. She looked down at the brand with confusion.

"Unfortunately, you can't pick and choose the assignments. The magic in your brand won't allow it," Raj explained matter-of-factly. "You get a comfy bed to sleep in. I will dismiss your tasks of cleaning the castle until this is over."

She glared at him. "The bed I currently have is comfy."

King Raj was silent for a few moments. "It's only sleep. Nothing more." He inspected his ringed hand. "I need you to trust me, Orison. I find this is the only way to gain it."

Running her hand down her face, she looked down at the brand again, unsure what magic it held in its fibres. She shifted in her seat, stirring the food she no longer had an appetite for; she rested her head on her hand. There were many times she forgot about the brand and after a month it had fully healed. Akin to Ashim's, it was a lion with a K as a third eye. It had become a part of her and she didn't feel repulsed to see it whenever she took a shower.

"Can I stay for one night instead of a week?" Orison looked down at her plate, toying with the spoon.

"No. Your assignments are non-negotiable," King Raj stated. "I can only apologise for the brand making you uncomfortable. That's how the magic in the brand works if you defy me." He cleared his throat. "I believe Mahrishan is quite fond and very protective of you. I have sent a letter to him informing of your absence."

Orison gawped at the king—a week in his bed, it was entirely absurd. However, refusal couldn't happen without feeling like she was being poked with a blunt object. Her hand trembled as it hovered over her brand, the ghost of the sensation still persistent.

"Enjoy your meal, Orison," King Raj declared. "I tried alternate ways to gain your trust. I didn't want to do this."

Despite her nerves threatening to overwhelm her, she took it as best as she could and enjoyed the rest of the meal. Afterwards, the guards escorted her out of the castle and took her to Ashim's apartment to collect some belongings.

Saskia paced in the small living room of the two-story cottage deep in the belly of Old Liatnogard. Her hands were on her hips and her skirts stirred up a breeze as she moved. The fire roared behind her, illuminating the white plaster walls. She came to a gradual stop and turned to face Riddle and Taviar, who sat on the sofa. They watched her diligently as she fidgeted nervously; they had to make a plan.

"Raj will reply soon, he's very busy," Riddle uttered.

Exhaling a breath, she closed her eyes. "I don't need him to be busy. I need him to tell me if Orison and Xabian are safe. He's had them for a month!"

Riddle pushed himself off the sofa and approached Saskia. He stopped her mid-pace and massaged her shoulders with his thumbs. She glanced at Taviar, who forced a smile. It had been two days since they sent the last correspondence—just to be ignored again. Her patience had equated to pure unadulterated anger. It was now the tenth letter.

"He's got to respond to this one, surely," Taviar mumbled.

Saskia shook her head, flexing her hands into fists. The pacing did nothing to quell her woes. Every negative scenario raced through her head. Only the discovaker told her Orison was alive; she didn't know why Xabian's wasn't working. The front door opening took her out of the rabbit hole that was her mind. Zade and Yil ran into the room, followed by a man and woman with dark skin like Riddle's.

"I want to formally request a meeting with King Raj in Haranshal and ask for Orison's and Xabian's freedom," Saskia whispered to Riddle.

Riddle's parents ushered the boys to the kitchen—no doubt giving them sweets or hot chocolate to induce a sugar rush; Saskia knew how it was. She created a silencer shield around them so the boys couldn't hear.

"I think that's a good plan."

A loud crash behind them had them all turning to the sound. Yil bellowed with laughter at the cabinet that had spewed out pots and pans across the kitchen floor. Riddle ran a hand down his face, shaking his head. Stifling a laugh, Saskia tried to calm her racing heart and focus on the meeting at hand. The family had come back earlier than expected.

"Submit a request with Idralis to create a portal. You'll be back in Fallasingha by sunset. Don't stress too much, Sas," Taviar tried to reassure.

With a sigh, Saskia nodded. "Yes, I'm going to have to try to relax."

Another crash and they glanced at the kitchen. "It's best to send the request off after this meeting, away from the racket of children," Taviar explained with a chuckle.

"I'm sorry for ruining your family gathering, I'm just so scared," Saskia divulged and swallowed the lump in her throat. "This is Fallasingha's future."

Riddle rubbed Saskia's back with a nod. This was supposed to be a moment for their family and to ignore royal duty; but when it came to King Raj's brutal reputation, it had to disrupt everything. If only he had replied to the correspondence.

Moving through the home, Saskia bid farewell to Riddle's parents, before stepping into Old Liatnogard and Misting away in a flurry of bluish-purple Mist. She had a letter to draft—to kick Raj into doing something.

TWENTY

The king's chambers took on an ominous feeling when Orison had no choice but to be there. Ashim had tried talking the guards out of the assignment on her behalf, but his efforts couldn't dissuade the guards from her fate. She was grateful he tried, at least.

Orison inspected the space. She observed how the white walls gleamed from the Othereal lights and how the doors to the balcony were closed as night settled in. A red corner sofa surrounded a coffee table; a dining table was against the wall. Her attention finally settled on the circular bed in the centre; she hated how inviting it appeared. It had two red satin sheets placed on it and she could see the shield, which separated the bed perfectly down the centre.

Noticing King Raj's absence, Orison clutched her satchel's strap in a white-knuckled grip and remained near the door, not daring to take another step into the room. Her heart raced at what the king might have planned for the week; he might make her steal from a wealthy family or kill somebody. Orison wasn't worried the king would try anything with her. Ashim had confirmed that King Raj wouldn't do anything inappropriate, it went against the fundamentals of Raj's protection and leadership over his staff. This barrier made Orison feel a little better.

When the door opened behind Orison, she jumped and shied away, not wanting to face whoever came in. A guard stepped into the room before King Raj appeared with an older woman in a violet dress beside him. She carried a pile of books and was smiling. The king regarded Orison and looked around the room with a pout.

"You haven't made yourself at home?" he asked.

She twisted her clammy hands against the bag's strap, shooting a glare at the king. Her attention shifted between the door to King Raj, wondering how far she could go before her brand activated. Orison refused to talk to King Raj; if she did, she might end up back in the dungeons at the number of insults she'd throw at him.

"The door remains unlocked, Orison. I won't lock you in." Raj crossed his room and sat on his royal-red armchair, clutching the armrests. A multitude of gold rings weighed his hands down. He gestured to the other woman to take a seat, which she quickly did so. "This is Sherifa; she is going to help you. Come, have a seat."

Orison darted out of the room. To her relief, no guards tried to stop her. Her boots thundered down each winding corridor; servants gasped and pressed themselves against doors as she sped past. She ignored the pressure building in her brand as she raced towards the nearest exit. When she got to the drawbridge, she took a handful of steps into the night before she crashed to the ground from the brand's magic. Her stomach felt like it was yanked out of her throat, she retched and expelled the contents of her stomach.

"*Cehen*." She jumped when she heard a deep voice behind her, where a guard stood in the doorway. Orison groaned as she tried to calm down. "*Cehen*," he persisted.

Staggering to her feet, whilst wiping her mouth, she reluctantly followed the guard back to the king's chambers. She returned to find King Raj and Sherifa were deep in discussion. A servant poured tea as the king inspected books. Orison clutched her side and glared at the king. She realised she couldn't get out of this and steadily approached the sofa.

"You look like death just paid you a visit," Raj commented, clicking his fingers.

Orison fought the urge to throw up again and leaned against the sofa. "What do you mean by *help me*?"

As she waited for an answer, her legs grew tired from her attempt to flee. Though Orison didn't want to sit down, she knew she couldn't stand forever and slowly sank into the empty seat beside Sherifa. Her bag fell to the floor with a heavy thud. Orison could hear the muffled sound of waves crashing along the shore from beyond the window. She wanted to run out of this room and hop onto the next ship out of Haranshal, then she remembered the brand and swore under her breath.

"Can you read the common tongue?" Sherifa asked.

Orison looked between Raj and Sherifa. "Yes, I can read."

"What about Fallagh?" Raj asked. Orison inched closer to the edge of the seat. "I'll take that as a no. You've been gone for three months; without constant learning, it's easy to forget. You'll know that with Mahrishan."

Orison frowned. She didn't understand how her ability to read correlated with sleeping in the king's bed; it didn't take a genius to fall asleep. She wrung her hands in her lap as Sherifa pushed a black leather book in front of her. It was as thick as a large brick, impenetrable and would hurt to carry. What confused Orison, was the fact the title read—*Fallasingha Royal Protocols*.

"Wait, how do you do have that?" Orison pointed at the book. "What's it doing in Karshakroh?"

King Raj smiled. "Don't ask questions you don't want the answer to." She narrowed her eyes. "We'll begin here."

Sherifa opened the book with her magic and it flicked to the first page. Orison still couldn't grasp how the book had gotten into King Raj's possession. She assumed there had to be multiple copies if the people in Alsaphus Castle weren't demanding for it to be returned. But Orison didn't want to learn about Fallasingha Royal Protocols. She had questions regarding other concerns.

"Wait," Orison said quickly. "Why are you giving me different tasks to the other Runners and does the brand have a traquelle?"

"I need to keep you where I can see you." Raj stretched. "And there is no traquelle in the brand, I can only trust you do the work."

Orison frowned. "So how does the brand know if we refuse the assignments?"

"The magic in the brand can sense your intentions to defy me after I've set an assignment and warns you that they are your duty to the Karshak Crown," Raj explained and shifted in his seat.

She gawped at the king—at least he didn't keep that a secret. Orison's attention returned to the book of protocols and decided to learn while she had the opportunity. Inching to the edge of the seat, Orison waited for Sherifa to teach her. It was her assignment and if she had to be a Runner, she must comply with Raj's tasks.

The king provided Orison with parchment and a stylus, then the lesson commenced. The royal protocols were long-winded and boring. Orison wanted to zone out, but she had to know this if she was going to claim the crown—if she ever got out of Karshak Castle. Sherifa performed her duties thoroughly and spoke clearly, regardless of her accent. It was like she was a royal advisor—maybe she was. This was an opportunity to learn about a country that was denied for her to discover beforehand. When Orison settled into it, she didn't find the task so bad after all. The book was a treasure trove and Orison wanted all the gold.

As the sun was rising over Haranshal, Karshak Castle came alive. Servants mulled about the warm orange corridors, cleaning the sand which accumulated from the winds throughout the night. Others were ensuring breakfast was underway. Most of the castle residents were asleep, aside from the guards stationed outside the king's chambers; swapped out for morning watch.

Servants filled the king's chambers, ready to clean away the sand. Ashim followed behind them, clutching a broom as he kept his head down. His curiosity about Orison's assignment was too great to ignore. When he got a clear view of the room, his gaze fell on the circular bed where Orison slept on her stomach. Beside her, King Raj lay on his back, snoring lightly. Ashim quickly noticed the shield down the centre of the bed separating them both.

Glancing at the other servants, Ashim swept sand across the room until he got to Orison's side. He crouched beside her and shook her shoulder. Orison jolted awake; her eyes flew open in a terror-filled stare that was like a punch into Ashim's gut. He shushed her, which helped her relax.

Sorry, he said to her mind. *Are you okay?*

Orison nodded and snuggled back into the pillow, closing her eyes. He looked around the bed with a frown; he knew her task couldn't be something as simple as sleeping beside the king. The other servants didn't pay him any mind—too engrossed in their tasks. Ashim was aware that if he procrastinated too long, his brand would activate.

Is your assignment only sleeping? Ashim asked.

This is a trust exercise. King Raj is also teaching me how to be a royal, Orison mumbled and turned away from Ashim.

Reassured, Ashim pushed off the bed and stood up. *I'll leave you to sleep, Little Queen.*

He ventured to the balcony and got to work sweeping sand from the red floor tiles. This wasn't supposed to be his job. He'd swapped with Erol, giving him the task of cleaning the castle stables so he could check on Orison.

Ashim lost himself in the work and swept until there was no more sand on the balcony. He ventured back inside and took a feather duster from a servant's bucket. He approached King Raj's bookshelves and climbed the ladder, dusting each shelf while straightening the alignment of each book.

A cough drew Ashim's attention away from the bookshelf. King Raj stood at the bottom of the ladder with his arms folded over his chest. The king's dark-brown hair was down—flowing to his waist like Ashim's—and his white pyjamas were creased.

"Mahrishan, good morning," Raj voiced in Karshakir.

Ashim climbed down from the ladder and bowed deeply. "Good morning, Your Majesty."

"I was expecting Beshankar." Raj shifted. "Never mind; continue."

Raj clicked his fingers multiple times as he made his way to the dining table and sat down. The ladder creaked as Ashim climbed back up to the higher shelves. He snuck a glance behind his shoulder at Orison; noting King Raj hadn't awakened her for breakfast.

As he cleaned, more servants came into the room with the king's breakfast. The crockery on the carts clinked together as they wheeled in trays of delicacies which smelled sweet—loaded with sugar or jam. His mouth watered at the smell of Ferkowl, the perfectly grilled sausages with eggs and bacon—loaded with spices. Though he craved a bite, he knew he couldn't while on duty.

"Have you had breakfast, Mahrishan?" King Raj inquired.

"I've had breakfast, Your Majesty," Ashim replied as he continued to clean.

His breakfast was a simple bowl of porridge. It was nothing like the delicious pastries laid out on the cart or the Ferkowl, which a servant placed in front of the king. The porridge had been bland in his haste to check on Orison.

"Have breakfast with me," King Raj requested. "Orison is asleep and I don't want to disturb her. We can discuss your worries."

Ashim climbed down the ladder and faced the king. "You require me to have a second breakfast?" Raj nodded with a smile. "It's not my place."

"I insist. Please sit," Raj said.

With a sigh, Ashim put away the feather duster and approached the table. He sat opposite King Raj, as a servant set down a bowl of Ferkowl—cooked in Ashim's favourite way. It felt wrong to dine with a king as a mere peasant; however, the king had requested it and it was his duty to obey.

As he tucked into his breakfast, Ashim mentioned Raj's strange behaviour since he had returned to the Othereal. Ashim talked about the simplicity of Orison's assignments; followed by everything that weighed heavily on him. These sorts of conversations made him admire the king; Raj always provided a listening ear. That morning's discussion let Ashim breathe with relief.

Lake Braloak glistened in the autumn sun. The trees surrounding the lake were painted with vibrant oranges and reds. Kinsley's boots crunched on leaves as she walked along the waterfront; her hands were in the pockets of her light-purple coat and her dark hair swayed in the breeze. As far as she could see, the Sirens weren't around; presumably in the dark depths of the water.

Aeson walked silently beside Kinsley, his auburn hair glistened like the leaves. This was a walk to quell the storm that was Kinsley's nerves. She had a plan to retrieve Orison and Xabian from the grasp of Karshakroh. She knew her fathers would say no if she confided in them; though they gave her a lot of leeway, they wouldn't agree to this. Kinsley puffed out a breath as she soaked in the crisp autumn air.

"Are you really not going to talk to your fathers about this?" Aeson asked.

Kinsley turned away from her boyfriend and stared at the calm waters with a shuddering breath. She already knew their answer would be no. Her heart broke from having to betray them. With or without her fathers' permissions, she would find a ship to Karshakroh and demand a meeting with Orison.

"I don't need to talk to them to know I'm going," Kinsley persisted.

"Then I'm going with you."

She came to a halt and turned to Aeson as he did the same. Having him go with her would take the blow from her fathers' worrying about her safety—and Eloise's. Kinsley fiddled with a button on her coat and looked at Aeson, sucking in a breath. If they were going to find the whereabouts of their ship, he would have to shift into either her father, Idralis, Nazareth or Saskia.

"You'll have to be the one who gets the ship's information; they won't trust me or Papa. Only three people; and Nazareth, at a push," Kinsley stated.

Aeson let out a nervous laugh and scratched the back of his head. "We're really planning this." He looked past Kinsley's shoulder, then into her eyes. "We're going to Karshakroh."

"It's the only way to get them home," Kinsley reiterated.

Aeson pulled her into his embrace with a soft kiss. "Where you go, I go."

Kinsley placed her hands on Aeson's chest and nodded. "And we need to tell Eloise the plan. She has some holiday leave from the castle. It'll be two weeks at the most to get in and get out."

"How long have you been planning this?" Aeson pushed Kinsley's hair behind her ear.

"Since Orison's birthday. I know they can't leave Karshakroh yet, but I overheard my father and Saskia are going to portal there soon and buy Orison's and Xabian's freedom. That's why we need the ship's information because then we know she's free," Kinsley explained.

Aeson rested Kinsley against his chest and held her close. She gripped hold of his coat, then closed her eyes, listening to the bird songs in the trees. Lake Braloak was always a place where she found peace when things like this weighed heavily on her mind. Plus, Aeson was there to guide her through the darkness.

Knowing that their plan had a stronger foundation, Kinsley felt confident that she could do this for the future of her country.

TWENTY-ONE

The streets of Haranshal were crammed with people going about their daily business. Street vendors yelled to bystanders, offering free samples of food or drink. The smell of spices and coffee hung heavily in the air, along with fruity smells mingling with tobacco from the various shops providing hookah.

People parted ways and offered Orison a safe route as she walked alongside Sherifa and another servant named Zariah. The books on her head wobbled precariously with each movement. She didn't know if King Raj meant this as public humiliation or another lesson in being royal. All she knew was that she wanted to hide; everybody on the street—besides the servants who accompanied her—were staring.

"Shoulder's back, spine straight," Sherifa coached.

Orison adjusted her posture, exhaled a breath and continued on her quest to walk at a normal pace as King Raj instructed. She itched to hold the books as she walked; Raj had strictly told her not to, unless it was unavoidable. It was another peculiarity about this assignment—Raj was teaching her how to be royal, even though he'd stopped that part of her life when he branded her a Runner. Yet, the teachings contradicted her servitude.

The books slid from her head when she turned a corner. Orison caught them in the crook of her arm, cringing that some pages got folded by the incident. Zariah tutted and glanced at Sherifa; she shook her head with a roll of her eyes.

"You didn't keep your back straight!" Zariah exclaimed.

Smoothing out the books' pages, Orison stacked them up and glanced in the direction of where they were heading. Her stomach sank to witness a steep cobblestone hill; it was a true test of her posture. Mustering up all her strength, she secured the books back on her head like a crown and stepped up to the challenge. Orison pushed her shoulders back and straightened her spine. She walked up the hill with a new determination. She felt the books wobble violently on her head, causing her to pause until Sherifa tutted under her breath.

The higher she climbed, the more laboured her breathing became. Due to the Karshak heat, sweat rained down her back. She felt light-headed and her mouth felt like she had swallowed sand; she desperately needed a drink. At the top of the hill, the books slid from her head and she gathered them in her arms as she rushed to a water fountain. Water had never tasted so refreshing at that moment; it dribbled down her chin and soaked the end of her braid.

"Why is King Raj doing this?" Orison gasped as she splashed water on her face.

When finished, Orison straightened up and secured the books back on her head; she slowly followed Sherifa and Zariah into a large, cramped bazaar. Despite King Raj saying not to touch the books, the bazaar made it unavoidable; people bumped into her enough times that she had to cradle them in her arms to catch up with the other servants.

"King Sila didn't teach you proper royal etiquette," Sherifa explained. "Raj's teaching you, instead."

Orison gawped, "But I'm no longer a royal if I'm his Runner."

The servants exchanged a look, which made Orison frown. She followed as they weaved through the stalls and people, deeper into the belly of the bazaar. Sherifa stopped at a stall that sold burlap sacks of rice. She spoke in Karshakir to the vendor, holding two fingers up; she flashed a brass royal insignia as payment. Zariah inspected textiles and spoke to the vendor in hushed tones. It made Orison curious—would she have to do these tasks eventually? The only task Raj had set for Orison today was to walk with books on her head to this specific market and back.

"Trust King Raj. He's doing this for your benefit," Sherifa said in a hushed tone. She clicked her fingers and the two sacks disappeared. "The Runner status is giving you the opportunity to learn everything King Sila denied. Accept the help."

Her comment made Orison pause. "So, it was never his intention to keep me?" She adjusted the books under her arm as Sherifa walked to the next stall. "I don't understand."

"Trust the process." Sherifa paused at a milk vendor and talked to the shopkeeper in their language. "King Raj has a reason for everything."

All this time Orison had denied herself of trusting King Raj—worried he'd turn out like King Sila, but worse. However, not once had she seen the tyrannical beast Xabian warned her about or why this beautiful country was an enemy nation. King Raj always checked on her wellbeing and she hadn't experienced any form of torture, like she had with Sila. There were many nights she could talk to King Raj about absolute nonsense over tea, which eased the weight on her shoulders.

Orison's gaze roamed over the milk. She stopped with a frown at one in particular—*Curpacot Milk*. A shudder ran through her, knowing how sickly sweet Curpacot was; the milk would only be sweeter. Curpacot made Orison think of Saskia and a heaviness settled in her heart, which made her sigh heavily. She couldn't wait to see Saskia again.

The entire market fell silent, pulling Orison out of her head. She looked around the market out of curiosity. Her mouth fell open when she noticed the royal guards, their hands on the pommel of their scimitars. Orison didn't understand why vendors and patrons were dropping to their knees; her attention fell onto King Raj in the centre of the procession of guards.

As the guards walked through each aisle of the market, they inspected each person's face. Orison fumbled with the books in her hand, worried the brand would pull for not having them on her head. Her mind raced with the idea that

Raj had placed a traquelle on her while she slept and now watched her every move. However, as she observed the guards, it made her realise they had no idea where she was.

"Your Majesty!" Zariah called; she waved her hands with a wide smile.

King Raj paused and glanced around the market until his attention settled on them, then it snapped to Orison. He said something to the guards, pointing in Orison's direction. They swiftly approached and Orison curtsied low when he was close. She straightened up and clutched the books to her chest. Her stomach twisted as she waited for the king's reprimand. To her surprise, there wasn't one; instead, his attention diverted to something else.

The king inspected the milk at the stall. He spoke to Sherifa in Karshakir before he spoke to the vendor; it earned him a stammered response. The vendor handed him multiple bottles of what Orison could assume was his best stock. Unable to take the king's nonchalant approach at her defying him, Orison clutched the books tighter and sucked in a breath as she plucked up the courage to say something.

"Sorry, King Raj, for not having the books on my head. It's so busy and I don't want people to get injured," Orison interrupted quickly to get it over with. She hoped the guards wouldn't arrest her.

At mid-conversation, the king turned to her. His eyes fell to the top of her head, then he looked around. "Your judgement is correct; it's not safe." He returned to the stall, filling a crate with a variety of milk bottles.

Orison blinked at his lack of anger. She looked down at the books, then at the king and the guards who stood silently around her. He chuckled when Sherifa said something in Karshakir. Every Karshakian she'd encountered loved their king.

"I came to take Orison back to the castle though," Raj finally announced in the common tongue; once he had finished with the milk. It made her heart pound against her ribs at the possibility of being thrown into the dungeons again. "You're not in trouble. I'm here to inform you we've been successful in waking Xabian. Do you want to visit him?"

All her worries melted away and she covered her gawping mouth at the announcement. He had managed to accomplish something she couldn't in the mortal realm. Raj had the decency to inform her of his success. When Raj extended his hand out, she didn't hesitate when taking it; then a blinding white light enveloped her.

The mud walls of the Karshak Castle Infirmary provided a much cooler atmosphere than other parts of the castle—a welcome reprieve from the scorching temperatures outside. The walls were bare, apart from the tapestries of the Karshak emblem of a lion with a mane of flames and a K as a third eye. Only a handful of patients occupied the beds as Healengales mulled about healing them, or creating elixirs in medicine bowls.

Orison followed King Raj into the infirmary; she kept her head down with her hands clutched together. The king filled the entire room with his presence alone and it felt like she had intruded on his space, despite the invitation. His bare feet padded on the stone floor as he went to a bed at the back of the room. Orison lifted her head to find Xabian sitting up and eating a bowl of what looked like beef stew. Xabian's eyes widened when he saw Orison.

"Orison!" he exclaimed.

She hurried to him and wrapped her arm around his shoulder. "You're awake! How are you feeling?"

Xabian looked down at his bowl. "I feel good. It's great to be back in the Othereal. How did you manage it?"

"Well, Ashim and Erol got us back through a portal," Orison said with a smile.

Her smile faded when Xabian's gaze fell to her clothes—the beige trousers and white tunic known for the Runners. She shifted nervously. Orison smoothed her hands over the tunic and placed her hands in the pockets.

"And they sold you into the sex trade, how compassionate of them," Xabian said with a malicious grin. Orison felt the words like a slap. He looked over her shoulder. "I hope you're punishing them adequately for it."

Orison baulked and glanced over her shoulder where King Raj stood. She hugged her arms and felt unnerved that Xabian's first thought of her position was a prostitute. No words passed her lips, despite the desire to stick up for Ashim and Erol; his comments were too shocking. Part of Orison didn't think Raj would subject her to that.

"Don't talk about Mahrishan and Beshankar that way," King Raj snapped. He stood beside Orison and guided her onto a nearby seat. "Orison isn't in the sex trade, Alsaphus. Don't speak so unjustly. Learn some respect, *tahn*?" He turned to Orison. "Are you okay?"

"I'm fine, thank you," Orison said. She kept her head down and tapped her thumbs together with a sigh.

Xabian scoffed and returned to his meal. An awkward silence fell over the infirmary, Orison didn't know what to say after the accusation. She didn't recognise this side of him; he reminded Orison too much of Sila in this state. His purple eyes flared as he regarded her attire again.

"Didn't you think to fight?" Xabian asked. "You should have fought."

"I did. They had guns," Orison spat. She stood up. "You need some rest to recover. I have to get back to my duties. I'm glad to see you awake."

She tried to walk away, but Xabian grabbed her hand. "I'm sorry for my outburst. I didn't expect you to become this."

"Us," Orison announced. Her gaze fixated on the brand that poked out of Xabian's white tunic. "It's happened to you, too."

Xabian set his bowl down. He tugged at his shirt to inspect the brand and his eyes widened at the discovery. His hands trembled when he ran a hand over the lion with flames to signify his servant status. Then his purple eyes flared.

He pushed himself out of bed, rushed to King Raj and slammed him against a nearby wall. Orison gasped and raced to the king's aid, but a guard dragged her back while others swarmed in.

"Why the fuck have you mutilated me?" Xabian shouted. He slammed Raj into the wall again, making him grimace. "Why?"

The surrounding guards drew out their guns and aimed them at the prince. Orison could see he wasn't going to back down; her blood ran cold to see purple forks of lightning underneath his skin. The guards pressed in closer. She knew if he didn't back down, he'd be dead.

"Xabian, stop!" Orison called.

He screamed when one guard grabbed him and threw him to the floor. Orison turned around, unable to watch as a Healengale plunged a syringe into the side of his neck. She covered her ears and squeezed her eyes closed when Xabian's scream tore through the infirmary.

A hand on her arm made her tense. "Let's leave here," Raj said calmly.

As Raj led her out of the infirmary, it took everything not to look at how far the Prince of Fallasingha had fallen.

TWENTY-TWO

Two weeks later, the castle bustled with energy as Orison pushed a cart filled with roasted meat down the corridor. The crockery clinked together with each snag in the flooring as she pressed on. A familiar tug in her chest drew her attention to Ashim, who approached with a cart of desserts. His gaze settled on the sunburn she had acquired on one of her days off. She tugged at the hem on her white tunic in an attempt to cover it, despite knowing it was useless because it extended to her face. Orison ignored his scrutiny and appreciated the breeze through the windows which cooled the burn.

She didn't understand why King Raj had ordered them to conclude their cleaning duties early and bring food to the East Dining Room, but only time would tell. Typically, the servants served the food, not Runners. Either way, they had to obey and not protest at the sudden change of duties.

Ashim nudged her side, then whispered, "I didn't know King Raj hired tomatoes as staff."

"Rude," she retorted with a grin.

Ashim chuckled, then beamed as he glanced down at his cart. He came to a sudden stop. Orison copied his actions and leaned on her cart. She turned to face him, only to suck in a breath as he took a step closer to her. He stopped and took in her features.

"But I find you a pretty tomato," Ashim whispered. He looked at her from head to toe. "I always find you beautiful."

His confession hung like a cloud above them. Orison blinked with surprise; out of all the things he could say, that wasn't what she was expecting. She sucked in a breath when he leaned towards her and looked at his lips, bracing for him to kiss her. Footsteps interrupted the moment. Ashim cleared his throat and took Orison's hand. She jolted when she felt him enter her mind and in an instant, she didn't remember why she came to a stop in the corridor. Only a strange feeling remained.

Shaking her head, Orison returned to her cart at the same time Ashim did. She glanced at him but thought better of asking him if he felt strange too. Orison noticed his unusually tense gait—the person who had joked about her sunburn wasn't there anymore. With a glance over her shoulder, she watched Xabian push a third cart down the corridor. She had an inkling that's why Ashim was suddenly tense.

The East Dining Room doors opened on a phantom wind; Orison pushed her cart into the room, behind Ashim. The room was on an outside veranda with plaster columns that had ornate flowers carved into them. The columns held up a flat platform to shield diners from the weather. Orison came to a sudden halt when she saw who sat at the marble table—Saskia! It felt like a dream seeing her again.

King Raj snapped his fingers multiple times. With a nod, Orison hurried over with the cart and uncovered the steaming dishes of roast meat and vegetables. She kept her head down as she plated up food for King Raj, recalling the servant's advice on the exact portions. With the metal tongs, Orison placed four slices of beef on the king's plate with a large spoonful of vegetables topped with gravy. The person before her wasn't the man she knew; this was the mask he wore when around Fallasingha officials.

The rattle of crockery drew Orison's attention across the table, where Xabian approached with a cart of drinks. He looked slimmer; his white tunic hung from his frame. In silence, he poured red wine into the king's goblet. Orison kept her head down and pushed the cart towards Saskia. Her tongs only grazed the beef before Saskia paused Orison's duties with a gentle hand on her arm.

"I can serve myself, Poppet," Saskia urged.

Orison curtsied, leaving the cart beside Saskia, she hurried away from the table. She stood beside Ashim, who stayed in the shadows with the desserts; together they watched Xabian as he served alcohol.

"You broke our agreement, Your Majesty," Saskia said sternly.

King Raj scoffed. "I don't know what you are on about."

"The one where you said you'll inform us if Orison and Xabian returned to the Othereal. Now I find out you've made Orison a Runner and Xabian a servant."

"I think I said I'll think about it." He tucked into his lunch without a care in the world. "She gets the job done," King Raj noted. "I don't know about sleepyhead over there; it's only recently he's bothered to pull his weight."

Orison clenched her fists. She wanted to shout at Raj that Xabian hadn't been sleeping by choice, but Ashim's gentle hand on her arm warned her to quell her anger. Orison didn't want the brand making her vomit in Saskia's presence. Then she remembered Raj's mask; he was saying these things to create a reaction, knowing the stigma he had with Fallasingha.

"I would like Orison and Xabian returned," Saskia said sternly. She looked at Ashim. "As well as freedom for Mr Mahrishan."

And one other Runner. Orison said to Saskia's mind.

"And one other Runner of your choosing," Saskia said quickly.

King Raj's eyes widened as he glanced at everybody in the room. "You drive a hard bargain, Advisor Saskia—Mr Mahrishan is one of my best Runners. And I don't know who else I would grant freedom to."

Orison realised Saskia's plate remained empty, evidence she had chosen to skip lunch for this meeting. While Saskia and Raj negotiated, the room remained silent and Xabian glared at Raj for the entirety of their hushed discussion.

"I can't wait that long!" Saskia exclaimed; her voice echoed around the dining room. Orison tensed.

King Raj waved his hand for Orison and Ashim to approach him; they obliged immediately. "The day after tomorrow, Mr Mahrishan and Miss Durham are going to Lhandahir with Mr Ahbarsh. I'll give proper instructions later. Once they retrieve my items, then they win their freedom; *if* you— Advisor Saskia—can also give me two million gold."

A dust cloud billowed out from under the broom that Ashim used to clear sand from Raj's bedroom balcony. He hummed along to himself as he worked, moving sun loungers to get the dirt underneath.

He briefly glanced at the servants confined to the castle who were busy cleaning inside the king's chambers and remaking the bed. A shadow passed in Ashim's peripheral vision and Xabian stepped onto the balcony with a broom in hand—he was a servant like the ones inside. Despite being treated with the same respect as the Runners, they couldn't cross unknown lands.

"Haranah told me you needed help," he said in perfect Karshakir.

"*Halek.*" Ashim straightened up and pointed to the right side of the balcony where he hadn't gotten to yet. "Help me with that side."

Xabian got to work with little protest. When King Raj was absent, the servants and Runners answered to Haranah, the commander—he wasn't as kind as the king. Diverting his attention from the Fallasingha prince, Ashim returned to work. He squeezed his eyes shut as a headache surfaced. Placing his broom down, Ashim staggered to the water fountain and gulped down water.

Xabian approached Ashim. "In Fallasingha, we have outlawed slavery. Your king won't scar me again," he hissed in Karshakir.

"You aren't a slave, Alsaphus, you're a servant." Ashim moved past Xabian and shifted another sun lounger to sweep underneath it. Xabian's silence slithered up Ashim's spine while he calculated his next words. "The brand isn't permanent; they can remove it when you're out of service."

Ignoring the Fae Prince's next retort, Ashim pushed aside his headache and continued to work. King Raj liked the cleaning tasks to have a personal touch, hence why he allowed no one to use magic. Ashim didn't care; the cleaning took his mind off the things he couldn't tell King Raj.

"What is your infatuation with Orison?" Xabian asked. Ashim stiffened and turned to the prince with a raised eyebrow. "I know the only reason Raj made Orison a Runner is because you set him up to it."

The grip on his broom tightened. "I'm a mere peasant. I don't tell the king to do anything. He decided while I was rotting in the dungeons. And I have no infatuation with Orison; get that out your head."

An uneasy feeling settled on Ashim's shoulders when Xabian's eyes flared purple. He knew something wasn't right with the prince. Ashim could secretly admit he was attracted to Orison; the feeling grew each day and the tugging in his chest when around her wasn't coincidence.

Footsteps had Ashim turning around. He breathed a sigh of relief when Haranah stepped onto the balcony. "Mahrishan."

The commander stood with his hands behind his back. Badges of honour adorned the left side of his white lapel; a red turban covered his long dark hair and his brown eyes glowed.

"Yes, sir?" Ashim asked. He already knew what Haranah was about to announce.

"I dismiss you early, so you can prepare for your journey to Lhandahir," Haranah ordered. Ashim bowed. "Let me inspect your side of the balcony first."

He was glad he had finished his side. Haranah walked around the balcony, running his hand along the handrail which Ashim had never forgotten about. The commander rubbed his thumb against his fingers with a satisfied nod.

Ashim watched him check under all the furniture and potted plants. Ashim covered everything twice in case more dust accumulated while he worked on other areas.

"Good work, Mahrishan. Rest, as you'll be required to depart three hours after midnight," Haranah explained. "Alsaphus. Get to work and stop eavesdropping."

"Thank you, Haranah." Ashim bowed again.

Ashim hurried through King Raj's bedroom and emerged into the main body of the castle. He navigated his way to the servant's quarters and hung up his broom in the storage closet. He dressed in his civilian clothes, which he stored there. Instead of using the moat to go home, he used the servant's secret tunnels, then prepared for the mission ahead.

The day before a mission was like clockwork for him. This had been going on for so long that Ashim no longer felt nervous, but keeping Orison's nerves at bay would be another story.

A dull thudding sound from the living room occupied the silence of Orison's bedroom; she knew it was Mahavu racing around like cats usually do. She tossed and turned for an hour, trying to force sleep, yet her mind wouldn't switch off—too full of nerves about her first real Runner assignment. With a huff of breath, she turned on her side and stared at the green floral print walls and chest of drawers.

Orison sat up, unable to keep still any longer; she stood and approached the door. The sound of Mahavu bolting into an unknown hiding spot greeted her. She always knew cats were peculiar. Orison crossed the threshold to Ashim's bedroom and looked around for Mahavu; but in the dark, it was impossible. Biting the side of her nail, Orison knocked on Ashim's door loudly.

She knew he was probably asleep. Orison knew how childish it would be to ask him if she could sleep in his bed, but she craved comfort. Orison looked around for Mahavu once again, not even seeing her glowing eyes in the dark. The Karshak heat kept the wooden floors warm, making the wait tolerable. When the door opened, Orison faced Ashim.

"Are you okay?" His voice was groggy from sleep. She could just make out his silhouette in the darkness, the shutters on the windows were closed and no moonlight penetrated the barriers.

Orison braced herself. "I can't sleep. Mahavu running around isn't helping." She looked at her feet. "Would it be weird if I asked to sleep in your bed?"

They had shared a bed before, back in the tavern in Roseview, but this was his personal bed; it felt like an invasion. An odd warm sensation filled Orison when the door opened wider; she prepared herself to make that step.

"*Oneshir,*" Ashim mumbled. *Okay*, she translated.

She watched his form disappear into his room. It was the first time she had stepped inside. Ashim turned on the lamp on the bedside table and she gawped at the simplicity of the room. The peach-coloured wallpaper was peeling, a wardrobe with a broken door sat in the corner and a bookcase full of books were in the other corner. Her cheeks heated at the pile of dirty laundry at the end of the bed.

Orison gasped at the reality of Ashim being shirtless as he sorted out the bed. He wasn't muscular like most shirtless men she'd seen in the Othereal. He had a bit of a belly and didn't have perfectly sculpted abs which most women swooned over. Realising that she was staring, Orison cleared her throat and averted her gaze.

"*Hara,*" Ashim said as he pointed to the bed. *Here*, she translated.

Glancing at Ashim, Orison climbed into the bed and settled down beside the wall. The bed sank down next to her as Ashim climbed into bed, his back towards her. She sucked in a breath when his skin brushed against hers. Ashim turned off the lamp, plunging them into darkness. Orison shook her head and pulled the sheet up to her chin, willing sleep to come. The sheets smelled like him, like a freshly lit bonfire and his cinnamon soap.

After a while, Mahavu resumed her running around in the living room; the thuds were less thunderous in Ashim's room. Cats were unnecessarily loud during the night. Orison exhaled a breath and counted to ten, hoping to get to sleep. The thuds of Mahavu's feet became almost soothing.

"Ori," Ashim said. She glanced over her shoulder with a hum. "Don't be nervous about tomorrow; think of it as an adventure."

"I think it's not knowing what our task is," Orison replied. She snuggled into the pillow.

She felt Ashim turn over and place his hand on her shoulder. "You'll be okay; I will protect you."

"I'm sure you will," Orison replied as he pushed her hair behind her ear.

Something compelled Orison to place her hand on his; Ashim held her hand and rubbed his thumb over her skin. When the pull of sleep presented itself, Orison's eyes closed and she relaxed.

Only Ashim could calm the storm inside her head, which wasn't a small feat. When sleep found her, she dreamt of traversing a vast desert land with Ashim guiding the way.

TWENTY-THREE

The darkness of night still hung over Haranshal. Ashim and Orison ventured through the narrow streets of mismatching architecture to the outskirts of the city where they were to meet Bahlir. Most of the people of Haranshal were still asleep; except for the minority who worked through the night or made their way home from the taverns.

Bahlir waited at the city's wall for Ashim's and Orison's arrival. A cigar hung out of his mouth as he worked. The horses shifted upon their approach; alerting Bahlir of their presence. He turned around and took a drag of his cigar.

"It's about time we worked together," Ashim said in Karshakir. He laughed and pulled Bahlir into a one-armed hug. "This is Orison's first real Runner assignment."

Bahlir pulled Orison into a one-armed hug and tapped her back. "Glad to be joining you on this special occasion."

Ashim watched Bahlir as he secured their bags to the three brown horses and checked their supplies for crossing the Haransha Mountains and the Karshak Desert. "Have you got enough elixir for the trip?" Ashim asked as he assisted with the horses.

Bahlir nodded. He took the cigar out of his mouth and stubbed it out on the wall. "The king gave me some before I retrieved the horses. I'll be fine."

A chuckle passed through Bahlir's lips and he shook his head. It made Ashim tense and he looked at Orison; she shifted uncomfortably and fidgeted with her hair. Ashim cocked his head to the side and wondered why their companion felt the need to laugh.

"King Raj only gave us two camels and there's three of us. Who is Orison going to partner with?" Bahlir asked in the common tongue.

"I'll be with Ashim," Orison said quickly.

Bahlir nodded. "He gives us three horses, but two camels. Ridiculous," he commented in Karshakir.

Satisfied that the horses were ready, Bahlir mounted his horse and glanced over his shoulder to signal they should do the same. Ashim turned to assist Orison onto the horse, but she mounted by herself with ease. Regardless, he approached and ensured she was okay before he mounted his horse. Ashim settled on the saddle; he patted the horse's neck and smiled.

"When they trapped me in Alsaphus Castle, I brought my horse into the castle library and rode it inside," Orison admitted with a wide grin.

"Anesh!" Bahlir exclaimed and laughed.

Bahlir began the first leg of their journey to the Haransha Mountains. Ashim used gentle pressure with his heel to his horse's side and followed Bahlir with Orison beside him. The horses' hooves clopped on the cobblestone path and they left the safe confines of Haranshal behind them.

She looked between the two of them. "Have you been to Alsaphus Castle before?"

Ashim nodded with a chuckle. "One of our tasks was to poison King Sila with Mortelock to scare him. Raj knew they'd get the antidote in time."

"It was you two?" Orison exclaimed in a shrill voice. "People died because of that."

Bahlir smirked over his shoulder. "Is Princess upset?"

"No," she blurted. "But you realise you have blood on your hands."

Stifling a laugh, Ashim knew Orison was oblivious to how many acts of crime they had committed because of their Runner status. The only thing that protected them from prison was the brand on their chest. If the authorities caught them, the brand showed that Runners weren't in control of their actions—they begrudgingly returned them to King Raj. Being a Runner meant do or die.

"You know the rules, Durham," Ashim teased.

Orison shot him a glare, causing him to laugh. Her anger diminished quickly; she yawned and shook her head. He didn't get a good night's sleep with her being so close. They had shared a bed before, but he didn't feel such a powerful pull towards her that time.

Bahlir rifled through his bag and outstretched his hand to give Orison something wrapped in cloth. Ashim raised an eyebrow until Bahlir pulled out another one for him. It was still warm. The aroma made him realise it was *pohamak* and his stomach growled. It wasn't Ashim's idea of a good breakfast, but he'd take it. Orison tucked into hers, her eyes wide as she inspected the food.

"This is *pohamak*," Bahlir explained. "Kharhem made it for this journey."

"It tastes amazing," Orison said with her mouth full. "Your husband did a good job."

Ashim relaxed in his saddle as he took a bite of his meal. He'd waited a whole month for this moment and the best person to make it had to be Bahlir's husband. Ashim had been too busy to ask if he could arrange a dinner to introduce Orison to the best food in Haranshal—in his opinion, at least. They all fell silent as they ate their first breakfast. It would be enough fuel for the gruelling journey ahead. Aside from this delicacy, they only had a bag of raisins, grain bars and nuts to keep them going until Lhandahir.

Taviar tapped his fingers on his stomach as he laid in bed. He hadn't been able to sleep soundly since learning about Orison and Xabian being trapped in Karshakroh. On his last mission to Karshakroh, the army had shot at him, deeming that the Fallagh ship he arrived on was a threat. They had swiftly returned to Tsunamal. Though Saskia assured Taviar that they were fine, aside from Orison with sunburn, it was a difficult stigma to break.

In his peripheral vision, multi-coloured lights made him tense and he lifted his head up. He propped himself onto his elbows and looked at the Teltroma on the bedside table. Reaching over, Taviar flipped the lid on the golden disc and King Raj materialised before him. He swore under his breath, grabbed his shirt from the floor and shoved it on.

"We're all men; you can keep your shirt off," Raj suggested.

Taviar looked over his shoulder at Riddle, who was fast asleep. He looked back at the king. With a sigh, he put a shield around him and the Teltroma. He was curious about why King Raj was calling in the middle of the night. He huffed out a breath and rubbed his eye.

"What do you require, Your Majesty?" Taviar asked.

The king looked at his nails, appearing bored. "Saskia has paid what I required. Now it will take a week to retrieve an artefact to win their freedom."

"A week?" Taviar baulked. "We need Orison and Xabian home now."

Raj smirked. "I can assure you it's keeping me busy. This is a test to see how strong Orison is. A week is ample to test her true queen material."

"Where is Xabian?" Taviar asked.

"We can't let him leave Karshak Castle; he is quite sick. Not from my doing, might I add. Some of my Runners are on missions to retrieve some medication, which he needs to take three times a day." Raj's chair creaked as he leaned back with a stretch.

The space around Raj was dark. He didn't know the king's whereabouts in the castle. He couldn't hear any screams of distress, nor pleas for freedom—like he assumed would be the case in Karshakroh.

Taviar looked down. "Is Orison well?"

"Very well. She's settled in nicely."

Biting his lower lip, Taviar asked. "And when she's done this, she gets to go home?"

Raj nodded with a proud smile—like he was doing Taviar a favour by keeping Orison in Karshakroh for months on end and ignoring all their letters. In his eyes, it wasn't something the king should be proud of.

"Of course," Raj replied. "You've paid the cost on their contracts. As long as Orison and Ashim are successful on one last job; they're free."

The announcement made everything roar around Taviar's head. He realised how expensive it was to free Runners from King Raj's grasp; like they weren't humans at all, but property to be bought. He'd heard rumours they gave Runners special treatment. Taviar had a brief look into the reason behind it—they weren't disposable, like regular servants.

"This shouldn't have happened," Taviar muttered.

"I can assure you it was necessary." The voice of Commander Haranah sounded from behind King Raj—speaking in Karshakir. He turned around before facing Taviar again. "It's late and your children will be getting ready for school soon. You look tired, Regent."

Before Taviar could say another word, the call ended. Taviar's heart raced as he lowered his shield and closed the Teltroma. He settled into bed, staring at the ceiling once more. Taviar held Riddle close when he rested his head on his chest. He continued to stare at the ceiling as he lazily rubbed circular motions on Riddle's shoulder.

The price for Orison's and Xabian's freedom still didn't sit right with him. When she got home, they had so much to prepare for. He suspected she would be fragile. Taviar had grown protective of her—like an extension of their family—and he couldn't imagine what she had faced while she was away. He didn't know what Orison would be like when she returned to Fallasingha, nor how much she had grown. Taviar hated the unknown most of all.

Every time Taviar closed his eyes, he saw Orison as the timid, scared person she was when under Sila's scrutiny. Taviar's thoughts changed to the Battle of Torwarin and he imagined how Orison's exile occurred. He could see Sila as he dragged Orison to the portal and forced her inside, despite King Idralis saying that it didn't play out like that.

Taviar kissed Riddle's head and closed his eyes. He would have to speak to Eloise and find a solution to help him sleep. All he could count on was Orison's determination to thrive.

Orison was falling asleep in her saddle as the sun cast out the night. In her half-asleep stupor, she could just make out the wooden shacks that rose out of the sand.

Yawning loudly, she followed Bahlir and Ashim over to a shack on the outskirts of the settlement. Upon closer inspection, it was a stable. She hoped they would stay here and get a tavern, then she'd get a decent night's sleep before going to Lhandahir. Bahlir and Ashim talked amongst themselves in Karshakir as they came to a stop. They quickly dismounted, whereas Orison felt too exhausted to move.

"Do you need help?" Ashim asked.

She gave a slight nod. He held his arms out and she pushed herself off the saddle. He eased her to her feet, holding her arm as she stumbled slightly and rubbed her eyes again. Waking up at the crack of dawn was nothing easy. Looking around, only a handful of lights were on in the various shacks lining the road. To her right, mountains towered over her; she could just make out a road shrouded in the shadows.

"Where are we?" Orison asked, fighting the urge to yawn again.

"Ghartah, this is where we swap the horses for the camels," Bahlir explained, guiding their horses over to the stables.

Ashim waved his hand and Orison followed behind him. She glanced absentmindedly throughout the stables; there were multiple horses and unicorns who appeared asleep. Orison tensed when smoke billowed out of one of them. Approaching the gate, she gasped at the green scaled dragon that slept curled up in hay. Dragons mostly kept to themselves in mountains; seeing one up close that wasn't a Nyxite came as a shock.

"Flying would be faster," Orison grumbled.

Ashim looked at her. "Not if there's a sandstorm. The sand damages their wings."

"So, why's it here, then?" Orison asked.

"Ghartah and Haranshal are protected by the mountains. Sandstorms aren't as ferocious as in the Karshak desert," Bahlir explained, peering into the dragon's stall. "The dragon is most likely somebody's pet."

With a pout, Orison turned her back on the dragon and followed Ashim towards the camels that towered over her. She audibly gulped, unsure how she would mount the saddle when she was barely awake; plus, she'd never ridden a camel before. Ashim clicked his tongue and the camels lowered themselves to the ground. Noticing she wasn't expected to climb filled her with relief.

She stood to the side as Bahlir and Ashim readied the camels for the next leg of their journey, amazed that they could be so energetic— despite waking up so early. A soft growl made her look over her shoulder. The dragon was awake and looked over the gate at her, Orison smiled and waved to it.

"Hello." Orison inspected the beast. "You're beautiful."

The dragon nudged her arm. Despite being intimidated by the smoke billowing out of its nose, she ran her hand over its green scales and saw her reflection in its green beady eyes. She scratched behind its ear with a laugh.

"Ori, we're ready," Ashim called out.

"Coming," she replied and turned back to the dragon. "Bye-bye."

Orison returned to Ashim and Bahlir, who were already in their saddles. She exhaled a breath as she approached Ashim. He took her hand and helped her settle in front of him. Orison gasped when he held her waist as the camel rose to its full height.

With a click of his tongue, they strolled out of the stables and were back on the road in an instant. Orison leaned against Ashim, getting comfortable as the swaying of the camel made her exhaustion increase tenfold. Closing her eyes, she gave into the lull that told her to sleep.

Twenty-Four

Orison awoke with a jolt; the grip on her waist tightened with her sudden movement. She blamed the firmness of her skin and heated cheeks to the barren desert environment laid out before her—instead of the steamy dream that woke her up. It involved her and Ashim. She'd never thought of Ashim in such a way before and didn't know why it had to happen when he was sitting behind her.

She squinted to look up, realising a black umbrella shielded her from the sun. Haranshal was a dream compared to the Karshak Desert; it rested beyond the mountain peaks of the Haransha. Orison's throat scratched from how thirsty she had become, as the temperature soared. She watched the air ripple in front of her as Bahlir took the lead; while she had been asleep, he had adorned a black headscarf to protect himself from the sun.

A skin of water appeared before her. *Are you okay?* Ashim asked within her mind.

I had a bad dream, she lied as she took the skin and held it to her chest. *But I'm okay.*

She couldn't admit that she had a sex dream about him—it was embarrassing. Orison didn't even know how he felt towards her. Orison looked at his hands on her waist; she would be lying if she said she didn't want to be more than friends with Ashim.

From the moment they met, Ashim had picked Orison up at her lowest, strengthened her powers into a perfect storm and always ensured her safety.

They were a team—like their minds were one and the same; like they had known each other longer than a few months. Her heart raced at the reality that she was falling head over heels for him.

Orison took a generous drink of water, trying to clear her thoughts. She forced herself to stop when Erol's lecture about conserving water surfaced to her mind. Orison handed it back to Ashim, who drank before putting it back in their satchel. It felt strange not having Erol around; Bahlir made a good replacement, but he always seemed shy.

With the many thoughts occupying her mind, she basked in the cool shade Ashim provided for her. Orison felt the pull of sleep again as the movement of the camel underneath gently rocked her. Her one comfort was Ashim's arm around her waist; slowly she covered his hand with her own.

Another drink? Ashim asked in her mind.

Orison shook her head. *We need to conserve it.* Looking over her shoulder, she could see that Ashim also adorned a headscarf to shield his head and face from the extreme conditions. Settling against him, she said, *You should use the umbrella.*

You need it more, Ashim replied quickly.

They talked between their minds to prevent sand from getting into their mouths, which would have happened if they spoke out loud. She looked at Bahlir, who appeared to be eating something. Orison cringed at the thought of food, even though she hadn't eaten anything since they left Haranshal.

Ashim took her hand and poured some raisins into it; she tried to give him half, but he shook his head profusely. Orison snacked on the raisins which quelled her hunger; a proper meal awaited them in Lhandahir. Orison felt Ashim's stomach growl on her back. A pang of guilt punched her gut, until she reminded herself that he was made for desert environments like this.

How much longer? Orison asked to Ashim's mind as she snacked.

We're almost there, Ashim replied.

Orison petted the camel as it turned its head towards them. It grunted a response and continued to follow Bahlir to their destination. With no sign of civilisation, Orison had to trust they were going in the right direction and relax.

Lhandahir was a small town with compact structures made of mud rising out of the desert; as if they were meant to be there—not an anomaly to a desolate environment. Narrow streets were a rainbow of colours with paintings and advertisements on exterior walls. Some paintings were faded from the gaps in the cloth tarps across the street that allowed the sun in. Occasionally, the narrow streets opened up to large squares where wooden stalls stood, selling textiles, trinkets, food and spices.

Ashim slowly navigated the winding streets behind Bahlir; they guided their camels towards the Runners' house. Ashim glanced over his shoulder at Orison, where she remained mounted on his camel, her mouth ajar upon her first glimpse of Lhandahir.

They entered a grand, empty square, where a bland building of many windows and no prominent exterior door spanned the street to their left. This view of the building hid its true opulence. It was one of King Raj's many vacation homes until he turned it into a rest area for the Runners on assignments. Ashim guided the camel down an alleyway on the side of the building and checked on Orison every few steps.

Bahlir unlocked the gate that blocked the end of the alleyway and it swung open. The dark depths of the alleyway opened to a garden area that showed off the mansion's true beauty. A small fountain sat in the garden's centre that sprayed a cooling mist for any visitors. Unlike the view shown to the public, vines crept up the exterior sand-coloured wall and framed the brown windows perfectly. A porch covered the entrance from the harsh sun. Ashim noticed the double front door was open; from within the building's depths, he could see silhouettes moving around.

He navigated his way to a smaller structure at the far end of the garden—the stables. When they came to a stop, Ashim helped Orison dismount from the camel and eased her to her feet. She held onto him as she adjusted to being on solid ground before approaching the nearby fountain to sit on its cool edge.

Ashim clicked his tongue and the camel groaned loudly as Ashim guided it into the stable. He relieved the creature of their bags required for the trip and removed the saddle. Ashim watched over the camel, as Bahlir settled his own into its little area.

Once he was certain that the camels were comfortable, Ashim gestured for Orison to follow him into the mansion. The covered porch provided a welcome reprieve from the stifling-hot desert air. As they passed through the front doors, they stepped into a grand courtyard. A planter of palm trees sat in the centre, surrounded by plush sofas where the other Runners sat. The courtyard showcased the mansion's three levels of walkways to its multiple rooms.

A Runner named Akhili sauntered up to the pair and grinned. He wore a bright orange tunic and he had lined his brown eyes with kohl. Akhili's lips were a deep shade of red from his lipstick. He threw his scarf over his shoulder as he stopped before Ashim, with a smirk.

"Mr Mahrishan!" Akhili shouted in Karshakir. The others giggled. "What have we told you? Stop taking foreign women to bed!"

More laughter filled the courtyard. Bahlir walked away, glancing over his shoulder and chuckling. Heat filled Ashim's cheeks and he checked on Orison; she looked puzzled, not understanding what they said.

"No foreign women are warming my bed," Ashim exclaimed. "Everyone, this is Orison; one of the new Runners. Some of you may have seen her at a party recently or around the castle."

One of the women, Hala, stood up and approached them. She adjusted her blue and gold dress. Her yellow eyes glowed. "This is Orison? Interesting! Hello," she said in the common tongue.

"Ahnes," Orison replied.

"You both have to share Room Two, king's orders," Hala announced in Karshakir.

Ashim baulked. "Room Two is a double bed. I'll share with Bahlir, if he's comfortable."

"The king will know," Hala said quickly, her attention averted to his brand.

Ashim sighed and turned to Orison. "King Raj wants us sharing a bed," he said in the common tongue. "It's an order."

"I don't mind," Orison admitted.

"I'm tired. We'll go up now," Ashim said to everyone.

He waved Orison along, navigating his way to the nearest staircase where a stained-glass window cast the wooden stairs with a rainbow reflection. Though Ashim didn't mind sharing a bed with Orison, he had wanted her to have the opportunity for some privacy on her first mission.

Each time Ashim stopped in Lhandahir to break up his journeys, he got a different room. After ten years of service, he'd stayed in every single room twice over—except for Hala's. She lived in Lhandahir and her task was caretaker for this home.

Ashim entered the first floor landing and turned right at the stairs, knowing Room Two's location like the back of his hand. He opened the door and stepped into the familiar small room with mud walls, a blue double bed in the corner and a glassless window to air out the room. A blue wardrobe sat in the adjacent corner to the bed, both of which sandwiched the door to the ensuite bathroom.

"I'll sleep on the floor," Ashim announced.

Ashim flinched when Orison smacked his arm. "Don't be ridiculous. We've shared a bed twice at this point; this is no different." He nodded, not being able to argue her logic. She disappeared into the bathroom where Ashim knew blue tiles would greet her. Orison poked her head back into the room. "Can I shower?"

"You don't need to ask permission," Ashim replied as he sat on the bed.

She grabbed her bag and disappeared into the bathroom. The door shut quickly and the latch clicked to lock her inside.

Ashim wondered why King Raj had made them share this room. He tugged his hair out of his ponytail, then rubbed his brand as he laid down and stared at the ceiling. Maybe the king had discovered something recently and was trying to make them figure it out. He continued with these thoughts until sleep pulled him in.

Music filled one of Lhandahir's many squares. The strum of lutes accompanied the sound of drums and tambourines, creating an uplifting sound throughout the stalls. Orison paused to watch the performance which created the uplifting harmony—until she realised Akhili and Bahlir were too engrossed in their conversation to know she had stopped. She jogged up to them; Akhili glanced over his shoulder and winked at her. Orison twiddled her thumbs, glancing at the performance once more. It wasn't their fault they had left her behind. Despite language lessons with King Raj, she remained quieter than normal from not knowing Karshakir fluently.

Orison passed a multitude of stalls with a variety of wares to sell. She saw numerous jewellery stalls and coffee being sold out of kegs at the back of a wagon. People cooked food from their stalls, sending rich spices out into the narrow streets, enticing people to buy. It took Orison back to her first time out in Haranshal, how everything had mesmerised her because of the rich culture. Yet she stuck out like a sore thumb, making people gawk at her because of her pale skin tone; compared to the usual darker complexion of the Karshakians.

Akhili fanned out his bright orange scarf and swished his hips as they approached a tent on the outskirts of town. The tent had a sign on the top, which signified a fortune teller— based on the design of a hand labelled with symbols. Orison didn't know why they needed a fortune teller; she only agreed to go with Akhili and Bahlir because she didn't want to wake Ashim. When Akhili tore open the flap, he put his hand up to Orison and Bahlir then strode in; the person inside gasped at the intrusion.

"Best wait out here," Bahlir instructed. He gently guided Orison away.

"Why?" She could hear Akhili talking in Karshakir to the vendor. "It's only a fortune teller."

Bahlir scratched behind his ear and leaned towards her. "Actually, it's a black market."

Understanding dawned on Orison and she gawped at the tent, then down at her feet. She had to admit there was an irony about people who were bound to King Raj and going to black markets for their wares. Orison quickly shook away the thought of them harvesting organs. The plausible reason could be another task from King Raj.

Sweat beaded across Orison's brow as the harsh sun beat down on her. She exhaled a deep breath as she fanned herself with her hands to cool herself off. Akhili emerged with something wrapped in brown paper, which he placed into a satchel at his hip. He retrieved the cigarette from behind his ear and put it in his mouth. He used his magic to light it and took a long drag. Based on the smell, it wasn't tobacco that Akhili smoked.

"Want some?" Akhili asked, extending the cigarette out. Bahlir took it and inhaled; smoke billowed out of his nose when he handed the cigarette back.

"No thank you," Orison said.

Akhili shrugged as he guided them over to a shaded area next to a building. He sat on the ground and held the cigarette in his mouth as he looked through the brown paper parcel. He talked and laughed with Bahlir while Orison remained silent.

"I don't feel comfortable with Xabian in the castle," Akhili admitted in the common tongue. Orison tensed and turned to them, curious about the nature of the conversation.

"Me neither." Bahlir took another drag of Akhili's cigarette.

Orison cleared her throat. "Me too; he's changed." She ran her hand through the sand beneath her. "I don't even know who he is anymore."

Akhili took a long drag of his herbs after Bahlir. "The devil must taint King Cervus' seed, I swear." Orison raised an eyebrow. "Every Alsaphus is evil. Never trust one."

"King Sila said I was an Alsaphus since calling in the bargain." Orison fidgeted nervously with her dress. She didn't want to be evil like Sila.

"Ignore that bastard. Sila didn't sire you." Akhili blew smoke out from his nostrils. "Or did he knock up some unfortunate soul?"

Orison quickly shook her head. His chuckle flittered along her skin and sent chills down her spine. She glanced at Bahlir, who had been unusually quiet since Akhili brought this up. He squinted from the sun with his head rested on the wall.

"Are you well?" Orison whispered.

Bahlir nodded. "I don't trust Xabian and don't want to say anything out of line."

Orison shrugged. Hearing their confessions didn't bother her. She had experienced Sila's wrath for months and Xabian had taken on his brother's ominous demeanour. The longer she dwelled on Akhili's words, the more she realised Xabian was more like Sila than she originally noticed. It was like he wore a mask that continued to crack as time went on.

Clearing her throat, Orison stretched out her arms. "Maybe... we should go back?"

"Good idea, I need to contact my Equal," Akhili replied. He stubbed the herbs out in the sand and used Bahlir to help him stand.

"I think your partner will like that," Orison said. Bahlir burst out laughing; her attention settled on Akhili who had frozen on the spot. "What?"

Akhili held up his right hand; a white scar lined the middle. "We're only friends. He isn't attracted to men, but we accepted the bond for the power benefits."

Taken aback, Orison pressed her hands to her heated cheeks. "Sorry for assuming. Erol told me that the Equal bond was soulmates and I thought everybody married their Equal."

When Akhili slung his arm over her shoulder, Orison tensed and looked at him. He smirked as they re-entered the town of Lhandahir. The spiced scent of vendors assaulted her senses once again and the sound of tambourines returned to her ears.

"You can be Equal and not marry each other," Akhili explained. "Yes, the Equal bond is soulmates, but fate fucks up sometimes. Which is why they created the loophole, so that you don't have to fuck each other's brains out to accept the bond. When you're around your Equal, it enhances your powers, strengthens you—I train weekly."

Orison nodded. "I only heard about it two months ago, so didn't know how it worked."

"I can tell Pretty Boy isn't your Equal," Bahlir suddenly announced. Orison frowned and regarded them both. "Xabian."

"Maybe I'll find my Equal and maybe I won't. Let fate decide," Orison declared with a shrug. "Have you found yours, Bahlir?"

"*Halek*, my husband is mine," Bahlir grinned.

Orison moved her hair from her mouth. "Kharhem is nice."

Deep down, Orison wanted to find hers. She had no choice but to accept the Othereal as home. She'd rather go through life with her Equal, but it all depended on fate. Orison couldn't fathom what they would look or act like; she only hoped they were kind.

They passed by a band playing for the people in the square. Akhili finally lifted his arm off Orison's shoulders and went to different vendors. Orison ventured to a stall selling hair accessories; she picked one up with a pink butterfly and turned to Bahlir.

"How does this look?" she asked, holding it to her hair.

Bahlir inspected it. "It's pretty; it brings out your eyes." He tensed and turned away. "May I request you don't put that in my hair?"

"I wasn't going to," Orison said as she checked her purse, then giggled. "You aren't Ashim."

Bahlir snorted with a laugh. "He would not enjoy that." She smiled as she handed over the coin. "I want to let you know I'm transitioning."

"I have a friend who is also transitioning," Orison announced as she put the hair clip in her purse.

Orison tensed when Bahlir looped his arm around her shoulder. "That's good to know." Bahlir stepped closer to Orison and steered her towards a spice vendor. Chili peppers hung from a wooden support beam, with bags and crates, in a rainbow of colours. "Stay with Ashim; he'll protect you against Xabian when you get free," he whispered.

"Why do you say that?" Orison asked, turning to him. "If Xabian gets better, I might be able to trust him again."

He sniffed some sticks of cinnamon to look busy. "Tell me, what are Xabian's gifts?"

Orison looked around. "He's a Tearager and Mindelate; why are you asking?"

"If you can trust Xabian, think to yourself—why was King Idralis the only person to tear down that fucking shield and get you out of Alsaphus Castle?" Bahlir uttered and inspected a stick of vanilla. "Why wasn't it Xabian himself when you destroyed the traquelle mirror?"

"How do you know about both of those things?" She stepped out of his grasp and placed a hand over her heart. "You weren't there."

Despite her better judgement, Orison followed Bahlir when he approached a fruit vendor. He inspected an orange, throwing it in the air and catching it before he turned to Orison with a grin. "The King has eyes and ears everywhere, Orison."

Orison thanked the fruit vendor when they gave her a cup of orange juice. She sipped on it whilst pondering over his questions. She thought back to the night of destroying the traquelle, how she enjoyed Lake Horusk before falling asleep and waking up in her bed like her escapade didn't happen. Other instances filtered through her head and more revelations presented themselves.

With a loud gasp, the cup she held fell into the sand at her feet. In a daze, Orison fell to her knees, oblivious to the juice that seeped into her dress. The reality stared at her like a malicious entity—the man she thought was her friend had been deceiving her the entire time.

"Motherfucker!" she screamed.

TWENTY-FIVE

Kinsley, Aeson and Eloise were in the middle of painting the bleak walls of Orison's former chambers when they made a terrifying discovery. Riddle raced into the room, with Taviar close behind. The entire space permeated with the chemical fumes of fresh paint. Gone were the paintings with depictions of war; replaced with pictures of flowers and dancing ballerinas.

Bypassing the meeting room, Riddle entered the bedroom where Eloise and Aeson stood at the foot of the bed. He moved swiftly past them and crouched beside Kinsley at the side of the four-poster bed. She extended a trembling hand towards something on the floor, fear etched into her features. Pulling back the valance sheet, Riddle gasped when he saw a loose floorboard which revealed a band of thorns surrounded by diamonds. For him only, the band of thorns glowed an angry red. Riddle raised the thorns into the air and frowned as he rotated the object to investigate what it meant.

"What is it?" Taviar asked.

Riddle's gaze drifted between everybody in the room. He looked at the band of thorns again and squinted as he tried to see who created it. When he looked into its creation, it was like looking into murky water—a shadow of a person stared back at him. Riddle's eyes widened when he saw what the curse did.

"Orison wasn't exiled by accident; it was this curse. I believe its intended use was to kill her in the mortal lands from magic starvation," Riddle explained.

Gasps filled the room, followed by frantic chatter. Not being able to think with all the noise, Riddle loudly shushed them. It was an extremely serious curse. He didn't understand why somebody tried to assassinate Orison this way. She had done nothing wrong. For a Fae, death by magic starvation was torture; it was slow and extremely painful. Riddle and Taviar had prevented Orison meeting that fate once and lived in fear of it happening again.

A familiar hand pressed into his back; Riddle looked at Kinsley. "Papa, do you know who created this?"

"No, the creator has concealed themselves." Riddle tilted his head. He placed the band of thorns on the ground and paused when he noticed the diamonds were also charmed—they glowed a soft purple. He used his magic to pick one up. "Curious."

"What's curious?" Eloise asked.

Riddle held up the diamond as he sat on the floor. "This is white magic for protection. These two charms completely contradict each other."

When he looked into the creator of the diamonds, Riddle covered his mouth. He saw the Desigle around Orison while she was asleep. It had created the diamonds—like a cloud creates rain—and dropped them into this little alcove under her bed, next to the thorns. It wasn't unheard of for a charm to create other charms; but why a Desigle would create more protection when it was already extremely powerful, confused him.

Riddle used the bed to stand up. He clicked his fingers and a velvet bag appeared in his hand. "I'm taking these and putting them in an iron crate where I can safely store them."

The charmed items disappeared into the bag with a wave of his hand. Riddle shuddered at the thought somebody would do this. Kinsley held him close; he rubbed her back and kissed the top of her head. He was glad his daughter had made the discovery; if she hadn't, nobody would have known how Orison had fallen into her current predicament. Now they needed to figure out why and who would do such a thing.

"So, you think it's the Desigle that prevented the thorns from coming to fruition?" Taviar asked, as Riddle approached the bedroom door with Kinsley. Riddle nodded. "Fuck."

"Fathers," Kinsley said. Both turned to her. "Is it safe to continue decorating?"

Riddle looked at the bag in his hand. "Of course, it's safe. You've done a beautiful job so far. If you find anything else, come to me immediately and I'll remove it. Don't be scared, Kins."

He turned, leaving Kinsley to pick up her paintbrush and continue with her decorating. Riddle was glad she had taken down the tapestry at the back of Orison's bed; and the terrifying demon-dog photo. The room looked welcoming now, not like the prison it used to be. He was proud of his daughter's decorative skills. If she wanted to decorate the entire castle, he would allow it—the castle would be better for it.

After Bahlir's revelation, Orison rushed through the double doors of the mansion where they were staying. Pure anger made her magic burn in her veins. She wanted to scream at the top of her lungs in frustration for trusting Xabian.

She entered a random room and forced the door shut, securing the lock in place. The room she entered was nothing more than a storage room, filled with a wide variety of furniture underneath white fabric.

With heavy breaths, Orison pressed her back to the wooden door and sank to the floor; her hands trembled violently. She held her head and tried to quell the roaring. Tears stung her eyes and she hugged her knees to her chest as she sobbed.

The familiar tug in her chest told her Ashim had approached. Above her, the doorknob rattled, followed by a knock. "Ori, are you well?" Ashim called out as he tried the handle again. "Do you want to talk about it?"

Orison's lungs burned; she couldn't catch her breath no matter how much she tried. "I want to be left alone," she gasped as she looked at the ceiling.

Through the door, she heard movement and averted her attention to it—evidence that Ashim would wait in silence with her. Orison placed her hands on her knees whilst twiddling her thumbs, unsure of what to say to Ashim.

"Hala made some cupcakes; do you want me to get you one?" Ashim asked. Orison remained silent and looked at the white sheets in front of her. "Or something else?"

Orison exhaled a breath. "Xabian could have got me out of Alsaphus Castle immediately."

A long silence followed before Ashim replied. "Is he a Tearager?" Orison made a noise to tell him the answer. "What a coward."

"When we broke the traquelle, he took me to Lake Horusk. Instead of setting me free, he brought me right back to my prison." Orison punched the floor out of frustration. "If I didn't fall asleep, I could have run like hell."

"You think Xabian made you fall asleep?" Ashim cleared his throat.

"Yes," Orison grumbled.

She jumped when Ashim Misted into the storage room. She despised the pitying look he gave her, but he was there and wanted to listen. Orison shoved her tears away from her cheeks and tapped her foot on the floor. All this time and she could have been free the moment they broke the traquelle.

Ashim settled on the floor. "You needed to endure that to grow." She couldn't deny he was correct. "At least you aren't in the dark anymore."

Orison hung onto his words and realised he spoke the truth. If Xabian hadn't kept her trapped in the castle, she wouldn't be here now. Orison wouldn't have gone into that battle in Torwarin and fought against her own people, or gone against Sila. Nor would she have met Ashim, the man who had become so important to her.

A hand on Orison's arm made her flinch; she blinked a couple of times to get herself out of her head. Ashim held her and she slowly eased into his embrace. She rested her head on his shoulder and let herself relax.

"Orison," he managed to get out. She lifted her head, taking in all of his features and the way his eyes glowed. Ashim cleared his throat. "It's my birthday tomorrow. Do you want to have dinner with me?"

"With the others?"

He shook his head. "Just us. I'll pick you up from a room at eight."

Orison grinned. She truly fancied that idea. "Okay, we can celebrate your birthday somewhere in town." Orison rubbed her hands together. "I'll use Room Three to get ready."

The thoughts of Ashim's birthday surpassed the turmoil she felt over Xabian's betrayal. Ashim remained in the storage room and listened to her thoughts for a long while, never judging and just letting Orison vent. They stayed in the storage room until Bahlir needed them to scope out their assignment.

The only sounds in the darkened corridors of the Lhandahir Catacombs were the scurrying of rats on the stone flooring, which was littered with bones. Water droplets—from cracks in the infrastructure—plopped into growing puddles; creating an eco-system all of its own with small plants growing from the bones of the deceased.

Falling rocks and sand bounced off the walls as a rope appeared through a small crack in the ceiling. A dark figure descended the rope and when they dropped, a plume of debris stirred under their feet. A second dark figure descended into the catacombs, smaller than the first figure—who helped them to the ground. Then a third larger figure followed afterwards.

The musty smell of something ancient greeted the trio, instead of the sweet lingering scent of decomposition Orison expected. Then she remembered they had stopped placing the dead down here centuries ago, according to Bahlir.

A heavy, malevolent presence settled on Orison's shoulders, which told her to leave—she pushed the feeling to one side. Orison shrugged off her cloak and took a step towards the dark corridor in front of her. Ashim pulled her back and she staggered into him, which made her look between the two males who were assisting her on this adventure.

"No," he warned. "It's like a maze; you'll get lost."

Orison realised they were at a T-junction. "What are we retrieving, exactly?"

Bahlir unravelled a scroll and angled the parchment into the light of the setting sun. "Today, we are locating the entrance to the Ifrit Lhahlish and acquainting ourselves with the journey. When we pinpoint the location, we'll make a plan and go in."

"Lhahlish means necklace," Ashim translated.

"What is an Ifrit?" Orison asked.

Ashim looked down the corridor and created a fire in the palm of his hand. "A demon."

Her eyes widened. "This is a place of rest."

"For the unholy Fae," Bahlir uttered, he waved them along. "Let's go, we're losing light."

It unnerved Orison that they had to steal a necklace from a demon. She didn't want to be deemed unholy for doing this mission and end up in a place as desolate as this. Ashim thrust his hand out and every flaming torch on the wall illuminated, casting light upon the bones for the first time in centuries.

Orison raced to Ashim and held his arm as they began their journey. The sound of shuffling feet made her look over her shoulder. She relaxed when she realised Bahlir walked behind them and urged her forward. An ominous presence continued to weigh on her shoulders, like she was intruding on something she wasn't supposed to witness.

She looked down when something crunched underneath her feet. Orison stifled a scream and pressed into Ashim when she realised bones covered the floor they walked on. It felt like a desecration, regardless if these bones were of the unholy. Thankfully, her boots protected her from feeling the bones.

A loud screech made Orison tense and inspect her surroundings. The screech could have been several things—rats or creatures that she couldn't name. Orison's heart raced and apprehension plagued her, warning her not to go any further, but Ashim pressed on.

The trio turned several corners, all of which looked exactly the same—only the amount of bones in the area was the differentiating detail. Ashim continuously looked into crevices with Bahlir calling orders in Karshakir, whilst Orison cowered away from the darkness. The catacombs were a maze, just like Ashim said; Orison had no doubt that she would get lost without either Ashim or Bahlir's presence.

Orison couldn't wrap her head around how many unholy Fae were down there, despite the glaring evidence. Some doorways held skulls perfectly stacked into an archway. In some rooms, spines had been used to make chandeliers with skulls as the candelabras. It was sacrilege, but then again, so were the Fae who were down there.

At a dead end, Bahlir came to a sudden stop at a narrow hole in the wall. He stood on his tiptoes and peered through, before muttering under his breath. Bahlir turned to Ashim and talked with him in Karshakir; he pointed to the hole and gestured to Orison. She inched away, fearing the unknown in this place. The ominous feeling increased in this section of the catacombs. She wanted to run back the way they came, but she knew she'd get lost and be food to whatever hid in the shadows.

"Ori." She turned to Ashim when he called her name. "The path is quite narrow. You may be the only person who can make it through."

Orison stepped up to the hole; she peered through and her mouth went dry out of fear. From her perspective, the space only allowed enough room to belly-crawl through sand; she hoped no bones lay underneath. With an audible gulp, she turned to the men, then back to the space. It took everything to remind herself they weren't collecting the necklace today.

"Can we not Mist?" Orison asked. A beige mist engulfed Ashim, but he stayed firmly where he stood. "That would be a no. Bahlir, maybe you could fit through?"

He stepped up to the hole and hoisted himself through. Orison winced when his broad shoulders scraped against the wall until he came to a stop. Bahlir wriggled around, his legs kicked out and he shouted in Karshakir. Understanding the Karshakir word for help, Orison stepped up to Bahlir in unison with Ashim and they dragged him out by his feet.

"I guess I have no choice then," Orison grumbled.

"Not now," Ashim reminded her as he took her hand. "Let's go back to the house."

They navigated their way back through the maze of tunnels. After taking a wrong turn, they almost entered a partially submerged section of the catacombs and had to back track through the ominous tunnels. Getting their bearings, it didn't take long to find the rope. Climbing the rope made Orison grimace. The rough material bit into her skin like a thousand needles and it took all her strength to lift her own body weight.

Back on the surface, night had fallen over Lhandahir. Orison scrambled out of the hole and staggered to her feet, dusting sand off her white tunic and beige trousers. The cold desert air cut into the thin material and made her shiver as she waited for the others. It felt good to not have death surrounding them. Shortly after, Ashim and Bahlir emerged out of the hole in the ground, Bahlir tugged the rope back to the surface then wiped dust off his clothes.

A wave of Bahlir's hand moved the stone that sealed the catacombs for one more day. Another wave had Orison and Ashim following him back to the house. Ashim and Bahlir frequently spoke to each other, while Orison's heart pounded, knowing that the necklace was her responsibility to steal.

Orison knew things could go terribly wrong from her inexperience. But she would risk everything for Ashim's and her freedom.

TWENTY-SIX

The following night, Orison walked around the largest square in Lhandahir holding Ashim's arm as he ate ice cream. Lanterns illuminated the stalls where vendors were busy cooking Lhandahir delicacies. The magic in the square kept the chilly desert night at bay. People drank at tables situated around a fountain; some people played chess.

Orison huffed out a breath as she placed a hand on her overfed belly, which groaned in protest at how much she had consumed. Everything in Karshakroh had been delicious and she had indulged for Ashim's birthday. She looked up at the sky, where her attention became fixated on a shooting star; Orison closed her eyes and made a wish for the mission to be successful. She turned to Ashim, who had tied his dark-brown hair into a ponytail with a couple of braids within. It made his features more prominent and his yellow eyes glowed like a sunrise.

"I think I'm going to explode," she groaned.

"Please don't." Ashim ate the last remnants of his ice cream and placed the empty bowl on the vendor's stand. Orison couldn't help but laugh and she groaned as her belly griped in protest, her hand clutching her purple dress. "Raj would not be happy."

Orison flopped onto a nearby bench. "Stop making me laugh."

When she looked up and over Ashim's shoulder, she could see all the constellations Taviar had pointed out to her. The outline of a stag, a bear and the scythe appeared within the stars. It made Orison pause as she gazed upon it. A memory surfaced, which she had forgotten until now—back when she destroyed the traquelle tying her to King Sila.

With a sigh, Ashim laid next to her. "The stars are beautiful."

Extending her arm out, she pointed to the stag. "For Fallasingha; for strength and prosperity," she recited, remembering that night. Ashim squinted at the stars. "Those are the three constellations we see in Fallagh."

"We only see them as stars. A stag, bear and a scythe," Ashim pointed them out.

He settled beside her and clasped his hands in his lap. His gaze roamed across the shooting stars in the sky. Orison wished for more things, but doubted she would have them granted—another wasted breath of asking Fallagh to protect her from the monster underground. She knew she was overthinking, but she couldn't help it.

Instinctively, Orison placed a hand over her brand. When she first saw it in the bathroom mirror, her hand had trembled over the lion's head. As time went on, she didn't know her body any other way and it oddly comforted her.

"I like learning that the stars have names," Ashim admitted. While there was cheering from a neighbouring table, his attention remained on the stars. Orison followed his gaze and was awestruck by the view. "It makes them seem alive."

She told Ashim about when she spent the night at Lake Horusk after destroying her traquelle. Orison described how she had felt the sand between her toes for the first time in weeks—back when she didn't know of Xabian's deception.

Something squealed into the air. She jumped when it exploded. It cast a twinkling red star into the sky, which dissipated as it descended to earth. Orison gawped when another one appeared in purple—fireworks. As the sky erupted in colour, she turned to Ashim, who watched them with awe.

"I think something knows it's your birthday," Orison admitted. She turned her attention back to the reds, golds, purples and silvers in the sky—mesmerised by the moment.

She looked down when Ashim held her hand. "It's a great birthday with you here."

Orison burst out laughing until her stomach griped. She met Ashim's gaze and stared into his glowing yellow eyes, making her feel safe. He leaned into her and stopped himself when Orison's breathing hitched. His gaze lingered on her lips and when she didn't pull away, he inched closer.

"Why do I want to kiss you?" he murmured.

Orison's heart skipped a beat as she pressed a hand to his cheek. "You can, if you want to."

He didn't need to be told twice as he softly kissed her. Orison smiled and moved in closer as they kissed.

"I've been wanting to do that for a while," Ashim admitted.

Orison looked at him, surprised. "You have?" He nodded with a grin.

Another shooting star made Orison wish for more nights like this—when they would be free and could explore Karshakroh at their leisure. Ashim gently squeezed her hand. She rested her head against his shoulder and sighed as they watched the fireworks above them.

"Happy birthday," Orison said quietly.

Ashim snuggled into her and kissed the top of her head. "Thank you." Orison tensed when he stood up with a playful grin on his face. "I think we should dance with the fireworks."

"I can't dance," Orison reminded him.

She groaned as he tugged her to her feet and steered her towards the others who were dancing to the tune of a lute. Orison allowed Ashim to move into position and guide her through the steps. During the dance, she kept tripping or standing on Ashim's feet; he merely chuckled and carried on. They celebrated well into the night, like their mission wasn't happening.

One of the dining rooms in Karshak Castle had golden curtains framing each archway that led to a balcony. The white plaster walls were bare, apart from the occasional intricately designed trellises in the shape of flowers. Decked out in the middle of the room was a large white rectangular table with a large vase full of reeds, which sat in the centre.

The double doors opened and people filed into the room. Queen Inatai of Marona, a woman with pale-blue skin and white hair, stepped into the room; she wore a white empire dress. Her emissary, Ohra—a male with the same complexion—accompanied her. Then came King Aarond of Valhaevn, a male with tree branches for hair. He was accompanied by a blue-skinned pixie with pink hair. Nazareth and Idralis were the last ones. The only ones not invited were Taviar and Saskia, because they weren't royalty. Also, King Raj loathed Fallasingha; hence, these people were rarely invited to the events.

Each guest took their place around the table. Nazareth had her hair down and wore a brown figure-hugging dress. She clutched the chair in front and waited.

These dinners were all the same and unless King Raj was present, nobody had permission to sit. On this occasion, it appeared he would be late.

Moments passed before King Raj strolled into the room. He wore a golden tunic with matching hair accessories. Showing off his wealth, he sauntered over to his spot at the head of the table. Everybody in the room was rich to some extent. Nazareth didn't see the need to flaunt their wealth; she considered it rude.

"Sit," King Raj ordered.

Each guest sat down at the table, Nazareth placed a napkin on her lap and got comfy. She looked up as King Raj grumbled something under his breath.

Servants filed into the room; Nazareth gasped when she saw Xabian amongst the servants—wearing the servant's attire. She had heard from Taviar that this had happened, but seeing it in person turned her stomach.

"With all due respect, may I enquire why the Crown Prince of Fallasingha is serving us?" Inatai asked. "It appears demoralising and makes Fallasingha look weak."

King Raj clicked his tongue. "He trespassed on my lands, therefore, he's my servant now. The crown princess also met the same fate."

Nazareth exchanged a look with Idralis. He cleared his throat. "And where is the crown princess tonight?" Idralis asked.

"Away."

From across the table, Nazareth noticed that Aarond watched her. He appeared just as anxious as she was to witness Xabian's change of power. Servants placed bowls of tomato soup in front of them all. Nazareth kept stealing glances at Xabian. He was too quiet as he filled everybody's drinks; as though serving King Raj was second nature. With the ring of a bell, the meal commenced and they dug into their soup. The spiced tomato flavour danced along Nazareth's tongue when she had her first taste.

"Is Princess Orison safe wherever she is?" King Aarond asked.

Raj leaned back. "Please, can we talk about other topics?" He drank his wine. "My servants are my business. How about what we've been up to?"

"You have Fallasingha royalty serving you food, Raj," Queen Inatai spat. "If you want to see change and form an alliance with Fallasingha, you can't have the only heirs to the throne sworn into your employment."

He rubbed the bridge of his nose. Everybody jumped when he slammed his fist onto the table, causing the cutlery to scatter across the table. "It's for protection. Orison is safe and so is Xabian. She has my other Runners to assist her. Now, can we please change the subject?"

Nazareth continued to eat, ignoring the way Xabian stood underneath an archway waiting to collect their plates. Though her curiosity grew from

Orison's absence, the king's growing agitation made the question die on her tongue. If the king said Orison was safe, she had to take it at face value.

"How have the repair efforts been after the Battle of Torwarin, Idralis?" Inatai asked.

Idralis wiped his mouth. "We have rebuilt most of the buildings that King Sila set alight. Thank you for asking."

"And now King Sila is dead," King Raj rejoiced as he ate some soup.

Nazareth looked nervously at Xabian when she heard him growl; his eyes glowed brightly. She looked around the table. The other royals didn't appear to notice his sudden change of demeanour, too engrossed in the meal. King Raj acted like nothing happened, but she noticed he grew tense from Xabian's reaction.

Gasps filled the table when Xabian slammed King Raj's head into the table, causing his bowl to topple off the surface and shatter at his feet. The soup spilled down the king's tunic and onto the floor—akin to blood. Xabian snarled loudly, even as guards with guns stepped out of the shadows and aimed their weapons at him. The Prince of Fallasingha grabbed a steak knife and held it to the king's throat. Panting, his veins pulsated with a glowing purple light; like forks of lightning lived underneath his flesh.

"Let me go, that is all I ask," Xabian snarled in perfect Karshakir. His voice didn't sound like his own.

Raj merely laughed. "When Orison returns with the artefact, you can walk out that door." He tried to get Xabian off him. "Have you taken your medication?"

"I refuse to take your poison," Xabian seethed. The forks of lightning under his skin climbed like vines up his face. "You're trying to kill me."

"I'm trying to help you." King Raj shifted under Xabian's weight. The guards around Xabian stepped closer, one pressed their gun to the back of the prince's head. "I don't require guards. I need a Healengale to sedate him," he ordered in Karshakir.

With a flurry of white smoke, a woman dressed in white appeared. Nazareth didn't recognise this side of Xabian or understand what the deal with medication was. Standing before her wasn't a prince—this was something else.

A couple of guards lowered their weapons, grabbed Xabian's arms and wrenched him off King Raj. Xabian struggled against the guards; he screamed his protest until his voice broke and they pinned him to the floor. The Healengale plunged a syringe of fluid into his neck, which made him collapse instantaneously.

"What have you done to Prince Xabian?" Idralis asked, his eyes wide.

King Raj fixed his hair, tutting at the soup that marred his shirt. "I haven't done anything. This is the price of going into the mortal realm whilst the Nighthex is ending."

"What the fuck," Nazareth breathed.

"He's unfortunately akin to his brother—stubborn," King Raj remarked. "I'm trying to help."

In a million years, Nazareth never expected King Raj to help Fallasingha Royalty. Everybody knew how much he loathed the nation. Maybe he took pity on Xabian's predicament.

"Are you helping both of them?" King Aarond enquired.

King Raj winked as he sat back in his seat, regarding his ruined meal. Nazareth didn't know how to interpret it as she watched Xabian be dragged away. Maybe making Orison his Runner protected her from what the prince had become.

TWENTY-SEVEN

Ashim woke up to the sun in his face, groaning as he rubbed his eye. He looked down at Orison snuggled against him with her head on his chest; her hand gripped his shirt. He gave her shoulder a gentle squeeze, then rubbed it with his thumb, feeling the soft green material of her nightgown. The night in Lhandahir was still fresh in his mind two days later— the food they shared and their first kiss. It felt right to kiss her and he wanted more, but he wanted to be free before taking the next big step in whatever their relationship led to.

Since they started sharing a room together, there had been many times Ashim had woken to Orison cuddling him—exactly like this with her head on his chest. He'd grown accustomed to it and it felt strange when she wasn't there. Waking up with Orison gave Ashim comfort and the awkwardness of it had passed quickly, to his relief. Ashim had been sleeping better since this arrangement had presented itself.

Orison blinked her eyes open and groaned as she stretched. "Morning," she mumbled, closing her eyes.

"Morning," he repeated.

She propped herself onto her elbows and gave him a soft kiss on the lips. Her eyes widened, realising what she did, but Ashim didn't mind. Orison cleared her throat. "Do you want to shower first?" Her voice was still croaky from sleep as she rubbed her eye.

"You go first, we have a big day ahead of us," Ashim replied.

Later that morning, they would retrieve the necklace. Though they would get dirty down in the catacombs, some sense of normalcy wouldn't hurt.

"You go, I'm too comfy," Orison said. She flopped back onto the bed with a grin.

Sprawling out, a playful expression spread across her face as she attempted to push Ashim out of it. He chuckled as he slipped out of bed and crouched on the floor; Orison's purple eyes shimmered with mischief in the morning sun as she regarded him.

"Do you want to go to the bathroom before my shower?"

Orison rolled onto her stomach and closed her eyes. "I fully intend to go back to sleep, having the bed to myself. Enjoy your shower, Mahrishan."

He laughed. The way his last name rolled off her tongue made his heart skip a beat. It wasn't mocking like how the other Runners pronounced it. Instead, it sounded like his favourite song he could hear repeatedly. When the thought of his last name being hers came to mind, he snapped himself back to reality. Ashim was unsure where that thought came from.

Standing up, Ashim gave Orison one last glance. She relaxed as she fell back to sleep and he slipped into the bathroom. The lock clicked behind him and he leaned against the wooden door as he panted, staring at the blue tiles. Going to the sink, he threw cold water over his face to calm himself.

He saw to his needs and showered quickly. They had to get to the catacombs soon if they wanted to be successful. Ashim didn't know how today would pay off. Would they leave Lhandahir with their freedom or watch it go up in flames? Like every errand he completed for King Raj, he had to keep an open mind. Shaking the negative thoughts away, he prayed to Othereal for a successful mission; although he wasn't religious.

After his shower, Ashim stepped back into the room as Orison woke up again and stretched out on the bed, looking at him. He had dried himself off and had dressed in black trousers and a white shirt; only keeping his hair wet so it would dry in the desert heat. He stepped to the chest of drawers for his hairbrush, glancing behind him at the sound of the bed creaking.

"I'm getting a shower," Orison announced and disappeared into the bathroom.

He nodded and kept brushing his hair. A knock at the door had him crossing the room to open the door—Bahlir stood on the other side. He had dressed in similar attire, with a satchel over his shoulder.

"We've not had breakfast yet," Ashim pointed out in Karshakir.

Bahlir strolled into the room and sank down on the bed with a huff. He glanced at the bathroom door when he heard the shower running. "I thought you'd be bright-eyed and bushy-tailed at the crack of dawn."

Shaking his head, Ashim checked himself in the mirror. "No, I couldn't sleep because of nerves." He pushed his hair over his shoulder.

"Freedom is on the horizon." Bahlir stood up and clapped him on the shoulder. "I'll wait downstairs."

Ashim pressed a hand to his growling belly. He felt too sick to eat but would force himself, only so that he had enough energy should anything go wrong. This was the most nervous he had been when on a mission because he was unsure what they were dealing with—especially when an Ifrit was involved. Yet it was the only thing that stood in the way of being free.

The dust in the Lhandahir Catacombs stirred as a wooden ladder invaded the land of the dead. Rats scurried away into the shadows where only the most nefarious lurked, yet the bones remained in silence, waiting to alert the evil of the intrusion. The oppressive energy down there was heavier the second time around. It was as though the shadows could pre-empt the future theft, knowing they would take something from its clutches.

Ashim, Bahlir and Orison climbed down the ladder much quicker than the last time they entered the soulless place. Orison dusted herself off and looked at

Ashim for guidance; he gave her a dip of his chin as he illuminated the sconces on the wall. Bahlir checked their equipment.

She steeled her nerves as Ashim and Bahlir conversed in Karshakir and glanced back at her every so often, as she toyed with the empty pouch around her neck. Orison clutched Ashim's arm for comfort as they began their journey into the unknown. The ever-increasing ominous presence had Orison rolling her shoulders to shake it off. Whatever it was, it wasn't happy about their second visit.

Orison had grown so familiar with the crunching underneath her boots that she no longer grimaced at the floor of bones; nor did she want to scream and run for the hills. The more alert she became of the sinister aura on her back, the more she clutched Ashim's shirt until her knuckles were white. Angering an ancient ghost wasn't a good omen for their task ahead.

Orison inched away from scorpions scuttling along the mud walls. She shied away from the rats that scurried between her feet; the vermin that made homes in the eye sockets of skulls. It took everything to press on and clear her thoughts of running to the safety of the ladder.

They navigated their way down the maze of Lhandahir Catacombs and multiple corridors that came with it. The trio ignored the growing number of bones that spread out around them at all angles. At the dead end, where the hole to the necklace sat, Bahlir came to a stop. He stood on his tiptoes and peered through before turning to Orison. Her stomach sank to her feet like it was being pulled under by quicksand. Everything within her screamed not to take that step. Yet her trembling hands let go of Ashim and she stepped closer to Bahlir.

Bahlir interlocked his fingers and crouched down. "I will help you."

Exhaling a breath, Orison placed her foot on Bahlir's joined hands. He pushed Orison up and she belly crawled into the small space; to her surprise, it was large enough for her. On the other side of the tunnel, gold glinted in her direction, beckoning her to come forward and seal her fate.

"Be safe," Ashim called through.

I will, she said to his mind.

Orison glanced over her shoulder at the two men, then crawled towards the golden hue. The sand beneath her hands slithered between her fingers, the feel of bones scraped against her nails underneath the coarse surface. She pressed on and tried to fight back the cringing that she felt, especially as the ominous presence grew stronger.

The crawl space opened to a treasure room and the sconces on the wall surprisingly lit up. Orison lowered herself down, brushing sand from her trousers and shirt as she took in the golden spectacle that reminded her of the Temple of Lioress.

There were golden coins piled high on a gigantic stone table; the surface's height came to Orison's shoulder, giving the illusion she had shrunk in size. Along the walls were scimitars with golden hilts. She turned in a circle, staggering to a stop. In the centre of the room, a horned beast appeared to be carved into the stone. Its eyes were closed as though asleep. Around their neck, was a golden chain with a large ruby the size of Orison's fist; the item which Orison had to steal.

"Forgive me, Fallagh," Orison whispered, sending a prayer to her deity.

Orison looked back at Bahlir and Ashim, who stood around waiting with bated breath. She tiptoed her way to the altar, where more golden offerings were strewn about. Orison's hand brushed against the stone where people had carved the Karshakir language into the mud walls.

At the foot of the creature, she looked up in awe at its gargantuan size. It unnerved her how alive it looked. Orison could have sworn she saw it breathing if she looked close enough. Placing her foot on a section of altar that wasn't covered in golden coin, Orison hoisted herself up.

Balancing on a thin ledge, Orison's skin bristled when she inspected the pores in the beast's stone skin. Her heart skipped a beat when she was sure it looked too realistic to be man-made. Reaching around the beast's broad shoulders, she fumbled with the clasp of the necklace with one hand, relieved when the large pendant fell into her spare hand.

Orison looked around when the chamber shook; dust rained down on the offerings. She swiftly slipped the necklace into the pouch she carried and climbed down the ledge on shaky limbs.

She made to take a step, but something warm wrapped around her waist. Her scream was trapped in her throat when she looked up. The beast's yellow slitted eyes bore into her as it lifted Orison into the air with a painful slowness. She struggled in the beast's grasp that was too strong. When it snarled, a terror-filled scream tore out of her. The creature threw her across the chamber, knocking the wind out of her as she landed in a heap near the exit.

"Orison, get out of there!" Ashim called out.

"Orison!" Bahlir cried.

She groaned as she came around, looking up at the beast; its yellow eyes continued to burn into her soul. Orison scrambled to the wall and attempted to climb through the hole to her saviours. It grabbed her by the ankle and yanked her into the sand with an ear-splitting roar.

Orison winced as tears streamed down her face; she scrambled to the wall of scimitars. Staggering to her feet and overwhelmed by dizziness, she groaned as she unhooked a scimitar from its placeholder. Her hair fell into her face and she panted as she adjusted her grip on the handle. The beast's growl engulfed her, like a second skin. Looking down at the weapon, she realised her predicament—Orison had no idea how to use it.

"Help me!" Orison shouted. "I don't know how to use a sword!"

"I do," Bahlir offered.

Orison glanced at the creature, then at the hole. "Then get here and help!"

"I can't fit—remember?" She whimpered as she narrowly ducked out of the way of the beast's punch. "I am a Protelsha, however."

It swung again; Orison screamed as she swung the sword blindly. Its giant fist slammed into the wall, sending coins toppling down with clinks. "What the fuck is a Protelsha?" Orison ducked again and tried to calm her breathing.

"I can control people if I sing," Bahlir replied. "My elixir prevents me from singing for very long, though."

A choked sound left Orison as she dodged another fist. "Help!"

Bahlir called to her. "When I can't go on, remember the movements."

Miscalculating the next hit, Orison cried out as it slammed her into the ground. The metallic taste of blood filled her mouth, which she spat out. Swinging the sword again, the beast roared as she connected with its next fist of fury. It paused when a melody filled the chamber in Karshakir.

It was instantaneous when Orison's arms moved without her doing, as she jammed her sword and sparred with the Ifrit. It was like she had been doing it for years. Orison forced her hair out of her eyes, continuing to slam the sword into the creature's flesh—with a cry. It roared with each successful hit.

Orison wailed when she misinterpreted its next move and it grabbed her around her middle. It slammed her against the table, into a plume of gold coins. She wheezed as she rolled onto her stomach. She managed to get herself onto all fours, spitting blood upon the sandy floor.

The melody in the chamber diminished when Bahlir's voice cracked. Orison baulked as she looked helplessly at the hole in the wall—it wasn't enough time. In one final desperate attempt, Orison threw the scimitar with a war cry. It slammed into the Ifrit's eye and the roar that it emitted violently shook the catacombs.

Seeing her opportunity, she raced to the hole in the wall and scrambled through. Tearing the pouch from her neck, she tossed it to Ashim who caught it with both hands. Orison scurried through the dirt that rained down on her from the Ifrit's continued pain-filled screams. Her gaze focussed on Ashim as he urged her forward; she couldn't hear his voice over the sound of the creature. Only when she saw his face fall did dread consume her.

The Ifrit grabbed her around the ankle and dragged her backwards. Orison screamed and clawed at the sand. When she turned around, the scimitar was still protruding from its right eye as it flipped her onto her back. It bared its teeth and grabbed a shard of bone from the ground. The beast pinned her to the sand whenever she attempted to escape. With a malicious smile, it snapped the bone in two.

"No, please don't!" Orison gasped.

She tried one last time to get away, but couldn't move fast enough. The Ifrit slammed the shard of bone into Orison's thigh with a sickening squelch; she let out a blood-curdling scream as excruciating pain numbed her body. Sounds of distressed sobbing echoed around the crawl space as she tried to flee. She collapsed in the sand as her world spun. As the Ifrit twisted the bone into her leg, she yowled from sheer agony. Orison lost her breath momentarily.

A loud groan came out of Orison and her lips trembled as she tried to drag herself to Ashim. The creature slammed the second shard of bone into the same leg with a sickening twist. Orison screamed until her voice finally broke as the pain increased tenfold.

Extending her hands out as her lower lip quivered in anguish, she needed Ashim to drag her out of this deplorable place. She cried with loud sobs when the pain became too much with each drag across the sand.

Hands grabbed Orison's wrist as the ever-increasing pain made darkness claim her.

Twenty-Eight

Pain. So much pain.

TWENTY-NINE

Ashim ran through the narrow streets of Lhandahir. His breathing was heavy and blood covered his hands as he cradled Orison. Her head lolled to the side with each step. The thud of Bahlir's footfalls trailed Ashim's, whose eyes burned with tears as he continued to run. He tried to keep Orison's leg elevated so she lost no more blood.

People gasped and stepped out of the way; each covered their mouths in shock. When a local baker offered them a cart, Ashim clambered into it and gently laid Orison down. With trembling hands, he tightened the makeshift tourniquet above where the bone shards protruded out of her leg. Bahlir hung his head in sorrow as the cart jolted.

"Please save her," he begged, as the tears flowed. "Please make her stay."

Bahlir pressed his fingers on her neck. "Her pulse is growing weak."

"Please," he begged as he rocked with the cart's movements.

Taking Orison's hand, Bahlir tried to sing once more to keep her in this life. Ashim held her close and sobbed loudly, unable to see her face through the tears.

THIRTY

"Come back to us, follow my voice," a strong voice sang to Orison. *"Follow my voice."*

Darkness pressed into her at all sides.

Orison could hear hurried speech in Karshakir in her momentary lapses of consciousness. She could recognise Ashim's voice anywhere, though she had never heard it with so much anguish and pain.

"Stay with us," the voice sang.

But the light cleaved the darkness in two.

THIRTY-ONE

A blinding white light cut across a great expanse of trees and wilderness. Orison staggered back and shielded her eyes until she blinked. She knew this light like an old friend; it crawled up her arm, offering a reprieve from the pain and hardships. Beyond the light appeared a sprawling city like Parndore, where children's laughter ran free.

"Tontemgoref," a deep voice named it.

Voices in Karshakir made her pause before she took a step into the light. Ashim's pain-filled scream echoed within the surrounding forest. He begged for something she couldn't understand.

"Stay with us," a different voice sang. It was an anchor; she felt it around her chest.

She returned to the light. Wanting a break from the pain of this life, she wanted to join those laughing children in Tontemgoref where she could be free.

Orison staggered away from the light when she heard Ashim say one word through the hurried Karshakir language in her conscious mind.

Tahanbashri.

THIRTY-TWO

Ice rattled around the glass in Ashim's trembling hand. As he stared intently at his hand, he saw flashes of Orison's blood that marred his skin like a phantom. Ashim squeezed his eyes shut, focussing on his breathing as he downed the glass of rum with a wince—not caring that the ice crashed into his teeth. Nearby, Bahlir paced King Raj's chambers, the smell of his cigar drifted around the area. Both turned to the chamber doors as they opened and two guards stepped through.

"Keep this information away from Xabian," King Raj ordered to somebody in the corridor. "Mahrishan, Ahbarsh, are you well?"

Ashim shook his head and popped the cork on the bottle of rum. He poured another glass and lifted it to his lips. The amber liquid sloshed onto the table from how violently he shook. He knocked it back and cringed at the burn. His head swirled as the alcohol settled in.

He rested his head against the bottle. "Please tell me Orison is okay."

A portal returned them to Haranshal in less than a minute. None of the guards allowed Ashim into the infirmary. Instead, they ordered him to King Raj's chambers with Bahlir to await the king's return from Entan. The wait was dreadful. Ashim needed answers.

"Yes, thank Othereal." Raj placed his hands on his hips and looked down at his black polished shoes.

Bahlir stepped forward. "What the fuck happened?" he snapped. "You swore that the Ifrit couldn't wake up because it was in an eternal sleep. Now look at the mess we're in!"

"I can only apologise for the miscalculation. My sources are clearly unreliable and I will deal with them," Raj promised.

Pouring another glass and knocking the liquid back, Ashim looked at the red curtains that billowed in the wind. The night made Haranshal look like stars had descended to the earth—a small bit of comfort from the roaring in his head.

Bahlir hurtled the pouch at Raj, who struggled to catch it. The pouch dangled precariously against his arm. "Well, there's your fucking consolation prize," he sneered before taking a drag of his cigar.

Picking up the pouch properly, Raj's face paled when he saw the amount of blood that stained the brown leather material. Ashim winced and lowered his head, staring at the floor; he dared not look.

"Are you certain Orison is your Equal?" Raj asked.

Ashim nodded. "*Halek.*" He poured another glass of alcohol. "There's no denying it. I keep feeling this tugging in my chest and it enhances my powers when I'm around her. I've never been able to illuminate an entire catacomb before; it's always been sections."

The king swore under his breath and grabbed the bottle from Ashim. He popped the cork and placed the bottle to his lips, chugging the rum straight from the source. Raj winced when he finished and wiped his mouth with the back of his hand. Shaking his head, Ashim only assumed Raj would know the implications of an Equal bond.

"What are the consequences if she died?" Ashim asked, not wanting to know, but needing to—for his own peace of mind.

Raj offered the bottle to Bahlir, who declined. "Have you accepted the bond?" Ashim shook his head, the answer made the king relax. "Nothing would happen. You'd simply walk these lands as those without an Equal.

However, if you had accepted, your magic would fizzle out as her soul is returned to Othereal. The bond connects your souls."

"So, I'd die?" Ashim asked.

The king nodded solemnly as he took another long drink from the bottle. It made him freeze and look at Bahlir, who gawped at the answer. Obviously, Bahlir didn't know that caveat either. Raj rubbed the bridge of his nose. Ashim jumped when he smashed the bottle on the floor and screamed.

"Are you well, Your Majesty?" Bahlir asked.

"This is a fucking mess," Raj spat.

Glass crunched underneath Raj's feet as he made his way to the sofa, collapsing into the plush material and ran a hand through his hair. Ashim glanced at Bahlir anxiously, as he adjusted his leather waistcoat and cleared his throat; feeling deflated when he noticed his glass wasn't full. Everything about this was indeed a mess.

Ashim cleared his throat, "When will they allow visitors?"

"Tomorrow," Raj announced, keeping his eyes closed. "You can sleep in the Royal Visitor Wing, Mahrishan. Room Twelve. You earned it."

Ashim paused, as he had never been allowed there before. "Thank you, Your Majesty."

He pushed himself onto his feet, bade the king goodnight and followed Bahlir out of his chambers. They parted ways and Ashim headed towards the section of castle that was usually forbidden to him. In the Royal Visitor Wing, Ashim took a long while to find the room, then succumbed to his emotions.

Ashim woke up to the cold kiss of a knife to his throat and a weight on his chest. He willed himself to keep calm as he opened his eyes, coming face to face with Xabian who pinned him to his bed. Purple veins glowed under Xabian's skin like forks of lightning; his eyes were like a thousand galaxies reflecting the rage inside.

"Good morning," Ashim said in Karshakir, feeling the knife dig deeper when he swallowed.

"What the fuck have you done to Orison?" Xabian snarled in the same language.

Casually, he wrapped his hand around Xabian's wrist. "What did you hear?"

"She's in the infirmary, nearly dead by *your* hand." Ashim cringed at Xabian's warm breath on his face as the pressure at his neck increased. "Like asking the king to mutilate me and make me a slave."

Slowly meeting the prince's gaze, Ashim's grip tightened on Xabian's wrist and he dived into his mind.

Inside the prince's head, it looked like a library. Built into rocky alcoves were wooden shelves with glass vases, which bestowed his memories. However, something was undeniably wrong. Ashim covered his nose at a putrid rotting smell permeating around Xabian's mind; the smell turned his stomach. Some alcoves had turned to stone with purple lightning appearing between the cracks. Ashim baulked in horror at the black sludge that dripped down each shelving unit. It was like the Nighthex had been consuming him.

Pushing aside his horror, Ashim inspected each memory, bypassing the ones snuffed out by the strange rock. It didn't take long before he found the memory of Xabian eavesdropping on the Healengales who were discussing Orison's treatment. He grabbed the glass vase from the shelf and threw it to the rocky ground. Ashim forced down the nausea as black, bubbling sludge landed at his feet. He retreated from Xabian's mind and dived back into reality.

Ashim gasped loudly as reality returned. He was relieved when the kiss of the knife left his throat. The chains suspending the bed from the ceiling rattled and it swung gently as a dark mass disappeared down the side. Ashim sighed with relief, rolling onto his side; he retched at the memory of the putrid smell in Xabian's mind.

"What am I doing here?" Xabian asked with a frown.

Ashim pretended to be tense and turned back. "What are you doing here, indeed. I didn't call for any assistance." Xabian looked around in a confused daze as he used the wall to help him stand. "I think you were sleepwalking."

"I should go back to my room," Xabian announced.

"Goodnight," Ashim said.

Xabian nodded. "Sorry for waking you."

Making a noise, Ashim collapsed onto the bed and waited for the click of the door closing to reverberate around the room. The cool wind stirred Ashim's hair and he huffed out a breath as he rolled onto his side to stare at the darkness. Sleeping alone felt foreign and despite the emptiness in his heart, sleep claimed him.

Healengales hurried around Karshak Castle's infirmary. Some were at their stations mixing elixirs in medicine bowls; some tended to guards who groaned in the beds and others cleaned. All communicated various jobs to one another as they worked.

The white walls looked iridescent in the morning light and the flags with the Karshak emblem on them flapped in the breeze that flowed through the open windows. It was much cooler than the rest of the castle, designed to aid in fast healing.

Ashim stepped into the room, Mahavu on his shoulder; he cringed as her tiny claws dug into his flesh. He looked around, not being able to see Orison. His heart raced with anticipation. King Raj had said they allowed visitations, but all the beds were visible to Ashim and they were full of guards. Ashim stopped a Healengale, who was passing by with a metal tray of utensils; she looked at him with yellow glowing eyes.

"Excuse me, where is Orison?"

"Let me finish this, then the head matron will see to your request," the Healengale announced.

Taking a step back, Ashim scratched underneath Mahavu's chin that earned him a loud purr. He winced as more tiny claws dug into his shoulder. Her tail flicked down his back as he stayed in the doorway, waiting to be reunited with Orison. After a few moments, a Healengale appeared, a white cloth covered her hair and her green eyes were piercing.

"Mr Mahrishan?" It took him aback by how she knew his name. "Follow me."

Ashim pushed himself off the wall and followed the matron along a corridor of other rooms. Unhooking the keys from her waistband, they rattled together as she sorted through them. The sun illuminated each door through the small windows near the ceiling.

"Why is she locked in a room?" Ashim asked, glancing over his shoulder.

"Protection from Prince Alsaphus," Matron replied. "King's orders."

He nodded in understanding. After the previous night's encounter, it was wise to have her locked in a room. At the end of the corridor, the matron slipped the key into the lock and it swung open after a click.

The white octagonal room greeted Ashim as he stepped inside. Wooden beams crisscrossed the vaulted ceiling where a window cast a spotlight in the centre and Orison laid asleep in a bed. The only other piece of furniture in the room was an elixir station pushed to the side near the door. Ashim frowned at a gold band around Orison's wrist where wires led to an identical ticking box that whirred loudly when the numbers changed.

The box read: *0-0-0-8-4*.

He crossed the room and moved Mahavu from his shoulder. Ashim held the cat close to his chest as he leaned over and pushed hair away from Orison's forehead. He exhaled a shaky breath as ran his thumb through her hairline.

"Sorry I couldn't stop it," he whispered to her.

Ashim's attention was drawn to the box as it whirred loudly: *0-0-0-9-0*. He shifted and looked down at Orison before it whirred again: *0-0-0-8-6*.

"What is that box?" he asked the matron.

The matron stepped forward. "It measures her heart."

Ashim nodded, crouching beside Orison as he placed Mahavu on her chest. The cat walked around, making little noises before purring and curling up under Orison's chin. He smiled as he moved Orison's hair from Mahavu's face. The cat blinked slowly as she relaxed. Everyone knew cats somehow had healing properties.

"Make sure she gets her strength back," Ashim said, petting Mahavu's head. The cat purred louder as she pressed her head into his hand. "I love you. If you love me, you'll make sure Orison gets better."

His gaze went to the matron who stood in the doorway smiling. Ashim inspected Orison's appearance; the cuts on her face were fully healed and she was no longer grey. He didn't want to peel back the blanket and check her leg after the injury incurred by the creature. It would also be weird in front of the matron.

"We got to you in time, thankfully," Ashim admitted to Orison. "Still waiting for the paperwork to say we're free. I'm sure Raj will give it to us soon."

Ashim scoffed out a laugh to himself as he traced over a line on the sheets. He was unsure why he was talking to Orison when she was unconscious; she couldn't respond. Lifting his head, it only just occurred to him that he was free after winning the necklace.

Resting his head on the bed, Ashim stayed in the tranquil room with Orison. He listened to the machine ticking away to her heartbeat. The whirring of the machine and Mahavu's soft purring lulled Ashim into oblivion.

The only sign that Ashim had fallen asleep was the matron placing her hand on his shoulder to wake him up. Lifting his head, he turned to the matron. "Visiting hours have ended, Mahrishan. Unfortunately, the cat can't stay."

He rubbed his eye with a groan and looked at Mahavu curled up on the pillow beside Orison's head. Ashim stretched with a yawn and stood up, still dazed from his nap. He scooped up Mahavu who wriggled in his arms with a growl; nipping at him. While trying to calm Mahavu, Ashim ran a hand through Orison's hair and adjusted her blanket.

"I have to go. I'll return soon, I promise."

Ashim held Mahavu to his chest; she continued to wriggle around with growls. He thanked the matron and vacated the room swiftly. Seeing Orison in that bed broke his heart. Ashim couldn't wait to see her smile and hear her laughter once more. With his hands tied, he could only focus on returning to his room.

THIRTY-THREE

A week later, a warm breeze flowed through Karshak Castle's infirmary. When the door to Orison's room opened, Ashim looked up from the side of her bed. He had been dozing in the chair beside Orison as Mahavu slept soundly on her chest. Since visitations were allowed, he rarely left Orison's side. Even when visitations were closed, he was always itching to return, needing to know she was okay. The machine still whirred to monitor her heartbeat and each time it lulled him to sleep.

"Good morning, Mahrishan," King Raj said in Karshakir as approached Orison, checking her over. "Are you well?"

"Morning, Your Majesty," Ashim replied glumly. He inched to the edge of his seat and fixed his clothes from the night before. He rubbed his hand over the stubble which had accumulated since he hadn't shaved since that fateful day. "I'm good. I will return to work immediately."

King Raj held his hand up. "No." The single word made Ashim pause. A scroll appeared in the king's hand; he extended it to Ashim. "I'm a man of my word."

Tentatively, Ashim wrapped his hand around the scroll. He already knew the contents because he had been waiting an entire week for it. Unravelling the scroll, his hand shook as he first laid eyes on his Runner contract. King Raj had kept it hidden away somewhere. A large red stamp covered the contract's terms, announcing his true freedom. Tears stung his eyes as he placed his hand over the brand.

"Thank you, Your Majesty," Ashim delighted.

"Erol was my first choice to gain freedom, however, he declined the offer," Raj announced. Ashim looked up at the king. "After forty years, he's understandably anxious about joining society. Bahlir has taken his place."

Ashim nodded. "Okay. That's fair." Clearing his throat. "Are you continuing Bahlir's treatment?"

"Of course I am." Raj glanced at Orison then at Ashim. "I'll give Orison her contract when she awakens, along with a proposition," King Raj continued. "I think you have some royal duties to uphold."

He frowned. "I'm not royal."

"Orison is next in line to the throne, Mahrishan. As her Equal, you will be her consort if you choose to marry," King Raj explained. Ashim stilled. "I can get an enchantress to remove your brand, if you wish."

Ashim placed his hand over his brand. "I wish for it to remain." With a nod, King Raj turned away. "Wait." The king turned back. "When will Orison awaken?"

She had been unconscious for a week now. Ashim craved her laughter, which was like his favourite song. He longed for the smile that lit his dark days and the comfort that her touch gave him. Her sacrifice won him his freedom, but he wanted Orison to be here for it.

"I'm unsure; her body has been through a great deal of shock." King Raj dipped his chin and fiddled with the keys on his belt. "Have patience, Mahrishan."

Turning to Orison, he settled beside her again, desperately wanting to hear her voice. He petted Mahavu, consequently waking her up; she purred at his touch. Ashim stroked a thumb on the bridge of Mahavu's nose the way she liked it, making her blink slowly. The cat sprawled out on Orison and stretched.

"Please heal her," he said to Mahavu.

Tiny claws came scarily close to Orison's throat, making Ashim's heart skip a beat. But in true cat fashion, Mahavu wouldn't harm people she liked.

He continued to pet the cat's sandy fur and rested his cheek on Orison's shoulder. Mahavu yawned, showing rows of razor-sharp teeth, then licked Orison. Ashim tensed and looked up when he saw Orison's eyelids flutter. She stirred and the machine on her wrist whirred louder.

"Ash," she croaked as her eyes opened.

He stood up, his chair clattered to the ground. "Ori? I'm here, Ori."

She slowly turned her head in his direction, lifting her hand to brush her fingers against his cheek. With a relieved smile, he crouched beside her and guided her hand to touch his skin. Movement out of the corner of his eye drew his attention to the door. Nurses filed in, wheeling a tray of medical utensils. Orison lowered her hand as she watched the spectacle.

"You're awake, are you well?" the head matron asked upon her approach.

Orison winced. "I'm feeling fine."

Ashim scooped Mahavu up and took a step back. Petting Mahavu's fur, he picked up his chair as the Healengales surrounded the bed, checking over Orison. He watched them check her leg where stitches criss-crossed over her thigh.

For the first time in a week, Ashim felt like a whole person. Orison's first words were calling for him. With her awake, Ashim felt he could move on and begin the next chapter of his life. He was free and could build his life without reporting to King Raj.

Ashim remained by Orison's bed for as long as he could, until the Healengales dismissed him and sent him back to his chambers.

Orison cupped a mug in her hands as Raj poured her some herbal tea. The sweet fruity smell emanated throughout the balcony of his chambers—like they were sitting near an orchard of strawberries and apples. She sank back in her seat, sipping the sweet drink. She admired the view of Haranshal with tranquillity, as she always did whenever she saw it. This enormous city had slowly become home.

"How is your leg?" Raj asked.

She massaged the large bandage on her thigh. "It's okay," Orison said truthfully. Despite having an Ifrit ram a couple of bones through her leg, it felt like nothing more than a pulled muscle. The king grinned while he ate a grape.

"I've been teaching you how to shield for a very specific reason. Why didn't you shield yourself this time?"

Orison grimaced. "I've gone without knowing how to shield for so long that I forgot I could do it."

He looked out at the city before them and pouted. They fell into a shared silence of eating and drinking. Orison had an idea that this tea party wasn't about celebrating her healing.

"You're a Mindelate, aren't you?" Raj finally asked. Orison nodded slowly. Raj extended his hand out. "Go into my mind and find the one of an old crone about five months ago."

Orison set her cup down and took Raj's hand. She dived into his head—to her surprise it was gold in appearance and full of moving pictures. As she looked through his memories, she found the one he talked about and dived in.

"You can't save the prince," a croaky voice echoed around the columns of King Raj's golden throne room.

The old crone was the seer she met in Parndore. She still had her eyes sewn shut, but her features had crevices with deep wrinkles and wispy white hair. The walking stick knocked against the stone floor as she approached where King Raj stood.

The king bowed. "Pleasure to see you again."

"Do you know why Alsaphus Castle marked Princess Orison as royal, though she holds no royal essence?" the seer questioned. *Raj shook his head.* "It foretold what would become of the prince. The castle protected itself."

"What's going on with Prince Xabian?" Raj asked.

The seer tapped her stick on the ground as she shifted. "He went into the portal while the curse was ending. It takes three days in the Othereal to clear. If the receiver of the curse goes into the mortal realm, the curse becomes permanent. That's a clause the enchantress didn't mention. The Nighthex will slowly consume him."

Orison's heart raced at the answer. It meant he was currently losing the battle in his head. So many questions finally had answers and she realised the reason behind Xabian's strange, erratic behaviour.

"Orison needs to buy a property with her Equal," the seer announced.

"Why is that?" Raj questioned.

"I've already said too much," the seer announced.

The seer walked away, leaving the bewildered king behind.

Orison pulled her hand away, severing the connection. The king remained silent as he sipped on his tea. She couldn't move as she contemplated what she had witnessed. Even though she didn't understand the seer's advice—like the first warning she had given—Orison refused to make the same mistake twice. The seer told her not to look for the prince and because she did, her life had turned upside down. Guilt hit Orison like a punch.

"Why are you showing me this?" Orison asked.

"I made you a Runner because of this prophecy," Raj explained. "I told you it was for protection and I also wanted to teach you the things Sila denied."

She cleared her throat. "I already don't trust Xabian. In Lhandahir, Bahlir told me about his actions while they trapped me in Alsaphus Castle. Maybe I shouldn't have trusted him from the start and I was a naïve bitch."

"Don't speak negatively of yourself, Orison. The Othereal is a foreign world to you; I would be in the same boat," Raj said quickly. "Given how much hatred Sila spewed at you, anybody nice would appear trustworthy."

Looking directly at the king, Orison asked, "The elixir you're giving Xabian, is that to slow down the curse?" The king nodded. "I pray he takes it."

They fell into a mutual silence as they basked in the shadows from the sun. Raj looked at his hand, then at Orison. She didn't want to go into his head again and discover more secrets that he kept from her. Except Raj didn't offer any more secrets; those were his to keep. Sharing that prophecy appeared like it took a weight off the king's conscience.

Tsunamal's docks were heaving with travellers and workers. Boots thundered on the wooden pier as men unloaded imports from far-off shores to Fallasingha. Ship's captains barked orders and the excited chatter of visitors made the entire atmosphere overwhelming. Ships of varying sizes bobbed on the ocean's waves.

At the beach, people relaxed with their children playing on the sand or in the water; some of them looked at the ships. Seagulls hovered in the warm air.

Navigating her way through the throng of passengers, Kinsley approached one of the grandest ships on the dock; with Aeson and Eloise by her side. Aeson adjusted the bag of their belongings—which was strapped across his chest—to endure a long voyage. The ship was solid wood and on its stern were three rows of windows which glistened in the sun. A carving of a mermaid was in the stern, with her arm outstretched. On deck, multiple sails hung from masts, one of which presented the Akornsonian emblem of a tree with an acorn—the emblem being the only sign that Kinsley had found the right ship.

She stood by a barrel and watched as one of the ship's men approached. "Excuse me, I need to speak with Vex."

"I'll get him for you." The shipman turned and his brown hair stirred as he returned to the ship.

Kinsley waited as butterflies fluttered in her stomach about her deception. Her fathers were going to yell at her and so would Saskia. She hadn't told anyone she was making this voyage. Exhaling a heavy breath, Kinsley ran a hand through her black hair. Eloise held her close and Aeson rubbed her shoulder for comfort. Regardless of her fate, she couldn't let panic get the better of her.

The creaking of wood turned Kinsley's attention to the ship. A man with a green and yellow embroidered tunic walked down the ramp and approached the triad. A large hat with a feather sticking out shadowed his face but the evidence of greying stubble showed through. There was no denying who the man was. She curtsied low when he stopped before them.

"What do you require?" He puffed his chest out, hand on the pommel of his sword.

Kinsley cleared her throat. "I know they have sent you off on a quest to retrieve Queen Orison and Prince Xabian, by King Idralis. My partners and I wish to assist you."

"Why?"

"I'm Queen Orison's lady-in-waiting," Kinsley declared. She stepped to one side. "My girlfriend is her personal healer and my boyfriend is her personal attendant. We're her staff and we have devoted ourselves to her service."

It was a gross exaggeration, but Kinsley would do anything to get on that ship. The captain's gaze roamed over each of them, placing a hand on his chin as he weighed matters up. Vex glanced at the ship, then returned his attention to the triad.

He gestured to the ship. "Your payment for passage is helping clean the ship and healing those who are sick. Understand?"

"Yes, Captain. Thank you." Kinsley curtsied.

"Follow me."

With another curtsy, Kinsley followed Vex up the docking ramp with Aeson and Eloise close behind. Once on deck, Kinsley steeled her nerves and walked across the platform. The lie got them on the ship and she was one step closer to helping Orison. The stairs creaked as she followed Vex towards the captain's office.

The office was an opulent room filled with gold and diamonds spilling out of treasure chests. Maps were strewn about on the captain's desk, along with compasses. There was a variety of fishing gear propped up against the walls. Vex gestured to the round table where there was a map laid out of their course from Yetnaloui, Akornsonia—to Haranshal, Karshakroh. Kinsley could see this was their only stop in Fallasingha before Karshakroh.

"Names?"

"What... what would you do with the names?" Kinsley asked.

Vex smirked. "I have to report them to the Regency of Fallasingha, then the kings of both Akornsonia and Karshakroh." Her heart hammered in her chest, knowing they would catch her.

Then Eloise piped up. "Eloise Aragh."

"Aeson Marshall," Aeson spoke.

"Kinsley Luxart."

The captain paused at her name and leaned across the desk. "Your father doesn't know you're here, does he?" She looked down. "That's why you're so nervous."

Kinsley stood up with a curtsy. "Sorry for wasting your time." She turned to leave until Vex spoke again.

"I didn't say you could leave." She sat back down and clasped her hands in her lap. "I am still giving you safe passage to assist your friend. Princess Orison doesn't know me; we need somebody she recognises. You three are a blessing in disguise."

She relaxed significantly at his declaration. "Thank you, Captain."

Vex inspected the keys on the wall; he plucked one up and placed it on the table. "This is your room. Lady Aragh, you'll be below deck with the sick. Lady Luxart and Sir Marshall, you will assist with dinner at five o'clock sharp. You may go to your room downstairs."

Kinsley stood up again and curtsied. Aeson took the key and led Kinsley and Eloise out of the captain's office. Once outside, Kinsley closed her eyes and basked in the sea air. Despite her fathers not knowing her whereabouts, she was on the ship. She would apologise to her parents when she returned home.

THIRTY-FOUR

Saskia's hurried footsteps echoed around the stairwell of Alsaphus Castle. Rounding the corner to the office, she could see Taviar through the glass doors. Crossing the threshold, Saskia used her magic to throw the doors open.

"Kinsley is on a ship to Karshakroh!" she announced breathlessly.

The correspondence she received made her race to Cardenk to check if another Kinsley Luxart had boarded a ship to Karshakroh. Only to find the home she shared with Eloise and Aeson was empty.

Taviar looked up from the legislation he was reading, eyes wide. "Are you sure?"

"I got the ship's log from the Sleeping Siren; Kinsley's name is down as a passenger along with Eloise and Aeson."

Throwing the piles of parchment down, Taviar pushed himself away from the desk and ran to the door. She followed him out of the office, picking up her skirts as she ran down the winding staircase. Her breathing came out in pants from running up and down the staircase.

Navigating their way to the castle entrance which led to Merchant's Row, Taviar threw the exterior door open and made his way into the street. Saskia continued to follow him outside, looking around at guards who paused when Taviar passed by like a thunderous storm. She noticed his hands balled into fists.

They swiftly made their way through Merchant's Row, all the way to Riddle Me This, where Taviar threw the door open. Saskia paused in the doorway when Yil and Zade looked up from some books set up on the cashier's desk.

"Where's your sister?" Taviar demanded, with his hands on his hips. The twins exchanged glances. "Boys, your sister was supposed to be looking after you today. Where is she?"

"Out," Zade answered.

Saskia's eyes widened. She glanced at Taviar when he let out an exasperated breath. "Zade Axel Luxart, where is out?"

"Tsunamal."

Looking down at her feet, Saskia fidgeted with her dress when an uncomfortable silence settled around the room. Taviar buried his head in his hands and crouched onto the floor with a loud groan. Saskia squatted next to him and placed her hand on his back. She shushed him and tried to calm him down.

"Where's Riddle?" Saskia asked softly.

"Helping family move to Tsunamal. Kins was supposed to look after the boys while he was there," Taviar explained. His eyes glazed over with tears as he looked at the twins.

Zade stamped his feet and folded his arms. "We are ten!"

"You should have found us immediately," Saskia reprimanded.

"We're fine," Yil retorted. "If anything happened, we could have gone to the neighbours."

She returned to soothing Taviar as his shoulders shifted while he broke down. It was unknown why Kinsley had kept this a secret from everybody. It had also been wholly irresponsible to leave her brothers to fend for themselves.

"Why couldn't she talk to us?" Taviar asked quietly. "We usually talk about everything."

"Maybe she was afraid we'd say no," Saskia offered.

"For Orison and Xabian to return safely to Fallasingha, we would have agreed. She only needed to talk," Taviar said.

Despite her anger at the situation, Saskia could only hope Kinsley returned to Fallasingha triumphantly with Orison and Xabian. Her decision was easily forgivable as long as she came home.

Ashim made his way through the winding corridors of the Royal Visitor Wing in Karshak Castle. The tunnel-like structures had intricate paintings decorating the walls, which were illuminated by Othereal lights in their sconces; with occasional breaks of colour. He clutched books to his chest, determined to get back to his chambers and study the Equal bond—to understand his connection with Orison better.

Room Twelve was at the end of a corridor. Ashim used his knee to steady the books and cradled them in the crook of his arm; he used his elbow to push the door handle down. After a week of staying there, the entire room was still the most luxurious sight he had laid eyes upon.

Stone brick walls greeted him, tapering off to the rocky alcove where the bed was suspended from the ceiling over a rock pool. Floor to ceiling arched windows looked over Haranshal, providing the perfect view of the ocean. A dining table sat in front of the window and near the door was a brown seating area around a fireplace.

"Ashim?" Orison called.

He jumped when he heard her voice and the books fell to the floor with loud thuds. Swearing under his breath, he crouched down and picked them up. Orison sat up in bed and her hand roamed over the white sheet around her legs. He extended his hand in front of him, not wanting her to move out of bed to assist him; knowing that her leg was still healing. She had to rest to get back to her full strength.

"Sorry," he blurted. "Go back to sleep."

"I wasn't sleeping, only resting. What are all those books?" The chains on the bed rattled as Orison inched to the edge. "Do you want me to teach you more of the common tongue?"

Ashim staggered to his feet and hugged the books to his chest. "Ah, anesh!" He laughed nervously, then looked down at them. Orison tilted her head. "You won't be able to read these; they're in Karshakir. Rest."

With a frown, she settled back. "Ashim Mahrishan," she said sternly. "Tell me."

He stepped closer to her with a sigh and nudged the door closed. "We're Equals."

"Well, it's about time you admitted it!" Orison exclaimed with laughter. Ashim froze and frowned. She tutted. "I thought I would have to say something."

"You... you knew?" Ashim stammered.

Orison guffawed. "Yes, I knew. I heard you say *Tahanbashri* in Lhandahir after the Ifrit incident." She looked down at her hands. "I was waiting for you to tell me after I woke up."

"Oh..." He cleared his throat. "I've been doing research on the Equal Bond to understand it, so I know what I'm getting into, if we accept." Ashim looked down at the books. "If I'm honest, I'm scared about it."

He clutched the books tighter when Orison tapped the space beside her. Ashim hurried over to the bed and walked over the stepping stones leading up to it. He placed the books on the bed before climbing on; the chains rattled with the movement and the bed swayed gently. Ashim kicked off his sandals and got into a comfortable position, then opened several books to bookmarked pages.

"Tell me what you discovered," Orison coaxed.

He tapped a section of the book, looking at Orison. "We already know the Equal bond is soul mates. But both parties must consensually accept the bond—by making love or exchanging blood on a full moon."

"Exchange blood?" Orison asked, taken aback.

Ashim ran his finger over the line. "To not go through the sexual route, both parties have to cut the palms of their hands and press them together for their souls to merge."

"So that's how Akhili accepted the bond," Orison muttered under her breath.

He paused. "Akhili is Equalled?"

Orison nodded. "His Equal isn't attracted to men; they accepted it for the power benefits. Now I understand how it happened."

Usually, all the Runners knew everything about each other. Akhili had kept that piece of information about himself well hidden.

Orison's hair brushed against the back of his hand as she leaned into the book, running her finger over the line which he knew she couldn't decipher. Ashim could smell the citrus scent in her hair and he could see her face furrowed in deep concentration.

"What happens if you reject it?" Orison asked.

Ashim focused on the books, flicking through the pages. "Nothing really." He massaged his arm as he read. "You'll always feel the pull of the bond and have enhanced powers when they're around. That's about it." He rubbed his chest, feeling that familiar tugging in his chest at that moment. "With how annoying the pull is, I think people accept the bond to make it stop. But the bond doesn't have to be romantic."

"Is that what that is?" Orison asked with her hand on her chest. "I thought I was imagining the tugging sensation whenever you were around."

He nodded in confirmation. "Anesh, you weren't imagining it." He shifted. "We could remain friends, we don't have to be involved romantic..."

"I love you, Ashim," Orison interrupted. His eyes widened. "I first realised it while we were in Lhandahir, when we were travelling through the city for the first time."

He closed one of the books. "You're not saying that because we are Equal?"

Orison's hand pressed to his cheek and made him gaze into her eyes. "This has nothing to do with the bond we may share. I don't know why I feel this way, but I do." She tried to move her hand, but he covered it with his own, keeping her there. He looked at her lips; she averted her gaze. "And I can understand if you don't feel the same way."

"I love you too," Ashim said quickly, before the moment slipped away.

She looked into his eyes and sucked in a shuddering breath; she relaxed at his admission. He pulled her into his chest and continued to scan the books between them. They needed to understand if they wanted the bond and consent to something that would change their lives irrevocably.

The city of Haranshal scattered across the shoreline. Homes and businesses on the winding road up to Karshak Castle loomed over the city like a watchful eye. The architecture clashed, but it's what made the city unique. Mud homes were more equipped for Karshakroh's tropical climate than the timber-framed structures.

Kinsley, Eloise and Aeson stepped off the Sleeping Siren, taking in the surrounding sights. The night air sent a chill down Kinsley's spine. She looked around from the dock, wondering where Orison would be; it could take her days to find her.

"Where would Orison be located?" Eloise asked Vex.

Vex shrugged. "I suspect the castle, but nobody is permitted to see the king." He walked past the triad to a guard that waited for Vex's paperwork. "Go find a tavern to spend the night. Meet me in the morning at nine when we return."

Aeson looped his arm around Kinsley and Eloise, then moved towards the city. He tried to guide Kinsley away from the docks, but she shrugged out of his hold, defying what Vex had ordered. She needed to see Orison and refused to be denied if she was in the castle.

Kinsley approached the guard, who Vex conversed with and placed her hand on the wooden table. "I request to see the king," Kinsley said sternly.

The guard laughed. "Doesn't everybody?" He stamped Vex's documents as she looked at the elven captain, who smirked and uttered the words *told you*. "Run along, ma'am."

"I'm Princess Orison's lady-in-waiting and I need to see her," Kinsley demanded. "Along with her other staff."

The guard glanced over Kinsley's shoulder at Aeson and Eloise who stood behind her. They both kept their heads down. With a sigh, the guard grabbed some paper and scribbled down a note. It disappeared into oblivion, then he drummed his fingers on the table. She smiled sweetly as she waited for an answer about whether this would work. It had to—Orison could vouch for them.

Another piece of parchment appeared on the desk shortly afterwards. The guard unravelled it and gave an exasperated sigh. He waved over another guard, clutching the paper in his hand. Kinsley pushed her shoulders back and smiled when the two guards communicated in Karshakir about her request. She was convinced she had gotten somewhere.

Dread overcame her as several guards holding manacles stepped out of the shadows. Kinsley's eyes widened with shock. Her attention turned to Aeson when he grunted, as guards shoved his hands behind his back and into the manacles. They did the same to Eloise and Kinsley—who cried out. The trio struggled in their constraints.

The guards talked in Karshakir. Kinsley had never been taught the language and didn't understand a thing they were saying. She whimpered when they dragged her away from the dock and they were all thrown into the back of an awaiting black carriage.

Being transported to Karshak Castle happened in a blur. Kinsley struggled against her manacles, watching her boyfriend and girlfriend do the same. She wondered if this was how King Raj treated all his guests. Hearing the loud click of the drawbridge being lowered, she tried peering out the window, but the guard in the back of the carriage quickly pulled the curtains closed.

The drawbridge settled with the scraping of stone. Kinsley gasped when she heard the crack of a whip; the carriage jolted as it resumed its journey into the castle. She trembled profusely, realising she had made a fatal mistake and should have listened to the ship's captain. Her desires had clouded her judgement.

A cry filled the Karshak Castle throne room as guards guided Orison inside. Three trembling figures were kneeling before King Raj, who slouched in his throne and stared down at them. One was wearing a lilac dress; another had a white dress on and the third one wore a white shirt with black trousers. Her gaze roamed over the manacles on their wrists, all of them chained together. Loud sobs escaped one captive. Orison's heart pounded against her rib cage, as she picked up the pace despite the guards' leisurely movements.

The nearer to the throne she got, the more she recognised the trembling people at his feet. A loud gasp escaped her when she realised it was Kinsley, Aeson and Eloise. She thought of Raj as an ally, but after doing this, Orison didn't know what to think.

"These assassins came off a ship from Akornsonia, claiming to be your staff. What do you want to do with them?" King Raj inquired.

Orison recoiled and looked at him. She placed her hands on her hips. "These are my staff, *not* assassins. I demand you unchain them at once!"

The king's eyes widened with surprise, clicking his fingers frantically. Guards stepped away from their posts and approached the triad with keys. They removed the manacles which fell to the stone floor with metallic clanks. Orison crouched before the three of them and pulled them all into hugs; thankful they were there, after not seeing them in months. They held her close, sighing in relief that they were no longer held captive.

"Are you all well?" she asked.

Orison checked each one of them over, finding nothing more than red marks from the manacles. She lingered at Kinsley, noticing her tear-stained face. Aeson wiped her tears away and kissed her gently before he tended to Eloise. It wasn't the type of reunion she wanted with her friends. Guiding them over to the nearby sofas, she ensured they got comfortable before she confronted the king.

"Apologies, Princess, we can't be too careful," Raj advised.

Orison turned around. "You should have spoken to me first before arresting them." He nodded as he looked at them. She balled her hands into fists. "Their presence here means my time in Haranshal and Karshakroh has ended. When is the ship home?"

"Nine in the morning," Kinsley said, with her head down. "Tomorrow."

She nodded. "Please prepare a guest room for my staff with adequate meals."

"Your wish is my command, Princess," the king declared.

Summoning servants, he spoke to them in Karshakir. Orison could only assume it was a request to get her friends' room ready for the night. She crouched before them once more, trying to reassure them that being here was okay. She had already established Raj didn't have the best people skills. When everything calmed down, she would have to introduce them to Ashim—Orison was excited to tell them everything.

"Can I take them to my chambers?" Orison asked. Raj nodded. "Ensure you send food there and give us notice when the room is ready, please."

Taking her friends' hands, she Misted all three of them to her chambers. With her training from Ashim and Erol, her range of Misting had improved; no longer did she get burnt out by transporting multiple people. She could do so much more with her power, thanks to her friends who she had made in the mortal realm; even if Ashim was so much more than a friend after discovering he was her Equal.

Kinsley, Aeson and Eloise admired the grand room that made up Orison's chambers, along with the magnificent view of Haranshal from the window and her bed's alcove.

"This is where King Raj put me after I won my freedom," Orison announced.

Kinsley tiptoed across the stepping stones towards the bed. "It's beautiful. I thought you were in a dungeon sleeping on the floor." She collapsed on the bed. "This is so comfortable."

"I've been staying with Ashim." Orison pushed her hair behind her ear. "Otherwise, I would have been sleeping on the streets of Haranshal."

Servants filed into the room, placing a buffet of food in the centre of the table. Aeson and Eloise were drawn towards it as they smelt the rich aroma of the various spices common in Karshakroh. The servants kept silent as they set plates down and poured drinks.

"Ashim?" Eloise asked as she looked at the dishes.

"He and his friend Erol prevented me from dying in the mortal realm. He's also been helping to improve my powers," Orison explained with a beaming smile. "And he's my Equal."

Eloise stumbled as she walked to the tower of plates Her jaw fell open as she focused on Orison, then at Aeson and Kinsley. The room suddenly fell silent, apart from the servants' shuffling feet while they were busy working.

"You found your Equal?" Kinsley asked as she climbed off the bed; chains rattled as the bed swung. "Have you accepted the bond?"

Shaking her head, Orison clasped her hands together. "We're both confused about what it means and when we figure that out, we'll decide if we want to accept."

Kinsley approached Orison. She took her hands and led her over to the seating area, where she sat her down with a grin. Shifting in her seat, Orison glanced at Aeson and Eloise who were choosing what they wanted to eat; the smell alone made her mouth water and her stomach growl despite the fact she had dinner earlier.

"You could have sent us a letter asking for advice. All three of us are Equal," Kinsley said, gesturing to her boyfriend and girlfriend.

Orison's jaw fell open. "You can have more than one Equal?"

"If you're polyamorous like we are," Kinsley said with glee. "But most monogamous people only get one."

A knock at the door made Orison move her hands out of Kinsley's grasp. She hurried across the expanse of her bedroom towards the door. She thought it might be a servant saying the triad's room was ready. When she opened the door, she gasped at Xabian who leaned against the wall; his gaze lifted to hers before he surged forward.

THIRTY-FIVE

Orison staggered back as Xabian pushed his way into the room. She pressed herself against the door and kept a close eye on him. She noticed his hands trembled as he rubbed at the stubble on his chin. The others didn't appear to notice as they ate their food in silence. Xabian advanced on Orison and grabbed her wrist.

"We need to leave, now," Xabian whispered.

Orison tore out of his grasp and glared at him. "We're leaving tomorrow." She gestured to her friends. "They're here with a ship."

Orison couldn't trust anything Xabian said after discovering he was an accomplice in Sila's sick game—despite her pang of guilt knowing that inside his mind, the Nighthex consumed him bit by bit. After Sila placed the curse on him, the man Xabian used to be didn't exist. Xabian paced around the entrance to Orison's chambers. He rolled up the sleeves on his black tunic and huffed out a breath; his purple eyes flared.

"King Raj is trying to poison me—the injections and pills," Xabian whispered. "He's trying to kill me."

Folding her arms over her chest, Orison pouted. "You can trust him; the medication is there to help you. You're sick and still recovering from the curse." She watched as Eloise approached. "Does the medication make you feel bad?"

Xabian shook his head and interlocked his hands at the back of his neck as he leaned his head back with a groan. He kept shaking his head and fell to his knees. Eloise hastened her approach and crouched beside Xabian, placing her hand on his back to comfort him. Unlike Orison, she had no way of knowing what was happening to Xabian.

Placing her hand on Eloise's shoulder, Orison said to her mind, *Xabian is being consumed by the Nighthex; he needs the medication to prevent it. He doesn't know.*

Orison watched as realisation dawned on her friend and sadness clouded her features. The grip on Xabian's back tightened until Eloise's hand glowed as she tried to heal him, but she tore her hand away when she noticed she couldn't.

"Answer Orison's question. What does the medication make you feel like?" Eloise coaxed.

Xabian looked up. "They stop my head hurting all the time and I feel calmer."

"Then that means the medication is working. I don't think King Raj is poisoning you, Xabian, if it's making you feel better." Eloise rubbed his arm.

Crouching in front of him, Orison stared at the prince. "Do you know what you're taking?"

He shook his head, then took out a metal syringe of purple liquid from a pocket in his trousers. Eloise painstakingly plucked it from his grasp. She examined it with a frown as she turned it over. Her hands glowed as she identified what was in the vial. Orison saw Eloise's shoulders relax, which indicated the medicine was good.

"It's Nuit Root, perfectly fine," Eloise said, keeping hold of the syringe.

"What does it do?" Xabian asked.

She looked at him, then her gaze fell on Orison. "It's a muscle relaxant, for when you feel angry. It'll make you feel as you described. You don't want to be an enemy, do you?"

Orison sat on the floor. *What does it actually do?*

Slows down curses, Eloise replied.

While Xabian rocked on the floor, Orison stifled a gasp when Eloise plunged the syringe into the vein in his neck. Xabian wailed as she administered the medication. He scrambled away from Eloise, holding his neck as he panted heavily with eyes widened in fear.

"You're on his side!" Xabian screamed.

Eloise sighed. "Your hands were shaking, I needed to make you relax."

"Traitors, the lot of you!" Xabian panted as he looked around, his eyes glazed with tears. He continued touching his neck where a trail of blood ran down onto his tunic.

The door opened and Ashim strolled in with Bahlir. His attention turned immediately to the prince who thrashed about against the wall. Orison winced at the spectacle, glancing at Kinsley and Aeson, who had abandoned their meals to gather around.

Bahlir crouched beside Eloise and cast a nervous glance at Orison, who looked at the floor. Exhaling a breath, he sang a song in Karshakir and closed his eyes. In an instant, the prince's face went blank and he suddenly became calm. The song quickly ended when his voice became strained and he breathed heavily. Pushing his hair from his eyes, he saw Xabian blink like he was in a daze. The prince was too far gone for anybody to save.

Nazareth walked behind King Idralis as he entered the office in Alsaphus Castle. She saw Taviar near the fireplace looking over a map that had some points marked with pins. Saskia was pacing the room, muttering to herself. A bad feeling settled on Nazareth's shoulders as they came to a stop before them.

The Regent looked up from the map and stood to shake hands with Idralis and Nazareth. He gestured to the armchairs opposite him. Nazareth sat on the edge of the seat to check on the map, which marked the ports along Fallasingha and Akornsonia's coastlines. She frowned and turned to her king for an explanation; he appeared just as clueless as he rubbed the stubble on his chin.

"What is this for?" Idralis gestured to the map.

Taviar sat back down with a heavy breath. "Good news first or bad news?"

"Bad news first," Idralis decided.

"According to letters from Kinsley, something is wrong with Prince Xabian. I don't know the details at this point and neither does she."

Nazareth's jaw fell open at the announcement. She looked at Taviar in bewilderment, then at Saskia, who had stopped pacing to listen to the conversation. Many scenarios flowed through Nazareth's head, like a grave sickness was to blame, or another curse.

"Do you know if it's an illness?" Idralis asked. With a solemn expression, Taviar shook his head.

"And what's the good news?" Nazareth pushed.

"The Sleeping Siren will embark on its voyage back to Tsunamal tomorrow morning. Our future queen is coming home!" Taviar announced.

King Idralis punched the air with a resounding *yes* before he sank back into his chair. Nazareth raised an eyebrow at him and returned her attention to Taviar. At least their search for Orison and Xabian had ended.

Idralis looked at the map and tapped Tsunamal. "I can get Nazareth to meet them in Tsunamal to assist with the journey home and monitor Xabian's condition." She made to protest, but he continued. "They'll need protection."

She couldn't deny about them needing protection. With a sigh, Nazareth moved her hair over her shoulder and slouched in her chair. Her only relief was her walking stick to tackle the countless narrow stairs to get anywhere. Tsunamal's brutal terrain and scorching climate always made her feel like she had done an intense training session with the army.

"Okay, I'll do it," Nazareth breathed. She stretched with a loud groan. "But you owe me chocolate at the end."

Idralis let out a laugh with a shake of his head. She needed the chocolate if she was going to climb all those stairs and risk the pain that followed from all the climbing. Nazareth had been to Tsunamal on some missions and almost always left in pain with a bruised ego.

"Fine, chocolate, if you insist. You have five days to prepare, Naz," Idralis declared with a smile. "I have a secret holiday home in Tsunamal they can stay in."

At least she had time to prepare, both mentally and physically, for a trip to Tsunamal. Part of her was almost excited to see Orison again, but she was most curious about Xabian. Nazareth wanted to know what had become of him.

The following morning, loud meows emanated out of an iron cage. Ashim tried to shush Mahavu as he walked on the docks towards the ship, but the cat continued to wail protests about being caged. Beside Ashim, Orison kept up their brisk pace and glanced down at Mahavu in her cage. She took the cage from his hand and held it to her chest; Mahavu quietened down slightly and her wails came in longer intervals.

Haranshal's docks were unusually quiet at eight in the morning; only a handful of workers and travellers roamed about from one ship to another. Even the beach was void of people. Captains hollered at each other and visitors excitedly chattered as they stepped onto Karshakroh's shores for the first time.

They approached a large ship with a mermaid carved into its stern, flanked by three rows of windows. The sight made Ashim's jaw fall open. He had been on many ships during his time as a Runner, but nothing this grand. He was so caught up in looking at the ship that it took Xabian all his strength to pull Ashim towards the ramp and snap him out of his reverie. Part of Ashim wanted to explore the staterooms, but he knew that was highly unlikely for a peasant like him.

Following everybody on deck, he continued to hear the sounds of Mahavu's wailing as he went up the stairs to the captain's office, where everybody crowded inside. He glanced at the cage in Orison's arms and rolled his eyes; Mahavu had taken to shoving her face into the bars before meowing. It wasn't time to let her out yet.

The captain's office had shelves full of memorabilia from many voyages and fishing equipment scattered around. The most notable feature was gold—lots of gold spilling out of treasure chests. Through the wall of windows, there was a faint line on the horizon where the dark-blue sea met the light-blue sky. A man sat at the desk, with a large feather hat, which he took off, revealing long strands of light-brown hair. Judging by the lack of glowing in his eyes, he was an elf. He gestured for them to have a seat; Orison settled down, talking in a hushed voice as she fussed over Mahavu.

"I'm Captain Vex. Nice to meet you, Queen Orison and Prince Xabian; with guests," the captain spoke.

Xabian baulked as he sat down. "Queen Orison?" He gestured to Orison. "She's a princess."

Orison looked up from Mahavu's cage. "I'm not a queen until my coronation, Captain."

"You're set to be queen?" Xabian asked.

"Yes, I am set to be queen and with Ashim as my Equal. He is my king consort if we get married." Orison returned to Mahavu when she wailed loudly.

He scoffed and shook his head. "What a fucking joke!" Xabian looked between them, then scoffed loudly. "Ashim can barely speak the common tongue and you don't know fuck all about the Othereal."

"King Raj has been teaching me daily," Orison retorted. "And Ashim can speak the common tongue, but he gets anxious." She turned to the captain. "Apologies."

Xabian sat back with a snarl. Ashim glared at the prince, then gave the captain a warm smile. He shook Captain Vex's hand as a way of greeting.

"I am Ashim, good sir," he announced.

The captain nodded. His brown eyes lingered on Xabian before returning his attention to Orison, then Ashim. Ashim wondered if Vex could sense there was something wrong with the prince. Orison stood up and made Ashim sit down; she sat on his lap and cooed over Mahavu as she growled.

"Do you have veterinary paperwork for the feline?" Vex asked.

"*Halek*," Ashim said. He fished the papers out of his pocket and handed them over. "She's in good health. No fleas and very good at catching mice."

Vex read through the paperwork with a nod. "Welcome Mahavu Mahrishan." He filed the paperwork away and looked at everybody. "I'll give you, Queen Orison, the royal suite—so to speak. It's underneath my quarters."

"Orison's already explained she's not queen yet. She needs a coronation," Xabian snapped.

Vex gave Xabian a lethal, calm smile as he handed Xabian a key. "I am aware, Prince Xabian. Get some rest and calm that temper. Your room is downstairs." The captain sat back; his leather chair creaked. "We also have running water; enjoy a soak in the tub or take a shower. This meeting is done."

Before Vex could hand Ashim his own separate key, Orison spoke up. "Can Ashim and I share a room, please?"

He looked around as the office fell silent, all attention was on them. Vex nodded. "Of course, be on your way, then. Enjoy the journey."

Ashim was glad Orison spoke up and that Vex asked nothing. King Raj's scheming antics in Lhandahir had strengthened their relationship in that way. It drove them to admit their feelings for one another.

Mahavu still wailed from her cage as Ashim followed Orison back onto the deck. As they made their way down the stairs, he couldn't help notice the glare that Xabian shot at him; his purple eyes flared by doing so. It made Ashim slow his pace until the prince disappeared through a door. It made little sense why Xabian would suddenly hate him again, until he remembered it wasn't the original prince who boarded this ship.

THIRTY-SIX

Orison covered her mouth as she tried to stifle a retch. She turned the door handle of the bathroom in their bedchambers; finding it locked. Another lurch of the ship against the waves had her stomach doing somersaults. She retched and tried not to vomit all over the floor as she used her magic to unlock the door—despite knowing Ashim was in the bath. It swung open and she hurried inside.

"Sorry," she managed to blurt out. "I won't look."

Wooden walls greeted her. It took everything to keep her eyes off the bath where Ashim soaked in the water. The toilet was nothing more than a bench with a hole in it, which dropped directly into the sea below. She crouched before it and violently threw up.

The ship rocked intensely again. Orison pressed a hand to her stomach when it sloshed around and she groaned loudly. She rested her forehead on her hand and waited for the nausea and dizziness to subside. She'd never had travel sickness before; however, Orison had never been on a ship before, either. There was something about the choppy movements from the sea and having no break from it, which made things worse. Orison could safely declare she hated travelling by sea and couldn't wait to get off the ship.

She heard water splash behind her and the rustle of fabric. A hand gently pressed to her back. "Feeling better?" Ashim asked.

Orison let out a weak groan as the boat rocked again. She did a double take when she realised that he was naked, with only a towel to cover his lower half.

Having already seen him shirtless, which she didn't mind; it was the fact that only the towel prevented her from seeing anything else—towels weren't the most secure clothing item.

"Sorry for ruining your bath; there was nothing in the room," Orison explained.

Despite her hair already being tied into a ponytail, Ashim pushed back a fallen strand. "I'd rather you ruin my bath than ruin the room, Little Queen." She groaned and pressed a hand to her stomach again as the boat swayed. "You've never been on a ship before, have you?"

"No." Orison closed her eyes as dizziness overwhelmed her. With a wave of his hand, a steaming mug of tea appeared. The scent of ginger filled the room. "Thank you."

She sipped it gently. Ashim remained by Orison's side, his bath forgotten for the time being. The door remained open and Mahavu came strutting inside. Orison smiled when Ashim let out an exasperated groan.

"You should have closed the door," Ashim said with a smile. "This cat watches me on the toilet and tries to swim in the bath."

Orison laughed, which she instantly regretted as her stomach lurched and cramped. She groaned as she curled up, holding Mahavu when she jumped into her lap. She had undoubtedly made a special bond with this animal.

"We have to go to Captain Vex's dinner soon," Orison groaned. "I don't feel like eating."

Ashim shook his head. "Don't go. Stay and relax here. You'll feel better than forcing yourself to eat."

She sipped on her tea, looking at Ashim over the rim. Most men would say she was being dramatic, to suck the sickness up and go regardless; but Ashim wasn't most men. This was her Equal. Orison gasped as he scooped her up; she held Mahavu steady on her lap as he carried her bridal-style into the room.

Their bed-chambers were too luxurious to say it was on a ship. A wall of windows encased in gold greeted them; looking through them, it was pure darkness outside. There was a double bed pushed against the corner next to the window, providing a perfect view to wake up to. A chest was at the foot of the bed and a large table in the adjacent corner—to eat in style.

Orison appreciated the way Ashim gently laid her down and set her cup on the window ledge. He grabbed some clothes from his travel bags and disappeared behind the divider as he got dressed. She snuggled under the sheets, allowing Mahavu to run around the double bed. Orison watched the bedroom door as Ashim disappeared; leaving her alone. Her head felt too heavy to lift, now that she was lying down. She stared at the wooden ceiling and noticed its rose looked like the sun. There were many unique and interesting details she had to explore on her voyage. The sound of the door opening made her look towards it; Ashim had returned with a wooden bucket and a dishrag.

It surprised Orison when he set the bucket down beside her pillow and he hurried into the bathroom with the rag; moments later, he placed it on her head. She held the damp cloth in place as she rolled onto her back, staring at the black abyss outside. Now she had permission to remain in bed, all she wanted to do was sleep.

"Is seasickness normal?" Orison asked.

"*Halek*," Ashim replied as he used his magic to free Orison's hair from the ponytail. "Get some rest. I'll tell Captain Vex you're sick."

Orison nodded and closed her eyes. After a few moments she drifted off into a dreamless sleep, where sickness didn't overwhelm her senses and she could relax in a warm bed.

The captain's chambers were luxurious—like Orison's and Ashim's room, there was a wall of windows and a panel on either side. An alcove underneath the stairs had a four-poster bed. Next to the wall of windows was a roaring fireplace. Ashim didn't think it was safe to have one on a wooden ship; regardless, it cast out the cold ocean breeze. A large circular table dominated the centre of the room.

A feast had been prepared for Ashim and the rest of the gang from Fallasingha. In the table's centre was a large decadent turkey, surrounded by links of sausages. A variety of roasted vegetables sat in silver platters; set upon trays were fresh crab and lobster, along with grilled fish. The banquet looked magnificent and succulent in the chandelier's warm light. Servants stood in the shadows, only coming out to serve wine.

Captain Vex sat at the head of the table, his plate topped with a variety of food. To his left sat Xabian who silently ate a chicken wing. Kinsley, Aeson and Eloise sat to his right. Ashim was at the foot of the table, where Orison would have sat if she wasn't sick.

Ashim looked down at the lobster on his plate; he swiftly removed the shell and large pieces of lobster meat adorned his plate. He placed the shell in a metal bin near him and sucked the buttery grease off his fingers. One of his favourite luxury foods was lobster, but he wasn't able to afford to indulge properly.

"It's a shame Orison isn't feeling well enough to join us," Vex said as he ate some chicken. Ashim nodded.

Xabian placed his knife and fork down on the table. "What did you do to her?" His hands balled into fists. "Did you poison her?"

"You'd be foolhardy to try to poison somebody with a Healengale as a friend," Kinsley retorted. "She has seasickness, not that it's any of your concern."

Ashim grinned as he piled his fork with vegetables and meat. It was different to the spiced food he ate in Karshakroh. There wasn't the kick of heat at the back of his throat; in some ways, it tasted bland. He sat back in his seat as he ate in silence.

"I wasn't talking to you," Xabian spat.

"As long as she rests, that's the main thing," Eloise interjected, turning to Ashim. "I'll go to your chambers soon and give her a remedy."

Ashim gave her a thankful nod, glad that a Healengale could give Orison some relief during her days at sea. It would help her in the long run.

"Miss Luxart, how did you get past your fathers?" Vex asked, to change the subject.

Kinsley wiped her mouth on the napkin and nodded. She explained how she came to be in Karshakroh, defying her fathers with a plan she had worked on for two months. Occasionally Aeson would cut in to explain parts she missed. Ashim looked between them and laughed when they initially thought Orison and Xabian were in danger.

"They were fine in Karshakroh, until Lhandahir," Ashim interjected as he ate.

The diners' attention turned to him. Clearing his throat, he licked butter from his fingers and explained what happened in Lhandahir with the Ifrit incident. Ashim glanced at everybody who stared at him in horror at the descriptions of the catacombs and the ordeal they had. He knew he should stop, but he'd never had the chance to vent about it before.

Xabian interrupted when he slammed his hand down on the table; it made everyone jump. "I still find it reckless that *you* took Orison to Lhandahir."

Eloise glared at him. "They didn't have a choice, at least she's alive and well, regardless of her current ailment." Xabian reached for his alcohol, but with a click of Eloise's finger, it disappeared. "You've had too much to drink. Servants, he's cut off."

Xabian baulked at her authoritative tone. Ashim remained silent as Xabian's purple-coloured eyes widened and focused on Eloise. As he continued to observe the prince, his heart sank to see a silent cry for help in Xabian's eyes; as though a kind part of him couldn't verbalise what he felt. Nobody knew how to help him, either. Somewhere, deep inside Xabian, there had to be a kind man.

"Apologies, I'm still getting used to everything that's happened since waking up," Xabian said more calmly.

With a sharp intake of breath, Kinsley glanced at him as she cut some steak. "We feel the same way, a lot has changed."

As she ate, Aeson placed a hand on her shoulder. Xabian's outburst had caused an awkward silence to settle around the room. Instead of a reunion, it turned into a battle of wits against a prince who refused to take his medication.

When Ashim looked at Xabian, the prince's gaze burned into him. He could assume Xabian was jealous that fate had chosen Orison to be queen instead of him being king. Plus, there was the fact it had chosen Ashim to be her Equal; something Xabian didn't know yet. Ashim didn't understand why Xabian had to be jealous about her being queen, especially in his condition.

"Have you ever been to Tsunamal, Ashim?" Kinsley asked; to break the silence.

Ashim shook his head. "Only passing through—we never stayed there when they sent us on missions to Fallasingha," he answered.

"I don't see why we can't spend a couple of days in Tsunamal," Eloise piped up. "Then we can Mist back to Alsaphus Castle. At least it wouldn't take two weeks on horseback."

Everybody, except for Xabian and Vex, nodded their agreement to the plan. They had to get to Alsaphus Castle somehow. The excitement made Ashim giddy, imagining what Tsunamal had to offer and what he would see. As he left Karshakroh, he braced himself for a new adventure in Fallasingha.

Ashim eased into the luxurious bed-chambers with a bowl of broth. He immediately checked on Orison, who slept soundly, with Mahavu curled up beside her. The only sign she had woken up during his time away was her change of clothes. He tilted his head when he noticed she wore one of his beige shirts. With a shrug, he moved towards the dining table at the foot of the bed.

He set the bowl down on the table with a clink. Judging by her sickly green complexion, she wouldn't want to eat anytime soon; but he requested it from the kitchens, nonetheless. Magic would keep the contents in the bowl hot.

Moving to the seating area in front of the bed, Ashim went through his bag and pulled out his book, *Cinderella*. With how much he had read the book, it was now more beat up than he would have liked; yet it was the first common tongue book he'd read from front to back. Settling on the red sofa, he lit a candle then tried to get lost in the story that he had become so familiar with. It took his mind off the tense dinner and Orison's seasickness.

"Ash?" A small voice tore him out of the story.

Leaning back, he peered over the back of the sofa. Orison was looking around, holding the flannel to her head. "I'm here," he whispered.

A red ribbon settled in the book; Ashim walked over to the bed and sat down. Orison groaned softly as the ship swayed with the waves. Ashim returned to his book, but couldn't concentrate; instead, he focused on Orison.

"I'm sorry for borrowing your shirt," Orison mumbled. "I was too hot in my nightgown."

Ashim looked up from his book. "I don't mind."

"Did you get any leftovers from the dinner?" Orison asked.

He glanced at the table. "I got some vegetable broth from the kitchens. Do you want me to get it for you?"

Orison nodded; he put his book aside and went to the table. He returned with the steaming-hot broth. She eased herself into a sitting position and took the bowl with both hands. Orison leaned forward for Ashim to place pillows behind her so she could sit back.

"Thank you," she said as she relaxed.

Ashim pushed her hair behind her ear. "You need it."

"Sorry for being weak," Orison said. "It's not befitting of a queen to be sick by the sea."

He scoffed. "Even the strongest people have weaknesses, Little Queen," he stated as he picked up his book. "You're not weak."

"Why do you call me Little Queen?" Orison asked.

"I forgot the word for princess, now it has stuck." Ashim smiled.

Orison looked at the black abyss outside. Ashim hoped she felt better the next morning. He didn't like seeing her suffer; nor did he want to be accused of poisoning Orison again. He would never do that to the woman who brought light to his darkness; especially the woman who was bound to his soul.

Tiny claws dug into his leg as Mahavu woke up and climbed into his lap. He petted her soft fur. He liked this little world they had created for themselves in this small cabin. In a way, this was Ashim's family and he didn't want to be anywhere else.

THIRTY-SEVEN

Sunlight streamed through the windows the next morning. At the sound of a knock on the bedroom door, Orison crossed the threshold from the bathroom, a hand on her stomach as it rolled violently. She opened the door to a female elf dressed in white, who wheeled in a large cart of food. Orison looked down at the two plates, mugs and a steaming pot which emanated the smell of coffee. It even came with a small bowl of food for Mahavu. The thought of eating made Orison want to run back to the bathroom. Outside the door, the deck was lively with the crew working on their various tasks.

The servant set the tray beside the table and curtsied before hurrying out of the room. Orison shouted *thank you* as the elf disappeared. Her gaze snagged on Ashim, who was still fast asleep on his stomach at the foot of the bed.

"Is that coffee?" His voice was muffled from the pillow.

Orison walked over to the cart; the covers clinked as she lifted them. "Yes. Do you want breakfast in bed or at the table?"

"Just give me a moment." Ashim groaned as he stretched with a yawn. "Are you feeling better today?"

"A little," Orison admitted.

She looked down at the fried breakfasts that awaited them. Her stomach turned at the sight of scrambled eggs—that was the last thing she wanted to eat. The sausages, ham and mushrooms on the other hand made her mouth water. When arms wrapped around her waist, Orison tensed, only to relax with a giggle when Ashim sat down beside her. He took a plate and Orison poured him a coffee the way he liked, with an equal amount of milk and two sugars.

She settled opposite him and scooped her eggs onto his plate, he exchanged them for his mushrooms. Usually Orison loved eggs, but if she ate them, it would be another day in bed. Orison tried to eat the rest of the food, ignoring her gurgling stomach. She slowed her chewing when Ashim put her portion of scrambled eggs into Mahavu's bowl. The cat gobbled them down with little purrs of happiness.

"Can cats eat eggs?" Orison asked.

Ashim nodded as he checked on Mahavu. "If they're cooked. Better Mahavu eats them if you can't stomach it." He chuckled as he returned to his breakfast, then he looked at Orison. She kept meeting his gaze over her coffee as she took small sips. "Ori... would you like to be in a relationship with me?"

She spat her coffee back into her cup and coughed. Orison set her cup down and tried to figure out if he was joking, but the seriousness in his facial expression told her he was serious. It was a simple question; she inched to the edge of her seat.

Before she could answer with a resounding yes, a loud commotion ruined the moment. In unison, they looked at the door; Ashim winced when he heard a loud thud. She wiped her mouth with a napkin and made her way across the room. When Orison opened the door to check, the sound of the commotion grew into a crescendo; men shouted and jeered.

"Ash!" she beckoned. Orison's voice wavered with worry.

He got to his feet and approached her. She covered her mouth at the sight before her. The crew stood around in a circle. In the middle, Xabian panted heavily as he sized up one of the elves, who stood in a defensive position. The prince's purple eyes flared like the Othereal lights and tendrils of wet hair hung down his face. Blood spilled from his nose and head.

With a hand to Orison's shoulder, Ashim stepped onto the deck. The crew roared when Xabian tried to throw a punch, but his opponent was too fast and dodged out of the way. Consequently throwing a punch into Xabian's face while distracted. He crashed to the ground.

Orison followed Ashim onto the deck, closing the door behind her so Mahavu couldn't get out. She hurried down the steps, ignoring her intensifying nausea as she watched Xabian grab the elf's arm. Orison retched when his arm snapped in two, bone jutted out of his skin and he let out an agonised scream.

"Stop this!" Orison shouted.

With hurried steps, Orison followed Ashim into the packed crowd. Finding a path to get to the front, she clutched the back of Ashim's shirt as they pushed forward. Through the dense crowd, she recognised Aeson as he pushed towards the centre as well. As the crowd dispersed, the true horror presented itself. Orison gasped to see the deck covered with blood and Xabian holding the elf in the air by the throat.

With a single look, Aeson shifted into King Sila. The resemblance made Orison stagger into Ashim, who held her close. Xabian did a double take at the appearance of his brother and dropped the elf in disbelief. So lost in a trance, Xabian didn't anticipate several other crew members who stepped forward and used their magic to render the prince unconscious. Ashim picked up some rope and bound Xabian's wrists together.

Orison followed the sound of heavy boots on the desk. Captain Vex stood nearby, his arms folded over his chest with a shake of his head. Other crew members came to aid the elf, who belly-crawled and choked on the oxygen he desperately tried to get into his lungs.

"Get Xabian into the cargo hold," Captain Vex ordered.

Aeson changed back into his normal self, pushing his hair from his face. "What will happen to him there?"

"He'll remain there for the rest of the journey, unfortunately."

Captain Vex crouched beside Xabian. There was a sad look in the captain's eyes about what had become of the Prince of Fallasingha—former heir to the throne—Orison didn't know if the captain knew what was happening in Xabian's head.

Six crew members picked up Xabian, the others parted ways as they carried him to the stairs which led below the deck. Ashim pushed himself off the floor and watched as the prince disappeared into the belly of the ship, never to see the light of day until the voyage was done.

Ashim walked on the upper deck of the ship. Before him was a vast ocean which stretched on for miles. He smiled at not seeing a hint of civilisation; it was oddly liberating. With his arm around Orison, they walked slowly while she got used to the movements of the ship. He knew she needed fresh air at some point—despite being sick. Ashim glanced over his shoulder as Eloise swept sand from the deck. She had given Orison an elixir as promised, but it was all she could do and nothing more.

The most unnerving thing about the ship was the crew—doing their chores like Xabian's outburst didn't happen. Even the elf Xabian attacked was back to work. Ashim wasn't sure if elves were resilient like that.

Ashim waved to Aeson as he threw a lobster trap overboard. It was also confusing that he hadn't been required to work to earn his passage; unlike Aeson, Kinsley and Eloise, who had to assist in cooking meals, amongst other chores.

"What's the matter, Ash?" Orison asked.

He snapped back to reality. "Just thinking about what happened earlier." Ashim pulled her closer and kissed the top of her head. "How are you feeling?"

"A little queasy," she admitted. Coming to a stop, she smiled up at him. "I never got to answer your question earlier. My answer is yes."

Ashim grinned and held her hand. He leaned towards her, planting a soft kiss on her lips. He lifted his head to look into her purple eyes. "I love you, Little Queen," Ashim said.

"I love you too." Orison stopped and pulled him in for another kiss. He smiled against her lips, pulling her closer. "Thank you for being there for me."

Ashim hooked his finger under Orison's chin and tilted her head up. "I'd do anything to see you smile."

"I don't think I would have survived the mortal realm without you," she admitted in a whisper. "You're my lifeline."

He kissed her gently again. "And you're mine."

Orison held him close. She closed her eyes as she relaxed against his chest. He wrapped his arms around her and gently rubbed her back. Ashim ran his hands through her soft hair and was comforted by the embrace.

"When we get back to Fallasingha, we can look at houses," Orison announced.

He paused. "Houses? Aren't we living in the castle?"

She looked around. "King Raj had a prophecy that we have to buy a home," Orison whispered. "I don't know the details as to why, but I think we should listen to what a seer says. Besides, it'll be nice having a holiday home to get away from royal duties."

"*Halek*." Ashim looked around. "We can do that, if it makes you feel good. Where is this home going to be and what will it look like?" He turned Orison around to face the ocean. "Would it allow us to go on more adventures?"

"I was thinking Tsunamal, it's got a similar climate to Haranshal," Orison explained. "And it's a port town, so we can go on lots of adventures."

Kissing her neck, Ashim rested his chin on her shoulder. "Okay. We can look for houses in Tsunamal; it will give us the freedom to explore places and I can easily go back home," Ashim explained. Orison nodded as she turned to him. "If it will put your mind at ease."

"The last time I ignored a seer's prophecy, I was exiled to the mortal realm. I don't want to make the same mistake twice," Orison explained. "But it did lead me to you."

Orison reached up and pulled Ashim in for another kiss. He kissed her softly and stared at the water. He could understand why she was adamant about following the seer's prophecy—she almost died while being in the mortal realm.

"I don't trust Xabian anymore," he whispered. "And neither should anybody else."

"I know," Orison said quietly. "I stopped trusting him in Lhandahir."

Ashim watched as she observed the deck. It became apparent she was checking that Xabian wasn't around; a symbol of how much trust she had left for him. Although they had chained him up, there wasn't anything to stop him from unchaining himself and wreaking more havoc.

"While talking to King Raj, I didn't believe the Nighthex was slowly consuming Xabian from the inside out." Orison looked around. "But after today's outburst, I don't have a doubt that he was telling the truth. He'll end up like Prince Neasha if he continues."

He leaned on the ship. "What happened to Prince Neasha?"

"We'll explain when we're back in Fallasingha," Orison said as she stood next to him. "Pretend to be his friend, but keep your distance."

That was all they could do. If they wanted to get to Fallasingha in one piece, they couldn't allow Xabian any insight into the fact they no longer saw him as a trustworthy companion. Ashim looked overboard, observing the way the ship created its own current in the sea.

A sense of foreboding dragged Ashim's stomach to the bottom of the ocean. If Xabian did indeed lose his shit, everybody on this ship would be doomed. Something he never wanted to experience. Though he was born and raised in Haranshal, being in the sea terrified him and being stranded at sea would be a living hell.

Seeing the ship partially submerged in water was troubling, though the shallow puddle Orison's boots entered was enough to not be of major concern. Supply crates for imports crammed the lower deck, save for an isolated corner. A lamp suspended from a hook protruding from the ceiling illuminated part of the room—the only indicator of where Xabian sat.

The water muffled the sound of her boots, only the swish of water announced her movement. She held her beige cardigan closed to stop the bite of cold; in her other hand, she carried a tray of food with a glass of water. After a few turns through the aisles of the supply crates, Orison approached Xabian—his head was low with remorse and manacles secured to a support beam held his ankles.

"Hi," she said as she crouched in front of him.

Orison slid the tray towards him. She was thankful he was being given a substantial meal of steak and mashed potatoes with peas. It was to remind him he wasn't a prisoner; just being kept down there for safety.

Xabian watched her through his hair. Orison forced a smile and held her arms, the interaction noticeably awkward. The temptation to run up the stairs was strong, but she forced herself to remain. Without saying a word, Xabian pulled the tray onto his lap and tucked in. She scratched her neck and looked at the water beneath her feet.

"Are you well?" Xabian asked. "I guess I was tired earlier. I hope Vex forgives me."

"I'm sure he will if you show good behaviour," Orison replied. "I'm feeling much better, thanks to Eloise's help. Are you?"

Xabian nodded as he continued to eat, then he set his cutlery down. When he tried to drink, his hand shook and water sloshed over his hand. Orison knew what he was going through—it was the side effects of the Nighthex consuming him. Little did he know, they had crushed a pill of his medication into his mashed potatoes.

"I heard you nearly died in Lhandahir because of King Raj."

She straightened up. "I... I." Orison grimaced. "Yes. And it wasn't King Raj's fault; he didn't know the Ifrit would wake up."

"He's so greedy, he doesn't care if you live or die," Xabian grumbled. "I got the brand removed as soon as he gave me that slip of paper. Hope you did too."

Orison closed her eyes and nodded. A lie—she was proud of her brand that was still etched into her skin and would remain that way. Her need to run to the upper deck increased. Keeping herself focused, she needed to convince Xabian to take his medication without hiding it in his food. He was being difficult on purpose. Shaking the thoughts away, she suppressed her emotions.

"At least we're free now," Orison stated with a forced smile. It earned her a glare. "Then we can prepare for the coronation and start rebuilding The Empire."

"Away from King Raj." Xabian resumed eating.

Orison's stomach lurched. "I think I need to get more medication from Eloise to stop the nausea."

"It's not very becoming of a queen to get sick so easily." Orison narrowed her eyes at Xabian. "Most people in The Empire believe you're weak because you don't know about our lands and then this adds to it."

Xabian spoke to Orison about their exile to the mortal lands. He tried to convince her she was weak for accepting help from Ashim and Erol. In the past, such comments would have hurt her; however, she knew this was a true Alsaphus before her. Deep down, he was exactly like Sila, like she should have expected when she first found out he was Xabian. Since her time in Karshakroh, she had grown a thick skin.

"That's a great story. But you would have died too if I didn't accept help." Orison folded her arms over her chest. "And for the record, Ashim is my Equal."

The words were out before she could stop them. Xabian's grip on his fork tightened until it bent in half; his knuckles were white and his eyes flared. "He's what?"

"I can't help the cards that fate has dealt me," Orison said sternly.

His eyes flared purple. Sila's famous scowl presented itself like the horror of Orison's nightmares. She rolled her shoulders and looked down at the fallen prince. She wouldn't be apologetic about what fate had done.

"He's corrupted you, that's what Karshakians do," Xabian snarled.

She moved away. "Enjoy your meal. Ashim has done nothing to me; he's not what you make him out to be."

Turning around, she walked through the maze of crates as Xabian shouted insults about Ashim at her. It was further evidence that nobody could trust him.

She didn't have the chance to explain that he was dying. It was selfish of Orison to want him to remain blind to his fate. However, for the safety of the people around her, she had to protect them and keep him in the dark until the timing was right.

THIRTY-EIGHT

Propped against the sofa in his chambers, Ashim glanced at the game board made from a broken crate. His attention lifted from his token to Aeson, who inspected the board with a frown. Ashim looked at Kinsley and Eloise who were giggling about something. It made him roll his shoulders, thinking the giggles were about him, but he knew they wouldn't do that. Aeson rolled the dice, which clattered against the wooden board. He moved his bronze piece until it landed on a Rokuba, subsequently swearing when he had to lose progress.

"Why do you have to go back?" Ashim asked.

Kinsley shook the dice in her cupped palms. "That's the rules. The Rokuba eats you and shits you out, then you're losing; you can only pray you avoid them, to be successful."

Ashim cringed as she played her hand, moving the silver Akornsonian coin ten spaces; she smirked when she climbed a ladder. He wanted to ask why, but he knew it was just how they played this strange game. They didn't have it in Karshakroh.

Everybody looked in unison when someone threw the door open. Orison stepped into the room; she tugged the beige cardigan around her as she approached the group and knelt beside Ashim. He could tell something bothered her after speaking to Xabian.

He looked down when Orison held his hand; she gave him a reassured smile. Hearing a joyous sound, Ashim turned his head in time to witness Eloise punching the air as she settled back on the floor; her green button narrowly avoided a Rokuba.

"What's wrong?" Ashim asked as he gave her a kiss. He tensed when realising they hadn't told anybody else yet. Looking around, Kinsley and Aeson were smiling at each other while they watched Orison and Ashim. "Did Xabian say something?"

Orison moved onto his lap, making Ashim hold her around the waist. "He thinks you've brainwashed me because we're Equal. He called me weak again."

"Nobody can brainwash you into being your Equal," Kinsley retorted with a scoff as Ashim rattled the dice in his hand. "There's the weird tugging sensation and when around your Equal, your powers are enhanced. You can't make that up. He can fuck off calling you weak; you survived the mortal realm with no training, for fuck's sake."

Ashim smiled at Kinsley as he rolled the dice. Kinsley's comment further proved it wasn't only him saying Orison was the strongest person he knew. As he kissed Orison's shoulder, she leaned forward and moved his gold coin seven times—feeling deflated when he landed on a Rokuba. He gently rubbed her back, but paused when a loud bang outside violently shook the entire ship. The chandelier above them clinked together and Mahavu chirruped.

It didn't have the same feel as the lurching of the ship when it glided over waves; and the ship hadn't made a loud bang before. The group exchanged glances with one another. Eloise focused on the door, then turned back to the group when the ship creaked loudly and shouting emanated from the deck. Her eyes widened.

"What was that?" Aeson asked as he rolled his dice.

Kinsley glanced at the door. "Somebody probably dropped some cargo." She looked around the group. "Let's continue."

Focusing on the game, Ashim tried to ignore the sound of running from outside the door. "Is this game popular in Fallasingha?" Kinsley nodded. "I still don't understand the rules. What do we get if we win?"

Eloise grabbed the dice. "Just winner's pride. It's intended for children. We're only playing it because you said you've never heard of it before."

With a nod, Ashim tugged Orison to lay against his chest as he watched Eloise play her turn. The triad looked up from the game board when Orison burst out laughing after Ashim made a fart noise against her neck. He smiled at everybody as he conjured the dice into his hands with a click of his finger. Shaking the dice, he rolled it across the floor and landed on a ten. More shouting and running echoed outside the door; it made him exhale a jagged breath as his heart raced. Something was wrong.

"No fair, you got a double," Aeson exclaimed. "Roll again."

His jaw fell open—another rule he didn't know. Using his magic to scoop up the dice again, he rattled them and rolled. He moved the gold coin accordingly and went up a ladder, surprised to find he was nearly at the end.

The entire room fell silent when a bell tolled from above them.

Everybody jumped when a pale-looking crew member threw the door open. He was panting heavily and stammering over his words as he pointed to the main deck. Mahavu watched with peaked curiosity. Everyone stood up and looked at each other.

"Evacuate!" the crew member rasped.

Ashim scooped up Mahavu and held her to his chest; his heart raced as he followed everybody out of the room. The floor felt uneven and going to the door was like walking down a hill. Ashim's eyes widened at a gaping hole in the bow. Purple flames licked the night air—like a malicious entity—and fully engulfed a mast along with its sails. People emerged from below deck with their soaking clothes clinging to their bodies.

Taking Orison's hand, Ashim guided her to the stairs that lead to the main deck. "What's happening?" Orison asked.

Hand in hand, Ashim jogged down the stairs with Orison and dodged crew members who ran in the opposite direction. He watched some of the crew try to throw sea water on the flames; it did nothing but make them flicker for a slight moment before they roared. Orison squeezed his hand as he led her over to where the lifeboats were being prepared. Her steps appeared to falter the closer they came. At the nearest lifeboat, Ashim whirled around and handed Mahavu to Orison, who cradled her to her chest. He held Orison's arm; tears glazed his eyes as he kissed her deeply. His hands shook at what he was about to do.

"Take Mahavu, get to the first available lifeboat. I love you," Ashim said.

Orison shook her head, holding Mahavu close. "No, you're coming with me."

Ashim closed his eyes and swallowed the lump in his throat. He pressed his forehead to hers as he kissed one more time. "I'm a Fire Singer, I need to help."

Kissing her again, he let her go and ran to the fire. The sound of Orison crying out his name in anguish cut him like a knife. He knew if he followed her voice, it would sway him to flee without helping the elves first. Her cries turned to screams, pleading for him to come back. Even if he went down with the ship, Ashim would utilise his powers.

Orison thrashed around in Aeson's arms as he held her around the waist; she screamed and tears streamed down her face. Her friend was trying to prevent her from running to where Ashim had disappeared through the thick cloud of smoke. All her cries hadn't swayed him to turn around. In defeat, she sank against Aeson with heavy breaths and he slowly lowered her to the floor. This couldn't be how she said goodbye to Ashim.

Aeson only let her go when convinced that she wouldn't run into the fire. Her vision was blurry from tears as she looked up at Mahavu in Kinsley's arms. She needed to check on Vex. With a boost of courage, Orison staggered to her feet and approached Mahavu.

She kissed and stroked Mahavu's head. "I love you. I'll be back soon."

"Orison, no!" Aeson argued.

Shaking her head, she stepped away from them and ran to the stern of the ship, avoiding Aeson's grasp. Trying to make her way up the stairs was like climbing a mountain. She needed to find out if Captain Vex was amongst the apocalyptic scene.

Opening Vex's office to find it empty, she closed the door and tried to run towards the top deck. Her knuckles were white against the banister as she ascended the stairs with heavy breaths. She could tell the ship was on a slight incline, increasing steadily as time ticked on. Her heart sank to find that portion of deck empty as well.

"Orison!" Kinsley screamed.

She spotted Kinsley with Mahavu, frantically waving her over as Eloise and Aeson waited by a lifeboat. Descending the stairs was easier than climbing; she hurried towards her friends—towards safety. She staggered to a halt when the ship creaked loudly; it felt like she was standing on a hill and watching the chaos from the top. The elves focused on the fire, rather than keeping the boat upright. Orison froze, wondering if there was anybody trapped below deck. When she got to the main deck, Orison's attention was on the stairs below.

Aeson shook his head as he ran to Orison. "Don't you dare go down there!" he ordered. She turned on her heels and ran to the stairs. "Orison!"

She grabbed the banister, ignoring her friends' cries of protest as she ran down the stairs, taking two at a time. Her feet thudded against the wood as she ran down the corridor and descended into the belly of the ship. Orison's heart raced and her stomach filled with butterflies. At the bottom of the next set of stairs, ice-cold ankle-deep water greeted her; the water fully submerged the next staircase.

"Othereal above," Orison gasped.

The sound of Kinsley shouting her name made her look up. Orison swore as she looked at the stairs one last time before she ran back to the main deck. She constantly glanced over her shoulder to hear if anybody needed help. With the utter silence, it was easy to assume it was only herself down there.

Orison ran back up the stairs, clutching the banister. She shivered from the sea water in her boots. Aeson was there to greet her in an instant; his face was stern from anger at her defiance. Who could blame him when he was there to protect her? He wrapped her in a red tartan blanket and grumbled about her behaviour. Orison kept looking for Ashim, but she couldn't see him amongst the crew.

"What is wrong with you?" Kinsley exclaimed in a shrill voice, checking her over.

Orison staggered into Aeson; the incline more intense than before. "I thought people were trapped, but it's empty," she breathed. "We're taking on too much water."

"What?"

Orison pointed at the stairs. "Water has completely submerged one of the stairwells."

Aeson ushered Orison along, her boots squelched with each step from being in ankle deep water. Her breathing was heavy. Crew raced around her and shouted commands in the Elven tongue, oblivious to the passengers. Looking around for Mahavu, she saw the little cat poking out of the blanket around Eloise's shoulders as she stood by a lifeboat. With each step, Aeson looked around to ensure everybody in his care were safe.

A burning mast came crashing down. Orison shielded her head for protection because of the screams that followed. Not wasting another moment, Aeson scooped up Orison and threw her over his shoulder. He ran across the deck towards the awaiting lifeboat and thrust Orison off to Kinsley, who held her in a vice-like grip until the lifeboat was too far down for her to jump back on the ship.

Sweat beaded across Ashim's brow as he tried to control the raging inferno that consumed the deck. He could manipulate the flames that bent to his will, but they didn't behave like normal and raged on when he told them to stop. The heat intensified and he grimaced as he tried to douse the flames.

A bell tolled, making Ashim glance behind him. Captain Vex rang a large bell from his office. His face was stern as he continued to ring the contraption. One by one, the crew shook their heads in defeat and backed away from the fire, dispersing towards the last remaining lifeboats. Ashim focused on every face as he looked for Orison, hoping she made it out before Vex called it quits. He could only see the tired-looking crew as they gave up the fight.

"Ori!" he shouted as panicked crew members shoved him towards the boats. "Aeson!"

When a break in the crowd presented itself, he raced towards the stern, wondering if they got off the ship safely. Scrambling up the stairs to his chambers made his thighs burn from the exertion. It was like climbing a steep hill.

"Ashim!" a voice shouted. Aeson ran up to him. "They're safe. I put them on the first lifeboat out."

He slumped against the handrail with relief, then reality hit him. Ashim ran to the chambers where he'd been staying, finding it empty. Mahavu must have been on the first lifeboat out with the women. Before leaving, his attention snagged on the bags they had packed. Deep down, he knew he should ignore them, but something compelled him to grab the one holding Orison's marionette doll and a few of his books before fleeing from the room.

"Now there's no denying that you're Orison's Equal," Aeson hissed when they reunited and fled down the stairs. Ashim gave him a look. "She did things as careless as that."

When their feet met the main deck, the sound of cracking made them look up in time to see another mast engulfed in purple flames. Ashim ducked and shielded his head as it collapsed in his direction with the sound of screaming crew when it smashed into the room that he had just been in. If Ashim had been a second later, he would have stared death in the face.

On the main deck, people scrambled into lifeboats and settled in. Ashim got pushed into one of the lifeboats and squashed shoulder to shoulder with the crew. He was relieved when Aeson settled in next to him with a grateful sigh.

The head crew member shot a bullet into the sky and shouted something in Elven; they lowered the boat with loud creaking sounds. Ashim watched with abject horror as the crew members who couldn't get on a lifeboat scrambled to the captain's office and kneeled on the floor; awaiting the inevitable. He tensed as he looked around at the other lifeboats bobbing around in the ocean, getting away from the rapidly sinking ship. He tried to stay calm as they descended into the cold ocean below them. From there, he had no idea how they'd get to shore.

Crew members swiftly rowed his lifeboat away from the sinking vessel. Ashim dared a glance at the ship when another mast crashed through the deck. A gasp lodged in his throat when he realised the Sleeping Siren sat on a forty-five-degree angle. Purple flames ate away at more of the ship as it went down. He panted as he held his head and averted his gaze quickly, rocking to get the image out of his head.

"We're safe," he assured himself. "We're safe."

Ashim raised his head and watched the ship sink below the ocean. When nothing but bubbles were the only evidence that the Sleeping Siren existed, a strange emptiness washed over him. The ship was supposed to be their haven until Fallasingha; now it lay at the bottom of the Falshak Sea, with the crew who couldn't get on a lifeboat. He lowered his head in remorse.

He sucked in a shuddering breath when he realised that they were nowhere near land and the crew needed the strength to row such a vast distance. Getting to Tsunamal was now in fate's hands and he had no idea if they would survive.

THIRTY-NINE

When the Sleeping Siren disappeared into the ocean, the remaining crew waited an hour before they dived into the water to salvage necessities and survivors from the wreckage. They gathered nets to fish for food, as well as cups to fill with sea water—their magic purified the water and made it safe to drink. All chipped in to gather and cook food. Once they retrieved an ample supply, they tied all ten lifeboats together where Ashim was finally reunited with Orison and the remaining passengers and crew went on their way. Nobody had the time to grieve the loss fellow shipmates or Captain Vex—only time to send a silent prayer to Lioress to let them into the afterlife.

In the days that followed, groups of crew members took it in turns to propel the boats across the ocean with their magic to keep on schedule; they were getting to Tsunamal, no matter what.

The freezing nights were the most torturous. By the second day, Ashim couldn't wait to get into a warm bed. No ships offered aid and were destined for Karshakroh, unwilling to return to Fallasingha. The Sleeping Siren's crew members had already come too far to turn back.

As a new day dawned, the lifeboats knocked together from the choppy current of the sea as rain crashed down around them. To Ashim's relief, the elves used shields to keep the rain out.

Ashim held Orison close as she tried to sleep off her sea sickness. Her skin was worryingly pale and her eyes squeezed shut; her hand was on her belly.

He hushed her and rubbed her arm, kissing her head. His eyes widened when mountains rose out of the ocean and his heart raced—land!

Tsunamal's tiered city came into view shortly thereafter, just as beautiful as the first time Ashim laid eyes upon it. However, the homes looked bland in the stormy weather, unlike the shimmering yellows that they usually were. It felt foreign to consider Fallasingha as his home; being there wasn't some mission Raj conjured up. He would live upon those shores—free. That thought alone had his stomach doing flips.

From the lifeboat, Ashim watched people scramble to the edge of the docks as they saw the approaching boats. The sounds of instructions echoed across the water and Ashim could hear calls for assistance and ladders. The crew looked exhausted, with dark circles under their eyes. He didn't know how to show his appreciation for their efforts—*thank you* wasn't enough.

As the boats came to a stop at the dock, the occupants had a ladder lowered down to them. Ashim gasped when a crew member lifted Orison up and placed her onto the first rung. He looked around and scooped Mahavu out of Kinsley's grasp, trying to balance the boat, which rocked as he stood up. He made his way to Orison and placed Mahavu on her shoulder. Sitting back down, he watched Orison kiss Mahavu and she began her ascent to Tsunamal. Despite the precarious situation, Mahavu behaved.

"Next!" a dockhand exclaimed. Kinsley was next to be ushered up the ladder. "Keep them coming."

Following the line of crew members, Ashim ascended the ladder when he was called forward. His hands trembled uncontrollably as he climbed higher and higher; feeling like he was climbing into the heavens, not daring to look down and lose his balance. Stumbling on the deck, a dockhand kept him upright until he found his footing and ran to Orison. She cradled Mahavu in her arms as she explained the situation to the person in charge of filing paperwork. The dock quickly filled with the ship's crew. Eloise, Aeson and Kinsley huddled together close to Orison, as they watched the exchange in silence.

Through the crowd, Ashim's jaw fell open when he saw the Akornsonian Emissary approaching Orison with a smirk. Karshakians admired Emissary Nazareth and she was a known celebrity; he was starstruck in her presence.

"I wondered when I would see my queen again." Orison turned at the emissary's voice. Ashim stepped closer. "Welcome home."

Orison threw her arm around Nazareth; the emissary held her close with a groan. She stepped back with a beaming smile as she guided Ashim towards her. "Emissary Nazareth, this is Ashim Mahrishan."

He wiped his sweaty hand on his shirt, then extended it out. "N-nice to meet you, Emissary Nazareth." Ashim bowed. "We hear a lot about you."

Nazareth smiled at Orison. "Starstruck, Mahrishan?" His cheeks heated and he looked down. She tapped his arm. "You're a good one."

"Sorry," Ashim mumbled. She shrugged as she checked Orison over. "I'm not used to famous people being around."

Orison stroked Mahavu and looked at the crew. "Xabian blew a hole in the ship and it sank in the middle of the ocean. We lost Vex and a handful of crew at sea."

The announcement made Nazareth dive into full emissary mode. She called orders and within minutes, the entire crew were in a two-by-two formation. With a click of her heel, she whirled around and guided everyone from the dock. Orison looped her arm around Ashim's and followed at the back of the procession. People gawped at them as they passed.

Along the shore, they passed various stores on the beach, each selling groceries or souvenirs. Sometimes there were cafés where people sheltered inside from the rain. Ashim hadn't been able to see these places before, usually the moment he was on Fallasingha soil he'd have to Mist somewhere far away, he never had time to linger. There were multiple anglers selling their catch and calling out sales, despite the weather. The unfamiliarity of everything overwhelmed Ashim.

In the centre of the promenade, they stopped at a set of narrow stairs winding up the mountain to the higher levels. Ashim noticed Nazareth sighed heavily as she conjured up a walking stick. The group ascended towards their accommodation—wherever that may be.

As they climbed higher, Orison's breathing became laboured and she leaned against the handrail as she pushed herself to continue. It seemed like they were climbing forever, until Nazareth went into a large empty square and leaned heavily on her walking stick.

Ashim's eyes widened when Nazareth created a large portal in the middle of the square. He'd only seen elf portals a handful of times; they weren't as powerful and could only allow travel within the Othereal. This one looked like somebody had run their hand through water as it materialised to show Torwarin. Nazareth guided each crew member through and they disappeared.

When the last one went through, the portal closed and Nazareth turned to the rest of the gang. "Let's continue. We have accommodation nearby."

They walked along in silence, taking occasional breaks until Nazareth pointed out a small alleyway sandwiched between the second and third tiers. Ashim wiped sweat from his brow and sucked in a breath. He followed Nazareth down the alleyway, unsure where it would lead to.

His jaw fell open as the worn stone path changed to orange tiles. Before them, stood a white stucco mansion with large windows overlooking the ocean. In the courtyard's centre was a large fountain, surrounded by seating areas and palm trees.

Ashim watched Orison relax because it was a home and not a dungeon—or a ship. He knew she hated ships with a vengeance. Nazareth beamed over her shoulder and guided everybody through the courtyard's entry gate.

When Nazareth opened the double doors to the mansion, Orison's jaw fell open. A large entryway led to an enormous seating area, where sofas flanked a stone fireplace. Grand archways led to various parts of the mansion she couldn't wait to explore. Her attention snagged on the curved wooden staircase, surprised to find a wooden stairlift—a rare device in Fallasingha. Orison didn't know something this luxurious existed in Tsunamal—she hadn't been able to explore when she was there last time.

"This is where we'll stay for a couple of days," Nazareth announced with her arms open wide.

Orison stepped into the home and untied her ruined boots which had fallen apart since being submerged with sea water. She ran her hand down Mahavu's fur and kissed her head as she kicked off her boots while taking in the grandeur. Looking up, an opulent chandelier loomed above her head.

At the sound of running footsteps, Orison noticed Kinsley, Eloise and Aeson disappearing upstairs to inspect the rooms. It was a beautiful home, something she strived for when she would look for her property. Ashim hesitated at the door, as if he wasn't sure if he should cross the threshold.

"What are you waiting for?" Orison asked, as she waved him along.

"I'm not allowed in this area, only the basement," Ashim said.

Orison stepped towards him, "Why do you think that?"

"In a royal house ..." Ashim gestured to a line in the orange tiles where it changed to white. "We can't pass that point when visiting."

Nazareth appeared out of nowhere. "You're more than allowed. Go and make yourselves at home," Nazareth reminded him. "Though there is a basement, I think a bed would be more sufficient."

Ashim hesitated again; Orison relaxed when he finally crossed the threshold. She held his hand, smiling and reassuring him that he deserved to be in that section of the house. He moved his arm around Orison's waist and petted Mahavu's head.

With a grin, Nazareth guided them further into the home, showing Ashim the large seating area and botanical garden through floor to ceiling windows. The longer they stayed exploring the home, the more Ashim appeared to relax that he didn't overstep boundaries. Orison guided him back towards the stairs to inspect their room.

"Do you want me to show you both to your room?" Nazareth asked.

"Please," Ashim said.

Nazareth sat herself on the stairlift and secured the belt around her waist. Ashim and Orison followed the whirring contraption up the stairs. Orison marvelled at the innovative lift, having never seen one in action. She realised how it could help so many people around the Othereal and vowed to get them rolled out across Fallasingha when she became queen.

At the top, Nazareth removed the belt and walked onto the upper floor. There was a set of double doors with a tree carving in them; she pushed the doors open and stepped into a grand bedroom. Orison placed Mahavu on the floor, allowing the cat to run off and explore.

It was an exotic room with sea-blue walls and coving to resemble the waves of the ocean. A large four-poster bed sat in the centre, piled with pillows in a plethora of bright colours—pinks, greens and teal-blues. From the open balcony door, a cool breeze flowed into the room. With the city sprawling out below them.

Orison ogled at such beauty. It was exactly how she'd imagined a royal's vacation home to look like—if not more. There was a golden archway that led to the bathroom, but Orison's focus was on the bed. This one was large enough to accommodate four people, something she had only witnessed in Alsaphus Castle and strictly forbidden from sleeping in. After four days sleeping while sitting up and pressed against the Elven crew, she couldn't wait to sprawl out and sleep.

"I'll leave you to get settled in," Nazareth said.

"Thank you," Ashim said with a smile.

Without being invited, Orison crawled onto the bed as Nazareth left and sank into the mattress with a smile. Ashim stood nearby, inspecting Orison and climbed in next to her. She hadn't realised how exhausted she was—until sleep claimed her as soon as her head rested on the mattress.

During his time as a Runner, Ashim wasn't permitted to experience Tsunamal's nightlife when on a mission. It was always work before pleasure. He had seen very little of Fallasingha; it was like this excursion was his first time in the country—everything was new and exciting. While sitting on a private veranda built over the ocean with the rest of the group, it surprised Ashim to find the nightlife as lively as that in Haranshal. So much so, he felt a pang of homesickness in his chest.

The centre of the table had a selection of food. Skewer kebabs lay in a dish, along with various spiced meats, fish, roasted potatoes and pizza. Another custom like Karshakroh—they made the food in restaurants to be shared with friends and family to build a connection.

All it took was the restaurant staff to recognise Orison and Nazareth; they organised the best table and provided a welcome home meal on the house. It felt like too much for her return. Yet these people clearly worshipped what Orison could provide for Fallasingha's future; and they were excited about her upcoming reign.

As they ate, Orison spun tales of what they endured before getting to Tsunamal. She divulged about the time she had nearly died in the woods, but Erol saved her; the ever-increasing situation with Xabian to keep him alive; then about Lhandahir and the ship sinking. Occasionally, Ashim interjected with details she'd missed or how they'd met. It fascinated people when they heard about his Runner status; nobody had asked him about it before.

"What is it about you and basements?" Nazareth asked as she ate some pizza.

Ashim's chair creaked as he sat forward. "It was a rule that when visiting royal residences, we had to sleep in the basement because we are of a lower class. After ten years, it's hard to get it out of my brain, you know."

Orison held Ashim's hand as he spoke in Karshakir. Nazareth appeared to be the only person at the table who understood what he said, for she laughed along with him. When Ashim noticed the rest of their group's bewildered looks, he caught himself; his cheeks heated as he took a kebab. Kinsley and Eloise exchanged glances, perplexed by what he had said. Exhaling a breath, he forced a smile.

"Sorry, I was explaining that my friend, Erol, used to break the rules. He snuck upstairs with some courtesans," Ashim said while drinking.

The comment made Orison spit her wine back into her glass and cough. Ashim rubbed her back with a few pats to calm her down. She laughed and shook her head—defying King Raj was unheard of.

Kinsley sat next to her. "Do you think we can go the long way home?"

"Why?" Orison turned the goblet in her hand.

"Oh, Ori," Nazareth called. "Cleravoralis is now enchantress territory. If you plan to pass through there, they might be apprehensive about Fae in their lands."

Ashim frowned—that kind of thing was unheard of. He didn't know what Cleravoralis was, either. When he checked Orison, she was drinking; but her posture was stiff and uptight, like something had rattled her about it. Because of his lack of knowledge about Fallasingha, he couldn't comfort her and tell her it was okay. First, they needed to know what had become of Xabian after the sinking and why he had done it.

Her gaze fell on Ashim as he ate some pizza. "I think a stop at Cleravoralis would be a really good call," Orison announced.

"Wait, couldn't we Mist to Cleravoralis?" Aeson proposed. "Kinsley did it before."

Nazareth raised her hand. "I can't Mist, remember."

"I don't know what Cleravoralis is," Ashim admitted.

"It's a city with a powerful tale," Eloise chimed in.

Kinsley sat forward. "I'll put the images in your heads." Her friend looked at her, knowing Orison couldn't Mist that far. "I'll Mist you to Cleravoralis. Then we can get horses from there."

It made Ashim frown and shift in his seat; he didn't know about the powerful tale with Cleravoralis. If it was a famous land, it made no sense for it to be given to the enchantresses; unless something bad happened. Part of him wanted to stay in Tsunamal and explore. He wanted to rest after ten years of running. He was fed up of being on the move all the time. But he couldn't—they had to traverse across Fallasingha to get to Alsaphus Castle. Orison's time as queen was quickly upon them.

Another part of Ashim wanted to remain living freely with Orison by his side, travelling over nations denied to him since he was sold to King Raj. He wasn't ready to take on the responsibility of King Consort.

There was no part of his childhood that involved being raised for royalty. He didn't know the first thing about his new role. Yet he had to step up to keep the crown out of Xabian's hands and stop Fallasingha from crumbling.

FORTY

The next day, Orison leaned against the handrail of the stairs. She panted heavily as she dragged her legs, which felt like dead weights, up to the highest tier in Tsunamal. Orison staggered towards a stone wall and slumped against it as she gasped for oxygen. Ashim copied her movement and gulped down air as he pressed his back to the façade. When she turned her head, she gawped at the grand archway and its adjacent stone wall that led onto a decommissioned watch tower. The only sign of its decommission was the array of tourists hanging out of the open windows to admire the view.

"Are you well?" Ashim gasped.

Orison winced and held her side. "I'm fine," she panted.

A part of her wished she had stayed in the mansion with the rest of their group, then her chest wouldn't ache with each breath. But it was her idea to climb this high, upon seeing a white structure on a hill.

She had been out with Ashim since mid-morning, heeding the seer's warning about finding a property. Orison had found a perfect home in a secluded area of Tsunamal away from prying eyes. It was like King Idralis's vacation home, except it was smaller.

Extending her hand out to Ashim, he took it; together they continued their journey through the archway. It led them to a courtyard where a grand white marble temple rose out of the centre. People mulled around and gawked in the shadows of the grandeur as they studied its intricate details—Orison and

Ashim were no different. Orison wanted to run inside the structure and explore everything, but Ashim came to a halt.

"Do you want ice cream?" Ashim asked, pointing to a parlour nearby.

"Yes." After the climb, it would make everything better.

Orison let him guide her over to the parlour; he blew a kiss as he disappeared into the crammed little shop. As she waited, she ventured over to the edge of the square that presented the full view of Tsunamal in all its glory. From up there, it was like she was in the heavens, looking down at the world. The beauty took her breath away—more than the wind. When Orison found an empty bench, she settled down.

"This is beautiful," she said to herself.

Kicking her legs in front of her, Orison admired the view; something Sila and Xabian had prohibited her from ever seeing. For the first time in the Othereal, she was free and didn't need to cower away from exploration or hide from tyrannical kings. She could be outside and feel the sun on her face with pure bliss.

The tugging sensation in her chest returned. It pulled Orison out of her reverie and she looked over her shoulder. Ashim approached with two goblets in his hand, filled with ice cream—one brown and one yellow. He beamed as he held them up. She admired how handsome he looked in the sunlight and the way his yellow eyes glistened. He kissed her gently, then grinned as he held out the brown ice cream with a smile.

"Did you order a chocolate ice cream?" Ashim said when he greeted her.

Orison's eyes lit up as she took the goblet with a second kiss. "After that walk, this is what I need. Thank you."

She pulled him to sit next to her so he could admire the view with her. They could see each tier of homes and businesses built into the mountains through the clouds. If Orison looked hard enough, she could see the ships setting sail to other nations. A pang of guilt hit her that the Sleeping Siren hadn't survived.

Orison shook the guilt away as she dived into her ice cream, savouring the taste. She put some ice cream onto her spoon and gestured for Ashim to try it. He let her spoon feed him; his eyes widened at the creamy milk chocolate flavour. Ashim dipped his spoon into his yellow ice cream and let her try it; her face lit up at the exotic flavour which danced around on her tongue. If she remembered correctly from Karshakroh, it was pineapple. When she stole some of his ice cream, Ashim couldn't help but laugh and shake his head; then he stole some of hers.

While they ate, he looked at the temple when a bride and groom made their way down the stairs. The couple beamed and held up their hands. Wedding guests threw flowers over them and cheered at the joyous occasion.

Ashim pointed to it. "Look, we can get married here."

Orison knew he meant it more of a blanket statement than an actual proposal. She could agree that in the future this would be a perfect place to host their wedding ceremony—if their relationship ever came to that. With the beautiful views and architecture, it was everything that she didn't realise she wanted in a wedding. She pointed to the couple coming down the stairs and leaned on Ashim.

"That could be us one day." She stared at the temple with a smile.

Ashim ate his ice cream. "It could, right in this spot."

"You want to get married in Tsunamal?" Orison asked, inching closer to him.

He shrugged. "Maybe. It reminds me of home."

Despite their relationship being so new, it didn't hurt to see a future together and plan out what could happen; like a normal couple. It wasn't like they were two people sold to kings with power in mind. It was no wonder they were Equals; their stories were almost identical. Almost.

"It kind of reminds me of Karshakroh too," Orison admitted as she held the ice cream to her chest with a smile. She recalled her time when she was in Haranshal and after so many months of experiencing the culture, she fell in love with it.

"I'm glad you feel that way," Ashim admitted with a smile.

Orison turned to him. "I didn't think I could fall in love with your country, but it captivated me to the point that a part of it is in my soul." She gestured to her concealed brand with a laugh. "Literally." Orison smiled as she reminisced. "I'm glad to have experienced Haranshal and that you showed me what a wonderful place it is."

With another kiss, Orison leaned her head on his shoulder. He rubbed her arm and smiled.

"Do you want to explore where we might get married?" Ashim offered.

Orison put her spoon in her half-eaten ice cream. "Yes."

She grinned as he took her hand and walked her towards the temple. The newly-weds had congregated in the centre, still having flowers thrown on them, giving Orison and Ashim hope that the structure was empty.

Orison picked up her skirts so she didn't stand on them. At the bottom of the steps, Orison looked up at the ceiling, where she saw various depictions of women in horse-drawn chariots, as well as angels and other creatures. She didn't know what they would find inside, but she took Ashim's hand and they made their way to the entrance.

From sconces secured to marble columns, flames danced and licked in the air. With a flick of Ashim's wrist, the flames transformed into little unicorns that galloped in a circle above the sconces. Orison gasped and staggered towards the flames in awe. Ashim puffed out his chest with a smug expression when she looked at him.

He realised people were staring, so he dropped his control of the flames and they returned to their regular dance. Ashim wrung his hands together and kept his head down as he followed Orison towards an enormous golden statue that grazed the ceiling. It depicted a curvy female with luscious hair down to her waist, her face in a soft, proud smile.

"Who's that?" Ashim asked, looking at the statue.

Orison dipped her hand into a bowl of Fallagh water. "That is Fallagh." She wiped the water across her temple, closing her eyes and sending a silent prayer.

He stepped up to the bowl and copied her actions. In Karshakroh, they didn't believe in religions; the act was foreign to him, but in this new culture he would copy the customs. Ashim observed the offerings of fruit at Fallagh's feet and bowed to her. Looking up at the statue, he was curious.

Ashim examined the statue. "What is she worshipped for?"

"In Fallasingha, we believe that Fallagh and Lioress created the Othereal," Orison explained. "We can find Lioress in Akornsonia."

"In Karshakroh, we do not think that. King Raj thinks there is another reason for Othereal's existence." Ashim leaned on the handrail that blocked them off from Fallagh. "I am just happy it exists."

Looping her arm around his, Orison kissed his shoulder and leaned against him. He continued to observe Fallagh. She appeared motherly as she gazed down upon them in the temple, as peaceful as a cloud on a sunny day. Along with the fruit, Ashim saw bouquets of flowers surrounding Fallagh's feet in a rainbow of colours. He assumed these were from the weddings held in this temple.

"It's a beautiful place for a wedding," Orison announced.

The words triggered something and somebody dressed in white stepped out of the shadows. Their dark hair was pulled back into a half-braid and cascaded down to their waist with a glistening white smile. "Are you here for a wedding?"

A nervous laugh bubbled out of Orison. "No, we're visiting at the moment."

"I can give you the tour of the facilities!" she exclaimed as she curtsied. "I'm Miss Alva, Your Majesty."

"Rise," Orison instructed.

The wedding planner led them away from the statue of Fallagh and through a door labelled *Private.* Alva guided them down a set of golden steps that led them underground—something Ashim didn't expect to see. An enormous golden chamber sat hidden underneath the entrance they'd just come from. Some Fae mulled about removing furniture from the last wedding performed there.

Alva continued through a set of double doors that opened up to an opulent corridor full of doors. She opened one, which showed off a golden bed chamber. The next room had saunas for relaxation. When they came to a lucky fountain, Alva insisted they throw coins into the water for prosperity. Ashim kissed his coin before he flicked it in the water, watching as it sank to the bottom. He softly touched Orison when he noticed she was pondering over hers before she tossed it into the water.

As they toured more of the venue, Ashim found he couldn't take the smile off his face. He didn't know where his relationship with Orison would lead to. The thought of marriage had always been something unattainable for him, but with Orison, he wanted to spend eternity with her. It felt right with her by his side. While they toured the wedding venue, he felt closer to her in a way he didn't know was possible.

When the tour ended, they walked down the temple steps hand in hand with the view of the setting sun—a testament of how long they had been underground. Tsunamal's homes glistened with gold in the golden hour light. At the bottom of the stairs, fewer people were strolling around. Ashim slowly came to a stop, then Orison squealed as he took her arm and whirled her around. She staggered into him with her hands on his chest, looking into his eyes.

"I want to explore," Ashim announced.

Orison laughed. "Your wish is my command."

Hand in hand, they left the square and descended the tiers of Tsunamal to other places of interest. Ashim could finally explore places off limits and enjoy the city like he hadn't done before. He could take in his new home to his heart's content.

Orison and Ashim stumbled into their bed chambers in fits of giggles. She approached the marble dining table, kicking off her shoes with a smile so large her cheeks hurt. Her hand covered Ashim's when he held her around the waist. Orison leaned her head to the side as he kissed down her neck, trailing a line across her shoulder. Her body heated with desire at his actions and she bit her lip, tilting her head for him to continue.

When his hands left her waist, Orison felt the emptiness immediately. Then she felt Ashim's gentle fingers in her hair as he pulled out the pin that held it up. Her hair cascaded down to her waist; she shook it out and turned to face him. Biting her lip, she lifted herself onto the table and pulled him into her as he kissed her deeply. While they kissed, she wrapped her legs around his waist and a moan escaped her when he kissed her neck. Orison's body heated when his hands travelled up her thighs; she could feel his desire as it pressed against her.

"Wait," she gasped. Ashim pulled away. "When is the full moon?"

Ashim looked at the night out the window. "Next week. Do you want this?"

Orison nodded and returned to kissing him. "Yes."

Part of Orison hated the bond—having to plan when to fuck. Accustomed to doing it whenever the mood struck her, she had to remind herself that was before, when she was using sex to escape the world. She was free now, with Ashim and with no need to escape her fate.

Her dress became loose when Ashim pulled the strings. She shrugged out of it, letting the fabric pool at her waist; Ashim removed her stay. As they kissed, she tugged off his white shirt and threw it to one side; then pulled the strings of his trousers. Orison's hand rubbed his bare torso as they shared another deep kiss.

"Bed," she gasped.

Ashim looked at her. "Okay."

Orison pulled him towards her, gasping as he picked her up. While they travelled to the bed; the rest of her dress slid off her waist and settled on the floor. Orison smiled up at Ashim as he gently laid her down in the centre of the bed. He hovered over her as he kissed her deeply, his hands massaging her breasts; making her moan into his mouth. There was no denying he was going to worship her tonight.

"You're so beautiful," Ashim said as he broke the kiss and took off his trousers.

"So are you."

As he settled between her legs, Orison could feel Ashim against her centre. He kissed her neck, running his hands through her hair. When they kissed again, he eased inside her, making her gasp and moan as she wrapped her arms around him. She ran her fingers through his soft, dark hair. Orison moaned louder with each thrust; this wasn't fast like the other times when she had men in her bed; this was slow and passionate.

They explored each other's bodies well into the night, switching positions and drawing out each other's pleasures. With a silencing shield around their room, they didn't hold back from the noises they created. When they finished, they were both deeply satisfied and fell asleep wrapped in each other's arms.

FORTY-ONE

The sun streamed in through the open windows of Idralis's holiday home. It illuminated the kitchen into a welcoming space, where a family could sit around the dining table. The wood in the black cast-iron oven crackled as the fire heated. Flour, along with cracked eggs, various bowls and dirty utensils were scattered around on the kitchen table. The kitchen was void of servants. Orison hummed as she whisked batter in a bowl. She gasped when Mahavu jumped onto the table and ran around.

"Mahavu!" she gasped. Setting the bowl down, Orison wiped her hands on Ashim's shirt that she was wearing and picked the cat up. "You're lucky you're cute."

Mahavu wriggled around in her arms. Setting the cat on the floor, Orison frowned at the flour on the table, noting Mahavu left no paw prints. Mahavu meowed incessantly loud as she weaved in between Orison's ankles. She tried to ignore the cat and returned to mixing the batter. Eventually, Mahavu's cries for her second breakfast became too difficult to ignore. Orison looked up from her mixing bowl and found that Mahavu had eaten her food in the middle, with the rest pushed to the sides.

"You're a strange cat. How do you not leave paw prints?" She set the mixing bowl down again and walked up to the cat's food, shaking the bowl so it appeared full again. "Happy?"

Mahavu hissed, making Orison straighten up and look at her. She never hissed or stood hunched over with her fur raised. The cat hissed again with growling noises, her attention on something behind Orison.

Heeding Mahavu's warning, Orison turned around. She barely got a noise out before a hand clamped over her mouth. Someone pushed her into the wall. Orison's eyes widened when she came to—Xabian was inches from her face, scowling.

"Don't say a word," he snarled. Orison glanced at Mahavu as she trembled. The cat continued to growl and hiss. "I'm here to save you."

He took his hand slowly away from her mouth. "I'm not going anywhere with you," she seethed.

The sound of footsteps made her fill with hope; she ran to the kitchen entrance. "Help me!" Orison cried as Xabian pulled her back with force.

Orison kicked against him with a scream, scrambling to find something to use as a weapon. A knife glinted at her; she barely touched it before a roaring purple vortex knocked the breath out of her. She turned to him as tears rolled down her cheeks. A scream tore out of her as he forcibly took her away from Tsunamal and her friends. No matter how much she begged, Xabian tightened his grip around her waist.

They landed in the clearing of a dense forest blanketed by snow. It was a frozen wasteland and the ice cut into Orison's thin trousers. Only her loud sobs broke the tranquil silence that the forest provided. Ice bit into her skin as she scrambled onto a rock, each breath clouded in front of her. Xabian paced in front of her with his hands on his hips. Unlike Orison, he wore a fur-lined black coat with trousers and boots.

"You're safe." He laughed. "You're finally safe."

Orison pushed her tears away with Ashim's shirt. "What the fuck do you mean?" She looked around as she shivered violently. "I was safe in Tsunamal with the group!"

She watched Xabian intertwine his fingers and continue to pace; he stared at the sky with a relieved smile. Xabian crouched before her, causing her to wince as he put a finger to her lips. "Shush, Orison. They are Karshakians coaxing you into their plan to kill you. Why would Fallagh bind you to a Karshakian unless she wants you dead?"

Orison snorted and spat in his face. He roared as he staggered back, covering his face with his hands. She didn't waste any time, getting to her feet and blindly racing down a path, leaving Xabian in the snow. The icy terrain made her bare feet numb, but she had to get away. She yelped and skidded on a section of black ice, crashing to the ground when Xabian materialised before her.

He snarled as he grabbed her, forcing her to her feet. Xabian shoved some trousers, a fur-lined cloak and boots at her. "Put these on, *now*."

Clutching the clothes, Orison shivered violently as Xabian pushed her towards a nearby bush. She staggered over there, feeling too numb and shocked to react to what he'd done. Crouching behind the bush, she shrugged on the clothes, breathing with relief to feel some warmth.

Orison spied on Xabian through the bush as she laced up her boots. He stood with his hands on his hips while he waited. As an experiment, Orison tried to Mist back to Tsunamal; however, each time she tried, she remained behind the bush. Xabian had evidently nullified her abilities somehow.

"Ready," she breathed as she stepped out of the bush's concealment.

Xabian turned around. "Let's move."

He trudged through the snow, not daring to look behind and see that Orison hadn't moved, in an act of defiance. The thought of running again was strong until she remembered he could Mist and she couldn't. Balling her hands into fists, she played along and followed the prince. Orison would pretend to be a damsel in distress while she waited for Ashim to set the world on fire to get her back.

Kinsley ran into Ashim's and Orison's bedroom; her heart thumped against her ribs. Hurrying to the bed, she frantically shook Ashim and looked at the door—hoping Orison would run through and say she was fine; though she knew that wasn't the case. Ashim mumbled something and rolled over to go back to sleep. She collapsed against the bed and panted as she tried to think of a solution. Another frantic shove on Ashim's shoulder made him stir a bit more.

"Ashim!" she shouted. He winced when she smacked his head. "Wake up, Xabian's taken Orison."

His eyes flew open and he sat up. "He's what?" Ashim grabbed his trousers from the floor and pulled them over his hips. "Where did they go?"

"I don't know. I walked into the kitchen as it happened."

Ashim ran out of the room, not bothering with a shirt. "Orison!" he shouted, like it would help anything. She watched from the bed as he ran down the stairs. "Ori!"

Several group members emerged out of their rooms, bleary-eyed from being woken. Ashim ran through each room, calling Orison's name with more anguish as he went. Kinsley felt useless just sitting there, trying to process what happened. Standing up, she crossed the threshold and stepped into the corridor, watching Ashim grab his head and slump against the wall—lost and frantic.

The others had quickly caught on that something had happened to Orison. Deep in the mansion, Eloise and Nazareth shouted for Orison and Xabian. For reassurance, Kinsley gently placed her hand on Ashim's arm. He shrugged her off and raced to the stairs, as though he expected Orison to walk through the front door. Kinsley couldn't shake off the sound of Orison's screams.

In desperation, Ashim ran outside and looked around, shouting Orison's and Xabian's names. Kinsley watched from the stairs as he panicked; it told her he wasn't the monster Xabian portrayed him as. The chance of Orison still being in Tsunamal was slim. Ashim ran back into the house, panting as he looked around; eyes glazed over in sorrow, clutching his head once more.

He shouted something in Karshakir as he ran to the closest coffee table, where he crouched down. Ashim shouted again as tears streamed down his cheeks. Kinsley descended the stairs and stood beside him.

"What's a dislaha..." Eloise emerged out of a nearby study.

Nazareth buckled herself into the stairlift. "Discovaker," she translated. "We need a map and something of Orison's!"

As Kinsley knelt by Ashim, his hands were shaking violently against the coffee table. She could faintly distinguish his frantic mutters in Karshakir—like a mantra. Mahavu brushed against him, attempting to comfort him, but it didn't help. Ashim petted her absentmindedly and continued to chant. Aeson ran into the room with a map and laid it down. He prevented it from curling up by weighing it down with ornaments found around the house.

Ashim drummed his thumbs on the table impatiently. He looked up when Eloise ran into the room with Orison's hairbrush. She handed it to Ashim like it was a weapon. He took a strand of her hair and recited the incantation in Karshakir. Kinsley settled down and crossed her legs; she held Aeson's hand as he placed it on her shoulder. Exhaling a breath, guilt gnawed at her that something more could be done; like hitting Xabian over the head for starters.

The strand of hair swayed like a pendulum over the map. It was the only thing that would tell them where Orison was. Kinsley silently prayed it would be in Tsunamal—until she watched the hair fall from his grasp; it landed in a forest area between Parndore and Cleravoralis.

Kinsley watched in awe as a flurry of beige smoke enveloped Ashim; evidently trying to Mist to the location. To everybody's dismay, he stayed firmly planted on the floor in King Idralis's mansion. Something blocked them from Misting to Orison. The idea made her blood boil and she clenched her fists. It was immoral to reduce somebody into such a panicked state.

Ashim spoke hurriedly in Karshakir as he looked at everybody. They could only stare at him in bewilderment as he raised his voice. Kinsley jumped when he smacked his hand down on the coffee table where the strand of hair had landed. A choked sob escaped him.

"He's saying somebody Mist him there," Nazareth translated.

"I can Mist you to Parndore, then you can make your way on foot," Aeson announced; Ashim turned to him. "Or horse."

Ashim shouted in Karshakir; he stood up and approached Aeson. He looked at Nazareth for a translation. "He said, I don't care. I just need to get her back," she responded.

"Get your bags packed and some supplies, then we'll go," Aeson instructed.

"Pack something warm, it's snowing in that area," Eloise advised.

Everybody stayed where they were as Ashim ran out of the room. Kinsley clutched the side of the coffee table as a bell tolled, reminding her of the Sleeping Siren—until she saw black smoke billowing out of the kitchen.

"Shit," she muttered under her breath.

In her panic, she hadn't realised the oven was on. Pushing herself to her feet, she ran to the kitchen with Eloise close behind. While the men were busy preparing to tear up the entire Othereal to get Orison back, their task was trying not to burn down Idralis's property.

Orison waved her arm for balance as she nearly slipped on some ice. She limped towards Xabian, using a large stick as a walking aid. The boots he'd given her were new, giving her blisters and consequently caused her to feel like she was walking on hot coals when she stood on jagged rocks. On the other hand,

Xabian had no issues. He vaulted over them like it was nothing and barely slipped. Her mouth was dry from being denied a break to get any form of water. She wasn't desperate enough to eat snow and Xabian hadn't allowed her breakfast either.

"Where are we going?" Orison groaned as she stepped onto another rock. Xabian ignored her as he traversed from rock to rock.

They'd walked until the sun began its descent on the horizon. If they didn't set up camp soon, they would be traversing in the dark. With the plummeting temperatures, they would get hypothermia and frostbite if they continued. Orison had doubts Xabian would ever stop, too determined to get far away from Ashim. The darkness was his friend now.

Reality set in that she wasn't getting an answer. Orison glared at his retreating figure and decided to be defiant. She came to a stop, regardless of what Xabian would say or do. She looked around at the wintery landscape; the wind played with her hair— that's when she saw it, the mouth of a cave.

Satisfied that Xabian was oblivious to her actions, Orison gave him one last inspection before she tiptoed over the rocks and swiftly entered the safety of the cave. She was determined to not have another Alsaphus keep her prisoner for long.

Inside the cave, the glint of a knife caught her eye. Approaching it, she staggered back when she saw it was in the grasp of a skeleton. With a grimace, she pried it out of the skeletal hand with sickening cracks, satisfied as she tightened her grip on the hilt. Orison could still remember what it felt like in Lhandahir to brandish a sword—she'd channel that if it came to it.

Venturing deeper into the cave, the light from outside diminished and she used the wall to navigate her way through the darkening shadows. Orison jumped when she felt splatters of water against her skin; regardless, she pressed on. Her fingers snagged on a crevice and she eased her way inside of it, clutching her knife as she pressed herself to the cave wall. She knew a shield was useless against a Tearager like Xabian.

"Orison!" Xabian shouted into the cave. She covered her mouth to stifle her gasp. "You better be in here!"

Adjusting her stance, she waited with bated breath for him to come closer. The sound of shuffling footsteps made her tense and hold her breath. Through the sliver of sunlight still visible from the mouth of the cave, Xabian's shadow grew like a malicious entity. He breathed like an angry bull as he searched. Orison jumped when he punched the wall and roared loudly. Her entire world froze when an answering roar shook the cave. Rocks rained down on her from the vibrations. She had never heard something so loud.

Orison screamed when hands wrapped around her wrist and dragged her out of the crevice. She struggled against Xabian's hold; with a grimace, she drove the knife into Xabian's shoulder. He hollered in agony and his hold loosened. Through heavy breaths, Orison rammed the weapon into Xabian's stomach; warm blood coated her hands as her knife sunk home a second time. Another roar vibrated the space, making her pause.

Needing to get away, Orison lifted her hand and rammed her weapon between Xabian's ribs and twisted. He howled as he dropped her to the ground. She yanked her knife out and staggered to her feet as she backed away to the mouth of the cave. Xabian held trembling hands over his injuries; blood seeped through his fingers—eyes wide at what he'd driven her to do. Orison watched the darkness at the sound of something growling.

The ground shook as something approached them. Orison's grip on the knife tightened and she picked up the pace at getting to the cave's exit. She slipped and crashed to the ground when a bear with large antlers protruding out of its head came into the light. Its one red eye bore into Xabian as it sniffed at his injured frame. Orison watched in horror as its paw clamped down on Xabian's middle and dragged him into the darkness. With a stunned stare in pure shock, Orison scrambled to her feet and ran from the cave as rocks rained down on her.

Outside, she dared one final look over her shoulder when Xabian's blood-curdling scream rattled the quiet, wintry air. She didn't care. Another glance and she took off running, ignoring the burning pain of the blisters on her feet and the snow-covered ground. Her only worry was getting away, cursing herself that she had discarded her knife on the cave floor in her haste. The trees would provide ample coverage and could disorientate Xabian if injured enough. It wasn't until she was in its dark confines that she veered off the beaten path.

In the dark, Orison jumped over tree roots and scrambled over snow-covered fallen trees; deviating her path frequently to confuse Xabian if he ever got out of the monster's cave. No, the bear wasn't the monster in this situation; it was merely protecting its home. It was Xabian who was the monster. Her legs burned as she picked up momentum, focusing on her breathing as she pressed on.

On her journey, she tried one last time to Mist somewhere unknown, breathing a sigh of relief when engulfed in purple night and stars. She felt herself to be transported into oblivion. Orison landed under the canopy of snow-capped pine trees and as soon as she gathered her bearings, she took off running. Her only focus was getting back to Ashim.

She was relieved at the sight of wooden huts beyond the tree line. She knew there would be safety in the unknown village and she could beg the people for help to get away from the barbaric prince. Continuing to run with a grimace as cramp lanced through her calf, she focused on her determination to hide.

The town was like a light-house to a ship close to running ashore, trying to coax it away from the danger. Orison's energy dipped as she pushed herself to her limits; regardless, she propelled herself further, despite her body screaming for rest. All she had to do was go a little further to the wooden huts.

Waving her arms and calling out as she got to the outskirts of town, Orison felt grateful that people walked through the narrow streets of the town. Finding the town occupied and not abandoned caused tears of relief to stream down her face. Women with babies strapped to their chests, carrying baskets of linen, paused their strolls to stare at the mysterious woman running through the trees. Orison raced towards them, only to skid to a halt in the snow when they looked past her shoulder, kept their heads down and went on their way. *No!*

Screaming loudly when yanked from behind, Orison clawed at Xabian's hand and kicked as much as she possibly could. "You think you can stab me and feed me to a Roetabarian?" he snarled.

"I don't know what that is," she cried.

She didn't give up the fight, trying to punch and kick her way out of his grasp, yet his strength overthrew hers. With a vortex of purple fire, the strange town disappeared once more. Her one chance of safety had diminished.

FORTY-TWO

Once in Parndore, Ashim quickly got to work. He didn't have the time or energy to stall for even a moment to take in this new destination. Despite being his first time in Parndore, he couldn't enjoy this visit without Orison by his side. While walking through the snow-covered city, he stole a cloak from the back of an empty chair outside a café to keep warm—much to the dismay of Aeson, who insisted he put it back. Ignoring Aeson's pleas, he secured the cloak around himself and covered his head to stop shivering. People didn't bat an eyelid as he scanned the packed cobblestone streets.

"Somebody needs that cloak, Ashim," Aeson hissed as he hurried beside him. "Give it back to its owner, we'll buy you a new one."

"There's no time. Orison needs me and I'm cold." Ashim shoved his hands into the cloak's pockets as he shivered. "Why live somewhere like this?"

He stopped suddenly, jumping when Aeson walked into him; then he gawped at the entrance of a tavern. If memory served him well, there were always horse stables at the back of taverns in Fallasingha. Ashim turned down a cobblestone street, his boots crunched in the snow, with keen eyes on the wall that led to the back of the establishment.

"What do you have planned?" Aeson asked, looking around nervously.

Ashim glanced at him. "Let me handle this."

He peered through a partially opened gate and pushed it open. He sighed with relief at the jackpot handed to him; two horses were at a hitching post already fully equipped for riding. One was smoky-black colour, which was eighteen hands—give or take. The other was a reddish-brown colour. He stepped forward before Aeson pulled him back.

He looked at the horses, then Ashim. "You're going to steal them?"

"The word you're looking for is borrow," Ashim told him.

Snow crunched under his boots as he entered the courtyard. Placing a gentle hand on the rump of the smoky-black, he ran it along the horse's side until he was face to face with the beautiful creature. The horse stomped its hooves and shook its head. It had character—the perfect horse to propel him through the forest for the search.

In quick succession, Ashim untied the reins and walked the horse so it faced the entrance. Using the mounting block, he sat in the saddle. Checking on Aeson, a sad facial expression masked his features—it was against his nature to do this. Ashim felt the guilt like a punch in the gut, remembering these people weren't subjected to this kind of thing. Stealing horses was second nature to Ashim; he'd stolen so many for King Raj that he'd lost count.

"Hey, you can't take those!" a patron from the tavern ran out. Waving their fist, their face was red in a fit of rage.

Ashim looked at him. "Royal business under the order of the Regency of Fallasingha!"

The patron baulked at what he said. Ashim gently squeezed the horse with his legs and it walked out of the courtyard. Its hooves clopped against the cobblestones on the street and people moved out of the way with surprised gasps. Behind him, Aeson shouted the directions to the forest. Ashim's bag banged against his back with each powerful move of the horse; he would sort that out when in the forest.

When the ground turned to an iced dirt road, he gave the horse another squeeze and it picked up the pace. Once in the forest's shadows, the sun was eclipsed by the trees. When they were far away from Parndore, they commenced the quest to return Orison to safety.

The pair had ridden well into the night until they could no longer see through the darkness— or stand the cold. Ashim tethered the horses to a tree. He melted the ice around their encampment with his Fire Singer abilities and a fire quickly roared from a pile of twigs he'd uncovered. While Aeson collected more firewood, Ashim killed a deer with a fireball. Upon Aeson's return, he pulled out a knife and helped skin the deer; then cut its meat into chunks for dinner or to use as jerky.

"We'll eat, get some rest, then set off again at first light," Ashim explained as he put the deer above the fire.

He'd been listening to Aeson's stomach growling for the past few hours; though his stomach also growled, they couldn't stop for food before this point. It would waste precious time, which they didn't have. The only time they stopped before was to relieve themselves and collect water.

Aeson poked at the meat with a stick, fire crackled from the disruption. "Just to let you know, this isn't a mission from King Raj; you're free now. You can't steal things in Orison's name; imagine how she'd feel knowing it's being used to steal."

"*Halek*, I'm sorry." Ashim lowered his head in shame. "My emotions possess me."

Aeson tapped Ashim's arm, forcing a smile. For Ashim, being free felt foreign. After ten years, it still felt like he should report to King Raj, as well as acquire artefacts and other wares for him. Deep down, Ashim knew he shouldn't have stolen the cloak, but his determination prevented him from thinking logically.

Groaning, he buried his head in his hands until something brushed against his leg; a piece of parchment lay at his feet. Ashim scooped it up and read the note.

'King Idralis and Regent Luxart have been notified of Xabian's actions. – N.'

Covering his face with the letter, Ashim sank back on the rock and exhaled a breath. He didn't like admitting he got his hopes up; he thought it was a letter from Orison saying she was safe. Ashim paused as a plan formed in his head—to tell her he was looking. With a click of his fingers, a stylus appeared in his hand. He tore off a piece of parchment and scribbled a note to Orison.

'We're looking for you, Little Queen. We'll do whatever we can to get you back to safety. Love, Ash.'

As the note flew into the night, Ashim watched it in awe. He turned to Aeson, whose face was full of focus. The fire flashed shadows across his features as he used a rock with a leaf on it as a plate—to distribute the venison. If he was like any of the Runners that Ashim grew up with, they wouldn't care how dark it became or how little food they'd had to eat. They would ride through the night until they retrieved Orison. Part of him wished he had Akhili, Bahlir or Erol as a companion.

"Can I send a letter to Kins and El?" Aeson asked.

Ashim swapped the stylus for his portion of the venison and tucked into it. It was delicious, regardless of the lack of spices—it melted on his tongue as he ate. After Aeson sent off the letter, he ate his own meal. Ashim itched to talk, but held his tongue. There were many conversation topics, but he didn't know if Aeson would communicate with him. Instead, he settled for a question.

"Do you think I'll make a good queen's consort?" Ashim asked, nervously tearing grass out of the ground.

Aeson chuckled. "Not if you keep stealing."

Tapping his feet on the ground. "You must understand, I've had to steal for King Raj since I was eleven."

"And you're twenty-two now?" Ashim nodded. With a sigh, Aeson continued to explain. "People don't like those who steal from the poor and give to the rich," Aeson explained.

Aeson rattled on about something else, but all Ashim could focus on were his words. No. Indeed, people didn't like those who stole from the poor. Despite King Raj's luxurious mask, Karshakroh was a poor country because of the multiple wars King Sila waged. It's what drove the orphanages to sell their best children to the king; it was the only way to pay their tithes. He rubbed his brand anxiously and sighed. If he took the role of consort, he wouldn't allow that to happen.

"Are you well?"

He nodded. "Yes. Memories," Ashim replied as he stared into space. "We should feed the horses; they must be hungry."

Ashim looked over at them, they were grazing on grass nearby. They needed more than that in their bellies if they were being ridden to look for Orison. He pushed himself off the rock and went over to the two horses; he used his magic to conjure up a basket of apples from thin air. His mind raced with endless scenarios as he distributed them to his steeds.

The crunch of snow woke Orison from her slumber. She rubbed her eyes with a groan, finding the fallen tree she had slept in oddly comfortable. Orison lifted her head and watched Xabian emerge out of the tree line, fixing his trousers and hair. His clothes were in tatters from the creature's attack and his dark hair dishevelled. His purple eyes flared.

Out of the corner of her eye, she noticed a folded-up piece of parchment. She picked it up and unravelled it. Orison covered her mouth when she saw Ashim's scratchy handwriting. She got all choked up and her vision blurred from tears, when he wrote he was looking for her. Even though she knew he would, the confirmation warmed her heart. She wiped her tears and checked on Xabian. Using her magic to conjure up a stylus, she ripped half the paper, then shoved Ashim's note in the pocket of her trousers. She quickly replied to his message.

'I tried getting away, Xabian found me. I miss you. – Love, Ori.'

A scream tore out of Orison when Xabian grabbed her ankles and pulled her out of the tree. To her relief, the message and stylus disappeared before Xabian could see it. She kicked and punched as he picked her up around the middle and sat her roughly beside a bonfire. Orison grimaced as she inspected her hand; it burned from being scratched against the tree. A popping sound made her jump, only to realise two eggs were in a pan above the campfire. It was a utensil Xabian must have found... and it was something that made a perfect weapon.

"Breakfast is nearly ready," Xabian announced.

Orison remained focused on the pan—how she could discreetly grab it and run. To wield it, Xabian would have to be looking the other way; possibly when he got a fresh set of clothes. Then she'd Mist far from there, if the blockade Xabian had placed on her power allowed it.

Xabian scrambled the eggs with a stick, muttering something under his breath as he cooked. He kept looking around, as though suspicious about something; maybe he knew Ashim would come to find them. Orison hugged her knees to her chest, not knowing what to say to him or what to do. She truly didn't want to say anything.

"We'll go to Lake Horusk. We'll be safe there," Xabian muttered to himself.

She tensed at that announcement. *Lake Horusk.* Of course, he would choose somewhere near Alsaphus Castle, but not so far away that he couldn't take the crown. The idea was gravely flawed, a Discovaker could find her in a heartbeat and guards might be sniffing around. Nobody would offer Xabian any remorse or protection—he would be a prisoner, never to see the light of day again.

"Why will we be safe in Lake Horusk?" Orison asked as she accepted the rock with scrambled eggs on it.

Xabian laughed. "Actually, I change my mind. The Karshakian can't get into Torwarin to save you. Idralis can fix your head and remove whatever spell they've put on you."

This was coming from a man acting exactly like Sila. The thought turned her stomach and her appetite diminished. Having not eaten since yesterday, she forced down her breakfast.

Bahlir was right, it was the Alsaphus Family who couldn't be trusted with anything. It had started with the bargain and her being kidnapped, then Xabian's betrayal from the very moment they met. She was thankful for King Raj's protection and showing her the prophecy. That was a king she could trust and she needed somebody like him to get her out of here.

"We should go to Torwarin," Orison said between mouthfuls.

Xabian tensed. "You think so?"

"Definitely, I need protection from the Karshakians." Orison felt sick saying it. But she needed to get Xabian imprisoned; the pan in front of her was one of her ways out. "It's going to be the safest option for me to get away and be protected from them."

"I knew you'd see sense, Orison," Xabian said. "We'll make you better."

They ate in silence. Xabian continued to watch every single thing that moved; rife with paranoia in case the Akornsonian army or Fallagh army emerged through the trees. By now, Orison knew a notification would have been sent about what Xabian had done.

When Xabian stood up to retrieve water from a nearby stream, Orison stood up and grabbed the pan. Cast-iron... perfect. She tiptoed up to him, careful not to make too much noise in the snow. Aiming the pan, she inched closer to the prince and adjusted her grip. With a quick glance around, she swung as hard as she could with a groan. The force of the hit made Orison jolt. Xabian's entire body tensed before he fell face first into the frozen stream with a splash.

"That's for everything," Orison seethed as she dropped the pan.

Running away from Xabian, she ensured she was far enough away from his sight to Mist in a purple flurry of night and stars. It cast her away from the forest and her captor. When she landed on the precipice of a hill, her breathing was heavy. She could feel the slight drain on her magic.

Her eyes widened as she took in the picture before her. A carpet of golden wheat swayed in the breeze with red painted windmills rising from it like giant chess pieces. Her mouth opened in awe at how beautiful it looked and how familiar it was. Orison had landed right where she needed to be—Navawich.

Trudging down the hill, Orison glanced behind her shoulder as she ran towards the wheatfield, her hair flowed behind her. Hiding in the wheat would be a good deterrent away from Xabian. She needed to get a horse from a farm. Wading through the long strands, Orison came to a white fence which led to a paddock full of horses.

She placed her foot into a gap in the fence, but whilst she was in the middle of climbing over, a voice made her pause, "I wouldn't do that if I were you." She groaned loudly at the sound of Xabian's voice. "Get here now."

Defiantly, Orison climbed over anyway; throwing her middle finger up at Xabian as she continued towards the building at the far end of the paddock. She could steal a horse. However, with Xabian close, she could ask for a ride into Akornsonia and report him to the Regency. Hurrying her steps, it was her chance to succeed.

Xabian materialised in front of her, making her stop; rolling her eyes, she went around him and ran. She didn't get far before Xabian grabbed her wrist and tried to drag her away; Orison drew her arm back, then punched him in the nose. With a cry of pain, he let go of her and she got free, the horses scattered as she continued.

Climbing over the next paddock's fence, Orison ran up the path that led to the farmer's home. The stairs creaked as she ascended. Under the shelter of the covered porch, she knocked loudly on the door and peered through the window. The farmer was taking too long to answer the door, so she knocked more intently. Orison turned around and gasped; she pressed her back to the door as Xabian approached.

He touched his nose, inspecting the blood; he glared at her and his purple eyes flared. Orison glanced at the farmer's home again; reality set in that he wasn't home. It was a plan that could have gone so well, but fate had other ideas.

"Looks like the farmer isn't around to help you," Xabian said with a sinister grin.

Her attention darted between Xabian and the horses; Orison chose the latter. In a heartbeat, she tried Misting to the horses, only for her purple night and stars to be consumed by a roaring purple vortex. She landed on the edge of an enormous crater in the middle of a snowy plateau. Teetering on the edge, her arms windmilled to balance herself, until Xabian pulled her back. She recognised it as the site of The Battle of Torwarin.

"Why are we here?" Orison asked.

"I killed Sila here," he mumbled. The answer made her hesitate. She looked at the crater, then at Xabian. "This crater is where I landed."

Wind tore at Orison's hair and her clothes as she looked at it. She was standing at the site of King Sila's death and now she couldn't deny King Raj's claims. Everything King Raj had said or did was for her protection. Her new captor was the man who killed her old captor—a tyrannical king for a tyrannical prince.

Clearing her throat, she asked the only questions she had, "Where's Sila now?" Orison turned to Xabian. "Did he have a burial?"

Though she didn't care about Sila, it was the curiosity which had spurred on these questions. Part of Orison hoped he didn't have a burial; a man that heinous didn't deserve any respect or honour.

"I ate him."

Orison's eyes widened in horror. The confession was grotesque and it made her feel queasy. She wanted a horrible death for King Sila, but cannibalism was never on the list. She wanted it to be slow and painful. Pushing her shoulders back, Orison realised Xabian was boasting; he had that malicious smirk once more.

"Do you feel guilty about doing that to your brother?" Orison dared to ask.

Shaking his head, Xabian spat into the crater. "Not anymore."

FORTY-THREE

Another day proved fruitless in their efforts to retrieve Orison from Xabian's clutches. As the sun was setting near a river, Ashim spread out a map on a tree stump, weighing it down with several rocks as he got Orison's hairbrush out. He recited the incantation in Karshakir as he held her strand of hair over the map. Ashim watched it swing like a pendulum before it fell out of his grasp. His eyes widened when he realised that she was in Navawich, near the Akornsonian border.

"*Cehen hara!*" Ashim shouted to the thicket of trees. *Come here.* When there was no reply, he kicked himself for speaking Karshakir. "Aeson!"

Out of the darkness of the trees, Aeson emerged with his arms full of firewood, his feet crunched on the stones beneath his feet. "Is something wrong?"

"Where are we?" Ashim asked quickly.

He clicked his tongue as he looked around. "I'm afraid I'm not too sure."

"*Khafsh,*" Ashim spat. *Fuck.*

"Pull yourself together, there's no need for that language." Ashim looked over his shoulder, with a raised eyebrow. He knew Aeson couldn't speak Karshakir. "My friends in school told me Karshakir swear words, so we could swear in front of our parents without them knowing."

Ashim grumbled several expletives as he pulled a hair from his own head. He recited the incantation again, watching his own hair swing like a pendulum and fall out of his grasp. *Old*... Ashim tilted his head and pointed repeatedly at the spot on the map. He had forgotten the common tongue—out of frustration. Running a hand through his hair, he turned to Aeson; he slammed his hand down on the second word.

"Old Liatnogard," Aeson said calmly. "We only need to stay calm."

"Stay calm?" Ashim scoffed as he stood up. *"Khafsh! Yohla Dhuffehphulorsh!"*

Aeson's jaw fell open. "Calling me a Dufflepud is unnecessary."

Focusing on his breathing, Ashim fanned himself as he tried to relax. The worst thing anybody can say in a dire situation is *calm down*. With his hands on his hips, he paced in a circle. Old Liatnogard was nowhere close to Navawich. Though the places looked close together on the map, the journey may be long—less time to save Orison.

A thud made him look over his shoulder. "We'd be faster Misting," Aeson said.

"How... how long by horse?" Ashim asked.

"Two weeks, give or take." Aeson scratched the back of his neck with a pout.

Ashim crashed to the ground at the news. They couldn't wait that long. Many incidents could happen to Orison and she might be imprisoned somewhere; as Sila had done not too long ago.

He tilted his head when he observed Aeson's attention flashing between the horses, then at the map. It told Ashim that a plan was formulating in Aeson's head, but he couldn't decipher if it was a good one. Ashim baulked in protest as Aeson swiped up the map. Aeson used his magic to conjure up parchment with a stylus to scribble a message that went off into oblivion.

"Now we wait," Aeson declared.

Ashim tapped his foot frantically; he always did it when he couldn't take the unknown. He sat forward and pointed at the stylus. "You talking to your girlfriends?"

"Better." Aeson's eyes were wild with the plan he'd set in motion.

"I want to say I'm sorry for..."

Wind stirring the forest floor cut Ashim off; he staggered back as a portal appeared in mid-air. The portal looked like somebody had run their hand through crystal-clear water; it grew as wind tore through the forest and stirred the snow. Ashim clenched his fists, anticipating a threat as the portal rippled before them.

King Idralis of Akornsonia appeared in an instant. "Did somebody need assistance to Navawich?"

Awestruck, Ashim couldn't form words to say to King Idralis, who was another celebrity in Karshakroh that people ogled over. The Elf King was such a big influence and help to his country, King Raj forbade any Runner missions in Akornsonia without Idralis' written consent.

"Are you well, Ashim?" Idralis asked.

Bowing deeply. "I am humbled to be in your presence, Your Majesty," Ashim said.

A warm laugh flittered through the trees. "Please rise, Ashim, you don't need to bow to me. I am a friend."

He couldn't help but bow again and take a step back, allowing Aeson to take the lead in discussions. Ashim fidgeted with the buttons on his cloak as he observed the horses and wondered if they left now, how they could return the animals to their rightful owners.

"What about the horses?" he asked.

Idralis gestured to the portal like it was an open door. "They can come through. We'll return them home. Come and enter Torwarin."

With a nod of reassurance from Aeson, they both stepped through the portal. It would be Ashim's first time in Torwarin or Akornsonia. The only good thing to come out of the ordeal was seeing the new places Ashim had only seen in paintings.

Soon after dinner, Orison pretended to be asleep on a mat within the snowy plateau where the Battle of Torwarin had commenced. The warmth from the fire brushed against her back as she waited, listening to the sound of Xabian's movements and breathing. It was the last time she would be in his clutches—she'd vowed to herself.

Laying there, she waited long after Xabian's breathing had relaxed, enough to know he was in a deep sleep. She bided her time until the fire ebbed away into a small flame—to the point she could see her breath whenever she breathed out. She shivered violently as winter embraced her.

Sitting up, her heart raced as her attention settled on Xabian. In the moonlight, she could see his silhouette as he laid on his side. Scrambling to her feet, Orison stalked over to him on her tiptoes, ensuring she didn't disturb the snow. Leaning over Xabian's head, part of her knew she could kill him in this moment. No. Something told her it wasn't the time.

With a grimace, Orison inched away as quietly as possible. She kept glancing at Xabian, freezing when he shifted and rolled onto his other side, then scratched his face. Orison prayed to Othereal that he would stay asleep.

Looking over her shoulder, she picked up the pace, using her magic to shift the snow over her retreating footprints. Orison's heart raced with each step. Satisfied she was far enough, she willed herself to Mist. Engulfed in a flurry of purple night and stars, she felt herself lifting off the ground and being carried away into oblivion.

Landing on her tiptoes, she teetered on her feet before righting herself. The Torwarin gate, a grand wooden archway that reached the treetops, loomed over her. Orison knew the magical wards around Akornsonia recognised her like an old friend and wouldn't deflect her too far from its safety.

Without hesitation, she bolted. Her ears popped as she raced across the border and into the dark depths of Akornsonian woodland. Once on the other side, Orison came to a gradual stop and keeled over, pressing her hands on her knees as she took time to calm herself. She pushed her hair out of her face and laughed to herself that she'd gotten this far on her own. Though as much as she wanted to relish in this great triumph, something in the back of her mind told her she wasn't safe yet.

The feeling of being watched made her sprint like a startled deer towards Idralis's cabin. Her breath came out in heavy pants as she pushed her cold muscles to work. Movement in her peripheral vision had her look from her right and then left, noticing Akornsonian guards that swung from the trees.

When one landed in front of her, she skidded to a halt, crashing to the ground when she slipped on black ice. Orison covered her mouth with a trembling hand when the guard pulled the mask from his face. She breathed a sigh of relief when she recognised Feud. He extended his hand out and helped her to her feet.

"Come with me," he instructed and swiftly moved on.

Orison didn't hesitate. More guards surrounded her with their hands on the pommel of their swords. All the guards were confirmation she'd made the right choice and she was free. Her feet crunched on the gravel path the further into town that they travelled. When Idralis's cabin came into view, Orison held onto Feud as her knees buckled. The elf kept her upright and guided her towards sanctuary.

As if owning the place, Feud entered without knocking and ushered Orison inside. A bleary-eyed Idralis came out of the room, wearing nothing but a blanket wrapped around his waist. His eyes roamed over each of his guards until his gaze settled on Orison. Idralis baulked and approached her, wrapping his arm around her as he led her to the sofa.

"Orison!" he gasped. "How did you get free?"

She held her hands out when the fire ignited of its own accord. "I waited until Xabian was asleep and then Misted to the gate. I ran like hell."

Idralis rubbed her arm as he sat her down. "You're safe now." He assessed the guards nearby, then he pointed to a guard nearest the door. "Please wake our guest and send him here at once."

Orison hugged her arms and looked around the room, hoping their guest wasn't Xabian who had somehow gotten into Torwarin. She shivered as she held her arms out to the fire, watching it lick the air; her heart ached at how it reminded her of Ashim. The rattle of crockery had Orison shifting in her seat. Servants approached her with steaming mugs filled with the undeniable scent of hot chocolate.

"I need parchment and a stylus," Orison gasped. She leaned on the back of the sofa, waving her arm to get a guard's attention.

A guard turned to her. "Why?"

"I have to tell Ashim where I am. He's looking for me," Orison explained.

The words died on her tongue as she paused at the sound of a familiar voice. She choked on a sob when she felt the familiar tug in her chest. Orison watched the door intently. Her thoughts of hot chocolate abandoned, needing to know if he was really there and she wasn't imagining things. When he appeared in the doorway, Orison broke down.

"Ash?" she choked out as she pushed herself off the sofa.

Orison and Ashim ran to each other. He caught her and embraced her in a tight hug, hand in her hair as he relaxed against her. She clutched his shirt as she breathed in the charred scent of him—of home. Orison never wanted to let him go. After what felt like an eternity, he stepped back as he inspected her face and hands, then pulled her back into his embrace.

"Did he hurt you?" Ashim asked as he pressed his forehead to hers. Orison shook her head. "Are you okay?"

"You came for me," Orison sobbed with a smile. He kissed her gently and wiped her tears away with his thumb. "You're here, you came."

"I've been searching every day. You're my horizon and I will always run to you, today and every day." Her body shook as she resumed sobbing. "I love you, Little Queen."

She buried her head in his chest. "I love you too." Ashim kissed the top of her head.

"We should get you a bath and a proper bed. I bought you some clothes when we arrived here and some books you might like," Ashim explained.

Orison rested her head on Ashim's shoulder when he picked her up bridal style. She clutched his shirt and placed her hand on his chest. He carried her through the threshold of Idralis's home and out into the night. She fell asleep to the gentle swaying as he walked her back to his cabin.

A procession of Akornsonian guards traversed through a snowy plateau. With Idralis by his side, Ashim adjusted the grip on the sword he borrowed. Everyone was sly-footed as they neared the camp where a fire licked the winter sky; it blinked out momentarily when a shadow passed over it. Metal sang as they drew their weapons, along with the sound of Xabian as he called Orison's name. Anger overwhelmed Ashim, so much so that the grip on his sword tightened into a white-knuckled grip. The prince wasn't getting away with this.

Ashim moved hastily past Idralis and the guards as he homed in on his target—Xabian. The prince didn't have time to react as he approached. Ashim pulled his fist back and slammed it into Xabian's face; he jolted and fell to the grass. He grabbed Xabian by the collar and continued to pound his fist anywhere he could. Channelling every ounce of anger, which had accumulated over the three days, into each hit.

"This is for taking Orison!" Ashim sneered in Karshakir. He punched the prince again. "This is for breaking her trust." Xabian covered his face as he groaned, but Ashim didn't want to stop. "This is for making her feel worthless."

Two guards dragged Ashim off Xabian as he went to strike once more; they held his arms back to prevent any more damage. Ashim panted, his hair hung in tendrils over his face. He watched Xabian roll on the floor and spit blood into the snow. Xabian touched his nose as he tried to recover from the assault. More anger presented itself as Ashim struggled against the guards, but they weren't backing down. Idralis calmly stepped forward and glanced at Ashim, before turning to Xabian.

"Prince Xabian of Fallasingha," Idralis bellowed. "You are under arrest for treason against the crown."

Out of the shadows, more guards surrounded Xabian. He cried out and thrashed as they used their magic to drop him to his knees. They clamped manacles around the prince's wrists, covered with vines, so he couldn't escape. Fear finally appeared on Xabian's face as reality set in. As guards hauled him up, Xabian hung his head and stared at the ground, he only cried out when the vines tightened. A scream tore through the plateau when a flash of blue magic sizzled along Xabian's flesh.

It filled Ashim with sick joy to see Xabian in pain. The man before him had hurt Orison—his Equal—and deserved pain in retaliation. She would have vengeance. Ashim watched it all with awe.

The guards communicated with each other in the Elven tongue, then they let Ashim go. He adjusted his newly purchased coat and watched Xabian struggle in his bindings like a fish out of water; his bindings became tighter with each movement.

In reality, Ashim didn't want to be there. He was desperate to return to Orison and check on her wellbeing. Ashim had only chosen to go with Idralis to apprehend Xabian and see justice being served; to get a few punches in before they imprisoned him.

Lightning crackled as the elves created a portal nearby; it shimmered in mid-air. Idralis stared down at Xabian with scorn as he commanded his guards in the Elven tongue. The guards picked up the prince and carried him through the swirling vortex, with Idralis following behind. From within the portal,

Ashim tensed to hear Xabian scream. He looked around the plateau, then took a deep breath as he stepped into the unknown.

They entered a dark and decrepit place that was void of life. Only the sconces on the wall illuminated the dark rocky walls, along with the thick layers of cobwebs which lined the ceiling, corners and doorways. Even rats didn't congregate there. The musty air made Ashim's skin feel filthy the longer he stayed. He turned when Xabian screamed again. The prince tried to fight his way out of the bindings as if he recognised and feared this place. Guards, with the Fallasingha crest over their hearts, stepped out of the shadows and joined forces with Akornsonia.

"Not the lower dungeons, please! Anything but the lower dungeons," Xabian pleaded. He cried out as the guards dragged him deeper into the darkness.

A Fallasingha guard pushed his shoulders back. "These are Regent Luxart's wishes for the safety of Fallasingha and beyond."

The lower dungeons had an eerie resemblance to the Lhandahir catacombs, except it wasn't used to house the dead. Memories of Orison's ordeal filled Ashim's head; it made him feel uneasy—something he desperately tried to shake off. With each step, his shoes sank into soft soil. At the end of the corridor, Ashim dared to look behind his shoulder to realise there wasn't a physical entrance.

"Please!" Xabian begged.

A loud metallic click reverberated around the lower dungeons, as a key turned in the lock of Xabian's assigned cell. Guards dragged Xabian inside and shackled him to the wall with manacles. Ashim covered his mouth as the Fallasingha guards plunged a syringe into his neck; they took it one step further by securing Normahlef berries around his wrists and neck. The berries made Xabian scream and plead for forgiveness—despite the fact that there was no forgiveness to be had.

As a group, Akornsonian and Fallasingha guards stepped out of the cell with Idralis. The head guard slammed the door behind him; it locked with a resounding click. In silence, they walked back to the dead end, where another portal materialised. With one last look at the dark corridor where they left Xabian, Ashim turned to face Idralis with a nod. Together they walked through the portal and emerged into King Idralis's cabin, where he would soon reunite with Orison.

"Where are the lower dungeons?" Ashim asked when the portal closed.

Idralis smoothed out his tunic, watching something out the window. "Deep in the Visyan Mountain range below Alsaphus Castle." He yawned. "You must be tired. Go back to Orison."

"I didn't know such a thing existed." Ashim toyed with the hem of his shirt. He was learning so much outside of Karshakroh. "Goodnight, Your Majesty."

"Don't worry about him Misting out. He has the Normahlef Berries and it's warded with the magic that bound you to the dungeons in Karshak Castle," Idralis explained tiredly. "We will discuss this tomorrow."

"*Halek.*"

With a bow, Ashim Misted back to his cabin. He groaned when he noticed Aeson had fallen asleep on the sofa. He had entrusted Aeson to keep watch, in case anybody else tried to take Orison. Ignoring his dismay, he was too tired to be angry. Ashim stumbled to his bedroom, where Orison slept soundly on her stomach. She stirred as he climbed in next to her; he shushed her as he got settled.

He wrapped his arm around her and felt her hand wrap around his; he kissed her shoulder as he closed his eyes. For the first time in days, Orison's safety wasn't a dream; she was there and out of danger.

FORTY-FOUR

Kinsley hummed to herself as she carried a large basket of laundry to the hut in Tsunamal's many squares. Within the hut, a chestnut horse stood leashed to a barrel which bobbed in a pool of water; a chain tethered the barrel to a waterwheel in the hut's centre. She put two bronzes in the box at the entrance and approached the pool, then crouched before the barrel as she threw her laundry into it, along with soap. Dirt scraped against her skin as she pushed herself off the floor and tapped the horse's rump. The contraption groaned as the horse walked its circular rotation.

With a huff of breath, she put the empty basket outside. Kinsley leaned against a support beam as she looked at Tsunamal; the city was quiet at this hour of the morning. The only noises were the cawing seagulls hovering in mid-air and the ship's crew when they came to and from the wharf. It was a simplistic city that she didn't want to leave, but Aeson had informed her Orison was safe in Torwarin.

She straightened up when Eloise approached with something in her hand, she skipped over the cobblestones as she neared. Once in front of Kinsley, Eloise opened her hand to reveal a chocolate cupcake. A smile spread across Kinsley's face as she accepted it; it was still warm in her hand.

"What's this?" Kinsley asked as she kissed her.

"The bakery was handing them out," Eloise announced. "They're delicious; I knew you'd like one." She smiled.

Kinsley ate her cupcake and checked on the laundry. She assumed the horse was bored with walking around in circles all day; especially in the Tsunamal heat. Her girlfriend sat on a nearby bench and stretched her arms out with a yawn.

When a flurry of orange mist appeared and Riddle materialised, Kinsley choked on her cupcake and covered her mouth. Her father stood with his hands on his hips, a stern look on his face. Kinsley gasped loudly when there was a flurry of green mist and Taviar appeared beside Riddle. Kinsley's stomach did somersaults; it didn't take a genius to know she was in deep shit with them—despite her being an adult. She had run off, leaving her brothers alone.

"Hi," she squeaked as she stepped closer to them.

Kinsley paused when Taviar glared at his daughter; his jaw tightened and he looked at Riddle for reassurance. She gulped audibly, placing a hand on her stomach as she exhaled a breath. Together, her fathers approached her.

"Is Ashim and Orison well?" Eloise asked.

Taviar looked at Eloise. "They're both fine, El. Kinsley, we need to talk."

With a nod, Kinsley lowered her head and prepared for the worst. She knew she should have been honest and told her fathers of her plan; stated that she was going, even if they said no. Though Kinsley knew her brothers could hold their own, her fathers were very protective of all three of them. Even as the days went on, she knew she had crossed the line.

"What were you thinking, leaving your brothers by themselves?" Riddle exclaimed.

Kinsley looked at her hands. "That I needed to save my friend from King Raj and if I was honest, you would've said no. But I needed to go for Orison."

A groan made her look up. Riddle paced in a circle and shook his head. He rubbed the stubble on his chin and ran a hand through his hair. Kinsley hated that she'd disappointed them, though the journey she'd taken wasn't up for debate. She had to do this for her friend—and she had succeeded. Orison was back on the right side of the ocean; finally safe in Torwarin and ready to take the crown.

"Kins, you could have told us," Taviar said sternly.

She nodded and tapped her foot. Kinsley didn't have any words to say; sorry didn't seem enough for her deception and dishonesty. Despite knowing her fathers would forgive her quickly, she didn't want to say anything to upset them further.

"I'm sorry, Father and Papa, I should have been honest and told you," Kinsley eventually voiced.

"You're lucky your brothers were safe," Taviar reprimanded.

Kinsley nodded. "I'll be honest in the future, Father. I'm sorry."

After all she endured getting Orison home, Kinsley had to admit to herself that despite disappointing her fathers, it was all worth it to bring her friend home—for a new Fallasingha to be rebuilt out of the ashes of Sila's reign. However, she didn't consider how busy her fathers were and the worry she had brought to them. When Taviar and Riddle embraced her, Kinsley welcomed it and breathed a sigh of relief.

They stayed liked that for a while until she took a step back and headed to the laundry hut. She watched bubbles escape out of the barrel as the horse trotted along. If her fathers were there, it meant they were taking her and Eloise to Torwarin. Once reunited with Aeson, everything would slowly get back to normal; everybody had to take it one day at a time.

With a handful of books from the library cradled against her chest, Orison hummed to herself as she made her way to Torwarin's main square. She came to a stop as she noticed each of the villagers had frozen mid-activity; all stared in the same direction. Orison's heart raced as her mind flooded with thoughts that Xabian was in the vicinity, ready to take her far away from the safety of Torwarin; until she heard the music.

A sorrowful sound of a piano trailed down the main street. If a voice accompanied the tune, Orison convinced herself it would sound like somebody was crying as they sang. That was why the villagers were all immobile as they listened to it.

Unlike the villagers, Orison followed the music. To pick up the pace, she ran a few times, eager to inspect where the mournful sound was coming from. She'd never heard anything like it before; judging by the villagers' reactions, neither had anybody else. Doubt crept into her belly, thinking it was a siren's call that lured the villagers to their doom and freezing them in place.

She came to a stop at a familiar building—her former cabin, back when Idralis had sent her to Torwarin for refuge. Plucking up her courage, she walked up the path to the front door, not daring to think of the consequences. Her feet crunched on the gravel as the music increased in tempo; the stairs creaked with each slow step.

Cupping her hand over her eyes to block out the glaring sun, she peered through the window; to her surprise, Ashim sat at a piano in the living room. His eyes were closed as his fingers danced along the keys like they were patrons at a ball. Ashim was far away from there; lost in the music like Orison had never seen before. Her attention snagged on the open front door. Orison leaned against the doorframe as the music raised to a crescendo before he played the final sorrowful notes and lifted his hands off the keys.

"That was beautiful," Orison commented.

Ashim jumped and whirled around. He gazed upon her in a wide-eyed stare, like she had uncovered one of his secrets. Returning to the piano, his fingers brushed over the keys in a soft caress. "It's called *Te Shahran*."

She crossed the space between them, then settled on the piano bench when Ashim moved along. Clearing his throat, Ashim played the first few notes again; a chuckle filled the space when Orison tapped a key—ruining the mood of the song.

"What's *Te Shahran* about?"

Ashim was silent for a few moments; his fingers hovered over the keys. "It's about a couple separated because of an arranged marriage and the bride sings about her lost lover. She is telling him she doesn't want the wedding and has no desire to spend her life with a stranger. Promising she would come back to him some way or another."

"Did they eventually?"

He shrugged. "I don't know. But I hope they did, like us."

With that, he resumed playing. This time, he added lyrics to *Te Shahran*. Now that Orison knew the story, it made her think about Ashim's journey to get her away from Xabian's clutches and keep her safe. Her vision blurred with tears at how similar their story was to *Te Shahran* and how Ashim had traversed Fallasingha to get her back. When the room fell silent, Orison lifted her gaze to meet Ashim's. His eyes roamed over her as he took in her features.

"Teach me," Orison announced as she wiped her tears away.

Ashim took the books out of her arms and placed them on top of the piano. He held her hands and placed her fingers on the keys. "It sounds sadder with two people playing."

He walked her through each of the keys. Orison quickly picked it up and when they completed a full tandem of the song, the sorrowfulness had increased tenfold. With two people, it sounded complete in a way it hadn't before—like two lovers were crying out in anguish at their heartbreak.

They spent most of the day playing various songs. Ashim taught Orison more songs from Karshakroh; some more cheerful than *Te Shahran*. It made her reminisce of the Haranshal markets and the beautiful streets of Lhandahir. It was like the events of the past few days had never happened.

The lower dungeons always gave Taviar the creeps, along with a heavy weight that settled on his shoulders; like an entity was watching him from the darkness. He preferred not to dwell there longer than necessary; in his opinion, it wasn't a place for the living. Only the most heinous prisoners were sent down there—to be forgotten and left to waste away. Xabian was the exception; people had the unfortunate task to check and feed him because he was royalty.

Guards flanked Taviar and Emphina as they made their way through the decrepit corridor. Their footfalls were silent on the soft dirt of the floor as they made their way to Xabian's cell. Taviar watched Edmund untie the keys from his waistband; they clinked together as they walked further down the corridor. At the end, Edmund slotted the key into the iron door and unlocked it. The door swung open with a creak as he gestured for Taviar to enter.

The cell had stone walls where sconces illuminated the space. Chains held Xabian's arms above his head. The prince's head hung low as he sat on an iron bed. As Taviar entered the space, hay swished along with the stone floor, his gaze fixated on the Normahlef berries on Xabian's wrists and neck. To catch Xabian's attention, Taviar cleared his throat loudly; he pushed his shoulders back and clasped his hands in front of him—the prince didn't move.

"This is no place for royalty," Xabian said weakly.

Taviar scratched his nose. He had the dreaded task of telling Xabian why he was down there and reveal the truth about why the king was acting so cruel. Emphina entered the room; she held up the skirt on her black dress until she stood beside Taviar. She stood tall as she regarded Xabian.

"For your safety, you have to be here," Emphina explained confidently. "I'm afraid to inform you that you're still cursed with the Nighthex."

Xabian's head shot up. "No! It ended!"

"It became permanent when you went into the mortal realm." Emphina stared Xabian down, sorrow in her gaze. "In time, you will slowly become the Nyxite and live the rest of your days as a dragon."

Xabian's breathing increased significantly; his eyes darted from Taviar to Edmund, who stood in the doorway. Taviar averted his attention when Xabian regarded him; he couldn't look the prince in the eyes. Even he couldn't deny that the curse had begun to consume Xabian; the speed was astronomical.

"You're lying!" The chains rattled as Xabian tried to surge forward, but he stopped short when the manacles went taut. Edmund stepped forward, his hand on the pommel of his sword; Taviar watched the guard captain closely. "You're lying," he sobbed. Tears glazed over his purple eyes.

"Think of it!" Emphina exclaimed, raising her voice for emphasis. "Your recent behaviour should be proof enough, kidnapping an ally and sinking a ship in the Falshak Sea." She scoffed and looked at him with scorn.

"You killed an Akornsonian ship captain. It could have brought war to Fallasingha when we've just gained peace!" Taviar shouted.

Their voices echoed around the dungeon. Taviar watched Xabian shrink in on himself; his head down in shame. He looked upon a man who was slowly deteriorating before his eyes. He couldn't help but blame himself for allowing Sila to curse his brother that night—but he was too scared to speak up against that tyrannical monster.

Xabian shook his head; the chains rattled as he tried to cover his ears to no avail. "Stop lying to me!" He looked at Emphina. "Let me out. I'll try to control it with the medication."

"Please," Taviar managed to say as he closed his eyes. "This is the only place for you to undergo the transformation in a safe and controlled environment."

Xabian's eyes were wide with terror and tears on his cheeks glistened in the candlelight. He looked expectantly upon Emphina, like she would assist in this situation. All she could do was shake her head. Taviar hoped the news was sinking in about what was happening to him and would accept the medication more willingly. Something told him he would put up more of a fight.

"Please, let me out; I'm sorry. I was only trying to protect Orison." He rattled his chains with a grimace. "Please."

Emphina clutched her dress. "Explain your eyes, Xabian."

A choked sound escaped Xabian as he looked at the ceiling; his body shuddered as he wept. The prince could not explain why his eyes glowed so vividly all the time—so much so that they could see the glow through his eyelids, which didn't normally happen. Xabian lowered his head, as if accepting the inevitable truth. The chains rattled more violently as he screamed in anguish as reality set in. This change would be long and torturous until he was the Nyxite for all eternity.

Taviar approached the door. "I hope we meet again."

Xabian's cries followed Taviar into the corridor with his entourage. The cell door locked behind them. Another scream made Taviar tense as he staggered to a nearby wall and took a deep breath to calm down after the ordeal.

Together, the group returned to the portal at the opposite end of the corridor. Taviar couldn't bear to look one last time at Xabian's cell; the guilt was too much for him to handle. He could have stopped Sila that night and because of his failure, he had given Xabian a death sentence. Only time would reveal the true scale of what Sila's choice had brought to Fallasingha and the rest of the Othereal.

FORTY-FIVE

Metal sang as two swords collided. Nazareth spun on the spot and brought her sword down on Orison, who swiftly blocked the attack with her own and pushed Nazareth away. With heavy breaths, they parried with swords until Orison swung her weapon towards Nazareth, who ducked and swept Orison's feet out from under her. She crashed to the icy ground with a yelp and sprawled out on her back. Orison's chest heaved from the onslaught.

Nazareth grimaced as she pushed her blonde hair from her sweaty face; she paced in a circle while trying to catch her breath. She looked down at Orison and aimed the butt of her sword towards her. When Orison grabbed the sword, Nazareth adjusted her stance and helped her to her feet.

"You said you'd go easy," Orison wheezed.

Shaking her head, Nazareth walked circles around her. "This is easy."

Without warning, she spun her sword and swung towards Orison, who narrowly blocked her. Metal thundered around the open space near Torwarin lake. Nazareth jammed her sword at Orison multiple times in quick succession, to the point she staggered back with her arms crossed above her head—their silent signal to stop.

Retreating, Nazareth lowered her sword. She knew she got carried away and forgot her opponent was a novice. This was merely a warm-up for Nazareth. Sheathing her sword, she crossed her arms over her chest.

"Why did you want to do this?" Nazareth asked as she tried to touch her toes.

Orison was silent for a few moments. "I didn't like feeling powerless."

"Ah." Nazareth shook her body out when she straightened up. "If you block at the right moment, you could throw me off balance and put me in a choke hold."

Throwing her head back with a laugh, Orison smacked her sword against the frozen grass. She shook her head before regarding Nazareth. "I'm not doing that."

Nazareth unsheathed her sword, holding it in front of her with a wicked grin. A silent challenge for Orison to grow a backbone and do it. The emissary was used to being thrown around. During her countless years of training, many of the king's men and women had thrown her all around this very field. Orison was too gentle and forgiving—when in battle, those two words didn't exist. If Orison wanted to feel powerful, she had to forget the meaning of them. She had to fight and toughen up.

"Okay. Imagine I'm Xabian and I'm coming to take you again." She surveyed the princess before her as she once again sheathed her sword. Folding her arms over her chest, she stared Orison down. "Would you just take it, or will you fight?"

Her friend baulked and looked around. The only people watching them were the other guards. She slowly made her way around to the back of Orison, stopping behind her. Nazareth grabbed her from behind with force. Orison cried out and threw her sword down; with a heave, she threw Nazareth over her back, sending the Elven emissary crashing to the ground. Before she could regain composure, Orison wrapped her arm around the emissary's neck and squeezed. Holding her breath, Nazareth tapped Orison's arm. She let go immediately, staggering back with abject horror at what she'd done to her friend. Nazareth merely sat up and held her throat.

"Sorry!" Orison pleaded. "Is your leg okay?"

Nazareth shoved Orison hard. "When in a fight, there are no apologies or remorse!" Her blood boiled. "If you don't want to feel powerless, repeat what you did right then—doing whatever it takes to survive. Think of how you felt when you rode into the Battle of Torwarin. *That* is the version of Orison I want to see in a fight!"

Taken aback, Orison nodded and collected her sword from the ground. Fumbling to her feet, Nazareth returned to a fighting stance; her sword sang as she drew it and aimed for Orison. She could see the fire in Orison's eyes, the fight she withheld, the anger that drove her into battle. In her reverie, Nazareth didn't have time to relax before she felt Orison, once again, using her foot to swipe Nazareth's good leg out from under her.

Diving into a roll, Nazareth landed on one knee as she blocked the onslaught of attacks from Orison's sword. This was what she had been asking of Orison, who had finally released that fierce woman from her cage.

Throwing Orison onto her back, Nazareth held her sword to Orison's throat. Both breathed heavily from the exertion of the battle, inches from each other's faces. Orison's eyes flared when they took in Nazareth. The emissary sank back onto her knees before settling into a kneeling position.

"Could I face Xabian like that?" Orison asked, breathless as she stared at the sky.

Nazareth made a noise. "You'll need a lot of training."

"Then we go again."

Orison stood up and held a hand out to Nazareth. With a grin, Nazareth accepted the invitation and they restarted their battle. She saw Orison as a dull blade which needed sharpening. By the time Nazareth had finished with her, she would be lethal.

The setting sun filled the wooden walls of the bedroom with a welcoming hue; casting shadows that stretched to the ceiling. Orison's head rested comfortably on Ashim's shoulder. She stared at her hand that rested on his bare chest, watching the way it rose and fell with each breath, as he slept soundly. It was peaceful, with only bird song to fill the silence—the first bit of harmony she'd had in days. If she could, Orison would happily stay in this moment for a lifetime, enjoying the little world she'd created.

Their current cabin wasn't on the lakefront where Orison was used to. If it was, her view would have been even more perfect; instead, she could see into the neighbouring home. Seeing an easel splattered with paint and multiple canvasses propped against the wall, one could assume the owners were artists who sold their paintings to the wealthy.

Orison settled with Ashim, closing her eyes as she willed sleep to return. His arm tightened around her and she relaxed within his embrace; wanting to remain in their peaceful bubble. Her tranquil world shattered with a knock at the front door. Her eyes fluttered open and she watched the window again, not wanting to get up. After a few minutes, another knocking sound filled the cabin. With a groan, Orison propped herself onto her elbow, feeling Ashim's hold on her tighten slightly before it eased. There was another knock, more insistent than the last.

Easing out of bed, Orison winced when Ashim stirred and turned onto his side. She put on her slippers and adjusted her orange dress before exiting the room.

Making her way downstairs, Orison plucked her lilac coat from the hook and slipped it on. She unlocked the front door and inched it open. To her surprise, Riddle stood on the other side, watching a light dusting of snow settle on Torwarin's streets. Taviar was by his side, his gaze fell on Orison.

Orison laughed with relief, grateful to see her fathers, as she stepped onto the porch. She closed the door behind her and accepted the hug; Riddle immediately embraced her. He rubbed her back with a gentle squeeze; his embrace spoke of safety and protection, which she needed now more than ever. When Riddle let her go, Taviar extended his arms and Orison stepped into his hug. She groaned with a laugh when he squeezed her.

"We're here to take you home," Taviar announced as he stepped back. "We have so much to prepare for with the upcoming coronation and getting a tutor to teach you royal protocol. I trust you'll learn quickly so we can stay on schedule."

Orison stepped out of Taviar's embrace and smiled. "King Raj taught me Fallasingha royal protocols while in his care," she announced. Her words made Taviar stiffen and raise an eyebrow. "It'll be good to get a refresher before the coronation."

"How?" Taviar asked.

She shrugged. "He wouldn't answer how he had the information. When are we leaving?"

"I was hoping now, while Xabian is imprisoned," Taviar explained. Orison glanced back at the house. "Unless we can't?"

"Ashim's asleep; maybe when he awakens. He didn't sleep when looking for Xabian," she explained. Taviar nodded and moved her over to a bench on the covered porch.

"We've taken everything from Idralis's Tsunamal home. He currently has a strange sounding cat in his office," Riddle announced.

Orison covered her mouth to stifle a laugh. "That would be Mahavu."

"Mahavu?"

Orison nodded with a smile. "She's Ashim's cat. If Idralis lets her out of her cage, she'll be quiet. You know how cats are; they hate being confined."

They both chuckled. When the door opened, Orison turned her head; she hated the sheer look of panic in Ashim's wide-eyed stare as he surveyed the outside. His hair was dishevelled, like he'd run a hand through it multiple times and he hadn't put his shirt on. She pushed herself off the bench, stepped towards him and rubbed his arm for reassurance that she was still there. He breathed a sigh of relief as he held her close and kissed her head.

"I thought he'd taken you again," Ashim admitted. He sounded breathless with worry.

Orison shook her head. "Taviar and Riddle are here to take us to Alsaphus Castle," she announced and stepped aside, gesturing to her fathers.

Ashim bowed deeply when he realised Orison wasn't alone. He stepped towards them and shook their hands as an introduction. Despite being tense, Riddle and Taviar greeted him with forced smiles. She couldn't blame them, after years of being told Karshakians were evil. Orison knew that in time, they would realise Ashim was a safe person to be around.

"Do you want to get ready, then we'll be on our way?" Orison asked.

Ashim looked down, his eyes widened and he covered his chest. Orison giggled and tried to hide the blush that crept over her face. She gave him a kiss and watched as he ran back into the cabin to get ready. It felt strange knowing she was going back to Alsaphus Castle.

"You don't trust him, do you?" Orison asked.

Taviar ran his hands over the bench. "Not at the moment, but I'm confident as I spend more time around Ashim, he'll be a valuable ally."

It was better than a flat-out refusal to realise he wasn't like the others. As they waited, butterflies filled Orison's stomach at what she'd see sooner—rather than later. The person Alsaphus Castle knew all those months ago had died in the Battle of Torwarin. She was returning to the castle as a newly forged weapon.

Walking through Alsaphus Castle's front doors felt like a betrayal. Each mission assigned to Ashim, which involved this castle, always meant sneaking through the servants' doorway. King Raj had forbidden Runners to use the front doors lest they got caught. It still surprised him how his brand no longer burned when he broke such orders now.

The entryway was breathtaking as all-white walls greeted him, complimenting the black and white checked floor. When Ashim last snuck into the castle, all the walls had been a dark wood adorned with pictures of war—someone had removed all the pictures. At the top of the grand staircase, Ashim's jaw fell open when he spotted a large painting of Orison on the throne; an artist appeared to have done it from their imagination.

Orison's grip on his arm tightened as they came to a stop in the centre. He glanced at her with curiosity. She was tense as she peered around the foyer, fear clouded her every feature and each exhale was slow. Ashim checked on Mahavu cradled in Orison's arm; she shifted as Orison's grip tightened slightly.

Patting her hand gently, "King Sila's not here," he assured.

She placed Mahavu in Ashim's arms, then grabbed the fabric of her dress and raced outside. Concerned, Ashim followed her with haste, watching her sprint down the gravel path towards the castle gates. He remained on the top step, fascinated by what she was doing, while he petted Mahavu's head. Ashim wondered if the sprint was something she had been waiting for since arriving in the Othereal.

Ashim gasped when she raced through the wrought-iron gates. Orison skidded to a stop and turned around. Her squeal of excitement resonated around the courtyard and into the castle; Orison jumped up and down, then fell to her knees. Ashim couldn't hold in his laughter and smiled. He kissed Mahavu's head followed by scratches under her chins. He jumped when Orison appeared before him in a flurry of purple smoke.

She kissed him, then Mahavu; her eyes were suddenly wide. "There's so much of this castle I have no idea about," Orison announced.

She took Ashim's hand and tugged him through the entry once more. He looked down at Mahavu as she shifted. Orison pulled him through the foyer. Ashim looked over his shoulder as he was guided through a sunlit green corridor full of windows.

"Where are we going?" he asked.

"We are exploring. Shields blocked half the rooms in this place when Sila was alive," Orison explained. "I wonder what the rooms hold. Do you think they're all bedrooms, or are they treasure troves?" She gasped loudly. "What if there's a second library?"

Ashim laughed. "Calm down, Ori. Let's explore slowly."

She came to an abrupt halt, causing Ashim to bump into her. "But..."

"All this is yours, Ori. You can spend years exploring every nook and cranny of this place; don't waste it all in a single night."

Orison regarded his words, then continued on their path. They ventured down a dark wooden corridor, void of light like the green corridor. She opened each door they came across, peering inside before moving on—until they emerged into another sunlit corridor. Ashim watched her disappear into any place deemed worthy of exploration.

They found the guards' training area—it resembled a dungeon with dark, high fortified walls; hay covered the floor. The only thing different was the apple tree at the back. They had piled all the weaponry into buckets or hung them on the wall. Upon Orison's and Ashim's presence, the guards stopped their activities to watch the couple. With a wave from Orison, she closed the door and Ashim followed her to the next room.

The next door they entered was a light-brown music room where white dust blankets covered all the instruments. Looking around, Ashim approached the one that looked like a grand piano; he perched Mahavu on his shoulder to investigate. Gripping the dust sheet, he removed it and the material billowed to the floor. He cast his eyes on the sleek black instrument and ran his hands over the polished wood. He opened the keyboard cover and played a few keys, eyes widening in awe that it was perfectly in tune.

"We'll come back here tonight, let's explore something else," Orison encouraged.

Glancing at the piano, then at Orison, he nodded and raced after her. They walked hand in hand as they entered another wing—some rooms were open, revealing empty spaces or drawing rooms. It fascinated Ashim that he never realised how large Alsaphus Castle was.

Orison's smile faltered when they got to the throne room and stopped at the closed door. Ashim gently touched her arm to comfort her as she sucked in a shuddering breath. On a phantom wind, the doors opened; Orison gripped Ashim's hand in a vice-like hold as she stared down the aisle.

The throne room looked as it always did. Large stone archways flanked a vacant space for balls or ceremonies; in the centre sat the throne on a raised dais. Ashim had only ventured into the throne room a few times when on a mission to steal artefacts from the royal vaults.

Shaken out of his thoughts, Ashim felt Orison let go of his arm. He watched in awe as she pushed her shoulders back. She clasped her trembling hands together and began her walk down the centre aisle. Ashim was her shadow as he followed; he didn't know why she appeared to fear this room, but he would be her light through the darkness.

At the end of the aisle, Orison climbed onto the dais and settled on the throne. Ashim watched her run her hands along the cold stone surface as she adjusted in the seat. He noted how uncomfortable she looked to be sitting there, despite the throne looking like they made it for her to sit on. All Orison needed was a crown and she'd be the queen he saw every day. Ashim maneuvered Mahavu into his arm.

"Sit with me," Orison said.

Ashim held Mahavu up. "There's not enough room for the three of us."

Orison stood up and pointed to the throne. Ashim bowed his head as she took Mahavu out of his arms. He eased himself onto the throne—the first time he would sit upon it. The stone material felt icy-cold, like the blustering winter wind outside. He had an inkling that the throne was enchanted and it knew he wasn't royal.

The throne warmed when Orison settled herself onto Ashim's lap; he held her waist and watched her hold Mahavu close while petting her soft fur. He thought it would feel wrong to sit on a royal throne—especially one of an enemy nation—but he found himself extremely comfortable, like it was something he was born for.

Orison faced Ashim. "This is where Sila forced me to become a Fae."

"We can leave this room if you want," Ashim suggested as he moved her hair so he could see her face better. "See something that doesn't hold bad memories."

She shook her head. "I need to get over my fear. When I take the crown, I'll have to spend a lot of time here. Might as well get comfortable."

Ashim rubbed her back and let her reminisce. The room fell silent, except for Mahavu's loud purrs. Orison stroked her sand-coloured fur and stared into space. Her admission made Ashim understand Orison's fear of the throne room and her silence when she stepped inside. Though he knew what Sila had done—regarding locking her in the castle, he didn't know the true scale of it. The room felt colder since she uttered those words.

"And this is where Sila cursed Prince Neasha with the Nighthex," Orison announced as she leaned against Ashim.

He tensed at her further admission and turned to her. Without being prompted, she explained the tellages she found and what she saw hidden within the pages. She told him how the Nighthex led Neasha to a slow torturous death, where Fallasingha Castle guards eventually slayed him in Cleravoralis. When she couldn't recall any further details, the story hung like a heavy cloud in the near-silent throne room.

"Was Xabian cursed in this room?" Ashim asked out of curiosity.

Orison shook her head. "That was in Sila's room on the night I arrived."

She continued to recall things from the tellages she had devoured. Her recollection of Xabian's last moment was truly harrowing; Ashim's heart raced and he shifted in his seat. Xabian had fought Sila until he couldn't bear the pain any longer; all attempts to prevent Sila taking Orison from her parents had failed.

After she stopped, Ashim couldn't form the words for what he felt. It was clear she'd been holding these stories in for too long and it was time the walls of the castle listened.

Forty-Six

Blindfolded, Orison extended her hand out as Kinsley guided her into her former chamber room. Their giggles cut through the silence whilst her feet scuffled along the floor for guidance. Kinsley burst into laughter when Orison bumped into the door frame; she chuckled as she righted herself. From behind, she felt a tug on the blindfold and it fell away. Orison gasped loudly as she took in the transformation before her.

The space was still disgustingly extravagant with the two marble mermaids that flanked the fireplace and held up the ceiling. It had been modified from a dark, unforgiving place to a welcoming environment with white walls; gone were the depictions of war, replaced by colourful paintings of flowers. Orison moved on to her former bed chambers; the dark walls were painted white. They had disposed of the tapestry of a battle and replaced it with a mural of a flower field. She faced Kinsley, who smiled expectantly at Orison as she awaited an answer.

"It's beautiful." Orison looked around the room in awe.

As she further inspected the space, they had replaced most of the furniture. Orison's friends had replaced the red sofa for a green one; her dining table and bed were a light wood instead of dark wood. Everything looked refreshed and no longer resembled the prison she remembered.

Regardless of its newfound beauty, the space would forever haunt Orison and continue to be the place where Sila imprisoned her. With all the furniture being in the same place, Orison could still see the time when Sila slapped her across the face in a fit of rage and later destroyed her bed.

Forcing a smile, Orison faced Kinsley. "You did this?"

Kinsley nodded, then glanced over her shoulder when Eloise and Aeson entered the room. She extended her hand out to them. "We all did."

Orison covered her mouth. "I can't believe you've done this." She whirled around and inspected the details in the paintings, running her finger along the brush strokes that made the flowers look real. "You're so talented."

"It's your coronation gift," Aeson explained.

"You didn't have to give me anything for that." Orison touched the sofa in awe at the difference. "The furniture is a lighter colour."

Kinsley blushed. "I picked it out personally."

Her breathing hitched as she crossed the threshold, coming to a stop in front of the fireplace. Flashes of memories invaded her joy. She could remember pacing in front of the fireplace when she first received the note from King Idralis—at the time she didn't know who sent it. Orison settled down on the sofa with a huff of breath.

"All of this is beautiful, thank you. All of you," Orison choked out.

Eloise settled beside her, tapping her thigh. "We can fully understand if you don't want to sleep here anymore, but we thought it would be good to see a new life brought into the castle. And we aren't only talking about Mahavu."

A laugh escaped Orison as Eloise pulled her to her feet. "Yeah, the memories are too raw right now to stay here. There's lots of rooms I now have access to. I'll find one with Ashim and then you three can decorate to your heart's desires."

The trio nodded in agreement. Orison called for Aiken, who instantly appeared. She curtsied low and gasped upon seeing the room's transformation; the servant collected herself and clasped her hands in front of her.

"May we have some wine, please," Orison requested.

"Certainly." Aiken curtsied once more before she disappeared.

They all settled into the chairs around the dining table. When Aiken returned, she poured white wine into golden goblets and placed the bottle in the centre of the table. As quickly as she arrived, she curtsied and left.

"Did Ashim explain what happened when Xabian took you?" Kinsley asked. She leaned forward in her chair as she swirled her wine. Orison shook her head as she took a sip, then placed her feet up on the table. "He was on it. Immediately wanted the discovaker, he was not taking no for an answer. Babe, how long was it before you were on your way to Parndore?"

"Around half an hour," Aeson said with a smile.

Kinsley shifted to the edge of her seat. "Half an hour! He searched the entire house twice for you and then he was gone; Aeson went with him."

Orison smiled to herself as she looked down at her glass of wine. She averted her attention to Eloise and Aeson as they recalled how worked up Ashim became from the experience. He'd been brushing it off every time she asked.

Aeson steered the conversation to how they got to Karshakroh. He explained about their plan and their jobs to gain passage. The more he talked about the ship, the more it made her remember the sinking; something she didn't want to recall yet. Orison listened intently as she sipped on the wine. It felt like old times and as if she had never been on an incredible journey of self-discovery.

Riddle leaned against the cashier's desk of Riddle Me This Antiquities and frowned as he inspected the band of thorns Kinsley had found underneath Orison's bed. It was the first instance where he had enough time to properly inspect the discovery; what he saw wasn't anything good. Something unnerved him about the two objects.

It was undeniable that somebody had tried to assassinate Orison by exiling her to the mortal realm, then have her succumb to magic starvation. Riddle was inquisitive about who would do something so heinous. The unknown grated on him like an itch he couldn't scratch. Before him, the thorns still glowed an angry red; the Desigle diamonds still glowed their soft white hue—both items contradicted each other in power.

He tried again to uncover the mystery person who'd placed a hex on Orison. As he pushed his power towards it, it was the same illusion of a murky lake, where a warped silhouette stared back. Retreating from the vision, Riddle glanced at the clock above the stairs leading to his home that read it was almost midnight—he'd kept the thorns out of their box for over an hour.

Cursing under his breath, Riddle never intended to keep them out that long—out of superstition that the curse could come true. He swiftly placed them back in their box and sealed it shut. Then his attention settled on the diamonds. Rubbing his chin, he drummed his fingers on the desk, he used his magic to lift a diamond to eye level.

Riddle inspected the Desigle diamond with awe. They were an anomaly in the Othereal and so rare that they were seldom published in books on enchantments. Riddle had been in talks with Emphina to understand why the Desigle, an already powerful enchantment, would create something to protect itself further.

"Papa." Riddle jumped and dropped the diamond in the box. He turned to where the voice came from, finding Zade standing at the stairs rubbing his eye. "I had a bad dream."

Riddle waved his son to come towards him; Zade did so and held him close. "Did you tell it to go away?" Zade nodded. "Okay, how about you help me, then we get some warm milk?"

"Okay, Papa." He lifted Zade up and sat him on the cashier's desk. Zade noticed the band of thorns. "That's not good."

Riddle shook his head quickly and returned to inspecting the diamond; the crystal twinkled in the light as he rotated it. The items were complete mysteries. Whoever placed this knew how to shield themselves from Charmseers. Zade swung his feet, they drummed against the cupboard door with dull thuds.

He intently watched Riddle inspect a second diamond. Riddle gently placed a hand on Zade's legs to stop him from swinging as he tried to concentrate, before he placed the diamond in the box.

"These diamonds are called Desigle diamonds, they're almost unheard of," Riddle explained to Zade. "It's the first time seeing so many up close."

Zade used his magic to pick up a diamond. "Some of my friends at school found a book in the library about them." He looked around. "I forgot the name, but apparently they create diamonds when a person who makes a Desigle forms a hex."

Riddle's attention peaked; he drummed his fingers on the counter. "I've never heard of such a book. Have your friends been sneaking into the castle?"

Zade placed the diamond back in the box. "The book is in the smaller library, in the East Wing." He returned to drumming his feet on the desk. "Can you not see who it is, Papa?"

"They hid themselves from my powers," Riddle explained, then looked at his son. "What is the title of the book your friends saw?" Zade shrugged. With a sigh, Riddle placed the diamonds back in the box and padlocked it. He slid it under his desk then helped Zade down. "Come on, let's get you to bed; you have school."

They climbed the stairs to the apartment. Riddle used his magic to plunge the shop into darkness as he closed for the night. Once upstairs, he approached the icebox, opened the wooden door and took out the milk. He grabbed a glass and poured some milk for Zade. He ensured it had honey to aid with sleep and cast the nightmares away.

Zade's words about the Desigle replayed in Riddle's mind. He needed to look in that library and get the book his friends were talking about. He had to have concrete evidence before he handed his findings over to Taviar or Saskia.

Shaking his thoughts away, Riddle used his magic to warm up the milk. He stirred the honey through and gave the glass to Zade.

"Here you go," Riddle said. "Get back to bed or you'll be too tired in the morning."

When Riddle was confident Zade had gone to bed, he climbed up the stairs to his own room. He smiled at Taviar, who lay asleep on his side, illuminated by moonlight through the window. Riddle climbed in beside him and held his husband close as he continued to mull over Zade's words and what it meant about the mysterious box downstairs. So many thoughts ran through his head; it took a long while for sleep to come.

Unable to sleep, Ashim stared into space while seated at the dining table in his new chambers. The room was illuminated by the Othereal lights that were turned down low. They cast the stone floor in an orange hue, enough to see the light-brown walls. Through the open bedroom door, he had a perfect view of Orison, who was sound asleep.

He watched Mahavu as she navigated her way across the back of the brown sofa; she came to a halt and stretched out, showing her claws. Her yawn showed her sharp teeth before she shook her body. Ashim set his cup down and inched to the edge of his chair. He knew what Mahavu had planned and was prepared to grab her.

"*Anesh*, Mahavu!" he warned sternly.

Mahavu ignored Ashim and sunk her claws into the brown fabric with loud ripping sounds as she massaged her paws. He pushed himself out of the chair so fast it clattered to the floor. He grabbed Mahavu to prevent her causing any damage. The cat hissed and wriggled in Ashim's arms. The bed creaked and when Ashim turned to the bedroom, he saw Orison roll over. He groaned loudly when he realised Mahavu had disturbed her.

"Stop," he hissed in Karshakir. "Sofa not for scratching."

"Is everything okay?" He whirled around at Orison's voice.

"*Halek*, go back to sleep," Ashim said.

In the dim light, he saw Orison's half-closed eyes from being woken up. Her blonde tousled hair fell down her shoulders as she observed Ashim's precarious situation. The cat still wriggled in his arms and hissed in protest. Since moving to Fallasingha, Mahavu was being more mischievous, determined to let everybody know she was unsettled.

Orison returned to bed and settled back down. "Come to bed."

He carried Mahavu to their bedroom, placed her on his side of the bed and climbed under the covers. Before he had a chance to settle beside Orison, Mahavu jumped into Ashim's space. With a shake of his head, Ashim pushed her out of the way and settled down, holding Orison close. He glanced nervously when Mahavu growled; he rolled his eyes and shook his head.

Ashim kissed Orison's shoulder. "We need to explore Fallasingha after the coronation."

"We do." Orison mumbled.

"Where do you want to travel to?" Ashim asked.

She turned to face him and pushed him onto his back. She rested her head on his chest as she wrapped her arm around him. Ashim rubbed her shoulder and thought of places to visit in Fallasingha. Like Orison, Ashim hadn't been able to explore a lot of the country. They could travel back to Tsunamal if they so dared, with their new home as a place to stay.

Orison snuggled into him. "Parndore."

The announcement made Ashim tense. He remembered the last time he'd entered the city, when he was overwhelmed with anxiety from Xabian taking her. Ashim sucked in a breath and tried to calm his racing heart, which beat painfully in his chest. A hand on his face made him look at Orison.

"What's wrong?" She wiped the tears away with her thumb. He hadn't known he was crying.

"That's the first place we searched when trying to save you from Xabian," Ashim admitted. "I was so scared, Ori. Scared he was going to kill you."

She pressed her hand to his cheek and kissed him deeply. His hand travelled up her back as he returned her kiss. They continued until Mahavu kicked Ashim in the leg and they parted. A quick glance over Orison's shoulder revealed the cat was massaging her paws into the duvet with loud purrs.

"You've taught me how to wipe minds," Orison said, as she rubbed his chest. "If he tried, I could have wiped everything."

Ashim nodded as he kissed her again. "I'm glad I taught you about that. Even if it's illegal in this country."

It was their secret. Due to its illegality, not many knew the true strength of Mindelates or the authentic way they could alter minds. The one person who couldn't know this trick was Xabian himself. Ashim couldn't think of what would happen if he knew.

"I'm glad you taught me that too," Orison mumbled.

He moved her hair behind her ear. "Ori." She lifted her eyes to his. "If Xabian ever tries to take you again..." Ashim sucked in a breath, "Wipe his mind until nothing is left."

She lifted her head up, eyes wide in shock. "Won't that kill him?"

Ashim closed his eyes. "Anesh." He played with the strap of her nightgown. "He won't die, just won't know anybody or anything around him. Then he can rot in a prison cell where he belongs." Realising that he sounded like the Karshakroh stereotypes, he shook his head quickly. "Sorry to ask this of you."

"I understand." She rested her head on his chest. "I'll do it, if I have to."

He kissed the top of her head and ran his fingers through her soft hair. Ashim hated that he had to ask Orison to do something so heinous, but it was the only way to ensure the safety of Fallasingha. Xabian wouldn't die if he had his mind wiped of memories. He would only be incapable of doing anything for himself; he would need people to teach him how to eat and toilet train him again. It would take years to relearn everything and it would be severely degrading.

"I'm sorry," he whispered.

Orison shifted. "Don't be. It needs to happen."

He nodded and snuffed out the lights. From what she told him, the friend Orison thought she knew never existed. Together, they would need to protect the entirety of the Othereal against the last living member of the Alsaphus Family.

FORTY-SEVEN

In the centre of the room, several mirrors surrounded a pedestal. Along the blush-pink walls were white wardrobes inlaid with gold embellishments. Pressed against the back wall was a matching vanity. A set of white chaises sat under the two floor-to-ceiling windows that overlooked the Visyan Mountains, where snow fell onto each peak.

Castle servants surrounded Orison—six of them held the hem of the floor-length gold ensemble they had placed her in; two others held the long train that trailed from the cape. Orison held Aiken's hand as she stepped onto the pedestal; when she was steady, the other servants let the dress drape down to the floor. She peered at herself for the first time in her coronation dress. It took her breath away as she caressed the soft gold material, shocked that it hugged her figure perfectly. It brought out her eye colour and the tan that still lingered from her time in Karshakroh.

"When did King Raj claim you?" Aiken asked as she fluffed out the gold fabric.

Orison looked down. "What do you mean?"

"The brand." Aiken straightened up; her gaze lingered on Orison's hip where the brand was.

Realisation dawned on Orison and she placed her hand over it. "When he made me a Runner in Karshak castle. Did Taviar and Saskia not inform you?"

"No." Aiken fussed over the dress again. "We should get an enchantress to remove it, along with the scar on your thigh."

"Both of them are staying," Orison answered more harshly than she intended, as she smoothed out a crease.

Aiken bit her lip. "But it's not very becoming of a queen."

"Are you asking Ashim to remove his brand?" Orison enquired; Aiken shook her head. "My decision is final. The brand and scar remain."

Aiken's shoulders drooped; she pulled out a pin from the cushion strapped to her wrist and tugged at the fabric on Orison's torso. She tightened the dress so it hugged Orison's curves more than before. Each servant was silent as they tugged and pulled at the fabric.

Orison clenched her fists until her fingers dug painfully into her skin. The thought of removing her scars had rage clouding her judgement; to calm down, she exhaled a breath and faced the mirror. She didn't care if they weren't pretty or becoming of a queen; it reminded her she had survived. In fact, she had fallen in love with them.

A servant tied Orison's hair up and pinned it in place with a hairclip as they fixed the neckline of the dress. Through the mirror, Orison smiled when she saw Ashim watching her from the doorway. He looked immaculate in a matching golden tunic; he had his hair pulled back into a low ponytail. Orison wanted to turn around and run to him, but the servants held her firmly in place. It felt like a farce to go through so much effort.

"What's happened with Xabian?" Aiken asked.

Her gaze stayed on Ashim. "The curse failed to end when he killed Sila. As a result, he's now imprisoned in the lower dungeons until it finally takes him."

Aiken made a noise and moved more of the dress around; she spread Orison's arms out. With an exhale of breath, Orison told the servant everything that had happened with Xabian—from his erratic behaviour in the mortal lands to kidnapping her. Orison explained she overheard Karshak servants discussing about Xabian holding a knife to King Raj's throat at a royal meeting; though she'd never been able to confirm its legitimacy. With each new story, the Viren's scowl grew, she tutted and tsked as she adjusted the dress.

With a glance at Ashim, "Stay with Sir Mahrishan," Aiken affirmed.

Orison glanced at him in the mirror. "That's my intention." The servants stepped back in unison to admire their work. Orison gasped at how much better the dress had turned out; she covered her mouth at how spectacular she looked.

Her appearance reminded her of the beautiful princesses she'd only ever read about in books. Gold fabric pooled around her; constellations crisscrossed along the skirt before a floral pattern made up the bodice. Though it was exceptionally heavy, she knew she wouldn't be in it for long. Orison knew she would be unrecognisable when she had her make-up on and the correct hair-style.

With the click of Aiken's fingers, the blossoming golden gown disappeared. Orison yelped and instinctively covered her body with her arms; until realising she was in a floor length, one-shoulder golden dress. Unlike the previous gown, it was light-weight; Orison held onto the golden fabric.

"This will be the dress you wear to the night ball," Aiken explained.

"It's spectacular," Orison said as she inspected it.

Orison turned around at the sound of footsteps as Ashim approached her. She smiled as she showed off the servants' work. Orison posed so Ashim could inspect the intricate details on the second dress; the same constellations filled the fabric and shimmered in certain lights. Up close, Orison could see that the same details were on his golden tunic.

"You're so beautiful," Ashim gasped. Orison felt her cheeks heat with his words. "I didn't know if it was bad luck to see a princess before her coronation, but tonight I want to explore."

"That's only weddings, Ash," Orison pointed out.

He made to talk again, but a loud gasp sounded from the corridor. "Sir Mahrishan, please return to your dressing room, we haven't finished!" a male servant shouted. Orison stifled a laugh and covered her mouth.

Ashim glanced at the door. "Oops. I'll pick you up before dinner."

Orison waved goodbye as Aiken turned her around. Through the mirror, she smiled as she watched Ashim leave; he blew her a kiss before he disappeared. It made her feel giddy with excitement to know that she could leave the castle without having to think twice; her excitement made her itch with impatience.

Cardenk's main town square had been transformed into a night market. Lanterns illuminated the narrow alleyways where people crammed together to shop for the latest wares. People exchanged goods and vendors called out the best sales. The smell of perfume and freshly baked pastries permeated through the air. Revellers from the pubs stumbled out of establishments and shouted their approval of the drinks they had.

Ashim drank it all in with awe; he gawped like a fish as he turned in a circle. Though they had markets in Haranshal, none were like this. He partially missed the smell of a thousand spices, which usually came from his favourite bazaar back home. Instead, he smelt the aromas of rich perfume, leather and alcohol.

When Orison pushed his mouth closed, he turned to her. "Your mouth is going to be a fly trap if you carry on gawping," she laughed.

"Cardenk is very beautiful," Ashim commented.

"Orison!" somebody called out. "Ashim!"

When Ashim turned towards the source of the voice, he witnessed Kinsley running up to them with a wave. Ashim waved her along and she pushed her way through the crowd.

"Kins!" Orison cried out; she groaned as they embraced each other with smiles. "I'm showing Cardenk to Ashim."

Ashim smiled as Kinsley held him briefly, then returned to Orison. From the corner of Ashim's eye, somebody extended a small white box to him. He opened it up to reveal a small cake inside with a light dusting of sugar and jam oozing over the edges. Picking it up, he sniffed it; when certain it was safe, he took a bite.

"With Mahavu getting settled, I think it's best if she stays with us in the lead up to the coronation," Kinsley offered.

"I agree. With all the preparations, I think it's best we don't stress her out," Orison said. "I think she'll be happy like that. What do you think, Ash?"

Ashim nodded. "It'll be best while she's settling into Fallasingha."

"That sounds great." Kinsley accepted a cloak. "How about I see if Aeson or El can join us, then we can show Ashim the beauty of Grandma Jo's?"

He frowned, unsure what would be beautiful about a grandma's place. Ashim's curiosity grew when Orison's eyes lit up with excitement—like he had poorly misconstrued what Grandma Jo's entailed. Orison tugged Ashim along, waving goodbye to Kinsley as she ran back in the direction she came from. Ashim wondered what they were going to uncover next.

Grandma Jo's wasn't a home at all; it was a lively bar. They had pushed tables to the side to create a dance floor. Some creatures played fiddles and pan flutes, while others drummed the bass with their feet. A variety of creatures danced to the heart-thumping beat. Some took it a step further as they roared with excitement and rocked drunkenly on discarded chairs. It reminded Ashim of Haranshal during King Raj's birthday; everything was merry in the city that day.

Ashim extended his hand out to Orison. Her purple gaze met his as she swallowed the mouthful of alcohol that she drank. "Dance with me, Little Queen."

Orison wiped her mouth with the back of her hand. She shook her head. "I can't dance."

He waved his hand expectantly. "*Cehen.*"

With a roll of her eyes, Orison took his hand and Ashim guided her to the dance floor. He observed the others, who weren't skilled at dancing either; they kicked their feet or performed wild jumps while laughing. To make Orison feel more confident, he wanted to show Orison a silly dance he did as a child.

He puffed out his chest, held Orison's arm in the air and trailed a finger down her arm. Orison watched his finger and gazed into his eyes as his hand held her waist. With a gentle push, he spun her around slowly; the wind caught her green dress, which wrapped its way around her legs like a snake. Orison stumbled and stepped on his foot.

"Sorry," she exclaimed.

Ashim chuckled. "I don't mind."

They eased into the dance. Ashim guided her to move her feet quickly to the sound of those who drummed their feet on the floor; Orison laughed as she looked down. Ashim used his finger to move her chin, so she looked at him instead of her feet. This dance was another way to show Orison his world. Her giggles warmed his heart; he laughed when she stumbled again and fell into him. Ashim kissed her softly before he spun her out of his arms and reeled her back in.

They both panted as he brushed her hair out of her eyes; she smiled up at him. Only now did he realise how silent Grandma Jo's Restaurant had become. A group of people dressed in black stood close to them. When he lifted his head, some castle guards stood nearby—all with stern expressions; some had their hands on the pommel of their swords. Orison's smile vanished instantly and she looked at her feet. Ashim clutched her hand for reassurance that she wasn't in trouble.

"Sorry for not asking permission to go out of the castle," Orison said with her head down. She pushed her hair behind her ear. "I'll collect my things." She moved towards their table.

"We're not here because you didn't ask permission," the lead guard with brown hair and green eyes said. The announcement made her turn around. "Come with us. There's an important matter to discuss."

Orison returned to the dance floor with their coats and they both shrugged them on. She took Ashim's hand as the guards led them out of Grandma Jo's. To get her smile back, Ashim swung Orison's arm like a mischievous child, but the guards' appearance had stolen every ounce of happiness she had. It made his smile diminish, too.

He gave her hand another gentle squeeze to tell her it was okay; they could go back to dancing soon. They walked a long while before the head guard found an abandoned barn shrouded in darkness; far away from civilians. Snow fell through the missing rafters.

"Are you going to tell us what this is about, Edmund?" Orison asked sternly.

Edmund clicked his tongue, then clutched his sword. "Prince Xabian has escaped the lower dungeons."

FORTY-EIGHT

Howling winds tore through the lower dungeons. Guards crammed into the space and stood in various alcoves, deep in discussions. Orison followed Edmund, Saskia and Taviar through the dilapidated corridors, with her hands shoved into her green coat's fur-lined pockets. As she neared Xabian's open cell door, a heavy weight settled on her shoulders—the same feeling that she had in the Lhandahir catacombs. In the doorway, Orison was greeted by a grotesque sickly-sweet smell, the stench so pungent it turned her stomach and she pressed a hand to her nose.

The scene before her was gruesome. The back wall of Xabian's cell was blasted out in a perfect circle of purple flame and three white sheets covered charred corpses. Orison gasped and her heart raced when she realised the flames were identical to the ones on the Sleeping Siren. It froze her to the spot as Saskia and Taviar navigated their way over the bodies to inspect the gaping hole. Orison noted the flames danced in the wind like a torn piece of fabric. The manacles that had bound Xabian were twisted and clinked against the wall; the Normahlef berries were scattered across the hay-strewn floor.

A hand on Orison's shoulder made her jump. When she realised it was Edmund, she stepped aside as he pushed past her gently. He stepped over the bodies and made his way over to Taviar. Edmund inspected the room with his hands on his hips.

"What happened?" she managed to get out.

Edmund's boots crunched on the debris as he crouched beside one of the corpses. "We were on duty in the castle and then the ground shook with a loud roar," he explained. "When the ones in charge of feeding Xabian didn't come back, I sent somebody to inspect the lower dungeons. The guard who sounded the alarm said something flew over the Visyan Mountains."

"Did you say something flew?" Orison baulked; her stomach churned with nausea.

"Yes, flew." Edmund looked at the hole.

"He can't turn, can he?" Saskia asked as she straightened up.

Taviar looked between everybody. "The enchantress said he couldn't."

Orison rubbed her hand over her brand as she thought of King Raj's assistance with Xabian. "We may need to speak to King Raj," Orison said absentmindedly.

The room fell silent as they turned in unison towards Orison. She noticed their wide-eyed stares, Taviar's tense posture and Edmund with his hand on the pommel of his sword. Orison didn't miss how Saskia clutched her dress. It wasn't a bad idea; King Raj was the person who found a medication to slow the curse.

"He's an enemy, Orison," Saskia said quickly.

Orison shook her head quickly. "No, he's not. Not to me."

"Are you sure about this?" Edmund asked. She stared him down, knowing this was for the best. He turned to Taviar. "Please assist Orison to the royal office so she can request an audience with King Raj."

Taviar gestured to the door while he stepped over the corpses. Orison looked over her shoulder and watched Saskia follow behind. When Orison returned to the corridor, guards flanked her and they made their way to the portal that led her there. She knew what people thought of King Raj, but if anybody had answers about Xabian it would be the King of Karshakroh—enemy or not.

Once back inside the main castle, Orison settled down into the leather chair that accompanied the large desk in the royal office. When she was queen, she would strip the dark walls and replace them with something not so ominous. A glance at the fireplace told her they had removed Sila's portrait, only a perfect square made of dust remained where it used to be. It felt like Orison was trespassing by sitting there. She was afraid Sila would step through the doors any moment, until she remembered this was her office. She shook off her feelings and pushed herself closer to the desk as she opened her Teltroma.

Orison told the Teltroma she wanted to contact King Raj. When she felt the familiar pull in her chest, she glanced up and felt relieved that Ashim had joined them. The Teltroma pulsated with a white light; she drummed her fingers on the desk and waited for King Raj to answer. She breathed a sigh of relief when he materialised. He had rolled up the sleeves of his shirt to his elbows and he had a sword in his hand. His light-brown skin gleamed with sweat.

"Orison, pleasure to see you again. I hope you are well," Raj said by way of greeting, with a grin.

"I've been well, thank you." The king sheathed his sword and adjusted his stance. "Prince Xabian has escaped the lower dungeons. We need advice."

When Orison looked around, Taviar and Saskia gawped at her casual demeanour with King Raj—no signs of tension. She knew it would be like this, after her time as a Runner, it gave Orison an eternal bond with King Raj.

"I daresay he hasn't been taking his medication," he mumbled.

Sadly, Orison shook her head as she looked down at the desk. She didn't know why Xabian refused to take his medication and why he chose to endure this. Despite her Mindelate abilities, she couldn't control somebody like a

Protelsha. Maybe if she was a Protelsha, he would be back to that person she knew when Alsaphus Castle was her prison.

The sound of heavy breathing made her look up. Edmund stood in the door with the other guards. Orison straightened up, curious about why he was out of breath and red in the face. He pushed his brown hair away from his face, then his eyes lingered on the projection of King Raj as he came to a stop.

"The discovaker isn't picking up Xabian's location," Edmund announced.

Raj smirked. "Enjoy your dragon hunt."

"He's not a dragon yet," Orison retorted. "And he's still cursed with the Nighthex; that's why the discovaker isn't picking anything up."

Saskia was silent before she announced. "Cardenk."

All eyes turned to her. Then it hit Orison like a ton of bricks. Saskia's cottage was the only logical place Xabian could be.

FORTY-NINE

Saskia eased the door open to her cottage. At first glance, everything appeared in order—from her collection of dresses to the fire roaring in the hearth. She inspected the downstairs area and opened the bedroom near the kitchen to find the entire space empty. A creak from upstairs made Saskia look at the ceiling and instantly she knew her conclusion was correct.

She picked up her skirts to ascend the stairs, keeping her steps light with a vice-like grip on the banister so the wood didn't creak. At the top of the stairs, Saskia saw light escaping underneath the gap of Xabian's old bedroom door. With a sigh of relief, Saskia lowered her skirts; she approached his room to confront him.

The firm knock resonated around the hallway, then the door swung open with the command of Saskia's magic. Saskia peered inside and almost staggered back with revulsion. Before her, Xabian was curled up on the floor with black leathery wings that protruded from his spine; his shoulders shifted with loud, audible sobs. After Saskia composed herself, she crossed the threshold.

"Are you well?" Saskia asked.

Xabian jumped and staggered back. His wings hit the chest of drawers with a clatter. He panted as he held his hand out. Along with the wings, fangs protruded from his mouth and his purple eyes flared brightly. It was like his body was at war with itself, torn between becoming a Nyxite or remaining as Fae. This was the first time she had seen Xabian since he returned to Fallasingha; she held back her emotions at seeing how far he'd fallen.

"Don't," Xabian barked. The voice that came out of him wasn't his; it was too deep and took on a growl like an animal.

"What's happening, Xabian?" Saskia asked.

Xabian looked around. "I don't know," he breathed. "But it hurts."

The curse was common knowledge amongst the castle staff, along with the fact that Xabian had refused his medication countless times. Saskia crouched before him. When she made eye contact with Xabian his eyes were bloodshot, half-closed and filled with tears. He looked like he hadn't slept in weeks. Xabian panted and each time Saskia tried to get close, he flinched away; she knew he was terrified of the dungeons. She gently brushed his hair away from his face. She had only seen him look this scared the night Sila placed the curse on him.

"I think this is from not taking your medicine, Poppet," Saskia said calmly. "I've heard you've been refusing it. But it'll make all of this go away."

Xabian squeezed his eyes shut as he rested his head on the chest of drawers. She rubbed his arm and shushed him to calm him down. It was history repeating itself. This was how the curse began for Xabian, right in this very room, with only Saskia to tell him everything will be okay. Saskia wrapped her arms around him and embraced him.

"Then the enchantress must be correct," Xabian breathed.

She paused as she rubbed his back. "What did the enchantress say?"

"I'm dying."

The confession hung like a cloud heavy with rain and thunder over the room. It was an ominous feeling to know he had accepted his fate. But Xabian still fought and denied the inevitable. Saskia hated the knowing—knowing that he could have prevented this if he hadn't been stubborn like Sila.

As he closed his eyes, Saskia took out the syringe and Normahlef berries from her pocket—instructions from Orison and Taviar. She tried to stop her hands trembling; this needed to be done. She had to betray the man she saw as her grandson. Fumbling with the syringe, she held him closer as she used her magic to secure the Normahlef berries around his neck. Xabian tensed.

"Grandma, what are you doing?" Xabian asked.

"Nothing, Poppet, I only want to comfort you."

Saskia squeezed her eyes shut as she plunged the syringe into his arm. Guilt slammed into her the moment the medicine drained into him. Xabian had come to her home for solace; instead, he found the opposite. Her hands trembled as he shoved her away from him, she landed in a heap on the floor. He pressed a hand to his arm as his eyes widened with the reality of her betrayal; he tugged on the Normalef berries.

"What did you do?" Xabian asked quietly. He stood up and checked the mirror as the wings and fangs disappeared instantaneously. "What did you do?"

Saskia shook her head. "This is what's best for you."

The door swung open and castle guards swarmed in with several enchantresses to assist them. She hugged her knees to her chest and pressed herself to the wall so they had room to work. The enchantresses chanted in an ancient language. Saskia watched in horror as Xabian crashed to the floor like a dead weight—unconscious and ready for transportation. His next prison was Cleravoralis, under the watchful eye of ancient power.

The first time Ashim had seen the training yards, it had taken on the appearance of a dungeon. Being inside the yards told him his thoughts were correct. The high fortifying walls reached to the overcast sky, sealing him inside the castle walls, where the sounds of clashing metal thundered around. Underneath his boots, the frozen hay-covered path crunched when he approached the lone apple tree. It not only had apples, it also had an array of wooden targets hanging from the branches.

Ashim stopped beside a barrel of swords to watch Edmund aim at one of the targets with a bow and arrow. He pulled back the bowstring then let his arrow fly. It hit an apple that dropped to the ground with a thud.

The guard captain whistled as he stepped over a log on the ground and picked the apple up by the arrow. Dusting snow off its blood-red surface, Edmund wrestled the arrow out and took a hearty bite. The cold seeped into Ashim's grey coat, making him shudder as he tightened it around himself, unsure why Edmund had summoned him.

"Aren't you supposed to hit the target?" Ashim asked as he shivered.

"Why hit the actual target when you can have a snack?" Edmund retorted.

Ashim's teeth chattered violently as Edmund placed his apple on a nearby tree stump and stepped back over the log. He got into position again, drew another arrow and nocked it into his bow. Edmund pulled the string back and released, the arrow slammed into another apple and caused it to fall. It was an impressive feat; each of Edmund's movements seemed effortless. Lost in his thoughts, Ashim jumped when the apple bounced off his head. Edmund's laughter filled the dungeon-like area.

"You were supposed to catch it!" Edmund exclaimed with a chuckle. He waved his bow around. "Do you want to try?"

Shaking his head, Ashim picked up the apple and brushed snow from its red surface. "I prefer swords, though no one has ever trained me."

Edmund put his bow away and looked through the barrel of swords. It became evident Ashim was called here as a test of strength. A sword sang when pulled out of the barrel. Edmund handed the pommel to Ashim, who took it and tested its weight in his hand. It was weighty and felt unnatural.

He glanced down at the sword. "Captain, may I ask a question?" Ashim piped up. Edmund looked behind his shoulder. "Have you found your Equal?"

"No need for formalities," Edmund reminded him. He was silent for a long moment then nodded. "To answer your question, yes. Unfortunately, she rejected the bond."

Ashim's eyes widened. "I'm sorry." He swung the sword at a mannequin to test its weight. "Well, Orison's mine, but I'm scared of accepting the bond. I thought I could get some advice."

"I don't need sympathy; it was five years ago." Edmund adjusted Ashim's posture. "I heard about you being Orison's Equal, hence why you're here. Even though I don't trust Karshakians, I've been observing you and I'm glad you're her Equal and not Prince Xabian. You bring her smile back."

"You've been observing me?" Ashim turned.

"To see if the rumours are true. But the fact you're holding the sword wrong says we have nothing to worry about." Edmund adjusted Ashim's grip; he felt his cheeks heat and averted his gaze. "The bond isn't a marriage, Ashim. It only intensifies your powers by being with your person; do you feel it around Orison?"

"*Halek*," he admitted. "My magic is always strongest near her."

"Good. If you accept, it's supposed to make you in tune with each other; like knowing if the other is in danger," Edmund explained. "Go."

Ashim swung at the training dummy, this time with renewed strength. "Did you become sick when she rejected the bond?"

"No, it's entirely a choice." Edmund said as he adjusted Ashim's posture again. "My Equal is happily married to somebody else and has made it clear she doesn't want to be near me. As long as she's happy, I'm happy. Even if I'll never experience the greater power the bond provides, I respect her decision and wish her the best." He looked at the dummy. "Stop talking and let's get to training, Mahrishan!"

The answers swirled around in Ashim's head, making it difficult to focus on the lesson in sword fighting. He practised well into the afternoon until his skin glistened with sweat underneath his coat. He poured all of his frustrations about Xabian kidnapping Orison into each swing of the sword. The training made him vow he wouldn't see Orison hurt again.

Outside the throne room, Orison hesitated before crossing the threshold. Despite the months of being there, imprisoned and then free; it was like a mental blockade that prevented her from crossing that line. She took a step but retreated and paced in front of the doors like a well-practised dancer. Clutching her head, Orison groaned loudly out of frustration and stepped up to the door again—only to stand on her tiptoes as though something actually prevented that final step.

"Fuck it," Orison grumbled.

She turned and hurried down the East Wing's corridor, towards her new bedchambers. Each hurried footstep away from the throne room reverberated around the corridor with the clicks of her heels. For Orison, it was ridiculous that she was destined to be queen and couldn't set foot in the place where she was required to uphold royal duties.

Orison paused at the foot of the stairs to her bedroom. "Stop being foolish; you know he is dead," she muttered to herself.

She balled her hands into fists and turned around; Sila wasn't here and no longer controlled her. With renewed confidence, Orison raced back to the door of the throne room. She whirled around as soon as she tried to enter. It was like the shield was back, except instead of an electrical wall—it was Orison's agonised screams when Sila turned her into Fae.

A hand extended out to her. "Do you need help?"

Orison's eyes glazed over as she looked at Taviar. "Yes, I would like that very much." She took his hand and with his assistance, crossed the threshold. "Can we redecorate?"

Taviar tapped her hand. "It's going to be your castle; you can do whatever you wish."

"Then I want the pillars removed," Orison declared. "It reminds me too much of that night."

He covered Orison's hand with his own as he walked her down the aisle. Orison desperately wanted to get used to the throne room. She needed to familiarise herself with the steps and get comfortable in a place that brought torture on many; including herself. The more she relaxed, the more she could envisage the room packed with Fallagh residents to congratulate her. It wasn't hard to imagine, with the amount of preparation everybody had to do.

"Will I ever be able to enter this space alone?" Orison grumbled as she settled onto the throne.

"I'm sure you will," Taviar assured.

So lost in her head that when she turned to her side, it surprised her to find another throne beside the stone one. They had beautifully crafted it for Ashim—if they ever got married during her reign. It was still settling in with her that she was going to be queen. She glanced at Taviar, who remained standing. He looked around with his hands behind his back, Orison wondered if he knew about the second throne beside hers.

An idea ignited in her head. If Ashim could erase her memories of the night she arrived in the Othereal, then she could enter the space strong and confident. However, Orison didn't want to forget that night forever. She'd only consider it if they could bring the memories back. Then there was the part of it being illegal.

"What are you thinking about?" Taviar asked.

"How I want to make you my advisor when I claim the crown," Orison announced. A smile spread across her face when Mahavu ventured into the room. She clicked her tongue, urging the cat forward. "And keep Mahavu at bay."

With continued silence, Orison tilted her head to inquire if Taviar would reject her request. She held Mahavu close when she leapt onto Orison's lap. Mahavu purred loudly as Orison ran her hand through her soft fur. Taviar stood in silence, frozen to the spot in a wide-eyed stare, until he blinked.

"Personally, I believe Saskia is the correct person for the advisor role, Orison," Taviar explained. She nodded earnestly. "But I'd be happy to continue as emissary."

Her smile widened as she nodded again with agreement. Orison had two staff members and there were still roles she had to appoint, like a job for Kinsley and Aeson. With guidance from King Raj and within Fallasingha, Orison almost felt ready for queenship.

Orison stood up and allowed Mahavu to settle on her shoulder like a parrot, then she made her way down the dais. There were countless times Orison had seen the cat perched on Ashim's shoulder; she saw it as a sign of trust and acceptance. Its only downside were the claws that pierced into her skin as Mahavu balanced. With a nod from Taviar, he led her back down the aisle.

She paused at the threshold of the throne room door. For the first time since she returned, Orison told her former self to let go; she was no longer trapped there. When she stepped back into the main area of the castle, it felt like someone had lifted a weight from her shoulders—a prisoner reborn into a princess.

"Ori," Taviar said. Orison turned to face him with a tilt of her head. "We found a band of thorns underneath your bed in your old chambers."

She froze and raised her hand to steady Mahavu. "Who put it there?"

Taviar shrugged. "Nobody knows, we're still trying to figure it out. It was put there with the expectation that you would die in the mortal realm by magic starvation."

Orison moved Mahavu to her chest before she staggered backwards, slamming painfully against the throne room door. Her eyes stung with tears and her breathing was shallow—somebody had tried to assassinate her in the worst way imaginable. Orison held Mahavu tighter as the cat snuggled under Orison's chin.

"Why did it not work?" she whispered. "A band of thorns always works."

Taviar nodded in agreement. "Well, it couldn't work because a Desigle created protection diamonds to stop it."

A loud sigh of relief passed Orison's lips. "A Desigle saved me?"

He shoved his hands into his pockets. "Yes, long before the enchantment ceased to exist."

"Thank you for telling me."

Orison walked past Taviar and continued down the corridor with the new information that roared through her head. The knowledge that the person who hexed her was almost successful sent chills down her spine—they intensified when she realised her assassin could be closer than she realised.

FIFTY

Orison emerged into Cardenk's main town square with Edmund at her side. She had dropped Mahavu off at Kinsley's home, as her main task was preparing for her coronation. Revellers from the pubs hollered loudly, drawing her attention to them and she watched them collapse into mounds of snow—too drunk to care or to move. Edmund had his gloved hand secured on the pommel of his sword—since Xabian's latest escapade, Taviar insisted a guard followed her every movement.

Together they entered the small market where a handful of people mulled about to gather their groceries. Orison had never seen it so quiet; usually the crowd was so large she was uncomfortable being pressed shoulder to shoulder with people.

While making her way through the first aisle, vendors reached over their table offering Orison free samples. She paused briefly to thank them as she took them. After five stalls, she had accumulated a small collection of hard candy that rattled around in her lilac coat pocket; she wanted to distribute it to the Luxart twins and Ashim. Turning down the next aisle, another vendor handed Orison a mug of hot chocolate. She cupped her hands around it with a thank you, the warmth seeped through her green gloves.

"Are you ready for the cleansing soon?" Edmund asked as he inspected a rug.

Orison paused. "Cleansing?"

"Every royal in Fallasingha must go to the Temple of Fallagh for a cleansing. You have to live in isolation for a week and cleanse yourself of this life to welcome sovereignty," Edmund explained as he moved on.

"I guess people missed mentioning that bit whilst preparing me," Orison admitted as she accepted a piece of apple bread from a vendor. "When does that occur?"

"A little over a week before the ceremony." He stopped at another stall to inspect a golden rose pin.

While she sipped on her hot chocolate, it struck Orison she had no idea where the Temple of Fallagh was located. The map of Fallasingha was sprawled out in her head, but she couldn't recall ever seeing the temple. Orison stared into space and took a bite of her apple bread as she tried to think of her journey. Despite the mysterious location, it appeared she had to go to accept the crown. The thought of being alone in a strange temple made her skin crawl.

"Where's the temple?" Orison asked. "Is it the Parthenon in Tsunamal? There's a large statue of Fallagh there."

Edmund shook his head as he inspected the other wares. "Nobody knows. It's a secret only a handful know about, it's forbidden from being on maps. Legend has it the temple moves based on what the cleansing desires."

"Have all the kings and queens of Fallasingha cleansed themselves?" Orison finished her bread as Edmund nodded. "And their spouses?"

"Yes." Edmund handed over some coin as he bought the rose pin he was looking at. "And if you marry Ashim, he'd have to be cleansed as king consort."

Orison held onto his every word as they navigated their way to another stall. She thought she would walk down the aisle of the throne room, say the royal oath and walk out as queen. That was only the tip of the iceberg. As she thought more about her upcoming destiny, the thought of being a royal didn't disgust her like before.

"How did King Sila get cleansed with how evil he is?" Orison asked.

Edmund looked around. "Each cleansing is different. King Sila had to go on an alcohol cleanse and enter sobriety to be king." They broke out into laughter. "That did not last for long, clearly."

The appearance of an elaborate royal red carpet made Orison's laughter diminish; she looked over at the intricate gold threading of a wolf howling at a moon. Orison immediately recognised this kind of carpet from the many bazaars in Haranshal. She rubbed her thumb over the fabric with a smile as she recalled her time there.

"We imported this from Karshakroh, specifically," the vendor explained. Orison's gaze shifted to the bald vendor behind the table. His pale skin complimented his orange beard. "It's beautiful, isn't it, Your Highness?"

"I'll take it," Orison said quickly.

"Don't you think it's odd to have a Karshak rug in Alsaphus Castle?"

Orison turned to Edmund. "Not to me and I want to get something that reminds Ashim of home." She turned to the vendor. "How much?"

"For royalty, it's free."

The vendor rolled up the rug and secured it into a large bag. Edmund took the bag and slung it over his shoulder. She thanked the vendor and handed him ten gold—despite his many protests; she insisted. Then she was back on her way through the market. The surprise would amaze Ashim and it would be perfect in their secret home in Tsunamal.

Night had fallen by the time Orison Misted back to Alsaphus Castle. She had spent most of the day in her home in Tsunamal, decorating it to her heart's content. She walked down the corridors, where the guards dipped their chins as she passed.

It had taken a lot of convincing for Edmund to stay in Alsaphus Castle and she hadn't told anybody else where she was going; she needed the alone time. The choice to be alone also contributed to the fact she had concealed ten bags of gold from the royal vaults within the Tsunamal home; she'd placed them in a safe hidden in the attic. Orison didn't know what compelled her to hide the money, but something told her to—just in case.

Hands wrapped around her waist as Ashim came into view. "You've been gone all day, what have you been up to?" He inspected Orison up and down, licking his thumb and rubbing a spot on her cheek. "Why are you covered in paint?"

She excitedly told him about Cardenk and her exploration of Tsunamal alone for the first time. A feat she never thought possible in the Othereal. Despite her elatedness, it didn't feel right to enjoy it as much as she did while alone—especially with Ashim being confined to Alsaphus Castle to study the common tongue.

As they approached the throne room, Orison and Ashim slowed down when they noticed a large gathering of guards in the corridor. The guards scurried into the shadows when somebody raised their voice—Taviar. Orison let go of Ashim and ran towards the doors.

Guards parted ways as Orison quickly pushed her way through the tightly compact formation and into the open aisle. She instantly recognised Taviar, Saskia and Emphina. They stood in a circle in front of the thrones and talked in hushed voices. Orison raced over to them. She refused to miss out on vital information if something was wrong; as princess, it was her duty.

"What's going on here?" she asked.

Taviar turned to her and looked at his feet. "There's been an incident."

She was taken aback, her gaze darted between the three of them. "What kind of incident?"

"Xabian has escaped Cleravoralis," Emphina said solemnly.

"What?" Ashim shouted. Orison whirled around, unaware he followed behind her, but there he stood—wide-eyed. "How?"

The Regent closed his eyes; Taviar appeared defeated by this unfortunate turn of events. They had assured Orison that Xabian couldn't escape this time and that the Normahlef berries had been reinforced with iron. Also, they'd told her his medication was hidden in his food and that his cell had more wards than she could count.

"He waited until lunch, when the wizards would take the berries off and lift the wards," Emphina explained. Her eyes glistened with tears as she covered her mouth with a trembling hand. "Xabian killed them all to escape."

Orison was aghast and held her chest as she tried to breathe properly. He had done it again—killed and fled. Xabian was out and more than likely prowling Fallasingha to find her; to get her away from all this.

"What if Xabian tries to take Orison again?" Ashim questioned. "I can't lose her again."

"Then it appears we must bring the coronation forward to prevent this. Can we transport Orison to the Temple of Fallagh at first light?" Saskia asked. She hugged her arms as she looked between everyone.

Orison tensed at the announcement. She'd only found out about the temple in Cardenk that morning and didn't feel comfortable going so soon. The world slowed when Emphina and Taviar nodded their agreement. Orison looked around when the room fell silent with the weight of the decision—all the guards had frozen as they waited to hear more.

"Will Ashim be allowed to come with me?" Orison managed to blurt out.

Emphina stepped forward and placed her hands on Orison's shoulders. "I'm afraid Ashim will have to stay here and await your return. We'll escort you to Fallagh Temple, but you must go on this transition alone."

As she looked at Ashim with tear-filled eyes, Orison extended her hand out to him. He pulled her into his embrace and kissed her forehead. Wherever Xabian had gone this time, he had once again torn her away from her Equal, due to his own denial.

Shadows adorned the light-wood walls of the meeting rooms, cast by the warm glow of the fire which crackled in the hearth. Unlike other rooms in the castle, this fireplace was a simple hole in the wall framed by a golden mantel. The room was one of the smallest in Alsaphus Castle; it was homely and roughly the same size as Ashim's apartment in Haranshal.

On the floor, sprawled out on the royal red rug, Ashim held Orison close as she rested her head on his chest. He pulled the blanket around her shoulders and played with her soft hair. It was their last night together before her cleansing; he didn't want to let her go, but her safety magnified his desire.

"I love you, Little Queen," Ashim declared as he kissed her head.

She lifted herself up and kissed his lips. "I love you too."

Orison rested her head to his chest again. Ashim held her closer and watched the fire dance in her eyes as he lazily stroked her shoulder. He despised the fear in her eyes with a passion; if he could, he would carry the weight from her shoulders.

"Are you well?" Ashim asked.

Orison kissed his chest. "More than well." He gave her a knowing look, a silent request that urged her to talk. With a sigh, she moved her fingers along his chest like it was a piano. "No. I'm too weak to claim the crown. Sila kept me blinded so much that I don't know the first thing about taking on the responsibility. I will fail."

"Don't say that," Ashim said softly. "Ori, you stole an Ifrit necklace and lived. If you can do that, you're strong enough for anything."

"But I had to get help." Orison sighed heavily.

"We all need help, Little Queen." Ashim kissed her again. "And you're never in this alone. You have me and all your advisors. You will be the best queen Fallasingha has ever seen."

She settled back onto his chest and closed her eyes as she breathed. He wiped the tears which rolled down her cheeks and kissed her head. Orison kissed him deeply and ran her hands through his hair. He could feel more of her tears against his cheek as she straddled his hips. The duvet fell to her waist; Ashim gripped the fabric of her red jumper and kissed her more, as his hands travelled underneath the material.

Orison pressed her forehead to his. They both breathed heavily. "I don't want to go anywhere if you're not coming with me."

Ashim moved her hair behind her ear. "I'll be right here when you get back, Little Queen." She kissed him again. "It's only a week, then they'll crown you."

Ashim wiped her tears as she sobbed out a smile; the first since this conversation started. He held her close as he breathed in the sweet smell of sugar and apple pies from her day in Cardenk. While she was away being cleansed, he would stay, ready to fight Xabian in whichever form he came in. It was time for a new generation to rule Fallasingha, one that wasn't Alsaphus; where the name alone didn't mean enemy.

Orison lifted her head and hovered over him. "I..." She swallowed audibly. "I think I want to accept the bond, Ashim."

He cupped her face and wiped her tears away with both thumbs. "You think, or you know for certain?"

"I know for certain," Orison breathed.

"I need a little more time," Ashim admitted.

Orison kissed him. "That's okay, I'll wait for you. I only wanted to let you know I'm ready and want you to tell me when you are." She snuggled against him and once again, he watched the fire dance in her eyes. "Please don't stop calling me Little Queen when I take the crown."

"Okay," Ashim said confidently. "I think it's stuck."

She drummed her fingers on his chest. "It definitely has stuck; it'll be weird for you to stop at this point." Orison looked up. "You're so handsome."

"And you're beautiful." He toyed with her hair and smiled. "After the week, you get true freedom in the Othereal. Then we can plan our future. We can be away from Xabian when he's locked in an iron box somewhere to stop him escaping."

Orison sighed and relaxed as he drew lazy circles on her back. Ashim hoped this talk had comforted Orison in a time of need; he didn't like seeing her scared. He moved her hair and planted soft kisses on her shoulder, then his hand roamed lower.

"Ash." He made a noise and glanced at her. "I love you."

"I love you too."

When her body fully relaxed, he realised she had fallen asleep. Ashim pulled the blanket over her shoulders again; he held her like she would disappear if he let go.

It would be strange not having his Equal by his side for a week. Like a piece of him would be missing if he didn't see the smile that lit a spark in his heart or hear her favourite stories. Despite all their time apart, Ashim would be there to welcome her home.

FIFTY-ONE

Servants carried trunks down the steps of Alsaphus Castle and secured them to the back of a gilded black carriage. The white horses at the front nodded their heads and shifted as more servants approached to ensure everything was in order; none batted an eyelash at Orison, who stood frozen in the entrance, her identity concealed with a white veil.

Aiken approached Orison and curtsied. "You look like a bride."

Orison lifted the veil; it cascaded down her back like her hair. "Have you seen a coronation blessing be done?" Orison asked.

"Put the veil back on," she hissed as she fussed over Orison's violet coat. Footsteps made Aiken look over Orison's shoulder. "Good morning, Sir Mahrishan."

Orison instantly relaxed at Ashim's approach. His arms wrapped around her and she melted into the longing kiss he provided. It was one that made her want to stay, to not enter that carriage and get cleansed; but royal protocol had bound her to this.

"Princess, I must stress you put the veil back over your face. You aren't to be seen until after the cleansing," another servant said from the door.

With one last kiss, Orison's lips trembled as Ashim carefully eased the veil back over her face. Ashim pulled her close and planted another kiss on her forehead, he smoothed out her veil with a forced smile.

"Everything will be okay," Ashim told her. "I'll be here when you return."

Orison nodded and looped her arm through his as he escorted her out into the wintery morning and eased her down the stairs until her boots crunched on the snow. Her fingers gripped the sleeve of his navy-blue coat as he led her to the carriage. Ashim pulled on the door handle and it clicked open. The carriage was dark inside, only the sunlight partially illuminated the plush red seats and the dark silhouette of Emphina, who sat in a corner with an embroidery hoop.

"You must let me go," Ashim whispered.

Her legs shook as she slowly eased out of her vice-like grip. Ashim took Orison's hand and she allowed him to aid her into the carriage. Once seated, Orison's vision blurred as tears stung her eyes; her heart broke at how forlorn Ashim looked when a tear rolled down his cheek. The door closed with a resounding click that sealed her fate. She was going to the Temple of Fallagh, whether she wanted to or not.

Orison extended her hand out one last time. Ashim held her hand as the driver hollered in a foreign language. With a crack of the whip, the horses commenced their journey. He held her hand until he couldn't hold on any longer and the carriage whisked Orison away into the unknown.

Night had fallen when the carriage pulled up at an isolated mountain. Orison couldn't take in her surroundings properly as she was immediately rushed out of the carriage. They jostled her through a stone door in the mountain's side, which sealed behind her as soon as she crossed the threshold. When Orison came out of her daze, she realised she was at the top of a stairwell illuminated by flaming torches and surrounded by figures dressed in red robes; each were unmoving and silent.

In unison, the robed figures led her down the stairs. With every step she took, Orison inspected golden writing carved into the stone walls, each scrolled hand prayed for life and prosperity in the Fallagh tongue. Due to the lack of visitors, no other languages adjoined the prayers.

They led Orison deeper into the belly of the temple. She glanced over her shoulder at Emphina, who trailed behind like a shadow. Even in that moment, they kept Orison in the dark about everything. While her head was a thousand miles away, her feet moved of their own accord to her destiny.

She turned so many corners it almost made Orison dizzy. Gradually, she became more disorientated until they came to a halt at another stone door. One of the robed figures pushed the door open; the scraping sound echoed through the dimly lit environment. Nobody moved until the lights came on in the next strange room.

One of the robed figures took Orison's hand and guided her inside. It opened to a simple bedroom with a double bed, a white chest of drawers and a further stone door which led to a bathing chamber with all the necessities. The walls had no decorations; it was all stone surrounding her. To make the situation worse, the room also had no windows. Orison shifted anxiously as the robed figures congregated in the doorway; they remained as silent as they had since she first arrived. All of them kept their heads down.

"This is to be your chambers for the duration of the cleansing," Emphina said.

The silence of the chamber pressed down so much that once the enchantress spoke, it sent goosebumps up Orison's arms and she covered her ears. It was as though Emphina disturbed the dead and if anybody talked, it was frowned upon. Orison rubbed her thigh as memories surfaced of the Ifrit attack in Lhandahir.

"And what happens while here?" Orison asked. She winced at how amplified her voice sounded in the chasm.

"A guardian will collect you at first light, then we will begin the rituals," Emphina carried on. "You must not leave this room unless given permission from the guardians, such as mealtimes. After the seventh light, we will escort you back to Alsaphus Castle and prepare you for the coronation as a new woman."

The idea of being trapped in the stone chasm made Orison's skin crawl. Along with the ifrit attack, it reminded her of what Sila had put her through and they merged—two of her worst horrors fought for the spotlight in her mind. It made her heart pound against her ribs. Part of her wanted to scream that she didn't want to do this anymore, but she couldn't allow the crown to fall into Xabian's hands—especially in his condition.

"Please, may I request permission to leave my room. I don't like being locked in anywhere," Orison said, with as much confidence as she could muster; though her voice still wavered when asking.

The guardians huddled together in a circle and whispered to one another about her request. Orison waited with bated breath for the outcome; she gnawed on the side of her nail at the anticipation.

"You may roam the halls and one recreational room during your time here," Emphina explained. "Get some rest; we'll collect you at first light."

Each of the guardians—along with Emphina—bowed. In a single line, they all left the stone chasm. Orison breathed a sigh of relief that they had left the door open and not sealed her in. Though her mind was too busy to rest, she had little to do, apart from following Emphina's instructions. Orison shrugged off her heavy winter coat and her veil, then got ready for bed. When she was in her pyjamas, she climbed beneath the sheets and tried to relax in this new environment.

At first light, Emphina woke Orison and handed her to a guardian, who guided her to a new stone chasm where the door was closed. It made Orison fidget with the white shirt they had given her, as butterflies waged war in her belly. The door swung open and scraped against the stone floor. Orison gasped loudly and staggered into the nearest wall at the sight before her.

The guardian gently took her wrist and tried to guide her inside. "No, please don't make me go in there," she panted with fear. The guardian turned to face her, but Orison couldn't discern what lay beneath the hood; their silence told her she had no choice. "I can't!"

A firm tug on her arm made Orison stumble through the chasm door. Her vision blurred with tears and out of terror, her heart raced. The guardian led her directly into the throne room of Alsaphus Castle. Its large stone archways towered over her and flanked an empty space for ceremonies. In the centre of it all, seated on the throne—was King Sila. The reassurance of the guardian's hand deserted her. Orison whirled around and ran to the door as it closed in her face.

Orison banged on the door. "Let me out!" she cried. "Please!"

"Do you enjoy defying me?" Sila snarled.

Everything froze at the sound of his voice, which echoed around the stone walls. Orison thought she'd never hear that horrendous voice again. She turned around slowly and staggered into the double doors; her legs trembled as she took in her captor. Slouched on the throne and sipping on his goblet of wine, his infamous scowl burned into her.

She barely got a word out before guards grabbed her from behind. Orison kicked and flailed in their grasp. Her feet connected with their stomachs and legs, as she tried everything to get free. Orison shrieked when they slammed her onto the floor and forced manacles of fire onto her wrists. Her heart pounded painfully against her ribs, as they hauled her up with an iron grip and dragged her towards the throne.

"You're supposed to be dead!" she screamed as they threw her onto the floor again.

Pain laced up her knee as she hit the ground. She groaned and kept her gaze to the ground to avoid King Sila's gaze, not wanting to face him again. He was dead. No matter what she saw, she had to remind herself this was her cleansing and wasn't real.

"Who helped you survive the mortal realm without me?" Sila questioned. The question sounded eerily familiar and made her skin crawl. "Who helped you defy me and make me look weak?"

Orison remained silent and hoped that whatever this was would go away. It felt like déjà vu; she'd been here before. The guardians must have known that Sila terrified her—the only explanation for this to be her cleansing. Sila stood and strolled down the dais, then crouched to her level. He sneered at her defiance, grabbed her face and forced her to look at him. She scowled at his yellow eyes.

"I didn't have help in defying you and making you look weak. I did it all myself to reclaim what you stole from me," Orison sneered.

With a snort, she spat in his face. Sila roared as he inched backwards. He covered his face as he tried to wipe it clean. She willed her manacles to disappear; to her relief, they did. Orison pushed herself off the floor, then ran towards the throne room doors as fast as she could. She struggled with the door handle, pushed the heavy doors open and staggered into darkness.

Orison fumbled around in the dark; her fingers grazed along a cold rock wall which gave way when she pushed on it. She hoped it would be the corridor where she would reunite with a guardian. Instead, Orison had returned to Alsaphus Castle's throne room, without King Sila's presence. She turned around to inspect the way she came; only darkness greeted her until she turned back.

"I just have to overcome my fear of Sila and cross the threshold," she realised. "That's my cleansing."

With a deep breath, she stepped forward and paused as if a shield prevented her from going any further. Orison balled her hands into fists, determined to accomplish her task and get it over with. She stepped back through the darkness, bouncing around on her feet as she prepared herself; then ran towards the throne room. Orison screamed as she threw herself through the open doorway and collapsed onto her knees as she panted. Glancing around had Orison laughing, she had made it into the throne room by herself.

Orison staggered to her feet and whirled around in the open space. The cold floor tiles bit into her bare feet, but she paid it no mind. Her laughter filled the throne room and she stretched her arms out with a bold smile. For the first time, she was here alone and had no fear.

"I did it," she gasped and held her chest. "Fuck!"

Her feet smacked on the tiles as Orison raced back to the door. She wanted to try it again; only this time, she dared not take a running leap. Back in the darkness, she faced the door and braced for the mental shield to push her back. Orison stepped up to the door and found there was no fear blocking her. She crossed over the threshold again and again; each time she laughed at how freeing it felt.

Her gaze went to the ceiling. "Thank you."

Though the guardians may not hear her in this strange space, she wanted them to know of her gratitude. It was the first step on a long road to recovery.

Back in the throne room, she hurried through the aisle and down to the throne. Upon reaching it, she sat on the seat and settled in. Her hands brushed along the armrests. She never thought it would be possible to find comfort in the throne room by herself—yet here she was.

"This will be mine and I will rule," Orison said to herself as she settled back.

"It's time to go now," a voice seemed to say.

Deep down, Orison didn't want to leave. But soon, all of Orison's limbs felt like she was being pulled. The earth spun until the throne room disappeared.

Orison woke up with a gasp. She recognised the stone walls of the chasm under the mountain, along with a white chest of drawers and a stone doorway that led to a bathing chamber. It showed she was back in her assigned room. It was as though her experience with Sila or Alsaphus Castle never happened—her heart raced enough to tell her it did. With the lack of windows, there was no indication about how long she had slept.

With a sigh, she smoothed her hand over the empty space where Ashim should be. Her heart ached to have him hold her for comfort. Orison missed civilisation and the sound of people's movements. Nobody talked to her there, except for Emphina. The sound of shuffling made her roll over; one of the robed figures stood in the doorway as silent as they always were. Orison sat up; her hands clutched the bedsheets as she waited for the dizziness to subside.

Dinner is ready, a voice said to her mind.

Orison eased herself out of bed; she held onto the bedframe and waited for another bout of dizziness to subside. It must have been magic that projected her to Alsaphus Castle; she tensed at the reality. A Projeer was amongst them and would be here for the entirety of her cleansing—something which made her shudder as she put on her slippers. Orison approached the robed figure and allowed herself to be led to the dining room.

Her time in the throne room still resonated with her as she walked through the labyrinth of corridors. She had proved to herself that she was strong enough to push Sila away and step into the throne room unassisted. It gave her hope that she could enter the coronation after the week with her head held high and make Fallagh proud. Her people would rejoice that they have a just ruler, not a tyrannical king.

FIFTY-TWO

A crystal ring hummed with power while it sat in a glass case within Riddle Me This Antiquities; it was called *the Siren's Tears*. The crystal was a deep blue, like the deepest parts of Lake Braloak where it originated from. When turned in certain lights, even the lake presented itself. It mesmerised everybody who laid eyes upon it; despite being rumoured to have been stolen from the sirens by a daring nobleman.

The case door opened and Taviar reached in with gloved hands. He carried the ring over to where his husband waited behind the counter with a customer. Riddle smiled at the man in a black suit who enquired about the ring for his fiancée, she stood beside him in a burgundy dress. Riddle used his magic to lift the ring up without touching it, then allowed the client to inspect it; he rotated it to catch the light.

"It's beautiful," the woman baulked with her eyes wide in awe. Her orange hair swirled down her shoulder like a tornado.

"Now, this is a hundred gold marks, due to its rarity," Riddle explained.

Taviar remained silent while they negotiated about the antique. He looked over the woman's shoulder when the bell rang, indicating they had another customer. With a touch to his husband's arm, Riddle dipped his chin while he discussed the ring's reported history. Taviar set out to introduce the next customer entering the shop.

While he made his way over, Taviar side-stepped out of the way of Zade as he ran past him and bolted up the stairs to their home. He glanced at the stairs to their apartment, then turned back around when the bell rang again and a dark figure fled the shop. He rushed to the door—thinking a shoplifter had snatched an artefact—and flung it open. Taviar looked to his right, only spying children playing hopscotch in the street, turning his head to the left he homed in on Ashim running away and crashing into people.

"Ashim!" Taviar called. "Stop!"

The Karshakian glanced over his shoulder before he rushed on. Taviar grabbed his coat and ran through the street to catch up; he apologised to the people he bumped into. As he gained more speed, he eventually caught up to Ashim. He clamped his hand over his shoulder and whirled him around. Ashim's eyes were wide with fear when they came face to face.

"Why are you running away from me?" Taviar asked sternly.

Ashim shook his head. He muttered in Karshakir as he extended his empty hands out and turned out his pockets. His hands shook violently, which made Taviar even more curious about why he fled the shop and appeared shaken up.

"*Mehanasha*," he said. *Sorry.* Ashim stepped out of Taviar's hold and hurried off.

"What are you sorry for?" Taviar baulked as he rushed after Ashim. "What did you do?"

He caught up to Ashim, took his arm and dragged him down a dark alleyway. Rats squeaked as they scurried into the shadows; it made Taviar wince and let go of Ashim. The only light in this alleyway came from the sun that shined down on Merchant's Row. Taviar watched Ashim mutter to himself and knock his knuckles together.

"Your son said you could help. I'm sorry. I don't think I can accept help; nobody trusts me." He dropped his head down. Ashim's words cut like a knife for Taviar. "I'm sorry."

"Has something happened?" Taviar asked, trying to gauge the severity of the situation.

Dark thoughts swam into his head. The possibility that Ashim spied for King Raj crossed his mind; if so, that would lead to another war. Taviar shook the thought away quickly; deep down, he knew Ashim wasn't a threat to Fallasingha. The man before him was like a scared deer since he set foot in the castle and Taviar had reports from Edmund that Ashim couldn't hold a weapon correctly.

Ashim knocked his knuckles together again. "I'm scare..." With a raised eyebrow, Taviar waited for him to spit it out. "I'm..." With a sharp intake of breath, Ashim made an apple of fire appear in his hand. "Don't know word."

Realisation dawned on Taviar; he instantly relaxed. "You're scared of being a Fire Singer?"

"*Halek*," Ashim mumbled, as he looked at his feet.

"Of course, I can help you. Othereal above, Ashim. You had me scared, thinking that something was wrong." He urged Ashim towards the street. "There's nothing to be ashamed of, you're not a coward," Taviar assured as they re-entered Merchant's Row. "Zade was right bringing me to you."

Ashim looked up. "That was Zade?"

"You can tell by the scar in his hairline." Taviar continued walking and guided Ashim through the throng of people. "Why are you scared of your powers?"

Ashim huffed. "Nobody taught me how to control it."

Realisation dawned on Taviar, making it clearer that Ashim needed help. They passed children who ran around or played jump rope. They bypassed the people going about their daily business, until they came to a large home in a courtyard. It was where the Fire Singers resided.

"Taviar!"

He turned at the sound of his name being called and saw the lead Fire Singer approaching them; her name was Helienya. The sheen of sweat on her skin indicated she had been training. Her fire-red dress complimented her black hair nicely; she looked like a live flame. With each swish of her hips, the bells on her belt chimed.

"Helienya," Taviar said with a bow.

"Does Zade need more training?" She tilted her head and looked at Ashim.

Shaking his head. "This is Ashim; he needs training today. Not my son."

With narrowed eyes, she pointed to Ashim. "You're a Fire Singer?"

"*Halek*," he mumbled.

Helienya tutted loudly. "Leave him with me."

She ushered him along, towards the large red door to the Fire Singer's quarters. Ashim looked over his shoulder; fear darkened his yellow eyes as he waved goodbye. Taviar waved back, knowing Ashim was in very good hands with people of his own kind. If they could help his son tame his gifts and shape them into a weapon, then they could help Ashim with no issues.

Sand coated the floor of the Fire Singer's domain. Charred wooden pillars were black and flaking from a few too many incidents. It was a miracle they could still support the upper floors. Fire Singers trained their powers—they either battled with swords made of fire or danced with flames in the shape of a Fae person. The most impressive were Fire Singers who could shoot a bow and arrow made entirely of fire.

Ashim ogled these people until he realised Helienya walked ahead of him. He ran up to her with more glances over his shoulder. It sent a chill up his spine to realise how versatile this gift was. His piqued curiosity worried him as he wondered when he'd get to the level of archery with fire alone.

Helienya guided him through an open doorway. The room made him pause. It was brick with two charred wooden sofas inside that faced each other; the smell of fire hung heavy in the air. It didn't resemble an office at all. She gestured to the sofa on her left and Ashim eased himself onto it—to his surprise, the uneven material was comfortable. As she sat opposite him, Ashim tapped his thumbs.

"What is your skill level?" Helienya asked as she flicked her hair over her shoulder.

Ashim looked down. "I can make fire go away and can create objects. That's it." His cheeks heated; he knew he should be more skilled at twenty-two years old. Ashim pushed himself off the chair and took a step towards the door, embarrassed by his lack of knowledge. "I'll be too much work. Sorry for bothering you."

"Sit," Helienya ordered. He sat back down immediately. "What have you been doing with your Fire Singer abilities to be untrained?"

"I didn't use them," he admitted. "I... I'm scared because I hurt somebody when using them."

She gasped loudly. "This is the greatest weapon you could wield, Ashim!" Helienya stood up and rushed to the door. "We better get started."

Ashim stood up and followed her back to the room of sand. He kept his head down as Helienya guided him through the space. He wasn't expecting to begin training immediately. He thought he'd have a few more days; but time wasn't on their side. The ones who were currently training halted their sessions to gaze upon him. Casting his fears aside, Ashim exhaled a breath and pushed his shoulders back. For Orison, he'd master this part of himself.

"Good afternoon, everybody. We have a new trainee. Ashim..." Helienya looked at him.

"Ashim Mahrishan," he replied.

Helienya repeated his name with a big smile. "Please make him feel welcome. Jared, you'll help Ashim with his abilities. He's starting with the basics."

When Jared emerged from the shadows, Ashim staggered back. Built like a bull, he had heavy muscles. He had shaved dark hair and his wrists were adorned with golden chains. Jared only wore black trousers with no shirt, his chest gleamed with sweat. Shaking away his doubts, Ashim hurried over to Jared as everybody returned to their activities. He didn't know what Jared would start him off with. Part of Ashim hoped it would be a simple exercise, as Jared led him to a secluded area in the back.

"Didn't your parents teach you about your gifts?" Jared asked, as he created a fireball and tossed it between his hands.

Ashim shook his head. "King Sila killed my parents."

His partner paused his movements. "Oh, I'm sorry." Ashim shrugged. He was a baby when it happened. "Can you make a sword?" Jared asked and shook his arms out. Ashim nodded. A sword appeared in his hand, but when he tried to touch the handle, his skin sizzled. The burn caused him to cry out and the sword vanished. "No! You need to shield your hand before trying to wield it."

King Raj was Ashim's only father figure and he was a Mindelate and Realm Walker. Nobody had told him the inner mechanisms of Fire Singer abilities before. Though he could make animals and apples using fire—along with lighting candles, he had seldom utilised his gift. But being a Fire Singer was a part of him and it was silly to hide it.

A shield surrounded his hand like a skin-tight glove. This time when Ashim recreated a sword and held it, it didn't burn his skin. "Like this?"

"Yes, perfect." Jared inspected the craftmanship. "Beautiful."

A laugh passed Ashim's lips as he looked at the sword and swung it around. The only sword training he had to go on were the afternoon sessions with Edmund—but this made him feel terrifyingly powerful. Jared created his own sword and got into position with a smirk, his pink eyes flared in silent question. To Ashim's surprise, this didn't make him scared. Another laugh filled their area and Ashim knew this would be fun. He positioned himself the way Edmund taught him and faced Jared head on.

"Let's dance, pretty boy," Jared said with a wink.

The comment made Ashim pause. A move which Jared clearly anticipated. He swung his sword in a swooping arch and seared a hole in Ashim's shirt. Blowing the steam away, Ashim shook his head and got lost in the euphoria of using his Fire Singer abilities.

The sunset glistened on the horizon of the Visyan mountains through the windows of Alsaphus Castle Infirmary. Beds formed a corridor down the centre of the room; each a few feet away from each other. The smell of various medicinal herbs lingered in the air. Ashim sat patiently on a bed, drumming his fingers on his belly. His head lolled as he tried to fight sleep that kept pulling him in; it was the first time he had felt close to full depletion of his power and it had made him exhausted.

Approaching footsteps made his eyes open and two shadows blocked out the sunset. He couldn't discern the features of them with the glaring sun, but he noticed something being exchanged, then the one to his right faced him. Eloise suddenly came into view; she unravelled the scroll as she read over its contents.

"What seems to be the problem?" Eloise asked as she put the scroll in her apron.

Ashim shrugged. "I feel fine, but Helienya insisted I come here."

He tensed when she placed her hands on the sides of his head. His eyes widened when her hands glowed white and his skin tingled. Eloise nodded and left his bedside to approach a herbal table nearby. The clink of glasses filled the silent space as she sifted through them. Eloise grabbed the bottle that she was looking for then returned to Ashim's bedside and shook the bottle.

"All new Fire Singers have to take this," Eloise stated as she took a wooden spoon out of her apron.

He raised an eyebrow. "But..."

"Usually, we reserve this for children. I don't know how it'll work for an adult, but we'll trial it." She popped the cork and eased some black sludge onto a wooden spoon; Ashim grimaced and inched away. "You're peculiar, Mahrishan. Not many Fire Singers start training their powers in adulthood.

This medicine will ease the strain on your magic supply while it's being tested to its limit."

Ashim watched her extend the spoon to him. He grimaced as he watched the sludge bubble and refused to take it. She shook the spoon; after a moment's hesitation, he opened his mouth and let her administer the medicine. The black sludge didn't taste like he expected—instead of something vile, it tasted like sour apples. He looked at the spoon and blinked in surprise at the contrasting flavour to its colour.

"It tastes like apples," he said.

Eloise smiled as she loaded up another spoonful. "Yes. Like I said, reserved for children, so it has to taste nice."

"Do I have to do this every day?" Ashim asked.

"Yes, until your magic is strong enough to handle all the elements that come with being a Fire Singer," Eloise explained.

When presented with a second mouthful, Ashim didn't hesitate and allowed her to do her job. He settled back on the bed. Maybe the reason he was so tired was because his magic was at the precipice of being completely burned out. She put the cap back on and disappeared back to organise the herb table.

"Can I leave?" Ashim asked.

"Wait ten minutes," Eloise called back.

He settled back on the bed and watched the clouds roll past the window. Ashim had enjoyed this day. It was the first time his abilities didn't scare him, and he felt like a god. With the other Fire Singers, he wanted to learn more and become as great as the archers or dancers in the training area. With this new lease on life, he could work to defeat Xabian if he ever harmed Orison. Best of all, he would be unstoppable.

FIFTY-THREE

The week went by in a blur. Every day, Orison had to face visions of Sila and confront him; until she grew so tired of resenting him that she forgave him for the pain. Orison realised it made her stronger. She found her walks into the throne room easier each day. On her first day out of the depths of the Temple of Fallagh, the sun stung her eyes. They didn't allow Orison to linger for long before being rushed into a carriage, then pulled through a portal.

As the carriage rolled to a stop outside Alsaphus Castle, Orison felt lighter. She no longer had a sense of dread to gaze upon the castle walls; nor fear of what lay inside. It felt like her soul was a bird that was trapped in a cage and finally set free. Servants hurried over to the carriage to open the door and swiftly lead Orison towards the castle. Yet, she couldn't see Ashim or anybody she knew. Her heart sank that nobody was there.

Orison approached the steps, then paused when she felt the familiar tug in her chest, followed by a voice saying, "Welcome home, Little Queen."

She whirled around to find Ashim leaning against the side of the carriage with a flower bouquet and a beaming smile on his face. Orison rushed to him and pulled on his shirt, which brought him into a long-awaited kiss. The bouquet rustled when he pulled her closer and their kiss deepened. She was finally home.

"I've missed you so much!" Orison exclaimed when she pulled away. "I love you."

"I missed you and love you too." Ashim kissed her again. "How was it?"

Orison played with his shirt. "They had me confront Sila every day until I forgave him." He sucked in a breath and ran his hands through her hair. "And I got over my fear of the throne room."

He kissed the top of her head as he handed Orison the bouquet. She held it close to her heart as he guided her to the stairs leading to the castle. Once through the doors, Orison lifted her head and her jaw fell open at the decorations that adorned the entrance. Royal-green banners hung from the ceiling rafters; they had covered entire pictures to accommodate tapestries enhanced by a golden stag emblem of Fallasingha.

"The coronation is happening in two days," Ashim told her. "They've been preparing since yesterday."

Orison gawped at the space; it had never looked so inviting. After her ordeal in the Temple of Fallagh, it certainly felt like a fresh start. When she took the crown, she immediately wanted to change the name of the castle to rid its name of Alsaphus. She would redecorate the walls extensively until no part of the Alsaphus family remained.

"What have you been up to while I've been gone?" Orison fell into him with a giggle. "Were you well?"

He gave her another kiss. "I've been training with the Fire Singers to control my power. It's been amazing," he explained.

"Do you still feel scared of your powers?" She watched as he shook his head with a smile. "You can say we've both been on incredible journeys this week."

Ashim took Orison's hand and led her through the castle. They went down multiple corridors until they appeared in the East Wing in front of a familiar door for Orison—where ivy grew out of it like a chain that held it closed. It creaked as Ashim pushed the door open and led her into the botanical garden beyond the door.

The botanical garden still took Orison's breath away as she witnessed plants of every size and shape. Hand in hand, Ashim guided her through a curtain of vines and deeper into the garden, where a light dusting of snow fell from the open roof. The statue of the female made entirely of plants was smiling—

usually, the statue looked like she was in a deep sleep. Ashim led her down many corridors decorated with plants where the butterflies and pixies flew around, playing with her hair before he came to a stop at the familiar gazebo on the water's edge.

"I found this during our week apart." The gazebo creaked as he stepped inside. "It's beautiful. We need music!"

Orison laughed as she joined him and handed over her flowers. She sat on the bench. Ideas whirled in her head about how they could get music. Then she had a revelation and with the click of her fingers, the Faunetta's Atlas appeared in her hand. It made her heart ache because this was one of the final gifts Xabian had bought her before everything changed for the worse. Her gaze fell to Ashim; his eyes were wide as he looked at the small globe.

"How about a dance from Karshakroh?" Orison suggested. She set the dials on the atlas to play music from his homeland.

Footsteps made Orison pause and follow the sound. "Welcome home!" Kinsley squealed as she ran up to her. Orison groaned with a smile as Kinsley pulled her into a tight squeeze. She was relieved when Kinsley let her go.

Movement over Kinsley's shoulder made Orison gasp. Bahlir stepped out of the shadows with his arm looped around his husband's. "Bahlir! Kharhem!" Orison called and ran up to the couple. "What are you doing here?"

"The coronation, of course," Bahlir said with a smile. "We arrived this morning."

"It's good to see you again," Orison said with a wide smile.

Kinsley threaded her arm through Orison's. "We must celebrate! I know the place."

Orison's attention turned to Ashim. "I'd like that..."

"Ashim, you're coming too. We haven't gotten together in a while. This could be the last time before you're queen." Kinsley fluttered her eyebrows with a pout. "Pwease."

Orison extended her hand to Ashim's and led him out of the botanical garden. With a click of her fingers, she sent the Faunetta's Atlas to their home in Tsunamal. They navigated through multiple paths as Kinsley walked ahead, chatting about various topics and what Orison missed while away. She noticed Bahlir and Kharhem talked amongst themselves, oblivious to the other discussions going on. For Orison, hearing her friends' endless chatter made her feel pleased to be back.

Merchants Pub was a small building nestled between a guardhouse and a butcher's shop in Merchants Row. Its timber-framed structure was like the majority of the buildings in the street. Through the arched front windows, one could see flurries of snow accumulating on the window ledges. Inside was almost empty, with only a handful of off-duty guards or castle staff members enjoying some lunch in the warmth of a fire.

Ashim licked hot sauce off his fingers and sat back in his seat; he looked down at his plate of chicken wings with a satisfied smile. His appetite had increased since training his Fire Singer abilities. He was constantly hungry and had to increase his portion sizes, due to the large quantities of magic he had to use. Across the table, Orison sipped on her pint of ale as she discussed her cleansing ceremony with Kinsley. Ashim placed more bones into the bucket in the centre of the table with a metallic clink, as he listened to every word about her meetings with Sila. His gaze settled on Bahlir and Kharhem, who ate their meals of chicken and rice silently.

"One of the guardians had to have been a Projeer, right?" Orison's chair creaked as a servant set down a pizza in front of her. "They never took off their hoods, so I never saw their eyes or ears to identify if they were."

"That's possible," Kinsley muttered as she wiped her mouth with a napkin. "Anyway, with the coronation—we have picked everything out now. Do you feel ready?"

"I don't think I'll ever be ready," Orison admitted as she grabbed some pizza.

Ashim frowned as she placed a slice of pizza on his plate, but she waved her hand. He took another chicken wing and pulled out the bones as Orison and Kinsley resumed their conversation. When it came to being a royal, Orison would be amazing. Ashim knew she was capable of it and so much more.

The bones clinked in the metal bucket as he dropped them in. "In two days, we will have Fallasingha safe from another Alsaphus. It'll be a stronger nation with more allies and peace amongst us all," he declared.

Kinsley nodded as she raised her cup of beer and toasted to the declaration. He smiled as he raised his pint of beer and as did Orison. Bahlir did the same, followed by Kharhem. They all clinked their mugs together with cheers. A change was exceedingly overdue within the entire Othereal. Ashim was glad to be by Orison's side to assist with it.

"Are you two staying or going?" Kinsley asked as she leaned against the table, noting that neither Bahlir nor Kharhem had taken off their coats.

Bahlir looked up from his plate. "Fallasingha is cold."

"The fire's raging," Kinsley pointed out as she looked at the roaring fire in the hearth, which warmed the entire tavern.

"They have come from the desert," Orison mumbled.

Ashim smiled. "If they want to melt, let them. It took me a while to get used to it."

After being raised in desert plains, he understood why Bahlir and Kharhem were reluctant to take off their coats, despite the warmth of the tavern. They were not used to the forest life with a four-season climate. Ashim still found it cold, but it got easier the longer he stayed in this part of Fallasingha. He wanted to be back in Tsunamal where it was hot. He was always happier in warmer climates.

Orison clicked her fingers in his face, which made Ashim blink several times. "Are you okay?"

"*Halek*, just thinking," he admitted.

She settled back in her chair and resumed talking to Kinsley and Bahlir, trying to include Kharhem, but he couldn't understand the common tongue. As Ashim returned to his thoughts, they strayed to those that included slaying Xabian and getting revenge for his parents' death. It should have made him feel sick, but instead, it gave him joy. He had been too young to remember his parents; regardless, he still wanted justice for a lost and broken childhood. Now that he had Orison, her protection was of utmost importance. When she was queen, they'd go on a hunt to slay a Nyxite.

Saskia's rocking chair creaked as she gently rocked in front of the large fireplace in Alsaphus Castle's office. She hummed to herself as she knitted a scarf; it would be good for either of the Luxart twins to get a new one. When the office doors opened, Saskia planted her feet on the floor and looked up from her knitting as Edmund stepped into the room. His face was paler than usual and his palpable fear made his movements slow. He bowed deeply in front of her, which made her more curious as other guards filed in behind him.

The chair creaked again as she resumed knitting and gestured to the sofa beside her for Edmund to sit. Saskia planted her feet on the floor again when he remained standing. He clutched his guard captain helmet to his chest, which he puffed out to stand tall.

"We still haven't been able to locate Xabian, Advisor," Edmund declared.

"Does Orison know?" Saskia asked as she eased herself to the edge of the rocking chair; her gaze roamed over each of the guards. They all gave her stern expressions, which told her enough. She wrapped her cardigan around her as she stood up.

Edmund shook his head. "We didn't want to put unnecessary stress on her after the cleansing. It was best to seek your advice on what we should do, going forward."

With her hands on her hips, Saskia looked at the ground and paced in her own little spot near the fireplace. She racked her brain about the best course of action. A shield would be easy to erect around the castle, but it was a useless solution with Xabian being a Tearager and it would harm Orison. Saskia twirled her brown wig around her finger as she continued to think, then stopped as she came up with a temporary solution.

"It's best we don't tell Orison, as stress now will not be good for the coronation," Saskia began. "A guard will need to escort her everywhere. We need to continue efforts in locating Xabian's location. We must have a team of the strongest guards to ensure he doesn't get into the castle, by any means."

One of the newest guards, a short man with a bald head, suggested, "Would a shield be easier?"

"Do you think a shield can stop a Tearager?" Saskia questioned. The guard shrank in on himself and looked at the others. "Ensure he doesn't breach the castle perimeter. Xabian may pose as a guard, check every guard's eyes for purple stars."

"Yes ma'am," all guards chorused.

She pushed her shoulders back. It felt good to be in charge again since she fell from Edmund's position. The power was intoxicating. She went to the desk and got out some parchment.

"I'll put out an announcement to the rest of the squadron," Saskia announced as she leaned on the desk with a stylus in her hand. "Then everybody is on the same page."

"Can't we lock him up?" the youngest guard asked.

"We've tried three times; he's escaped each time," Edmund answered.

Saskia wrote a note and used her power to duplicate it several times over. She distributed them off to notice boards in each guard station. With the number of guards on duty, Saskia hoped Xabian wouldn't breach the barriers they had set—wherever he was lurking. Though Xabian's motives were still unclear, it still troubled Saskia that nobody could find him.

The possibility he had found a cave to dwell in gave her some comfort, but it wouldn't be a permanent solution. He'd have to find a home eventually because he was no longer welcome in the castle. In the best-case scenario, he would hang around until he found that home and then be on his way. But the worst-case scenario was something Saskia didn't want to contemplate or speak of out loud. It was her job to ensure the coronation was a success and try with all her might to stop a fallen prince from claiming the crown.

FIFTY-FOUR

Two days later, castle servants surrounded Orison like a well-rehearsed dance. Orison stood on the pedestal in Alsaphus Castle's dressing rooms. It was the second time she had seen the dress that the servants had pinned her into over a week ago; it looked just as beautiful as the first time she had laid her eyes upon it. The sun glistened in the mirror; it indicated the beginning of what would be a long day. She was to take the crown at sunset.

Orison exhaled a heavy breath as the servants fussed about with her clothes and clasped the cape to her shoulders. They fixed any loose bits of thread on the hem of her floor-length golden ensemble and smoothed it out. The train expanded well past her feet and took several servants to hold it up so she didn't fall over. A group of them sewed her dress at all angles so it conformed to her figure; others pinned her hair up and dusted her face to make her look as regal as a queen should be. She still found that it was too much.

When she wasn't getting puffs of powder in her face, Orison managed to look over at Kinsley and Eloise who sat in floor-length golden dresses with their hair pinned up. The dresses weren't nearly as extravagant as Orison's. Kinsley fixed the clasp on her heels and checked on Eloise, who closely observed Orison.

"Do you need any water?" Eloise asked as she stood up. The gold dress complemented her dark complexion well, it brought out her green eye colour splendidly. "You look a little pale."

"I think it's all the powder," Orison said with a nervous laugh.

"I'll get you a drink," Eloise tutted.

Eloise's shoes clicked as she hurried to a drinks table. She poured a glass of water and placed a straw inside. She extended the glass to Orison, who took a generous drink, not realising how thirsty she was. Orison teetered back onto the pedestal and saw something glisten out of the corner of her eye—a tiara with tear-drop diamonds.

"Thank you," she said to Eloise. Orison turned to a servant. "Will I be wearing that?"

Aiken smoothed out her dress. "Until your crowning, yes."

Orison faced Kinsley with a smile; she laughed when Kinsley waved around a glass of alcohol. For the past three days, she had been in full celebration mode, excited for the moment her friend would change everything. Orison had the straw of her water pressed against her lips as she took another drink.

"You look so beautiful," Kinsley said. "Ashim's going to be in awe."

Heat rose in her cheeks at the thought of Ashim. The concept of him looking equally regal made her heart flutter and her body heat up. She knew the servants would do something to accentuate his appearance and make him look like a king with his queen.

"I think we're almost ready," Aiken exclaimed with a smile as she examined her work in the mirror.

Orison peered at herself for the first time as Queen Orison Durham—and she truly believed it. She was no longer a mortal peasant apprenticed by a lowly baker.

As the day drew on, the castle filled with guests from far-off lands; Orison couldn't possibly remember them all. The foyer was loud with bustling chatter and the alcohol flowed freely. Everybody waited for one thing—to be allowed into the throne room, where the coronation would commence. Some of the wealthier patrons, outside of royal ties, had attended the castle to witness the coronation of a new era of Fallasingha Royals.

At the top of the stairs, Ashim allowed servants to fix the cufflinks of his golden tunic and smooth out any wrinkles. A surge of anger swelled in the pit of his belly. He hadn't been able to move an inch of his own accord since he woke up and he felt like a puppet. Bahlir and Akhili stood beside him; both hid their amusement at Ashim's misery behind a gold encrusted goblet as he pretended to drink. It only made Ashim more frustrated.

Over the servant's shoulder, Ashim's gaze lifted at the sign of movement from a nearby corridor; his jaw fell open when Orison came into view. It was the first time he gazed upon her in her final coronation outfit. The silence of the room was shattered by a chorus of gasps, followed by excited chatter. Ashim, on the other hand, was speechless. The servants had made it so she radiated with beauty. As she approached him, her purple eyes sparkled when the Othereal lights hit them at the right angle. Everybody in the room seemed to disappear and it was only him and his Equal in the entire world. Ashim extended his hand out and Orison slid her hand into his with a graceful grin.

"You look absolutely incredible," Ashim said. She smiled and leaned in to kiss him until a servant hissed loudly. Both thought better of it and stood beside each other. The room returned to a lively chatter as she looped her arm around Ashim's. "It's almost time."

Orison nodded and picked up a glass of champagne from a waiter. She downed the champagne—much to the protests of servants—and winced. It made Ashim pause and look at Bahlir and Akhili, who both watched her in a wide-eyed stare. Ashim knew Orison was bound to be nervous; she was, in essence, becoming another person. A servant hissed again.

"This is the first time seeing a coronation," Bahlir admitted in Karshakir. He smiled as Kharhem appeared beside him. "And my husband's."

"It's my first time too," Ashim admitted.

Coronations were rare when the majority of people in the Othereal were immortal. Ashim was pleased that the first coronation he witnessed was his

Equal's. It felt special this way. Though she held no royal blood, nobody protested the decision to make her queen. Everybody had become fed up with the unjust ways the Alsaphus line bestowed upon people in their own lands and surrounding areas.

"We can celebrate tonight," Ashim whispered into Orison's ear. "After the party, if you aren't too tired. I want to take you to our home in Tsunamal."

Orison looked around for any servants and gave him a quick kiss. She'd already ruined her lipstick by drinking the champagne; a kiss wouldn't hurt. A servant ran up the stairs with a palette; they dabbed a brush into a pink colour and reapplied the lipstick Orison had erased. Ashim caught Bahlir, who was trying to stifle another laugh. He shook his head with a smile and tapped Orison's hand.

As he gazed upon the packed foyer, he saw King Raj who toasted the air with a dip of his chin and gave Ashim a little wave. Ashim waved back and checked on Orison. Of course, King Raj would be here to cheer them both on; he'd helped Orison while she was in Karshakroh. Then Ashim watched Idralis approach Raj, their clothes clashed—Raj was wearing a golden tunic and Idralis was wearing something which resembled an orange leaf.

Trumpets filled the foyer and like a startled deer, Ashim looked around for a threat. The entryway fell silent as the trumpets continued; each guest smiled, giddy with excitement about what the trumpets entailed. It signified the coronation was about to commence.

"Welcome, guests, please make your way to the throne room. It is time for the coronation of Princess Orison Durham," a man bellowed.

Ashim turned to Orison as everybody filed out of the foyer; her smile faltered as she pressed a hand to her stomach. When she looked at him, he could see that her next smile was false; fear darkened her purple eyes. This was a new chapter. They had nothing to fear.

Joyous orchestral music filtered out of the throne room door. Orison stood before the threshold. She desperately tried to reinforce her nerves while servants made last-minute adjustments to her dress and touched up her make-up and hair. Beyond the doors were her future and legacy; it would make her leave behind her mortal life to serve the Fae. She knew she was capable, but the responsibility was a terrifying thought.

When the clock chimed, two guards opened the doors and the orchestral music amplified tenfold. Orison pushed her shoulders back as people in the throne room, who sat on pews, turned to gaze upon their new queen. She smiled at Idralis, then Nazareth, who gave her a small wave with a proud grin. They hadn't been able to talk while she prepared for this moment.

It was time to take the first steps to her destiny. Orison began the slow walk towards the dais of the throne where an elder enchantress stood on a pedestal with a crown and a golden sceptre. Ashim stood to the right of the enchantress, whose focus was entirely on him, as he pushed out his chest with a proud expression. Kinsley stood by his side, along with Eloise. To the left of the throne stood Taviar and Saskia, they provided more smiles at the prospect of her future.

Orison exhaled as she tried to forget her worries—such as failing to remember her vows. She was too scared to look around at the people who watched her closely and judged her worthiness to rule. At the halfway mark, a bone-rattling bang followed by a blinding white light exploded across the throne room. It knocked Orison off her feet, which sent her flying into one of the pews and everything went black.

Her ears rang when she came around, along with a heaviness that pressed against her legs. When she opened her eyes, she squinted at the blinding white light until it dissipated to reveal a cloud of thick fog. Orison touched her ear with a trembling hand, when the ringing subsided, feeling something warm and wet on her fingers. Her eyes widened when she pulled her hand away to reveal blood. Orison's shock was short-lived, replaced with horror at the terror-filled screams that echoed around her.

As her gaze settled on the room, she gasped at the gaping hole in one of the throne room walls, encircled by purple flame. There were bricks scattered around the floor. Collapsed archways left a pile of stone in their wake, where arms and legs hung out of the rubble haphazardly. Orison's stomach rolled and she forced down the urge to throw up.

The weight on her legs lifted, replaced with pain. Inching away, she came face to face with Bahlir; blood ran down his head from a large cut above his eyebrow. Akhili joined him, his orange tunic torn and his hair dishevelled with dried blood; along with a man with light brown skin she'd never seen before. Bahlir eased Orison to her feet, brushing off the debris from her dress and checking her over for injuries.

"Where's Ashim?" she managed to ask, unable to see through the smoke.

"I don't know," he replied.

Akhili turned to the stranger. "Mikhail and I will go and help the injured."

Though distracted, Orison nodded. Her heart raced and her stomach sank as she listened to the sound of babies wailing and people crying out for loved ones. Peering through the smoke, Orison saw Kinsley run into Aeson's arms and he held her close. The buzz of excitement was gone in an instant, replaced with sorrow and horror.

With the click of Orison's fingers, the heavy coronation dress disappeared and in its place was her evening dress. If she had to run, it would be easier than the heavier dress she was to be crowned in. Orison kicked off her heels and ran to find Ashim amongst all the death and destruction.

She avoided looking at the deceased as best she could, their hands and heads often protruded out of large slabs of rock, wood or glass. Orison skidded to a halt with a gasp and staggered into one of the remaining chairs; her focus on the elder enchantress who had a shard of wood speared through her chest. The crown and sceptre were scattered on the floor, covered in the blood which dripped from the enchantress' hand.

Gentle hands whirled Orison around. A choked sound escaped her when she felt the familiar pull and Ashim's embrace enveloped her. Her hands trembled violently on his back; the feeling of his golden tunic soft under her hands.

"What happened?" she asked in a shrill voice. "Are you well?"

"I'm okay." Ashim checked her over.

She turned to check on Kinsley, Eloise and Aeson. "Are you well?" They all nodded. She made her way over to Taviar, who held Saskia close. Aside from some cuts on their heads and arms, they appeared fine.

Orison turned in a circle, her attention snagging on the gaping hole in the room again. Wind howled through the gap like a beast, the purple flames licking the air. As she took in the destroyed throne room in all its entirety, Orison's knees buckled and she collapsed into Ashim, who eased her to the floor.

She held her breath, clutching Ashim's hand as Idralis knelt beside an unconscious Nazareth. The Elf King was silent as he checked the emissary's pulse, his shoulders visibly relaxed; it was the only sign Nazareth was okay. Behind Idralis, King Raj scrambled over a pile of rubble, his golden tunic torn and his hair hung limp in the bun, at his shoulder.

A dark void blocked out the light emanating from the collapsed portion of the throne room. Orison's eyes widened when Xabian materialised on a pile of rubble, leathery wings protruded from his spine that folded behind his back. His smirk was pure evil as he stepped down from his perch and fixed the cufflinks of his black shirt.

Idralis and Raj stepped into Xabian's path, each with a sword drawn; Orison could only assume they obtained them from fallen guards. With a wave of Xabian's hands, he threw the swords across the room. The weapons clattered to the stone floor and skidded away; neither of the kings could retrieve them. Xabian approached the dais in a casual walk; he came to a stop at the crown. He crouched down, picked it up and admired it in his hands—like it was a prize he had won. Then he faced Orison with a malicious smirk.

"I believe you were about to steal my crown."

FIFTY-FIVE

Orison baulked as Xabian strolled further up to the dais. She inched away from him as he admired the crown once more. Those uninjured cowered from the prince. Taviar's grip on Saskia tightened. The fallen prince merely glanced over his shoulder when somebody fled the room with a scream, calling for guards or Healengales to assist.

Bahlir, Idralis and Raj had reclaimed some weapons— poised to strike. They took the place of the guards who were absent from protecting everybody from Xabian's wrath.

With bated breath, Orison waited for Xabian to continue his rampage. The veins along Xabian's skin glowed purple and he scratched at his neck —as though he was fighting to control the Nighthex. When he resumed moving, he had the same swagger Orison had grown to fear in Sila. She wanted to run but couldn't bring herself to move from her place on the floor. Xabian moved the crown around his hand and looked directly at her.

"I'm only here for my coronation," he said. Orison's skin crawled at how much he sounded like Sila. "I was next in line before you came along. You should have waited your turn, then this—" He gestured to the throne room. "Wouldn't have happened."

"Nobody tried to steal your crown," Saskia spat. "You aren't worthy."

Xabian's glowing gaze fell on Saskia with a scowl. With a wave of his hand she screamed when she was engulfed in a purple vortex of fire and in a second—she was gone. Orison shrieked and pushed herself onto her feet.

"What have you done with her?" Orison yelled.

"I have banished her from the castle," Xabian snarled. Orison gawped. "You know, Orison, it wasn't an accident that you were thrown in the portal. It was me."

"What do you mean, banished? And how were you the one to throw me into the portal?"

Xabian approached her. "She spoke out of line." He looked around. "I realised you would take my place as next in line. Before the battle of Torwarin, I cast a band of thorns to kill you in the mortal realm." Xabian pointed at Ashim, "But that Karshak fucker helped you stay alive. If he wasn't in the mortal realm, my curse would have worked. He ruined my chance of killing you!"

Tears stung Orison's eyes as a trembling hand covered her mouth. "You were trying to kill me by starving me of my magic?" she cried.

His malicious chuckle flittered along her skin. "If the curse didn't render me unconscious, I would have enjoyed watching your suffering." Bahlir was right, Xabian was like his brother, Sila, in every sense of the word. Underneath his friendly façade was this heinous monster.

"You're a sick man, Alsaphus," Ashim growled.

The cursed prince held up a hand. It warned that if he pushed, then he would end up with Saskia. With a wave of Ashim's hand, a sword of fire appeared; he adjusted his grip with a scowl on his face. He took a step down from the dais. The fire crackled with Ashim's control and he swung at the fallen prince. Orison screamed when a vortex of purple fire engulfed Ashim and he disappeared before her eyes.

"You failed because you created it while the Desigle still protected her. The reason Orison found her Equal was because of you," Kinsley shouted with a laugh. "You don't like Ashim, yet you brought their fates together!"

Orison staggered into the throne when Xabian waved his hand. A vortex of purple fire engulfed Kinsley and Taviar; Eloise screamed before it engulfed her as well. All of them were gone. Banished from the castle, never to cross through the gates again. Orison's only relief was that Riddle, Zade and Yil weren't there. The three of them chose to stay at home because of how busy it would be.

Xabian looked at the ceiling and sighed as guards filtered into the room. "The entire staff of Alsaphus Castle are hereby dismissed from their duties and need to leave the castle immediately." The guards lowered their weapons; they looked at one another with puzzled facial expressions. "Leave before I make you!"

The servants hidden in the shadows all ran to the nearest stairwell; some shielded their heads as if Xabian would injure them. Some guards from the back of the formation ran after the servants, much to Edmund's protests to stay in line Consequently, Edmund disappeared in a vortex of purple fire. With no guard captain, they all raced towards Xabian and tried to take down the prince before he could do more harm than good. Xabian banished each of them from the castle with a single wave of his hand.

"You can't fire every single person; how would you take care of yourself?" Orison spat. Her heart raced at the scene before her. "This is a mistake."

"I've looked after myself for months. I can do whatever the fuck I want with my power!" Xabian screamed. "You don't control me!"

Without Ashim by her side, Orison could only watch as the situation grew worse. Xabian raised the crown above his head. He smiled as he viewed the golden design that looked like roses with thorns. He placed it on his head.

He bent down and grabbed the sceptre. Xabian closed his eyes as he recited the vows in the Fallagh tongue to swear himself into kingship. Orison froze with horror as the crown glowed and the golden material tarnished.

The crown's magic ate away at the metal until it was black and encrusted with green moss; like the magic didn't approve of this new ruler. Xabian screamed in pain as he fell to his knees, but he kept going. Lightning and wind erupted around them into the crown, which made him scream louder as a blinding white light made Orison shield her eyes.

"The crown is rejecting him," Raj whispered.

Mid-sentence of his vows, Xabian snarled through gritted teeth. "One more word and you'll be where the rest of them are!"

He continued to chant the vows, the light strengthened, like the morning sun was in the throne room. The ground shook violently, so much so that Orison lost her footing; she crashed into the throne with a grimace. She lifted her head and watched out the window as the sky became as black as night and more lightning vaulted around the castle.

As the final words of the vows echoed around the remains of the throne room, Orison turned around to bear witness to Xabian on the floor. He panted heavily with a hand over his heart and eyes squeezed closed; through his eyelids, Orison could see the unnatural glow. Then a malicious smile spread across his face as he staggered to his feet.

"For my first ruling as king, I hereby banish Orison Durham from Alsaphus Castle," Xabian snarled, looking at everybody who remained with her. "Along with everybody else who is not a descendant of the Alsaphus family."

Orison's eyes widened and she stepped forward. "No!"

It was all she managed before a purple fire engulfed her. She lost touch of the throne as she felt herself being lifted. Orison screamed as lightning tore around her in a swirling vortex of nightmares. It ripped away her breath as it threw her into the unknown.

FIFTY-SIX

The amount of people gathered outside of Alsaphus Castle was unfathomable. Crates lined the road that led to Cardenk, all labelled with family names. Babies and children cried while parents discussed amongst themselves in rushed voices about where to go. People tried to run back to the castle, only to get thrown back by a shield around the property. When Tearagers tried to take down the shield, a powerful force shot them back and they lay in an unconscious heap in the frozen grass.

Orison pushed through the throng of people. She grimaced when another Tearager crashed into a tree when hurtled back from the castle gates. As she walked, she overheard people explaining to one another that the business they had in Merchants Row had been owned by their family for over hundreds of years—it was all gone. Homes where children had been born and raised now sat empty. Her stomach rolled violently and she threw up on the side of the road.

To make this many people homeless with the click of a finger was beyond sickening; especially in the heart of winter. It made her want to go back through the gates and shove a knife through Xabian's chest, but she knew the shield was too powerful if Tearagers couldn't get through. She needed to find the Luxarts, Ashim; or King Raj and King Idralis.

"Princess, please, my baby," a woman pleaded through sobs. She rocked her new-born child in her arms. "Where are we going to go?"

She teetered on her feet; with so many people, it was difficult to discern where helpful people were. Orison found a white veil to signify that a Healengale was present, she pointed to the group. "Wait with the Healengales while I figure things out."

"We were in the middle of dinner when Misted here. What's happened, Princess?" a guard asked.

"I don't know, everything happened so fast," Orison said wearily. "I'll try to help."

When she felt the familiar tug in her chest, it guided her to Ashim. Orison ran to him and threw her arms around him; all she felt was relief that he was safe. He held her close and kissed the top of her head. Orison could hear his pounding heart through his shirt. None of this made sense—her mind raced with a plethora of questions.

Ashim's hold on her tightened. "Are you well?" He pulled away and brushed the tears from her face with his thumb; Orison didn't realise she had been crying. Ashim kissed her gently.

"I'm fine. Just scared. Is everyone else well?"

He pointed to an area nearby. Idralis and Nazareth conversed with people from the castle; alongside King Raj, accompanied by Akhili and Mikhail. They offered coats and blankets to people stranded in the snow. It made Orison realise how cold she was, in nothing but a thin dress.

Orison took Ashim's hand and made her way over to the kings. Every few steps, people stopped Orison to ask her questions she didn't have answers to; people with injuries from the throne room begged for help. It was absolute chaos. It took everything to keep her emotions in check and show she was a stronger leader.

"Has anybody seen the Luxarts?" Orison asked.

King Idralis secured a black coat around her bare arms and Orison held it close. She paused when she heard sobbing nearby; she turned on her heels and followed the sound. The only sign that Ashim followed was the persistent pull in her chest.

The sobbing led to Saskia who sat in the snow holding Zade and Yil between boxes of crates labelled *Luxart* and *Aragh*. Orison breathed a sigh of relief. Turning in a circle, she found Riddle and Taviar nearby. They talked to each other in hushed whispers as they mulled over what had become of their family home.

Riddle raced over to Orison. "None of our family has room for us," he gasped. "I've lost my shop and my home. What am I going to do for a job?"

"Every single one of you will come with me and Ashim to Tsunamal. I'll help you find a new shop when we get there," Orison declared. She turned around and found Kinsley and Eloise crying into Aeson's shoulders. "Are Kinsley and the boys well? What about Saskia?"

"I'm fine!" She exclaimed.

Taviar nodded. "Yes, everybody is okay, thankfully. So is Eloise and Aeson."

She breathed a sigh of relief. Orison had to figure out how to help the rest of the people. The shield around the castle prevented her from sending out any official royal correspondence for aid. She had left her Teltroma in her home in Tsunamal. Orison groaned as she tried to think of how to give the people of Merchants Row basic necessities; like a roof over their heads to shield from the freezing temperatures.

King Raj approached her; he looked down at the parchment in his hand. "Where are the hotels throughout Fallasingha?" Taken aback, Orison didn't know how to answer that question; nobody had advised her.

"I'll assist you," Taviar said as he took King Raj to a quieter area.

Orison turned back to the castle. She needed to get justice for these people. With Ashim's help, she climbed on top of a crate to see if the Tearagers had any success; each one had given up. She couldn't have the entire Merchants Row community homeless and jobless at the hands of a cursed prince. It wasn't too long ago the Alsaphus family made the shield to keep her in the castle; now it was to keep her out.

From up there, she could see Bahlir and his husband helping reunite children separated from their parents. Two nations who should be enemies came together in a time of urgent need. There had to be a solution. She crouched down and jumped into Ashim's arms; he eased her to the ground. Orison ran her hands through her hair as she tried to think. They'd have to start with the most immediate issue.

She conjured up some parchment and a stylus; writing to Emphina to ask for assistance with getting these people a campsite. From Orison's knowledge, Cleravoralis should be large enough to house the people before her, even while they were rebuilding. The rebuilding process would also provide jobs for families and bring life to the city.

The parchment flew off into oblivion; Orison tapped her foot as she waited for a response. If Xabian hadn't gotten in the way, everybody would have been celebrating for days—but he caused this dilemma. Within moments, a piece of parchment landed in her trembling fingers. She unfolded the sheet and looked down at it.

"Where to now?" Ashim asked, exhaustion written on his face as he slumped to the ground beside Zade and Yil.

Orison looked at the parchment in her hands. "Cleravoralis."

COMING SOON

The Fallasingha Chronicles
Book 3

Coming Soon

Thank You

L.J. Kerry hopes you have enjoyed your time in the Othereal.
If you liked what you read, please leave a review wherever you like.
By leaving a review, you help L.J. Kerry get this book into the hands of more readers.

Thank you for reading.
Have an awesome day!

ACKNOWLEDGMENTS

The Moon Denies Rulers is now in the hands of readers and I'm so sorry about the cliff hanger!

Thank you so much to my team of beta/sensitivity readers for reading through the horrible early drafts and crafting it into what it is today.

A huge thank you to my awesome attentive editor Dianne M Jones. This book is much larger than The Stars Plot Revenge and she still did a phenomenal job at making this the best book possible.

To Z.K. Dorward who made my amazing map, it's absolutely stunning. And the amazing Mad Schofield for letting me use your beautiful artwork for my under the dust jacket art.

Thank you to all my social media followers who showed excitement for The Moon Denies Rulers and couldn't wait for its release.

Thank you to my mum, Margaret. Thank you for always encouraging me to become a huge bookworm from an early age. A huge thank you to my sister, Emma, for also supporting me and helping me come up with plot points.

To you, the reader for taking a chance on a small author.

Glossary

Animunicate (*Ani-muni-cate*) - A type of Fae who can communicate with animals through the mind.

Aquaenix (*A-queen-ix*) - legendary creature from the Phoenix family. Possesses water instead of fire.

Carchaol (*Car-kale*) - A mythical creature which is a snail with eight appendages. Causes adverse effects on the Fae when it eats them.

Charmseer (*Charm-seer*) - A type of Fae who can see enchantments

Desigle (*Des-idgel*)- A powerful protection spell. Prevents enemies from coming near somebody who has a desigle placed on them. It also binds the spell creator to the subject, so when they are in immediate danger the spell creator gets Misted to their location.

Eryma (*Eri-ma*) - A mythical creature of a pig with poisonous flowers which grow out of its back.

Fire Singer - A type of Fae who can manipulate fire to their will.

Illusage (*Ill-you-sage*) - a type of Fae who can create illusions.

Mindelate (*Mind-el-ate*)- A type of Fae who can read and manipulate minds when directly touching somebody.

Mist - Type of Fae magic which allows Fae to travel from one destination to another over long distances.

Nighthex (*Nigh-thex*)- A curse placed on the people of the Othereal. By day they're fae, by night they're Nyxite; a rare form of dragon.

Normalef Berries (*Nor-ma-leaf bear-ease*) - Type of berries to nullify Fae powers.

Othereal (*Other-eel*) - The magic realm where the Fae, elves and other magical creatures live in isolation from the mortals.

Projeer (*Pro-jeer*)- A type of Fae who can create hallucinations.

Protelsha (*Pro-tell-sha*) - Type of Fae to control movements through songs

Realm Walker - A type of Fae who can create portals and help people transport between realms.

Roetabarian (*Row-ta-bear-ean*) - A mythical creature which resembles a bear with deer antlers.

Rokuba (*Rock-ooba*) - A mythical creature which resembles the snake but has the head of a beautiful mortal woman.

Shifter - A type of Fae who can change into various animals or people.

Tearager (*Tear-age-er*) - A type of Fae who can tear down shields.

Tellage (*Tell-age*) - A magical diary for Fae royalty which contains all their memories until their demise.

Teltroma (*Tell-troma*)- A golden disk used to project one user to another for communication.

Traquelle (*Track-elle*) - tracking spell watch her every movement through a mirror.

Viren (*Vi-ren*) - A sub species of Siren, but they lure mortals into forests instead of water.

PRONUNCIATION GUIDE

Characters

Aeson (Aye-son)

Ahbarsh (Ah-bar-sh)

Aiken (Aye-ken)

Alsaphus (Al-sa-fuss)

Aragh (Ah-rah)

Beshankar (Be-shank-car)

Eyam (Eem)

Idralis (Idra-lis)

Mahrishan (Ma-rish-han)

Nazareth (Naz-a-reth)

Neasha (Knee-sha)

Orison (Or-eye-son)

Sila (S-eye-la)

Taviar (Tave-ee-yah)

Xabian (Zabe-ee-an)

KARSHAKIR TRANSLATION

Ahnes (Ah-nes) – Hello

Anesh (A-nesh)– No

Cehen (See-hen) – Come

Diacerre (Dye-ah-see-ah) – Carriage

Dohrashmah (Dough-rash-ma) – Demisexual

Ferkowl (Fur-coal) – Breakfast bowl

Halek (Ha-lek) – Yes

Hara (Ha-rah) – Here

Inhanashra (In-hana-shra) – Infirmary

Khafsh (Kar-fsh) – Fuck

Lahralor (Lah-ra-lor) – Discovaker

Lhahlish (La-lish) – Necklace

Lohar (Lo-har) – Look

Mahavu (Ma-har-voo) – Sand

Mehanasha (Ma-hana-sha) – Sorry

Ohrahnarsh (Oh-rah-narsh)– Orphanage

Oneshir (Oh-nesh-ear) - Okay

Pohamak (Poh-ah-mak) – Potato and chicken pancake

Tahanbashri (Ta-han-bash-ri) – Soul mates a.k.a Equal

Tahn (Tan) – Right

ABOUT AUTHOR

L.J. Kerry is an author based in England. She's an avid reader turned author with some of her favourite genres being Fantasy and Dystopia.
Kerry likes to spend her free time playing video games and travelling.

www.ljkerrybooks.com/links

ALSO BY

Praise for The Fallasingha Chronicles

'I'd recommend if you're looking for a fantasy story with a diverse cast and a lot of plot twists.' – Blanche Maze, author of *Darkest of Thrones*

'The Stars Plot Revenge had me captivated from the beginning!' – Megan Wolters, author of *Souls*

'I feel like I have been on a journey and I need to continue it.' - Goodreads Reviewer

'The Stars Plot Revenge was epic, I was completely enchanted and sucked into the fae world.' - Reviewer

'This book will take you on journey.' – Goodreads Reviewer